There Are Other Ways to Score

By Jovana Iv

© 2020

COPYRIGHT

There Are Other Ways to Score

By Jovana Iv

Copyright @2020 By Jovana Iv

TABLE OF CONTENTS

PREFACE

The idea came to me when I was thirteen: a girl who is challenged with popularity, fame, perfectionism and all the perks that come along with celebritism, all thrown at her at from her first breath. I had already started writing by then and knew that this story was different, something I would always come back to and ponder on. I grew up with these characters, and as my personality developed, they developed, too. By the time I was twenty, I had finished and rewritten the text three times and tried to publish it, but I got either rejected or asked to change the names of the characters and locations. Therefore, I decided to wait.

A few years later, I started reading my latest version and found so many stylistic flaws that had to be altered. This time, I was older and more educated, my vocabulary more vast. I simply knew – *I need to write this again and I am ready now.* It took me one year to perfect the text to the point where I was more satisfied with it than ever before.

I would like to thank everyone who in one way or another contributed to creating and publishing *There Are Other Ways to Score*: my friends, who patiently listened to me when the book was the only thing I talked about and who stayed with me even after I hadn't met them for months while I worked to complete it; my sisters, who listened to me and gave me advice whenever I had doubts about how and what to write; my guy, who always understands when I want to skip his hockey games in order to write.

Of course, I also thank my copy-editor and illustrators, the amazing team who polished and decorated this book so that it now looks so attractive and presentable.

Jovana Iv

CHAPTER 1

The photo session finished late that night. I crawled into the car and just lay on the back seat. My legs were swollen, my spine almost bending in pain. The last thing I remember was falling on my bed with a thought: *When I wake up, I will be on the cover page of the most popular women's magazine in Europe.*

"Jane, this is absolutely fabulous!" pierced my ears.

"Beatrice, shut up!" I roared, covering my head with my blanket.

"You've slept enough. Come on! You've got to see this!"

I lifted my head with tremendous effort. The new issue was there, in front of my face. Beautiful I stared at myself, surrounded by titles that simply did not matter.

"Are you thinking the same thing I am?" I asked my best friend.

She assigned words to my thoughts. "Nobody will buy this issue for the content."

"Yeah. If I don't sell every single copy, nobody ever will."

I dressed and went to the dining room. Angie and Lana were already there.

"Hurry up, we've been waiting for you to start with Bea's salad," Angie said and attacked her bowl.

"How do you feel, Jane?" Lana asked me.

"Are you asking me as a manager or as a friend?"

"Both."

"Like a star!"

We all laughed and Angie threw a slice of cucumber at me. When I returned fire with a tomato, Lana continued.

"Well, you should, cause you definitely are one now. Girls, shall I tell her now, or wait?" The three of them shared confidential glances.

"Ah, no! You will not squint at me." I pushed my salad bowl away, pouting.

"Wait," Bea decided with a naughty smile. "Now eat the salad. I put love and effort into it."

They were persistent in their secrecy and kept me nervous for the whole day. I knew it was something big. I tried to relax by watching TV and revising for my exams. I did not go to regular school, of course. My father organised everything so that I could focus on my career to the utmost and develop it cleverly, on a good foundation that guaranteed longevity. I got books and a tutor from time to time. I wanted to master languages that would help my career most, so I studied Spanish and Italian. I had started off as a model, then diverted to acting, but I knew fashion would always be my main job.

Finally, in the evening, we gathered again in my and Bea's apartment. We did not go out much at the time, mostly because I was becoming more and more recognisable in public. I had come a long way from the cute, fluttery cowgirl that moved to the fashion capital four years ago. Then, I had been known as the daughter of Brad Andersonn, one of the most successful businessmen in the world. Now, the media was constantly writing about the dresses I wore, the TV commercials I did and my first film, *Never Get Back*. For that reason, we organised get-togethers in the spacious apartment Bea and I shared.

"OK, it's high time," I said as I poured us wine. "I'm listening."

"Well, I'll be straightforward," Lana began, "'cause you deserve it."

"Oh, yes, I sure as hell do." I sipped some of the delicious Chilean product.

"Well, you're now on the cover of the most read magazine for ladies. Why wouldn't you be on the cover of the equally ranked magazine for gentlemen?"

I was not sure I heard her correctly. "What?"

"The editor-in-chief called me this morning. He wants you on the cover of *Toned*."

My first reaction was to swallow the wine instead of choking on it. And then I thought, *finally*.

I grinned. "When?"

*****

It took me less than a month to conquer the whole world. Dad advised me to do projects slowly, so as not to shine and die out quickly like a spark. Instead, I became a global star with a few successful projects behind her and many more ahead.

I was indeed proud of myself. But what I was most satisfied with in those days was lying on my nightstand. I read it every night before going to sleep. It was a neatly written invitation to a friendly football match between England and Ukraine. Four tickets were folded inside the envelope, which had arrived one week after my *Toned* issue was published.

I love football. It all started when I moved to England. It was inevitable. In Texas, we didn't pay much attention to it – only for international tournaments, and only sometimes. In Europe, the atmosphere is different – especially in England, where football is said to have been invented. I attended matches frequently, although at times it was a bit of a hassle since people recognised me wherever we went. Still, I did not want to give up that weekend satisfaction whenever I had time to attend.

It was not the football match itself that excited me. I could find tickets for any event I wanted. The girls and I had already decided we would spend one month the following year in Germany being part of one of the greatest events on Earth – the FIFA World Cup. However, this was an invitation coming straight from Matthew Vance, the coach of the English national team. For me, being invited to a game by the national coach meant that I was on a good path to becoming a long-lasting icon, not just a temporary cute girl who people would forget unless she either made another good movie or was part of some kind of salacious scandal. Matthew Vance had been a good friend of my father's for years, but I knew he hadn't invited me only for that reason. If it had been like that, he could've done it earlier. I was making a name for myself now. That was why the girls and I got invited.

That weekend, I was fully prepared for the event. We chose our clothes carefully and read about the players who would be at the pitch that night. We set off to Wembley on time – early – to have a drink, relax and warm up before the game. I was positively nervous because in less than an hour I would see Joshua Hadleigh on the pitch. He was unquestionably the most attractive and successful young player in England and the dream of many girls. The girls and I had talked many times about how great it would be to attend football games as a girlfriend of one of the players. My wish, like many others, was Joshua.

However, there was something I wasn't prepared for.

We left the car and walked slowly and casually, trying not to attract too much attention. Our guards were dressed like us – in jeans and jackets, a scarf here and there – and we headed to the café as a group.

A bus entered the driveway and stopped close to one of the entrances, far in front of us. We continued walking, but I wasn't paying much attention to what the girls were saying. Suddenly, it clicked that it might be the players on the bus, and my heart leapt. I hushed the girls and sped up my pace. *I'm finally gonna see Joshua Hadleigh.*

The door of the bus opened and they started coming out.

But those weren't the English players.

They were Ukrainians.

I slowed down but still continued to walk, unsure what or who to look for. I didn't recognise most of them; there were only a few faces that I must have seen some time ago on the TV. When he came out, I didn't recognise him either, but it seemed to me that I had always known him.

He stood out, simply by being himself. He was bigger and wider than the other guys. It was funny how he had to turn sideways a bit to exit through the door frame because of his shoulders. Even his hair was a different shade of blonde than his teammates'. He carried a team bag in which a magazine was poking out. I saw the big first letter and instantly recognised "my" *Toned*.

Shivers ran down my spine. But that was nothing compared to the cold sweat and goose bumps that covered me when our eyes finally met. I was blunted, unable to hear, feel or see anything but him for that too-brief moment. Even my breath waited to come out. When he smiled at me, I swallowed hard, realising my mouth was agape and dry.

"Jane, is everything alright?" Bea asked, moving her eyes from me to his direction and back, while I still couldn't move mine off of him.

"Yes," I whispered. They had to go and he was the one to turn away first, for which I was somehow grateful because I felt I could remain there, staring at him, for hours.

In the cafeteria, I tried to focus on the conversation with the others and not to think about the guy from the parking lot. But it wasn't easy, knowing that I would see him very soon on the pitch. Suddenly, I realised that the VIP seats we had were too far from the pitch to see anything, and I didn't like them anymore. The next moment, my mind was concerned with how to solve that problem. I really wanted to see that guy a bit closer up.

As if he could hear me, Matthew Vance walked in with a guard next to him. He scanned the room and, having seen us, approached. I stepped out and shook his hand. I couldn't help thinking that my father would be proud if he were there to see me.

"It is my great pleasure to see that you ladies have accepted our invitation," he said.

"The pleasure is ours. There is no better way to spend a Saturday evening."

He treated us to a quick drink and we chatted about the game, the preparations for the next year's tournament, which he was delighted to hear we would attend, the players for tonight, the enemy…and then I decided to ask:

"I apologise in advance and want to highlight that I am not ungrateful, but I have one little concern about our seats tonight. I appreciate the VIP seats, but we both know how far out they are. Do you think it's possible for us to move a bit further down? Closer to the field?"

He laughed, said 'Of course', and asked to be pardoned for a few minutes. He made a phone call while we finished our drinks and returned with good news. He finished his drink, bid us farewell and went to the changing room. Some twenty minutes later, the guard who had accompanied him earlier came with our new tickets.

We would be seated in the very first row, the closest a visitor could possibly get.

We headed up to the stands after I gulped down a shot of pure vodka to relax and warm up a little since the weather in London wasn't very warm and welcoming. If it wasn't for the lights, it would have been downright gloomy.

The girls noticed something was going on with me but did not want to ask, assuming that I would explain everything later. I, on the other hand, couldn't wait for the game to start and was as anxious as before an important shoot. When the players finally came out, I jumped from my seat and started scanning the faces of the guys in blue, completely ignoring the hosts. He wasn't any of them. Even from afar I could see that. All of them were too skinny, their shoulders too narrow. And then I looked more closely at a guy who didn't wear blue, but black. *Oh, he's a goalkeeper.*

On the big screen, he was smiling calmly, confidently, and the sight of him tickled me more than the fact that I was at the stadium with Joshua Hadleigh. I didn't even look for him.

The game started and I lay back in my seat to take a breath and try to control myself. I wasn't supposed to cheer for the opposite team. It became clear to me that I had switched sides as soon as the blonde, broad-shouldered goalkeeper walked off to his end of the pitch, far enough from my eyes. The atmosphere heated up quickly as the ball rolled nonstop from one side to the other. It seemed that the Eastern Europeans hadn't come to the Island unprepared. Despite it being a friendly match, they obviously wanted to win.

And they were the first to score, at thirty-four minutes. It was another blonde guy, but this one had longer hair, more bleached than blonde. Nikolay Pavlov. I had heard about him because he was loud, outspoken, aggressive and the top scorer of the Ukrainian first league two years in a row. Also, he was wanted by the best European teams, but he kept refusing them, thus raising his price.

He definitely raised it again now, having scored against one of the best goalkeepers in the world. Harold Dare played for the best team in England and was competitive with the current goalkeepers from Germany, Italy, France and the Netherlands, who were much older and experienced.

During the break, I was sipping tea and couldn't sit still in expectation of the second half of the game, when Lana raised her head from her phone. "Girls, I think our team is in trouble. These Ukrainian guys here are not at all naïve. I've just checked them in more detail, and apart from the scorer, who's now the most precise in the country, three guys have just been transferred to major European teams, and at this moment, the goalkeeper is considered the best in the world."

I choked on my tea. "The big guy?" I asked.

"Yes," Lana said. "Last season he received only twenty-one goals, which, together with this season's results where he's again performing impeccably, makes him the goalkeeper with the longest record of not being scored on." I was impressed. "And if he continues this way, every important sports name thinks he will win the Golden Glove next year."

Interesting, I thought.

The game began again and my focus was still on the blonde guy. Where had he been hiding? How come I had never heard much about him? Probably because the media was more focused on domestic players and those from Western Europe than on these guys.

The second half proved to be much more intense. The English team were attacking, but whenever they lost the ball, they had to run back to defence. The guest players didn't just want to keep the result. They wanted to score again, even by risking being scored on.

Their wishes came true when a striker from their lines got close to our goal. He was so far forward that the English defenders couldn't keep up with him, so he created a good opportunity for himself to shoot. But since his move would be too obvious, he decided to pass the ball to a second forward who was closest to him.

And who scored smoothly, with his head.

I almost jumped, but, expecting that Bea would put her arm over me, I just uttered a satisfied *Yes* to myself.

The players in blue celebrated, but modestly and without much showing off or boasting. The goalkeeper in black was all smiles when the camera caught him on the big screen. I couldn't help thinking how beautiful, honest and captivating a face he had.

The game continued and nothing changed, but it was interesting to watch both teams trying to score more. The English team did not give up until the end, but it didn't help them. The goalkeeper in black was like a big, wide wall cemented over the whole space between the posts. No ball could pass by him.

When the final whistle blew without stoppage time, nobody was disappointed. Even the English fans were generally appreciative of the good game they saw and the lesson their team got. Now they could see their strengths and weaknesses a year before the tournament.

On the pitch, the players shook hands and exchanged jerseys. It had always been a pleasure to watch that on TV, and now also in person. The photographers and reporters swarmed the pitch to get their shots and interviews, while I stared up at the screen, waiting to see the blonde goalkeeper without his black jersey in a close-up. Joshua Hadleigh was not important at all.

For a second, I lowered my head to complain to Bea about how they weren't focusing on the right guys again, when I saw *him* running towards *us*!

I couldn't say anything, I couldn't move, my mouth turned dry instantly. I swallowed hard, wanting someone to pinch me and wake me up. *He can't be coming here! No way! But where else would he be going? Somebody wake me up! Or not! This is like the most amazing dream I could ever fantasise!*

He was approaching us. I couldn't blink or even turn my gaze away from him. When he got closer, I looked at his eyes and couldn't stop staring. I felt absolutely captivated.

He removed his jersey. Now he was at arm's length. I could see the lines of his face, his eyes. They were blue, clean ocean blue. He smiled again. I saw sweat drops on his face and in his hair. I wanted to touch it so badly I almost moved my hand towards it. If I hadn't been paralysed, maybe I would have. He looked me straight in the eyes, making me shiver. Then he lifted his arm and gave me his jersey.

Only then did I become aware of the rain of flashes that surrounded us. I was thankful because they woke me up and prevented me from looking like an idiot. I moved my hand, which felt so heavy now, and took the jersey. He smiled again. I couldn't. He left. I sat, stoned.

I drifted off again, becoming oblivious to the flashes of the cameras. The girls gathered, protecting me. I was still in a state of ecstasy.

"Maybe it's better to get lost," Angie said. She took me by the arm and we moved towards the exit.

Getting off the stands wasn't easy now, but we managed with the help of the stadium security. When we finally sat, I realised I was breathing heavily.

"That was the most romantic encounter I have ever witnessed!" Lana squeaked.

"It was," I confirmed, still in my trance.

"Totally unexpected!" Angie added.

"Exactly." I was still struggling to catch my breath.

"Correct me if I'm mistaken, but has a guy just totally, absolutely swept Jane Andersonn off her feet?" Bea was shining in triumph.

Normally I would throw something at her, but this time I had no choice but to agree silently. They started laughing while I was still lost in my thoughts, clutching his wet jersey and recalling the lines of his face.

CHAPTER 2

The following day, I woke up fresh and shining, although I hadn't slept more than three hours. I was too excited. I hadn't talked to the girls much when we'd arrived home. I simply couldn't. I had locked myself in my room and lain in bed with the jersey, recalling everything that had happened, for hours, till my body felt truly exhausted and I fell asleep.

In the living room, the girls were gathered for breakfast, all of them with their laptops. When I joined them at the table, Lana pushed a cup of coffee towards me, and they all looked at me, smiling. I smiled back before we started laughing out loud.

Then they started showing me videos, photos and news articles about last night's events at Wembley Stadium. Now, in the videos, I could see that *my* goalkeeper politely shook hands with the other guys and then headed towards us. He had avoided a few reporters and photographers before getting close enough that I'd noticed him.

There were many photos of me just staring bluntly in his direction. It was obvious that I was confused and mesmerised. Thank god the little makeup I had put on was still neat and clean. As he was getting closer, you could almost see my eyes growing.

The moment he gave me his shirt was captured a million times, from every possible angle. I wish I had smiled. Now, I knew very well I couldn't have even if I'd wanted to. Still, I didn't regret anything.

I also liked the articles. They made us all laugh.

JANE AND YANOV IN SECRET RELATIONSHIP.

THE CLASH OF TWO STARS.

YANOV SCORED LAST NIGHT.

Then, later that afternoon, Angie found a video from a press conference in Kiev.

"You gotta listen to this, Jane. I even managed to find subtitles." She showed me her phone.

There were four players giving statements: the two scorers, my goalkeeper and one more whose name I didn't know. Angie fast-

9

forwarded it to the end. "I guess at the beginning they talk only about football. But listen to the end."

She was right. The reporter asked out of the blue if we had been dating away from the eyes of the public, to which Yanov charmingly laughed and replied, "That's not a sports question." Then he pushed the microphone away and got ready to stand up as somebody in the background announced: "The conference is over."

My heart was pumping as if I was a thirteen-year-old girl, in love for the first time. I had watched the same video a few more times when, close to five o'clock, the doorbell rang. Bea opened it and, after a couple of seconds, returned with a large bouquet of colourful African daisies, reading out loud: "To Jane. Their colours remind me of your beautiful face. Alex Yanov."

The girls screamed while I jumped from the couch and took the bouquet and note from Bea, as if to double-check she had read it correctly. When it was in my hands, I couldn't quite believe what was written on it. I wondered if the handwriting was his or the florist's, then realised I was being childish.

However, childish or not, I felt that something about this guy was different than with all the guys I had liked before.

I had never really been in love in my nineteen years. There were some guys I had liked, but never anything serious. Oscar from home in Dallas had always been a friend – a best friend – despite his parents' encouragement to hang out more and get married later, which would make both our ranches boom. Jonathan, Angie's brother, was temporary, just a flicker in all the excitement of moving to London and meeting new people. And, of course, everything was subject to my career. I could not and did not want to compromise on that. It had always been my job first and then everything and everyone else second.

On top of that, my father had clearly set out for me a long time ago that I should never, ever get involved with men who could be bad for me; meaning no men who were bad influences, who could inhibit my career or who were in any way worse off than me. At every point in my life, when and if I wanted to date, it had to be a good guy – successful, committed and serious. No jokes.

This was partly to protect me but mostly for the family reputation. In his world, the name Andersonn was not to be smeared in any way. It was enough that the spelling was unique and there were no other Andersonns anywhere in the world, so if you typed our name in any search engine you could get to know everything about us. Coming from a working-class family in London, he had sweat blood to create the life of success and luxury he'd always craved. His great-grandfather was of Norwegian descent, thus the specific last name spelling. He was always proud of that and used it to create a unique brand. After he moved to the U.S. to pursue a further upgrade in his business, he had made the name Andersonn an institution. No person in the world read newspapers and didn't know about him.

That was why everything about our family had to be as clean as possible, even when it came to simple things, like me dating someone during my adolescence. "One day you will understand that for us, there must be no chance of failure nor of bad or indecent news," he once said while lecturing me, "no matter how trifling it might be."

Therefore, I never really felt safe involving myself with someone seriously. The guys I'd met were never serious enough, neither to grab my attention nor to confront my dad. Dating me inevitably went hand-in-hand with standing up in front of Brad Andersonn and proving oneself. No one was brave enough for that, which at times made me sad, but mostly it protected me from men who would hurt or use me.

But this Ukrainian guy, who I saw for the first time on the evening of the game, who saw me for the first time too, was courageous enough to walk across the pitch and give me his jersey in front of thousands of spectators and millions of people watching on TV. It was as if he had stood up and said, *This is my girl*. Being the best goalkeeper in the world, he had a lot to lose if this went badly with my father. But nevertheless, he did it. That brave attitude gave me pleasant tickles in my stomach.

That feeling kept me almost immobile for the next two days. All I did was visit the gym and study in my room. We didn't go out, because Lana thought it best to stay quiet for a time after the events at the stadium. Nevertheless, I enjoyed my break from the outside world with a grammar book for my Italian course, in which I was supposed to take an exam towards the end of the year.

I chose to study Italian and Spanish, mostly for work. Dad advised me that it would always leave a very good first impression when discussing and signing contracts, that it would show I was serious and ready to fully commit. He spoke fluent German and Norwegian, which he claimed was one of the reasons he was competitive in the market. He would tell me how he could see he'd won just five minutes into a meeting with Germans and Scandinavians, only because he spoke their language to them. Therefore, I thought it smartest to take up the two languages of fashion. And I did well.

On the third day after the match, when I was beginning to be deeply disappointed, thinking the flowers were the last I would see or hear from the Ukrainian goalkeeper and the fairy tale that had just started was over, I received another bouquet. This time, elegant, purple roses that felt soft and smooth to the touch and instantly filled the whole apartment with an irresistible scent.

There was also a note.

With his number on it.

Write to me, if you want. I know I'd love you to. It would give me great pleasure to see you again at a distance as close as that night at the stadium, but before anything I want to give you respect and choice. Alex Yanov.

P.S. I wanted to go for something more original than red roses, so I chose these. They remind me of you from the Toned *cover, where I took my first close look at you.*

This time I was the one to scream. Upon reading the note, the girls were as ecstatic as I was.

We spent three hours discussing when I should write to him, and in the end, came to a decision that the most natural time would be that same evening. I wanted to go with something simple and I just sent – *Hello.*

I think my life got shorter by twenty years because of the adrenaline that rushed to my brain when I clicked send.

But it lengthened by thirty when I got a reply half an hour later.

Hello, Jane.
- *How did you know it was me?*
There is no one else from the UK who would text me.
- *Haha. Cheesy.*
I hope you didn't think that of the flowers.
- *Definitely not.*
I couldn't think of another way of sending my regards without appearing impolite.
- *No worries. The flowers are perfect. Classy is always good and genuine.*
I will do something genuine again if you let me.
- *You already did.*

I smiled as I remembered the incident at the stadium.

If you mean enraging every newspaper in the world, I apologise. I didn't think that would cause such havoc.
- *No need to apologise. I loved it.*

Really?

I thought for a few seconds before I replied, my heart pounding excitedly.

- *I loved every second of it.*

Would you love then to spend a couple more seconds with that same guy?

By then, my breathing was fast as if I had been running. I pinched myself, understood that it was all happening and calmed down enough to reply – *When?*

Tomorrow. If you don't have any obligations.

Now I really jumped off my bed.

- *Where?* I asked.

In London, of course.

- *You would come to London?*

I will come. If you want to go out for dinner with me.

Having fought back the shock, I texted back – *I will.*

Alright, then. I'm gonna book tickets now. The choice of restaurant is yours, since you're a local.

My brain was still struggling to understand. The guy I'd seen only once, three days ago, who lives on the other side of Europe, will jump on a plane to spend a few hours with me!

- *Alright.* I confirmed. *But what about your training?*

I am on deserved rest. After we won against your guys.

- *Congratulations!*

Thanks. It was a wonderful evening. ;)

- *Haha. It truly was memorable. :)*

I'll pick you up at five. Is that alright?

- *Sure.*

I made sure to sleep a lot that night because I didn't want to show up for my first important date with black circles under my eyes. Before breakfast, I hit the gym for an hour of cardio and then commenced my day almost light-headed and with positive tingles about the upcoming evening. I even found what I was going to wear, although the previous night I'd been a bit concerned, like every woman would be. I chose a simple, elegant light blue dress, knee-length, and plain, white court shoes that matched a small envelope clutch bag.

Needless to say, I couldn't eat all day, although I liked everything the girls ordered. But at a quarter to five, I wished I had. When I was all ready and adding a final touch to my makeup, my stomach roared. I rushed to the kitchen to grab a bite of anything, so as to prevent embarrassing myself in front of Alexander. The moment I opened the fridge, the doorbell rang. I froze.

"I guess you will eat in the restaurant." Angie laughed with the girls.

I sniffed at them because all four of us knew I probably wouldn't be able to eat at all.

I composed myself, grabbed my bag and opened the door.

He was there, in all his size, packed neatly into black trousers and a jacket over a white shirt. His hair was messy in an attractive way and his eyes sky bright. *Now I know why I wanted to wear blue,* I thought. He then smiled and captured me again, like that evening at the stadium.

"Hello, Jane."

"Hi, Alex."

"Ready?"

I nodded and started through the door, but not before I announced that I was leaving to the girls, who I knew were standing just behind the wall, trying to peek and hear everything.

"You all live together?" he asked in the elevator.

"No, only Beatrice and me." I didn't dare look at him, although I could feel his eyes on me. *Oh, no, you won't confuse me again,* I thought, already flustered like a teenage girl. "Beatrice is the blonde one," I added.

"I know."

"How?"

"Everyone knows Jane, Beatrice, Angelina and Lana."

"Even in Ukraine?"

"Okay, in Ukraine the majority are probably guys."

Unexpectedly, I laughed, and then stopped, wondering how I had managed to.

In front of the building, there was a black Mercedes. He opened the door for me, which confused me even more because I was used to only my bodyguards doing that.

He passed me his phone to put in the location of the restaurant we were headed to. "You feel comfortable driving here?" I asked.

"You mean because you guys drive on the wrong side?"

I laughed again. "Yeah, it took me some time to get used to it when I moved here."

"I guess you'll see in the next thirty minutes how I'm doing. Don't distract me too much and hopefully we won't end up on the opposite side of the city."

We moved into the busy London traffic.

"How was your flight?" I asked.

14

He told me how everything was smooth until the moment he reached immigration at Heathrow. The officer was checking his visa for too long, then he called his colleague over, who instantly recognised him as "that goalkeeper who flirted with Jane". They let him go, but then the first one realised the most probable reason he had come to England and jokingly wanted to send him back to Kiev. After that, kids started recognising him in the terminal and he had to inconspicuously find a taxi and get lost.

"Yeah, after what you did on Saturday, everyone here knows you very well."

"I could see. In Ukraine, it's different. I don't know how I would deal with constant watch from people and bodyguards like you do."

"You'd get used to it."

"Says the girl who has grown up with them."

I laughed again.

We arrived at the restaurant and I realised I was a little more relaxed than when we met, though my knees still shook in excitement. He stood next to me and I took him by the arm. His cologne filled my nostrils. If anyone was looking at me at that moment, they would have seen hearts above my head. I was totally mesmerised by this man.

When we entered, the hostess instantly recognised us. I saw it from the change on her face.

"We have a reservation under Yanov," I told her. She nodded and led us to the table. "I hope you don't mind," I whispered to him, "but if I'd given my name, we wouldn't have peace at all."

He held me around my waist. "I most certainly don't mind," he whispered back, sending goose bumps up my whole body.

When he sat opposite me, I was a bit relieved because his closeness and cologne gave me tickles and vibes that absolutely confused me and would sooner or later have made me look like a complete idiot. But while he was sitting there in front of me, I soon became more aware of his piercing eyes, and smile, and hair, and big, strong hands, his wide shoulders, the shirt that fit him perfectly...*Is he for real?* I caught myself thinking.

Thankfully, I had studied the menu the day before, so I knew immediately what to order and what to recommend to him. I could see that I impressed both the waiter and him with my knowledge, so that gave me back a bit of my confidence.

"So, Yanov, tell me about yourself," I said after the waiter left.

"Like when filling out friends books in school?"

"What's that?"

"You know those notebooks your friends give you to fill out, and you write your name, age, favourite sport, actor, animal, etc."

"We've never had that, but that's what I meant. Please, continue." I smiled.

"I was born and raised in Kiev. I started playing football when I learnt how to talk, when I was actually able to say that it was something I really wanted to do."

"And your parents took you seriously when you were two?"

"Not really, but I showed them later that there was no other job for me."

"You are very committed."

"To everything I like."

Again I got those confusing tickles.

"Nobody had played football in our family before. All of them have what I would call…jobs that I'd never do."

"You mean boring?"

"I'm just being polite." We both laughed and he continued, "My mother is a lawyer and a clothes designer in her free time. My father is an IT technician. I've got one sister. Older. She is in charge of finances for a publishing house in Ukraine. We grew up happy, provided with everything we needed. Now I live in my apartment close to my club's training grounds. My best friends are most of the guys from the national team, but if I have to pick someone who stands out, that's Luca Ferreira. He lives with me—"

"The Brazilian guy?" I interrupted him.

"I should have guessed you'd have heard of him." He laughed.

Of course I knew of him. Every woman on Earth knew. Luca Ferreira was highly popular among football fans, both guys and girls. He was interesting because of his unusual story. Back in Brazil, nobody really believed in him. Not even his family. But one Ukrainian coach noticed him at a summer camp in Europe and offered him a position playing for the junior team of the best club in the country. Ferreira accepted and moved to Kiev, planning for Ukraine to be his step before Spain or Italy. But after a couple of seasons, he decided to stay in Ukraine. He liked living there and the friends he'd made. He would often refer to them as family.

Apart from his unusual story, he had the saddest pair of eyes that melted the hearts of all women who watched football. He had a baby face but still was tall and strong, and his build was perfect for magazines and sports commercials. Thousands of girls referred to him as the sexiest sportsman in the world.

"In my free time, when I don't sleep, I study physical education since I'm trying to complete at least my bachelor's degree for now. And if I'm not with books, the guys and I like to camp inland, or I hang around with my sister and parents, playing tennis."

"That sounds like a very lovely childhood and an interesting social life, very well balanced with your job." Since I had calmed down and regained most of my confidence, I took a sip of wine and looked at him over the top of the glass. "No girls?" I winked.

He smiled again, took his glass and bent a little over the table. "No," he said and winked back.

"You expect me to believe that?"

"Yes. There was one. But not anymore. How about you?"

"No."

"You expect me to believe that?"

I laughed. "Yes."

"Let me put it this way: you expect me to believe that there is no—"

"Has never been," I corrected him.

He looked at me in wonder. "—that there has never been a man in the life of Jane Andersonn?"

"Exactly." I was satisfied with the expression on his face. Finally, I had managed to confuse him. "My father is the only strong male figure I've had in my life. Nobody's ever interested me enough."

"Well, taking into consideration that I am sitting here, that's very flattering."

"You're welcome." I winked at him again.

I was suddenly aware of the sparks between us. And I wasn't even trying! I was just being myself. Relaxed. I laughed at his jokes that were so obviously unintentional.

When the food arrived, we continued with more general conversation about sports, art, modelling, reading, family, geography…We would slide from topic to topic so naturally that I forgot how stressed I had been at the beginning of the meeting. We realised we both had a wish to visit Fiji but never had the chance, that we both liked equestrian competitions and knew how to ride, that we were mad about cheesecake, and when it came to cars, we'd both opt for a Mercedes.

He opened up more about his childhood and told me how it wasn't always easy to pursue his career, which his parents didn't take as seriously as he did, especially his father, who, coming from a poor family, was afraid his children would end up the same. His mother was the more supportive one, but she was often torn between her husband and her son.

I, on the other side, shared with him how my family had always been strict with me, how my mother didn't support me but my father always had; how, since I was the only child, I had the burden of being both a son and a daughter; how I'd decided to move to the U.K. when I was only fifteen, having realised I had better chances alone than next to my mother, who couldn't help nagging me about how I had better turn to business and more serious matters.

I told him all this so easily, not afraid he might abuse it or laugh at it later with his friends. I knew stories about footballers, but to me, he was not even close to any of them. With that innocent face and those eyes that were devouring everything I said with the utmost attention, he was my picture of a perfect guy. I had met many men, but no one had managed to intrigue me as much as he did. As I had thought that first time I'd seen him – he stood out simply by being himself.

In all the excitement, we reached the dessert. I was surprised I had managed to eat at all. It was probably the mix of my hunger and his pleasant personality that relaxed me enough.

When we finished, I somehow felt sad that the night was over. We had to move, and on the way to the exit, he again held me by the waist. Outside the air was fresh and cold – no rain, surprisingly. We entered his car and continued talking, and I had almost forgotten how sad I was when we stopped in front of my building.

"Should I escort you upstairs?" he asked in a voice that sounded like something from a sixties romantic movie.

"I'd love that," I whispered and left the car. I felt like a girl from those old movies. A normal date! He'd picked me up, opened the car door, treated me to an elegant dinner, escorted me. I didn't think such a thing still existed. I almost smiled to myself.

"So, Miss Andersonn," he said when we reached the door of my apartment.

"Yes, Mr Yanov?"

He was standing in front of me, not touching me, which confirmed the respect he was determined to give me, and I liked him so much more for that.

"Will I get the chance to see you again?" He looked me straight in the eye, paralysing me again.

"Depends…" I uttered, unable to turn away.

"On what?"

"If you admit that the English team have better players."

I said it so coldly that it definitely didn't sound like a joke, but he still laughed.

"I admit it," he said.

"Then yes."

"This weekend?"

I almost choked. "Today is Wednesday."

"Yes. I have a game on Saturday. On Sunday I can be back here. Unless you have things to do, of course."

"No!" I said, a little too eagerly, knowing that even if I had, I would reschedule everything.

"Then Sunday."

"Sounds like a plan. I'll pray for the weather."

He smiled and approached me. Our faces had never been so close. I traced his cologne again. I wanted to kiss him so badly. Instead, I lowered my head and...

Hugged him!

I knew the very same moment I must have looked like the weirdest girl to him, but I didn't care. I liked my head on his chest and his arms around me. I inhaled his smell one more time before I stepped back.

"Thank you for a wonderful evening, Miss Andersonn."

"Thank you, Mr Yanov."

When our bodies separated, I was girlishly disappointed. He walked towards the elevator as I looked at him longingly.

Then he turned. "Hey, Jane?"

"Yes?"

"Better players, yes, but not a better team." He winked. I opened my mouth, wanting to rebel jokingly. "Too late," he cut me off with a smile. "We already scheduled the date."

I was still laughing when the door of the elevator closed after him.

*****

I was so ecstatic that my first date with Alex Yanov went perfectly that positive energy was almost radiating off of me. I used the remaining three days until our next meeting to be productive and finish one project I had signed up for, which would put me in all the major shopping malls in the country. On set, everyone said how pleasant it was to work with me despite that they'd expected a nasty, spoiled, demanding brat. By Saturday afternoon, I was exhausted and ready to rest and chill in front of the TV watching Yanov in his national league game. It was on at the perfect time on a weekend evening, when I had finished all my obligations and definitely didn't feel like going out for a drink – not knowing that I could watch him play instead. He didn't know about my intentions since I had hidden them, saying the girls and I had plans. I was way too proud to admit I liked him that much.

I sent the girls to the city, prepared popcorn and lemon water and sat in front of the TV, ready to indulge.

When he appeared, I again got those pleasant tickles. He was so handsome, so committed, so serious. It contributed to his overall attractiveness, that attitude with which he played, how he was confidently calm, a feature that probably contributed to him being the best goalkeeper in the world at only twenty years of age.

His team won and he again wasn't scored on. It was half-past eight in the evening when he texted me.

We won.

As soon as he entered his locker room. That warmed my heart.

- *Congratulations! How was it?* I replied straight away.

2:0.

- *Great job!*

Thank you. We're going for drinks now. See you tomorrow at ten.

- *Looking forward to it.*

We planned to spend the whole day together since he had never really explored London, only visited when playing games. He had to be back in Kiev the following morning for his regular training, so he booked a return flight for the same day.

It was interesting, being a tour guide. I dressed up as casually as I could, but we still attracted many eyes. Thank god, the majority of them just smiled and decided not to approach. There were no incidents that ruined that perfect autumn day.

He told me what he wanted to visit most, and one by one we ticked off the items from the list. When it started raining, we hid in a not-at-all fancy café for a cup of tea and laughed at how we were having a typical English afternoon break. We walked a lot that day, laughed, walked up and down Hyde Park because somehow it always happened to be in our way. The time passed so quickly, even though the day was full of events. We forgot about food – when we realised we were starving, it was too late, so we headed straight to the airport and decided to grab a quick bite together there.

It was so funny doing normal things with him. We ended up in Subway with wraps and Coke and joked endlessly about how we would rot in hell for being so unhealthy. Then I saw myself in the mirror for the first time that day and started laughing and hitting him.

"Why haven't you told me my hair has curled up?"

"'Cause I didn't want to. You look cute."

"Cute or like a sheep?" I tried to fix it, to no avail.

"Yeah, like a cute sheep."

I threw a ketchup bag at him. He was probably the first person who could call me a sheep and make me laugh at it.

When the moment of parting came, I again had mixed feelings of sadness and joy.

"Thank you for the funnest tour of London, Miss Andersonn," he said in front of passport control.

"You're welcome, Mr Yanov. But you still haven't seen everything."

"I know. I'd like to visit again."

This time I got closer to him, my chest almost on his, my eyes set longingly on his a few centimetres above mine.

"When?" I almost whispered.

He raised his hand to move the hair from my face. When he touched my cheek, I shivered. He could almost see it.

"When would you like me to?"

His hand was on my neck. I closed my eyes and almost moaned.

"As soon as possible."

"Then as soon as possible." He kissed me on the forehead.

That touched me deeply and I hugged him again, as hard as the previous time. It felt heavenly good to be in his arms, those big arms that were so skilled in their job, so powerful, that controlled everything. I felt I could just rest in them, not worried about anything else in the world.

CHAPTER 3

"As soon as possible" was the following Thursday, which came unexpectedly when his coach released him due to good results and decided to take the second goalkeeper for the game that weekend. He'd received the news on Wednesday afternoon. "I knew instantly where I was gonna be today," he told me during lunch.

The rain was heavy and nonstop. We still managed to do some sightseeing, which was better with fewer people around, and, hidden under an umbrella, we were quite safe from curious eyes.

Still, our shoes got wet after hours of walking over endless puddles, and we had to take a break. I knew we would go to either my apartment or his hotel, but the latter was closer and thus the smarter decision. I was nervous but knew that only what I wanted would happen.

I removed my boots, socks and jacket and went to the toilet. My hair was a mess, so I fixed it with the simple hotel comb. I washed my face, mostly to cool it down – I could feel it burning from excitement. It was my first time being alone with a guy in such a small space.

When I came back to the room, he had already put our shoes next to the radiator and was preparing tea.

"You read my thoughts," I said.

"Yeah, but not well enough yet to see if you want chamomile or green."

"Chamomile, please."

"No honey, I guess?"

"You guess well." I walked to the window over the soft, thick carpet to check the view. It was stunning. I love London for its beauty, even when it rains.

"Does it also rain in Kiev like this?" I asked. *Weather talk! For goodness sake, Jane!*

"Not like this. And not for the majority of the year."

"You like it there?"

"I love it. I think it's the best place to live, if you have the assets to enjoy it. Many Ukrainians don't, so they cannot see its true charm and beauty. I consider myself lucky."

"I understand what you mean."

"What about you?"

"I love London. It feels like home more than Dallas does." I turned, and he was lying on the bed in jeans and a white T-shirt. He looked more attractive than ever.

"You feel like watching something?"

I could only nod, knowing that the next step was lying next to him.

I sat on the bed, and he passed me the remote control. "You choose."

The first thing that caught my attention was a documentary series: an overview of every World Cup, starting with Uruguay in 1930, four tournaments per episode. We looked at each other, agreed with our eyes at the speed of light and then laughed at it.

I decided to finish my tea while sitting. I needed to relax. He was helping me, as if he could feel how nervous I was. We started commenting and discussing the games, and he was surprised by my knowledge of some players, facts and events that only a committed football fan (a guy) would know.

"To be honest, I learnt most of these things when I visited the FIFA World Football Museum in Zurich," I admitted.

"You've been there?" He was impressed.

"Of course I have. It was the first thing I did when I finished the project in Zurich." He still stared at me in awe. "What? I told you I was not an average female fan who just cheers and squeaks when guys remove their shirts."

"Yeah, I could see how you react to that."

I burst out laughing uncontrollably, so hard that I had to put aside my cup of tea and hold my belly. "You're so funny, Yanov." I was on my back, still trying to catch my breath.

In a second, he turned onto his side. Although he was lying beside me, because of his size it seemed as if he was above me. I froze again under his eyes.

"And you are the most beautiful woman I've ever seen, Jane Andersonn."

The eyes that absorbed me then would follow me forever. I couldn't catch my breath, but I didn't need it. We looked at each other, both serious, without a trickle of humour. I felt a vibrating joy in my chest. He moved closer. He could read my thoughts, and I his. His warm fingers touched my cheek and then moved to my shoulder. I closed my eyes and parted my lips just a little, still stiff.

When he touched them, it was like electricity running through my whole face and body. He was soft, and smooth, and gentle, his teeth just briefly clenching me. I was surprised at how my hand responded by rushing to his hair that I'd wanted to touch since he'd approached me at the stadium. Everything that I had wanted since then was infused in that first touch of our lips.

I pulled myself closer to him, wanting more. Now his arm was on my back, all the way to my hair, where his fingers held me possessively. And it lasted. Lasted perfectly long.

I almost moaned when he left me, when I realised I actually needed that breath. His eyes were the only thing in my view. They smiled at me.

"This was perfect," I whispered.

He placed a kiss on my forehead. I squeezed him into a hug, inhaling the smell of his chest.

*****

Maintaining a long-distance relationship was not so difficult for me at the beginning, since this was all new to me. Alex was giving me loads of attention whenever and however he could. We chatted during the day, we got to know each other's schedules and habits, friends and stories from work. Whenever he could, he flew to London. I didn't want to go to Kiev yet. I considered that too big a move, and I didn't think my father would approve of it. "My daughter going to some young man's house who she just met a few days ago? No way!" I could almost hear him saying.

After a month of seeing each other, we couldn't keep hiding anymore. The reporters and photographers, and regular people as well, posted about us on social media, and it was pointless to be quiet on the topic. We knew that if we kept saying "no comment" to every question that we got about our relationship, we would lose sympathy, interest and support from the public.

The public who genuinely loved us and our story.

I consulted Dad before confirming anything. That was a long and exhausting conversation, where I explained myself, Alex, his intentions, my feelings, what I thought was right, why I accepted a guy who lives thousands of kilometres away, why I thought we could work, why we were more than a temporary spark, what I planned with him, what I thought he planned with me and if that seemed to be long term, and numerous other questions I answered without getting frustrated or upset. I knew that wasn't allowed with him and would ruin it all.

"Anyway, I'd have to check him. Not that I don't trust you, but he's getting too close," he said over the phone.

"No problem. You know you're more than welcome here in London any time you want." I let out a breath of relief, sensing the discussion had come to an end.

The following day, Alex was in London and we finally walked out of a restaurant holding hands, heads up. I didn't notice any flashes, but half an hour later Bea messaged me a screenshot of a fresh article. By the end of the day, our holding hands had caused havoc across the media.

Being used to all that, it was much easier for me to deal with all the questions, followings, false assumptions, nonsense and everything that goes hand-in-hand with status like ours. Alex, on the other hand, was learning how to behave in all this. Reporters followed him – even his team's trainings became more frequently visited by foreign journalists, some of whom would even wait in front of the training grounds and the building where he lived.

I helped and advised him. I discovered that he was a person with a very calm personality. He didn't get upset almost ever. He was rather shy. He didn't like talking about his private life in public, and to too-intrusive questions, he preferred to only smile indefinably instead of getting upset.

And journalists liked him even more. While some other guy would brag to everyone about how he was seeing the most beautiful woman in the world, Alex would just nod and smile mysteriously.

I was growing fond of him at the speed of light.

My career was booming in that period. His also. It seemed like our energies together created an unstoppable force that could conquer anything. I didn't have to look for projects. So many came to me that I could choose carefully and pick those that would be in line with the image of myself I wanted to create.

Alex did excellent in his games. He played friendlies, national games, league games; in all of them, he was like a stone wall. He did receive a couple of goals, but it didn't spoil his statistics. He was still by far the best goalkeeper on the planet, with German Dieter Lahrman behind him by eight goals.

The end of November was approaching. Some Christmas decorations were already appearing in the streets of my favourite city. I was getting ready to go for dinner with Alex. His plane had landed two hours ago. He had gone to the hotel to change and was on the way.

The doorbell rang too early. Still, I went to open it, thinking that he might have decided to surprise me.

And I was indeed surprised.

"H—hi, Dad," I uttered in shock.

"Hello, Jane," my father said. I was completely paralysed with shock and fear. "May I come in?"

"Oh, yes, sure." I moved aside, letting him in.

When I closed the door, he turned, looked at me from head to toe, and then smiled.

"You are going out?"

"Was about to."

"With that Yanov?" I nodded. "Hm…You look great."

"Thank you."

My brain was heating up. I didn't know what to tell Alex and how to explain that our date was cancelled. He had run straight from his training to catch the flight to make it for dinner with me. I was happy to see Dad, of course, but he could definitely have chosen a better moment.

"I am lucky that I caught you at home."

You should've told me you were coming, I wanted to say, but I knew that was not an option. That kind of rudeness had never been allowed.

"Where are you two going?" he asked.

"Only to the Balmoral for a light dinner. Then for a drink in Sky Garden."

"You'll sleep at his place?"

I wanted the earth to open and devour me when he was so blatantly straightforward about such topics. But it had always been like that. And although never entirely used to it, I had to accept it and answer truthfully because, somehow, he always knew when I lied.

"That was the plan, yes," I confirmed.

He didn't look upset. That was a good sign. "Is Beatrice here?"

I nodded and showed him to the living room.

Bea greeted him. He was like an uncle to her since her father was one of his most respected partners and friends. Dad handed her a little red velvet box. Bea's mother had sent her an old pearl bracelet for her next photo shoot. She thanked him and understood she was supposed to leave us alone.

Dad asked me about work and my upcoming projects, advised me on what to do before New Year's and what to schedule after the holidays, and then the doorbell rang again. I looked at him, asking for permission to move.

"Let's go." He stood up and waited for me to go in front of him.

There was no chance to warn Alex that the most dangerous man in the world – according to some – would be waiting for him on the other side of the door, so I prayed for him as I made my way through the hall.

26

When I opened the door, I saw his face change from joyful to worried immediately upon seeing my expression. I didn't jump to hug or kiss him, instead stepping aside so my father came into his view.

"Alex, this is my father, Brad Andersonn," I uttered with difficulty, barely audible.

I saw a cramp on his face and how stiff his back became, but that didn't prevent him from talking.

"Nice to meet you, Mr Andersonn. I am Alexander Yanov." He held out his hand.

"Nice to meet you too, young man." Dad accepted his shake. "Finally."

They both laughed.

"Jane told me you were planning to go for dinner. Would you mind if I join?"

"It would be my pleasure," Alex replied, so calmly that I couldn't help admiring him.

"I would suggest that we first attend one exhibition I have been invited to and then go to a restaurant of my choice."

"Sounds ideal."

They both looked at me.

"I'll just get my bag and coat and we can go," I murmured nervously before rushing to my room.

"How was your flight, Mr Andersonn?" I heard Alex ask, and by the time I returned, they were casually chit-chatting. That encouraged me immensely. Whether he wanted to or not, Dad chased away one hundred per cent of the men who'd tried to have something with me. But this one seemed to resist his pressure. At least for now.

The exhibition in the Wallace Collection gallery was impressive. It was organised by one of Dad's partners and his wife, who were very supportive of young artists and enabled them to show their masterpieces. Dad wasn't much into paintings, but he recognised and respected talent, and he was very well aware of how much importance his name carried next to the names of these painters. He also had a rather controlling approach to media when it came to ventures like this. For example, he would give small interviews, but newspapers weren't allowed to publish anything if he wasn't happy with the outcome of the event. That attitude had saved me from lots of gossip and vulgarities that I definitely didn't want attached to my image.

Having left the gallery, we headed towards Hydesick, Dad's favourite place in London. I knew that he liked the Balmoral also, but by changing plans he wanted to show who was in charge and to see how Alex would behave and accept it.

And Alex was doing great. He took part in every conversation on any topic Dad brought up. He seemed to be versatile in all fields, from sports – of course – to politics, geography, agriculture, economics. I could see Dad was impressed. Later, I would say that to Alex, who I could see was trying, but not in such an obvious way. He was scared but had good control of himself.

"So, right now, you are the best?" Dad asked him after a sip of red wine.

"That's what they say," Alex confirmed.

"Who are 'they'?"

"The statistics."

"How long do you plan to stay on top?"

"Forever."

We all laughed.

"I like that ambition. Try to make it real."

"I will."

Alex sounded reassuring, even to me. As the evening progressed, he was more and more confident about himself. I was proud – of him, of my choice.

After we finished the main course and the second bottle of wine, I was more relaxed and got into the conversation more easily. But when Dad gave me the look that meant *Leave us alone for a while,* I froze again.

We've always had good communication. He taught me how when I was young, and he was my only supporter for whatever I wanted. I learnt to understand what he meant without words. I liked that because we were so close, and I needed that closeness with one parent when I couldn't have it with my mother. I was aware that some conversations would always be stiff and unnatural due to the fact that he is a man, but we still had them, regardless of how embarrassing they might be.

Nevertheless, despite how well I knew him, he could still surprise me. I knew there was a part of him somehow that was unknowable – the part that I would never entirely understand. That is why I have always respected and been afraid of him.

And listened to him, unequivocally. Therefore, when he looked first at me, and then to the toilet, I knew I was to get lost and leave Alex to his mercy.

In the bathroom, I saw how pale I was and that I needed a retouch. I stayed for around ten minutes and then decided it had been long enough.

It melted my heart when I saw the two of them laughing. It was good. Everything was good.

When I returned to the table, Dad suggested that we skip dessert and go for another bottle of wine. Our conversations became more trivial and relaxed. Dad enquired about Alex's lifestyle, daily schedules, how often he exercised, went out, saw his parents, and he then praised him for managing all that so well. Then Alex asked him about his daily routine and how he managed to stay fit with so much office work. I was truly impressed by both of them.

Still, it was such a weight off my mind when dinner came to a close. It was almost eleven and time to leave the restaurant.

"Where should I take you, Mr Andersonn?" Alex asked when we sat in the car. "Or should I drop Jane off first?"

"Dad often stays at my place when he comes," I said.

"I understand you two wanted to spend the night together," Dad said bluntly.

"Well, we wanted," Alex answered him.

Dad started laughing, and then the two of us laughed as well.

"Sorry to mess with your plans, Yanov. It has nothing to do with me being an asshole. But I would really like to spend some time with my daughter."

"I understand, Mr Andersonn."

Later, when we separated in front of my building, I could only hug Alex before Dad and I headed up to the apartment. The two of them shook hands again.

"Till next time," Dad said, which was rather encouraging.

In the elevator, he was the one to break the silence.

"He is a smart guy. I believe you're not bored with him."

"Not at all."

"And committed. And not a kid."

"He is definitely mature for his age. What did you ask him while I was away?"

"How the hell he dared do that at the stadium." He laughed again.

"I keep wondering the same. Tell me, please!"

We entered my apartment.

"He said that it was one of the moments he knew he had to do something, even though he was frozen with fear, otherwise he would regret it the rest of his life."

I felt warmth in my chest.

"That's pretty honest," I said.

"I agree. That's why I like him so far."

I smiled and hugged him before heading to my room to prepare for bed. We were tired and he was exhausted from his trip, so we decided to wake up early the next morning and start off with the gym and then have breakfast together before he took a flight to Dusseldorf, where he had a meeting.

Back in my room, I was free to check my phone.

- *What was that! :O* was Alex's message.

No worries. You did great.

- *Glad to hear that. All okay with you?*

Yes. Everything is fine. How do you feel?

- *Like a crocodile chewed me for a couple of hours and then spit me out out of mercy.*

I had to put my face into a pillow to silence the laugh.

The following day, after I saw Dad off at the airport, I told the driver to rush as fast as he could to Alex's hotel. We spent the rest of the day together, talking about our impressions from the previous night. Somehow, we both felt everything was alright with that scary man who happened to be my father.

CHAPTER 4

Things could not have been developing better for Alex and me. The first half of his football season was coming to an end and he was still the best at what he did. On the other side of Europe, I was also getting better at what I did. Together we conquered the market. That was an effect I had neither hoped for nor expected. Apparently, we helped each other's careers. I received more offers than I could accept, some of which were difficult to turn down. Projects lined up one after another to the point that I had the whole following year planned.

But what I was excited about most was a completely new type of fashion show that I signed up to do in Italy. The idea was that part of the show would be a music video with a local star and the other part a live performance with the same singer. It was something different, and after discussing it with girls, Dad and Alex also, I was sure that it would be an absolute hit world-wide. It required time, dedication, exercise and dancing, but I was willing to do anything.

I felt I would have the energy for it after my winter holidays, which I planned to spend in the Tatra Mountains in Poland with Alex and his friends. He suggested the trip to me at the beginning of December. Since one of his friends had a cottage in an area called Zakopane, popular for skiing and snowboarding among Europeans, they usually spent a few days of their winter break there.

I liked the idea; since he'd already met my best friends and my father, it was only fair that I get to meet some of his people. I felt it was the right time to spend a few days together, as we'd have been dating for nearly three months by then. The only condition was that I stay with the girls for Christmas.

With our families based in America, Bea and I didn't want to deal with flying there and back at the time of year that was busier than normal. The additional rain and snow that regularly caused flight cancellations and delays were something we didn't want to ruin our plans.

Thus, we spent Christmas morning at Lana's place and moved to Angie's family home later in the afternoon. By then, Angie's brother Jonathan and I had almost forgotten that anything had happened between us; we were just acquaintances who chatted casually. He even joked how I should get him some of Alex's used jerseys so he could sell them.

In all the rush, we managed to organise presents for everyone. I got my mom a ruby necklace and my dad a suit from his favourite tailor in London. He, on the other hand, was more generous and sent me a toy plane with the signage of his private jet, which meant that I now had a way of easily moving around Germany the following year during the World Cup.

We had talked on many occasions about how it would be difficult for me to attend all the games I wanted if I had to worry about booking plane tickets, dealing with standard airport procedures or, even worse, driving between cities. I would never make it from one stadium to another if two important games were on the same day. It was already clear by then that I would be following England and Ukraine at the tournament, but even before I met Alex, Dad and I had agreed we would attend some American games together, both as a sign of respect to our home country and due to his connections with the coach and national team management.

With so many obligations, plans and expectations, a private plane was the asset I needed. Dad always took care of everything.

*****

I landed in Krakow in the early morning of the 27th of December. I was alone, but the security staff at the airport had been informed that I would come and they should be ready to assist me if required. I landed earlier than Alex, so I waited for him in a café at the arrivals terminal. It snowed heavily outside. He would be arriving with two of his friends from the club. The others were either already at the cottage or would join us later in the day.

The invitation to spend a week in the Tatras was extended to the girls also, but we decided it would be best if I went alone. I needed to confront all his friends alone, as he had mine. I was a bit anxious because the world seemed to be divided into two groups: one half was fond of me and thought I was kind, cute and lovely, while the other half also liked me, but found me bitchy, arrogant and spoiled. Alex's friends had to fall into the former.

I was also stressed about the language barrier. I was to be the only non-Ukrainian/Russian speaker in the company, so I knew that if they persisted in talking in their native language, it would be purposefully to isolate me.

However, one hour into our trip I was already assured that I had nothing to fear. Nikolay Pavlov and Ivan Rostov were so relaxed and laid back that I hadn't stopped smiling since we'd met. We hit it off immediately when they accepted my hand, but instead of a shake, they each kissed it.

"I had no idea there are still knights in Ukraine!" I said, delighted.

"Well, we are a country that develops pretty slowly," replied Nikolay, and we all laughed.

They took my bag and we headed towards the rental car. I wasn't easily noticeable on my own, but the four of us together started gathering too much attention, so we just bought some coffee and set off quickly. Alex and I sat at the back, while Nikolay and Ivan settled in the front, where they constantly, brutally teased each other.

"Do you guys often roast each other like this?" I asked.

"Yes. It's like showing love," replied Ivan.

"Exactly. Normally, Al is included, too, but we've decided not to give him a hard time while you're around," said Nikolay.

"That's very considerate," Alex said, "after the way you both pestered me on the flight here."

The farther we went out of the city, the thicker the snow curtains were. The atmosphere in the car was great. It reminded me of one time when I went to the mountains in Montana with my friends from Dallas: Oscar, Vanessa and the Stevenson twins. Daniel and Harold were the only ones with driver's licences then, so they drove while the rest of us drank in the back of the car. We got stuck in the snow when Daniel, listening to music a little too enthusiastically, slid off the road. We weren't scared. We couldn't stop laughing, actually.

This time we didn't get stuck off-road – just in traffic – but we were still having fun. Everyone seemed to be in a celebratory mood; even people in other cars were already drinking beer and wine in broad daylight. We decided not to follow their example, though we planned to have some drinks that evening.

The cottage belonged to the parents of Alex's friend Sergey Lomin. His mother was Polish, so the spacious modern hut had been in their family for decades. It was in perfect condition, with an excellent floor and radiator heating system and a wooden interior and exterior. I fell in love with it the moment I saw it.

The majority of Alex's friends were already there. Only one more group was expected to arrive later that evening due to flight delays. When we arrived, Sergey and Danylo went out to greet us and show us where to park.

The inside was warm and welcoming. I smelt cinnamon cookies and mulled wine being prepared, along with some roasted meat.

"This already feels like home," I couldn't help saying.

A curvy lady with white skin and thick, black hair put back with a headscarf came into the living room. Behind her followed a slender brunette.

"Thank you," said the black-haired one, holding out her hand. "I'm Dasha, Danylo's wife. And this is Mila, Igor's girlfriend. We're the cooks of the group."

"Definitely a pleasure to meet you. The whole place smells wonderful."

The others started coming in from all sides and introducing themselves. I apologised in advance for mixing up names since only a robot would remember all eleven new names, most of which I had heard for the first time then, and some of which I couldn't even pronounce properly.

After that we sat for lunch, starting it off with a shot of the strongest alcoholic drink I had ever tried – horilka – which Alex explained to me later was a mix of honey and strong vodka. They were crazy about it, but I stayed away. I preferred the mulled wine that the girls had prepared perfectly.

In the evening, the remaining five people joined us: three guys and two girls. All of the guys played for the Ukrainian national team. Most of them also played with Alex in the same club in the Ukrainian First League, except for the few who were in the Western European leagues. Playing for the club often made them too busy to meet, so they loved international games because they frequently brought them together, keeping them in touch. They also made it a tradition to gather every winter holiday somewhere. And, as they said, every year the size of the group increased as guys kept getting married or finding girlfriends.

"But this time last year, no one ever even thought that at the next holiday, Jane Andersonn would be sitting with us," Vlad Starovsky said while we all sat in the living room lit by a fireplace and a colossal Christmas tree, sipping more mulled wine infused with cinnamon, apples and oranges.

"Especially not with this guy," added Ivan, pointing at Alex.

By then I had been told how everyone was beyond shocked by what Alex had done that evening at Wembley Stadium.

"I was there, also, and couldn't stop staring at him," Oksana, Vitaliy Koval's wife, said while I was helping in the kitchen. "Vitaliy was waving at me, but I just couldn't get my eyes off Alex. We had no idea what he was about to do. And when he gave you the jersey, I thought, *Jesus Christ! This guy must be absolutely insane!* I mean, to do this to Jane Andersonn! I was sure your gorillas would grab him over the fence, break his back and stuff the jersey into his mouth. But on the contrary, you two were so cute!"

"The guys haven't given him peace since then," said Sofia, wife of Mihail Hrichko. "Neither have we. He's always been that good guy from the neighbourhood who all parents like and wish for their daughters. He dated seriously only one girl for a year – it didn't work, he ended it politely and calmly."

"He is still nice in that way," continued Oksana. "You know how guys can be horny and talk about girls, tits and asses all the time. Alex gets involved only briefly in such topics."

"And then: ta-da! He approaches the hottest woman in the world! Just like that! Out of the blue!" Sofia said. "And he never even brags about that."

"Has he asked you to praise him in front of me?" I joked.

They giggled. "Jane, you have the most caring, sweet, patient, committed and understanding guy in that whole group," said Oksana. "If he had liked me, I would've married him instead of Vitaliy for sure."

"Me too!" added Sofia with a laugh.

The evening was full of jokes and stories from their life in Kiev. They all spoke English, even when talking to each other, which made me feel truly comfortable and easy at heart. How could I ever worry that my boyfriend, who was such a wonderful person, would hang around impolite and unpleasant people?

Sometime after midnight, the fire had dwindled out, and in the darkness we realised how tired we were from the plane trip and drive up the mountains, so we decided it was time for bed. Sergey's parents normally rented the cottage, so there were ten bedrooms in total: two on the ground floor and four on each of the two floors above, plenty of space for eighteen people. Alex and I got a room on the first level with a view of the mountains.

I liked the bathroom, too. It was decorated in blue and black tiles but still warm. It had both a shower and a bathtub. At that moment, I felt that a bath would make me fall asleep in the water, so I opted for a quick shower. Alex went after I finished. I loved the kindness and consideration he constantly showed me. In his visits to London, we'd spent the night together many times, but he had never tried anything. We'd just hug and sleep in each other's arms. Even though I felt more and more relaxed in his presence, I was still scared of crossing that boundary. Somehow you expect a lot from Jane Andersonn. I had always been expected a lot of. And when it came to sex, where I didn't have experience, I wasn't able to have the same confidence I did in everything else. I didn't want to disappoint.

Still, I knew he wouldn't put me down, whatever happened. I believed our bodies would understand each other when the moment came.

I had almost fallen asleep thinking about that when he lay in bed and hugged me from behind. I turned to give him a goodnight kiss and rest my head on his chest. I could place my whole body there, that's how big he was.

He kissed me on the forehead, placed his arm on my back and then kissed me again, on my lips this time. And that's when I felt the tickle that ran from my mouth, through my chest, down to my legs and belly. I wanted more of that kiss; I liked the feeling. He pulled me closer and kissed me more deeply. I hugged him and moaned. The tickles in my belly intensified into a fire. I scratched his back, wanting more. That desire was stronger than ever – stronger than my fear.

He rose over me so all the light I could see now was coming from the gleam in his ocean blue eyes. Suddenly, I wasn't tired anymore, or sleepy, or even tipsy. My mind was clear, the clearest it had ever been. And it wanted him.

He looked into my eyes and understood the desire before continuing to kiss me up and down my neck. The purple top I had on was minimal and easy to move aside. He cupped my breasts and started kissing them, too. The power of that feeling made me gasp and curve, asking for more. When he bit them, I perceived that as pain and immense pleasure simultaneously. All I could think was that I wanted more and why hadn't we done this before.

My fingers were in his hair and on his back, pulling and scratching, asking for more pleasure that he was so excellent at giving.

And then he started moving down. His lips were between my ribs, making their way lower, around my navel. I became aware of the pool of fire that ignited lower in my belly, and I felt the urge for it to be extinguished. I would have given anything to have it satisfied.

When he removed my underwear, I felt ablaze. I didn't recognise my actions. I could always control my behaviour, but with this, all my barriers collapsed.

He separated my legs easily, and I was totally unprepared for what followed. I was almost screaming as I squeezed him, curving under his touches that became more and more intense. One orgasm followed another, and another, and another; every time I asked myself if I was capable of more. I felt I would completely dissolve into liquid.

For the last stage of this crazy ride I had never even thought was possible for a female body, he put his fingers inside me and used them together with his tongue to take me down the wildest road I'd ever ventured. I saw lights, even though my eyes were closed. I felt pleasure and pain, power and weakness, eternity and the importance of a moment.

Lying next to me, while I struggled to even my breathing, Alex smiled. I slowly became aware of how quiet the house was. As before, his eyes were the only source of light. I was ashamed to look at him. Remembering my actions, I felt embarrassed of the naïve yet insatiable desire of an innocent girl.

He broke the silence. "Jane Andersonn, you are much more than a man could wish for."

"You mean horny like a spinster?"

He laughed. "I'd rather call it promising and pure. Your desire surprised me."

"It surprised me, too." I turned to him. "Alex, why didn't you—"

"Not tonight, Jane. We're both tired from the trip. I want it to be special and long, and for you to feel strongly everything I want to do to you."

That naughty tickle again sprang in my chest. I hugged him and, in a matter of minutes, fell asleep.

Over the following few days, we enjoyed skiing and snowball fights. From breakfast to dinner we passed the time in the surrounding sports centres. I stuck to skiing, while some guys also did snowboarding. Alex wasn't one of them. He was too big to balance on the board, which was endlessly amusing to his friends.

It was fun enjoying the natural snow then taking breaks in cosy cafés with tea, hot chocolate and biscuits. I felt I was on vacation and my battery was being recharged. I spoke to the London girls only in the evenings, when I had time to check my phone and email. They were envious and we decided that next year they would join us.

I got around the kitchen well, too. The cooks in charge, Dasha and Mila, told me what to do so I helped whenever I could. Though I'd rather have been doing something else, I didn't want them to think I was lazy or rude. Still, I enjoyed and appreciated being with Alex 24/7. It was the best gift I could get for Christmas. And I was beyond happy to see that we got on pretty well when we spent more time together.

The day of the 31st of December was pretty chill. We decided to stay in and prepare drinks, music and fireworks for the barbecue that evening. We would continue skiing in the new year.

Around three o'clock, when everything was ready, Nikolay suggested that we take a nap since we wanted to stay up past midnight. But I wasn't sleepy. The day was sunny and our room was bright with rays. I was sorting through my suitcase and wardrobe, deciding what would be the best to wear that night – something between casual and classy – when Alex entered and locked the door behind him. The way he was looking at me gave me goose bumps.

I was still holding one of the dresses in my hands when he approached and hugged me. I dropped the dress and gave him a light kiss, which he prolonged gently.

His finger was cold when he touched my cheek and then moved it down the side of my neck, over my breasts and waist. I couldn't take my eyes off his, and when he grabbed my hips and pulled them flush to his, I knew he could see in my eyes how my body reacted to it. It was comforting to see that he was as excited as I was.

He removed my shirt without breaking eye contact. I helped him out of his and once again was amazed at how firm, strong and handsome he was. It excited me to know that this guy was mine, entirely mine.

He kissed me gently on the neck, giving me shivers, and then turned me around and started kissing my back. My nerves were on edge, reacting frantically to every touch of his lips and tongue. His hands didn't give me peace either, and when he used them to unlatch my bra, a wave of heat sprang to my head. The lace fell on the floor, and he squeezed my breasts. I felt both shameless and shameful. How come I liked everything he did to me? How did he know everything that I liked?

I moaned before turning back to kiss him. Our chests were tight together, and I realised I was way too excited and needed to get rid of the clothes that now almost suffocated me. I unhooked his belt and unbuttoned his jeans. They fell down easily. He pushed me demandingly but gently onto the bed and then pulled my jeans off, still wordlessly maintaining eye contact. He was looking down at me, and that excited me like nothing before. My whole life, there had never been a man who could overpower me, be superior, tame my stubborn will and make me feel desired as the strong woman I was. All of them succumbed to me, were scared of me, listened to me, wanted me, but never made me want them. They were all scared boys.

Until this one, who was standing in front of me. In that moment, I admired him and wanted him more than anything. I wanted to give him everything just to get him in the end. It wasn't just a sexual wish. I had resisted sex many times before. Now I wanted all of this man: his body and his mind.

I pressed my lips to his lower belly, my nails in his back. I rolled my tongue around his navel and then slowly to the band of his boxers. With no experience, somehow I knew what I was doing. I felt his movements, his breathing; I could almost hear the beating of his heart.

I pulled down his boxers and he gasped. When I started kissing him and exploring with my tongue and lips, his fingers in my hair squeezed. I continued with more eagerness. I wanted to show him that I knew, even though I had never done it. But after a few moments, he pulled me by the hair.

"Jane, don't... please." I looked up at him. "I won't be able to control it."

I smiled, kissed his belly again. He bent over me and helped me out of the last of my clothes. The room was still bright with the dazzle of sunbeams through the window, and I felt more exposed than ever. The whole picture had a romantic touch.

I moved back on the bed and lay on my back, and he encircled me with his arms, completely covering me. He started kissing my belly, then up, between my breasts, over them, up my neck, finally reaching my face. With every touch, I curved and grasped and tore his back with my nails. All the things I imagined a man doing to me, he was doing. The fact that we clicked so perfectly warmed my heart and made me love him. All of him.

I felt him between my legs, and at the thought of what followed, shivers ran down my spine, covering me in a cold sweat. I knew he was waiting for my approval, so I moved under him, placing his hips right where they should be. He looked at me; I smiled, touched his hair and pulled him to a kiss. He understood the affirmation and moved slowly.

I didn't think it would be so easy. But it was. Smooth, gentle and effortless. When he entered me first, a little, he asked me with his eyes if he should continue or not, to which I replied by pulling his hips deeper. He was as surprised as me.

There was no pain, only a new kind of pleasure. Pleasure that rose with every move he made. My nails were now cutting into his hips, asking for him to give me more. He didn't want to rush, although I wished for that climactic moment. He built it up slowly and intensified it to the point I thought I would not be able to endure.

I wasn't aware that I was moaning, nearly screaming. I only knew the satisfaction he was giving me, and I demanded more of it.

Suddenly, when his moves became more forceful, I felt him touch one spot he hadn't touched before. It seemed to be the source of all the pleasure I was receiving. I screamed and gripped him stronger. He understood what I wanted and repeated the move, touching the spot again, and again, and again.

Everything in my eyes infused into the colours of some abstract painting. Those colours moved, liquid into liquid. And I became liquid, spreading over the soft sheets. I could almost hear music, the pleasant sounds of a forest, and birds chirping, a stream rushing. I felt absolute bliss.

His kiss on my cheek was what awoke me from my daydream and dispersed all the colours of the painting. I realised I was staring at the wooden ceiling. I turned my head to him. He was smiling. I smiled back and curled into his hug. He was so warm.

"This was a perfect Christmas gift, Yanov."

"I agree, Andersonn. Never had better."

"Including that table football when you were eight?"

"Including that." He kissed me on the forehead. "However, speaking of gifts…" he rolled over me to the night table and took something out of the drawer. I moved up to a seated position, still naked and absolutely relaxed about it. He passed me a little black velvet box. I was as excited as a child.

"Wait." I didn't want to open it before giving him my gift. I reached down to the floor and pulled out from under a pile of clothes a slightly bigger red velvet box and handed it to him. "You first."

Inside the red box was a black leather bracelet that had reminded me of him the moment I saw it while looking for gifts. He sometimes wore things like that but complained they would always tear after some time. This one I made sure was good quality.

"Wow, it matches my new gloves," he said.

"You're gonna wear it when you play?"

He clicked it on his right wrist. "Always." He bent over to kiss me. "Now, your turn."

I knew it would be something pretty that I would like because he knew my taste. Or maybe we had a taste for the same things. Perhaps I cared for him enough that I would love anything he'd choose for me. Either way, I expected to love whatever it was.

However, I didn't expect the rose gold diamond love knot earrings I had seen on a gloomy, rainy day in London when we'd hidden from a surprise storm in a jewellery shop. I had looked at them longingly but never said a word. I'd wanted to go back for them but somehow never had time.

But he'd seen that and understood everything from my look.

"Alex, how did you…" I said breathlessly. "When?!"

He answered me with a kiss.

"Merry Christmas, Love."

CHAPTER 5

The beginning of the new year was successful for both of us. Alex was still the best, though Dieter Lahrman, the German national goalkeeper, was just behind him. Lahrman was older and much more experienced, so it was only natural. However, Alex was determined not to let him take over and worked harder every day.

My projects placed me on the pages of every magazine and newspaper that mattered in my industry. The Italian project I helped pioneer – a new way of promoting clothes through an active fashion show and music video – was a good move. Shooting for the video lasted for two weeks and took place in Abu Dhabi in the United Arab Emirates because the weather there in January was perfect for outdoor projects requiring a summer vibe. It was exhausting, with long working hours, but everyone on the set was inspired, enthusiastic, creative, relaxed, and willing to work and give their best. I enjoyed every minute of it, as well as the show that followed at the end of February. I also had to take up dance classes before and during the project, but it was all fun. It wound up being a substitute for the gym since I didn't limit my hours to the required time. I stayed longer, working until I was either completely exhausted or had mastered the moves.

The main idea was that I model different swimsuits, beachwear and summer clothes in the video and then perform with the singer live in front of an audience, wearing one of the outfits from the collection.

People loved it. It was all worth the risk. The designer became a superstar overnight and the video of my performance with the Italian singer circulated on social media nonstop. Literally the day after the show, I got an offer for another project of the same type, this time with two world-renowned pop/rap singers whose song and video would be presented for the first time at a fashion show in New York.

I was ecstatic.

However, there were some headlines circulating in the media that I didn't approve of and that made Alex angry.

Petrov is Pumping up to Score Against Yanov and Win Jane Over

Jane German Bride to be, Assures Beller

Bianchi: 'I Will Bring Jane to the Italian Stands'

'Jane is the Only Reason I Worked Hard to Get to the World Cup Final Stage': Joyce

Robin Braam Says He'll Give Jane a Tulip First Thing When They Meet

I mostly managed to ignore them, but for Alex, it was difficult not to react to assumptions and statements that his girlfriend would leave him as soon as she met some other footballer. Normally, Dad and I would deal with such writings in our way: making them apologise and stop. But this time the articles were so numerous and came from so many parts of the world that we couldn't keep up. And they were piling up as the World Cup approached. I decided to ignore them as long as the positive stories were the majority, but there were some instances when it was impossible for even me to stay cool-headed.

It was getting worse and more lascivious every week. At the beginning it flattered me, since all those guys were good looking and many girls' dream, but when I saw how it affected Alex, who was by nature calm and quiet, I no longer found it funny. I promised myself I'd give them a hard time if I ever met them.

At the beginning of March, I was getting ready to go to Kiev for the first time. I had been mentally preparing for weeks since it meant inevitably meeting Alex's parents. He joked about it, saying nothing could be more difficult than meeting Brad Andersonn, to which I would always reply that however difficult it was, Brad Andersonn was still only one parent, while I was about to confront two. On top of that was his sister, who scared me almost as much as they did. I got lucky that she would be away the first weekend I planned to come.

I managed to squeeze my working week into four days and took off on Friday morning for Kiev. Alex picked me up after his training, and we went for lunch and a long tour of the city. It was chillier than in London but still pretty. It was interesting to see where he went to school and had his first trainings, and what his favourite spots in the city were (a quirky cinema, a cosy restaurant and a hidden park).

His apartment was lovely as well. Spacious, white, bright, simple, clean and neat, in the Pechersk District, in the city centre. You could see two disciplined men lived there. Luca Ferreira was away in Brazil, where he had a couple of trainings with his national team, so he was not going to play the club game that weekend.

That was great for us; it was fantastic to be alone somewhere that was not a hotel. It was even more exciting for me to have sex at his place – all over it. I felt that somehow I was leaving parts of myself there, something that would make him miss me even more when we were apart.

The following day, he headed to the stadium before me to have a short training and warm up before the game. Oksana and Dasha picked me up and we went to the game together. Fortunately, nobody except for my closest friends knew where I was, so, not worrying about reporters, we were free and relaxed on the way to and while entering the stadium. The security were the first to realise what was going on – Jane Andersonn had come to Kiev – and they led us to the stands without any issues.

The first game of Alex's I attended was as perfect as it could be. As before, he didn't receive any goals, his team won 3–0 and he ran across the pitch to come and give me his jersey. This time I didn't freeze, instead giving him a long kiss so that all the photographers had time to shoot it and announce once again to the babbling bastards whose girlfriend I was.

After the game, I had bigger concerns than the stupid comments of empty-headed footballers who were rising above themselves. We were about to go for dinner with Tanya and Olexiy Yanov.

Alex and I drove to his place to have a quick shower and get ready. I was starving but couldn't think of any food that wouldn't give me nausea. I made sure everything I wore was perfect, from my jewellery – Alex's Christmas present earrings and a miniature necklace – to my medium-heel brown boots and pearl white velvet dress. I didn't want his designer mum to find a single flaw.

We arrived at the restaurant before them, which was a good sign. I didn't want us to be late, make them wait and then have them say I distracted their son too much.

But after Tanya Yanova warmly hugged me when she saw me – before even kissing her son – I knew I had watched too many movies with evil mothers-in-law. She was simply beautiful at her fifty-two years of age, clad in lavender with a matching set of dangling earrings and a large golden necklace. Her hair was a well-maintained blonde, short and layered, and her makeup appropriate and just enough, with emphasised eyes and red lipstick. The way her smile shone is something I always think of first when somebody mentions her.

Alex's father was the reason his son was so handsome and charming. I recognised the same shoulders and height, the same attitude and manner of speech. Only his hair was different: black with a few white patches. He looked great in a navy blue suit and could still make girls' eyes turn. With the combination of these two people, it was no wonder Alex was so attractive. I could just imagine how stunning his sister must look.

I relaxed a few minutes into the dinner after a shot of spotykach, another favourite drink of the Ukrainians that I again didn't find very appealing. I still managed all the shots during the evening so as not to embarrass the Andersonns. We leisurely discussed many topics: my job and plans, Alex's plan to stay for another year in his club and the reasons behind it, our plans for the upcoming summer, and the most important event of the year – the FIFA World Cup.

It turned out the Ukrainians were pretty confident about the outcome of the tournament. If I wasn't dating one of the players, I would have found it funny and even daring, but since I knew and saw how committed Alex and his friends were, I agreed that there was a lot to hope for and that the world would see an exciting competition.

"Just don't let them enrage you to the point that you lose yourself," said Alex's father. "Your opponents will use whatever they can against you. And now, with Jane around, they have more material."

"Are you referring to all that stuff in the papers?" I said and instantly bit my tongue.

"Not just in the papers. They are everywhere. On the TV, in every news outlet I read. You two cover almost all the sections – sport, showbiz, celebrities, lifestyle, recently music as well. Only politics is missing."

"And obituaries, honey," Tanya said. "As long as they're not there, it's good."

We all started laughing, changing the atmosphere from slightly stiff to relaxed again.

"I just wanted to say that this time it will be intense. Alex knows what I'm talking about."

The two of them looked at each other.

"I know," Alex said.

"Don't let them use what you two have to their advantage."

I squeezed Alex's hand under the table. That was exactly what he needed to hear.

After that evening, his mood was different when it came to the salacious articles and assumptions. He was more relaxed, especially when he saw that for every ugly thing somebody said, there were dozens of great ones that admired and praised our relationship that we'd managed to nourish over long distance while each developing two rather successful careers.

In the end, other people's opinions didn't even matter. All we cared about was how we felt with each other and how that impacted the professional sphere of our lives. And things were going from good to great.

*****

Since my parents were busy in the U.S., we all agreed it would be best for them to meet the Yanovs in Berlin. Dad was a big football fan and planned to take a month off to attend most of the games in Germany, and Mom with him, so they were both working around the clock to finish as much as they could before the tournament. Having the family meeting in Germany meant I could postpone that stress for a couple more months and devote myself to a particularly exciting upcoming project.

Namely, a few days after I returned to London, Dad called me to announce two big things. One I already suspected: naming Lana as my official agent. She had already been doing a lot more for me than a friend would, taking care of many issues she wasn't responsible for or obliged to do. Dad would delegate proposals to her that he didn't have time to study, and she dealt with them excellently. We already behaved as if she was my advisor and agent, but I couldn't make it official without Dad's approval. And now, according to him, my career had become too much for him to take care of. After the movie *Never Get Back*, The Wembley Incident (as many referred to Alex's giving of his jersey to me), and especially the musical fashion show, my name appeared everywhere and every day, and the offers I was getting rained like heavy London showers. If he didn't want to neglect his job in order to give me a chance to develop mine to the maximum of my abilities, he had to delegate the work to someone, and no one else was more capable than Lana, who was educated, already had experience in the field, and was my best friend as well.

Of course, that meant she would have to give up her modelling career, but she had shown on many prior occasions that she enjoyed working as my manager more than posing in front of the camera. All the excitement about the fashion world that Bea, Angie and I still felt, in her case had faded after the first couple of years. She saw becoming my agent as an excellent step forward in the new chapter of her career.

The second news had actually prompted the first. The straw that broke the camel's back was an offer from the agent of a German singer. The girl had made a track that was one of the official songs of the World Cup, and she wanted to make a video for it starring the girlfriends and wives of the players. One girl per country. No pay. Instead, all the money would go to charity.

Most of the girls had already been chosen. Only a few countries were left, including England and Ukraine. They weren't sure which one I would choose but knew I had to be in the video.

I loved the idea and wanted to take part. Since I had the luxury to choose, I decided to do it for Alex, to once again show the world whose faithful girlfriend I was and that our love was strong enough to "pull Jane Andersonn away from England", as the papers would write later.

The production was in Berlin, and it started as soon as I accepted. Two days after Lana informed the singer's agent, I was on a plane to Berlin. In my hotel room there was already a package waiting for me with a female version of Alex's jersey set. I immediately tried it on and sent him photos. He was as proud as he could be and was sure I would steal the show from the other girls.

However, Lana and I confronted an issue in the very first meeting. Lana had anticipated it because she had done her research but didn't want to say anything since it seemed improbable.

But it did happen. In the meeting room, we were warmly welcomed by the producer in charge and his assistants, and after the initial chit-chat, he got to the point.

"Listen, Jane, I know we offered for you to represent Ukraine or England, but there is another, better role I'd like to suggest. Namely, we haven't yet chosen a German girl. We have Debora on standby, Friedrich Larsson's wife, but we have to face the facts – all people will remember from the video is you. And it somehow isn't fair for the representative of the host country to be overshadowed. You got me?" I nodded, although I still didn't see what he was aiming at. "Therefore, we came to a sensible conclusion to put you as the face of the Cup."

"What does that mean?" I asked.

"That you represent Germany," Lana said.

"Germany and the whole tournament," added the producer. "You would have a black and white jersey set, which is almost neutral, two flags, ours and FIFA's, and be in the climax of the video."

Lana and I sensed each other's rage and fought it back only because of our good manners.

"Sir, that's very flattering of you – of your whole country – to want me as their face," I said, "but I am not going to wear a German jersey after everything your players have shamelessly said about me."

I stood up and we left before they had a chance to say something in their defence.

That night in the hotel I was disappointed more than angry. I understood their point, but they clearly didn't understand that I could never accept such a thing. I was also a bit hurt. Being in that video was natural, it went without saying that I should be involved. How could the most famous girlfriend of a footballer be omitted from a video that included the most famous girlfriends of footballers?

When Alex called that night, he noticed immediately that something was wrong. I had planned not to tell him, since I knew how enraged he would be, but I also felt bad lying to him and it spilt out.

He was upset and swore in Ukrainian.

"Love, it's fine," I said. "It doesn't matter. I've got lots of work to do with or without this."

"I know, but it would be great if you took part in it. Imagine my girl really, meaningfully contributing to the World Cup. It's like a dream come true for me, too."

"Something else will come up, I'm sure. Or for the next tournament."

"I can't believe they actually let you go. That they will allow themselves not to have the most important girl in that video."

At that moment Lana burst into the room, squeaking with happiness. "Change of plans!"

"How?"

"I've just finished a conversation with the producer's right hand. They offered us a new contract. I amended it a bit and now it's perfect."

I put Alex on speakerphone. "We're listening."

"They realised they couldn't venture such a project without the main star, so they reverted to the previous idea. You will represent Ukraine, in Alex's jersey. In the climax of the video, you'll be waving two flags, Ukraine's and FIFA's, with the German colours in the background."

I jumped off the bed screaming with joy. "Sounds ideal!"

*****

When everything was over, I headed straight to Ukraine to spend the weekend with Alex and meet his sister. The video was set to be released at the beginning of April, when everything was compiled and combined into four perfect minutes. Filming hadn't required much effort since there were so many girls, and I finished my part in three days. Alex, his teammates and I were looking forward to seeing it with the excitement of little kids. That huge Ukrainian flag over the famous German Olympic Stadium would be a hard slap in the face of every German who had ever said anything bad about me, Alex or Ukrainian football.

Alex had a game the weekend I would be in Ukraine, and he planned that I go with his sister so that we could have time to talk and get to know each other. I dreaded it but couldn't refuse. Whenever I felt scared, I remembered how he had handled my dad when he showed up out of the blue, and I braced myself.

It turned out, yet again, that I had worried more than necessary. Yes, Maria was a brisk and cunning blonde with a bitchy face that I never liked on women, but she was also interesting and respectful. She loved her brother and wanted him to be happy. That was all. She spent the night with us in Alex's apartment since Luca was home in Brazil again, and the next morning we jogged together, went on a short shopping trip and then headed to the stadium. It was a fun morning. Maria had good taste in clothes and we helped each other choose some pieces. We agreed to play tennis the next day and then she'd leave us alone, as she said.

*****

Since April and May were going to be my busiest months of the year so far, I decided to visit Ukraine one more time during the first weekend of April. After that, Alex and I wouldn't get a chance to meet until I returned from the U.S. just after my birthday at the end of May. Two important projects were scheduled for me: one in England and the other in New York. The former, a commercial, was almost routine. But the latter, the musical fashion show, would keep me for a month, as it was more intensive and complex. Then I would spend a week in Dallas since I hadn't been there for almost a year. Dad wanted me to, plus, I hadn't seen Mom for a long time. And, honestly, I missed the ranch, my best friend Oscar, horseback riding, the evening fires and accompanying stories. I needed to get in touch with all that again.

Alex was very understanding, for which I was immensely grateful. Thus, I didn't tell him I would be visiting one more time before the big break. I wanted to surprise him.

The security guard at the entrance of his building was sweet enough to give me the key to the apartment and let me go upstairs, promising he wouldn't say a word to Alex when he came back from a visit to his parents'.

When I went out one more time, it looked to be minutes before rain, so I rushed my shopping for ingredients for the burgers I intended to make. I also found the wine he liked and ordered cheesecake from his favourite confectionary. I was so busy in the kitchen and excited to see his reaction when he returned that I didn't notice a new pair of black sneakers in the entrance hall.

When everything was almost ready, Alex texted me.

I'm leaving the house now, going to the apartment. Seems like it's gonna rain cats and dogs here.

- *Haha, it's becoming like London.*

Yeah. Thank god I'm used to it by now.

I started preparing the table. I put out a new tablecloth, plates and cutlery, and napkins with hearts that I somehow didn't find cheesy at all, but rather cute. The whole arrangement broke the plain simplicity the men of the apartment adhered to. When I finished and put the food on the table, I thought about how perfect it would be to have some candlelight. But the rain had started already and there was no time to go to the shop again. Alex would be home any minute.

I knew I had seen something in Luca's room when Maria had stayed there last time. I vaguely remembered an old candlestick on the shelf next to the window, so I quickly strolled over to his room.

Where I absolutely, definitely didn't expect to find him.

Sleeping.

In his boxers.

I almost gasped loudly but put a hand over my mouth. My first reaction was to scream – or swear – and back out of the room.

But I couldn't.

Instead, I stared.

He was tired, breathing deeply. His chest was rising up and down while he lay uncovered among four or five big pillows. His hair was messy but still slick with gel. His mouth hung slightly open.

All of the big muscles of his sportsman's legs were easily noticeable under the untamed light that came in through the curtains. His whole body was naturally tanned from genetics and childhood days on Brazilian beaches. Even while sleeping, he posed for a magazine cover. Everything about him looked just right and in place.

He was perfect.

And so desirable.

Look at this! I used to be his fangirl. And now he's lying in front of me, fully exposed. Any woman would give anything to be in my place. I could have him so easily. It takes only…

But then, terrified of my own thoughts, I stepped back, closed the door a little too harshly, and ran back to the kitchen.

To hell with the candlestick! I thought, bent over the washbasin, breathing fast and nearing a cold sweat. *What was that?* I couldn't believe my imagination. *Have I really just thought about doing it with…*

No!

I cut my thoughts short and splashed my face with cold water. I had to compose myself.

I pulled it together just in time. I was sitting on the dining table, apron still on, when Alex came in.

"Surprise!" I cheered.

"What? How? When?" I jumped into his arms and he lifted me in the air. "You've made all this?" He gestured to the food. I nodded. "You're a wonder woman. You managed to jump on a plane and come all the way here without me noticing anything, and even made this feast." He kissed me. "You're amazing, Miss Andersonn."

I felt terribly bad for what had happened minutes before he came, so I hugged him hard and, with all my strength, pushed the prohibited thoughts to the far end of my mind.

"It's good that you've cooked a lot. Luca is back," he said when we sat down to eat.

"I know. Why didn't you tell me?"

"I didn't know. Yesterday he said he wasn't sure if he'd make one flight or the next one. Seems like he managed the first. I've just seen his shoes now."

You're so stupid, Jane, I thought.

"How do you know?" he asked. "You guys met?"

"No, I just went into his room to take the candlestick, but I gave up after I saw him sleeping."

"Yeah, if he landed this afternoon he might sleep till tomorrow morning."

However, an hour later, while we were still on the burgers, we heard footsteps.

"Що ти приготував, Янове? Пахне добре![1] Oh, damn it! Jane! I'm sorry."

But it was too late. Before he ran back to his room, I had already seen him in his boxers again. A glimmer of my previous thoughts surfaced again, and I went red.

---

[1] What did you cook, Yanov? Smells good!

I managed to compose myself by the time he returned, fully dressed now in shorts and a T-shirt.

"Nice to meet you." He held out his hand. "I didn't know you were here."

"Only just," I replied, surprisingly calm. "You wanna join us?"

He turned out to be a sweet guy, the good boy from the neighbourhood "all parents liked and wished for their daughters", as Sofia had described Alex on our winter holiday. Nothing like the pretentious guy from the underwear ads and sports magazines covers. And the two boys seemed to get along well. They joked in the same way, bullied each other equally, had an understanding without the need to finish sentences. I was happy Alex had someone like I had Bea, Angie and Lana, since those friendships were so rare. I quickly forgot about how I'd felt when I first saw Luca. At the end of the day, wasn't that a normal reaction for a woman to an almost naked, good-looking man in front of her?

*****

The perfume commercial in England required no effort compared to how much patience, will and strength I had to invest in the creation of the music video in New York. The Italian project back in February had been a venture, a first time. This one didn't have the luxury of risk. No one was allowed to fail: not the singers, the production, or me. There were times on set when I felt utterly exhausted and couldn't even remember what my next move was supposed to be. However, when everything was over, nobody could help feeling that we had done a great job and that the show and video would be an absolute hit. The premiere performance was scheduled for the first week in June, seven days before the beginning of the World Cup.

On the plane to Dallas, I didn't want to think about it until my one week off was over. All that was on my mind was the family lunch, followed by an evening ride with Oscar and drinks and stories by the fire.

Dad picked me up from the airport and we drove straight to the ranch. The first person who welcomed us was Sophie – our maid in charge, as well as my nanny and substitute-grandmother, since all my grandparents died when I was very young. I always liked her because she never commented that I was too skinny nor bothered me to eat more, like other grandmas might. She understood me well and loved me like one of her own grandchildren.

The second person was my substitute-grandpa – Arnold, our ranch foreman. He had been part of our family almost as long as Sophie and was one of a handful of people my dad completely trusted and relied on when it came to the ranch. Arnold had taught me how to ride almost as soon as I had learnt how to walk. He was the reason I was fond of horses from a very young age.

It felt nice to see Mom as well. We hugged and talked during the lunch, laughing about both trivial and personal things that had happened while I was absent. We had come a long way in our relationship from the fights we used to have. She finally accepted my career choice and was at peace with it. Now, instead of criticising me, she was proud. I still didn't know if she ever felt guilty for not having believed in me and for humiliating my first attempts at acting, but I didn't need to. I had my father's support, and that was enough. Josephine Andersonn could now be my friend, and we both seemed happy to be on those terms.

When I saw Oscar that evening, the moment was like one from a movie. I was on my horse at the spot where our ranches bordered, our usual meeting place, when he appeared, galloping towards me. I couldn't wait and jumped my horse over the fence. We slid off our horses at the same time and ran towards each other. When he hugged me and twirled me around in the air a couple of times, I realised he was bigger and more handsome than ever.

"For god's sake, Jane, never ever go away for so long again!" He squeezed me one more time.

He wanted to know everything about Alex, from The Wembley Incident until now, and about all my projects: how I managed them, what was next after the summer and the World Cup. We couldn't stop talking. That's what I love about him – it always feels as if we've never lived apart. Whenever we meet again, we just pick up where we left off and all the months apart collapse into a few hours.

When I finished catching him up, we had already gathered around the fire with beer and whiskey alongside the other workers from his ranch.

Suddenly, our jokes and laughter were halted by gallops approaching.

"Are we expecting someone?" I asked.

"Surprise!" Oscar announced as I turned towards the sound. I squinted in the direction of the incomers and cried out in joy. They were my other friends I'd gone to school with, children of the owners of neighbouring ranches – Vanessa, who was the same age as Oscar, three years older than me, and the blonde twins Daniel and Harold Stevenson, who were in my grade. When we were kids, I hadn't liked the two of them because they always teased me and stole clips and ribbons from my hair, but as we grew older, we'd become good friends. The five of us always used to hang out together after school, even studying and doing homework to finish faster so that we could go out and play. I rarely saw them after moving to London. Oscar was an exception since we had always been close, but I was still beyond glad to see all four of them. We stayed up until late in the night, drinking, joking and making plans for the summer after the World Cup because they didn't plan to go to Germany. Football just wasn't their thing here in the U.S.

After two days of enjoying revisiting the life I used to have in Texas, I started missing Alex more than I had in the preceding days. Really badly. My birthday was approaching, I was surrounded by people who loved me and cared about me, and still I wasn't happy. I tried to fight it back, but my mom noticed.

"Honey, you wanna talk about something?" she asked over breakfast, once Dad had left.

"It's weird. I don't know how to express it, nor should I."

"Why?"

"I'd feel bad for saying it. It'd be ungrateful."

"It's Alexander, isn't it?" I looked at her and managed a smile. She nodded. "I knew it. I just wondered when you'd bring it up."

"So, what do you think? How can I change my mood and not look sad on Sunday?"

"Think about Wednesday, when you will be on the plane to Kiev."

"I'm trying, but it's been almost two months. It's driving me crazy."

"Just focus on the moment when you'll hug each other. The more you miss someone, the more intense the emotions are when you're reunited. And in the case of true love, distance can only bring you closer together." She kissed me on the head and nudged me gently. "Come on. Let's go choose your birthday cake."

The day before my birthday, everything was already organised and Mom and I could relax in the spa centre. Vanessa joined us later to help me shop for a new dress for tomorrow. She asked if her sister, Abigail, could also come to the party since she'd unexpectedly announced that she would come home from Chicago for a couple of days.

I remembered Abigail vaguely. She was the younger of the two and never spent much time with us. She went to private school in Chicago and continued university there, visiting home seldom, so no one really saw much of her. I had no objection to having her over the next day. The more people the merrier.

When we arrived to Andersonn Ranch, we had a quick bite and Vanessa and I headed to the stables. We took a couple horses to meet Oscar and the Stevenson brothers for a friendly race before sunset. The guys brought some drinks and we took turns racing and cheering each other on. I loved the adrenalin I felt and was happy to see that my riding skills hadn't deteriorated over the past year. Oscar was, however, unbeatable. Even Daniel and Harold couldn't keep up with him, and they were slimmer and lighter. Oscar was invincible, like a professional jockey.

On the way back, I was exhausted and only thought about the last evening beer I'd have with Dad, Mom and Arnold, and the cold, soft sheets of my bed. I could barely concentrate on what my friends were saying.

"Who the hell is that?" Harold said suddenly.

We all turned our heads towards where he was looking. Two figures on horses rode in our direction, along the fence. The sun was behind them, so at first all I could see were silhouettes. But the next moment, my eyes widened in shock. *No, it can't be!*

One of the riders I recognised instantly. I had grown up watching Arnold and horses. But the other one was too good to be real.

I didn't realise my mouth was agape. They were still approaching and I simply couldn't believe my eyes.

"Is that...?" Vanessa whispered.

It was. He wore jeans, a plaid shirt, cowboy boots and a hat. He rode surprisingly skilfully and looked absolutely breath-taking.

"Alex!" I screamed. "How?"

He rode up next to me and, reaching over, took me by the waist. "Did you really think I'd miss your birthday?" He bent his head to kiss me while our hats hid us from the observing lot, who cheered in awe.

I fell in love with him again.

It turned out that he had planned this ages ago but didn't want to tell me.

"You surprised me in Kiev first. Now it was my turn," he said.

At the house, we all sat for a welcome drink for Alex, who told us everything. He had first spoken to my father to ask him out of respect if it was alright for him to come to his ranch and surprise his daughter. Alex had been so smart in dealing with Dad that I couldn't have been prouder and happier. Dad had liked the idea and helped by sending a driver for him to the airport and suggested that he surprise me during our sunset ride.

"I didn't know you were so romantic, Mr Andersonn," said Daniel.

"Only on rare occasions," my mom replied, "but then he nails it." She bent over to kiss him on the cheek. She was almost as excited as I was.

"I also wanted to check how good a rider he was," said Dad. "That's why I sent Arnold with him."

"Be careful, man. With this guy, you'll always be under scrutiny," Oscar said to Alex, and we all laughed.

I was exhilarated. I couldn't let go of Alex's hand, wanting to show him everything around, still not believing that he actually came.

The final, happy moment was at the end of the day, when Dad didn't appoint any room to Alex. We could sleep together in mine, which meant that Alexander Yanov had completely won over Brad Andersonn.

My birthday kicked off in a festive family atmosphere. Both Dad and Mom took the day off, so we had a long breakfast and then all four of us headed for a ride afterwards, mostly to show Alex around. The weather was perfect, sunny, fresh and bright, not too warm. I couldn't have been happier.

In the early afternoon, my birthday cake with cherries was delivered and the kitchen was on fire under Sophie's surveillance. Oscar's parents, Alejandro and Maribel, came to see me and spend the day with us, and the Stevensons arrived shortly after them.

I was sitting with the rest of the younger crowd at the back terrace, from where we had a nice view of the fields, when Vanessa arrived with her sister.

A silence fell over the group the second they showed up – a silence so sudden and uncomfortable that it's only funny in retrospect. No one, not even I, could help staring at Abigail's colossal, enormous boobs. I saw Oscar's face and immediately turned to Alex, who also had the eyes of a child who had just seen a huge piece of candy. I saw red.

She wore jeans and a plain T-shirt, which technically didn't disclose anything, but they could not be concealed. *They can't be real!* But they were. I could tell. I had seen way too many plastic ones not to be able to distinguish. *This is outrageous!*

"Hi, I'm Abigail," she said amiably, but for me it was over. I didn't like her.

Oscar was the first to jump in, too eagerly in my opinion. "Hi, Abbey! Remember me? I'm Oscar."

"Of course!" She hugged him. "The hottest cowboy around." Oscar had stars in his eyes.

56

She looked at us. "Hello, Jane! Long time no see."

Alex pushed me to stand up.

"Yes. Long time," I replied curtly. My eyes were still moving from her face to her boobs and back up. *This seriously isn't fair!*

"Hello, Alex." She held out a hand to him. "I'm Abigail, Jane's neighbour."

I was looking at his face while he greeted her, waiting to see where his eyes would go, but, satisfyingly, they stayed only on her face. He controlled himself well, unlike Oscar, who was mesmerised like an imbecile.

"She's Vanessa's sister," I whispered to Oscar later. "You can't try anything."

"Why not?"

"Don't be childish."

"I'm not. Maybe I'm serious."

I elbowed him in the ribs. "Just because she has big boobs doesn't mean she has a big heart."

"Are you jealous?" he laughed and I elbowed him harder, this time in his belly.

Luckily, Abigail wasn't jumping around pushing her balloons into everyone's face. Taking the boobs part out, I could even say that she was fun and friendly, but it took me time to stop being bitchy and talk to her politely. She didn't seem entirely stupid as I had assumed, but actually pretty interesting – which made Oscar even more excited.

"I'm proud of you," I told Alex later when we had some time alone.

"Why?"

"For not staring like an idiot at her boobs."

"What boobs?"

I burst out laughing. He hugged me and kissed on the head.

We had lunch in the house and afterwards went out on the big terrace to enjoy the sunset, a crackling fire and the cherry cake. Arnold played some country music on the guitar and we all sang along. Even Alex knew some of the lyrics. It was an evening as perfect as it could get. I was happy, satisfied and grateful to have all of my favourite people around.

Except for the London girls, but we promised each other we'd make up for every missed day during the summer, especially over the next month of sport that was starting in less than three weeks back in Europe.

*****

Following our return from the U.S., time was flying at the speed of light. I attended Alex's last game of the season, witnessed his club winning the trophy, then rushed back to London to complete a couple of interviews. A few days later, I was on the plane back to New York to perform at the live musical fashion show, which caused havoc in the room. At the press conference that followed, we received only praise, and in the days after, when videos started rolling out across the media, long-term success was guaranteed. The whole collection sold out in a matter of minutes upon release.

After that, all I had to do was prepare for the World Cup, pack my suitcases and move to Germany for a month. The first stop was Berlin, where we would attend the opening ceremony. Then we would head to Hannover, where Ukraine was scheduled to play against the Czech Republic in their first match.

Alex and his teammates were ready and enthusiastic. After years of preparation with Milan Andreyevich, an ex-player of the best Spanish teams and a promising coach, they aimed high.

On the eve of June 9th, I zipped my last suitcase, locked the apartment behind me and headed towards the airport, from where a plane would take me to what was for many people – including myself – the centre of the universe. At that moment, and for the next thirty days, nothing on earth was more important than football.

CHAPTER 6

As the tournament approached, and especially following the World Cup music video, the articles about me leaving Alex for other guys, footballers bragging about how they would win me over and other such rubbish were present in every edition of every paper, every single day. And the Germans were annoyingly, strikingly standing out.

Leon Plans to Give Jane Jersey, Too
'I Will Find Her and Bring Her to our Game': Petrov
'Yanov Was Just Lucky to Meet Her First', Says Beller

I knew that most of them were taken from reckless or passing statements these guys had given and decorated to the point of distaste; but the incessantness of it all and the fact that these immature boys kept joking about Alex and me, without caring at all how it could impact us, had been upsetting me lately. I wanted to put an end to it. Especially for Alex, who still stressed about it and couldn't hide it, as much as he tried. I wanted him relaxed and ready for his games, not with his mind somewhere else.

The day before the opening ceremony at the Olympic Stadium in Berlin, the girls and I woke up late and decided to get ready, go for a little shopping, take a stroll through the city since the weather was beautiful, and have breakfast out. Dad had chosen us a hotel in a good location within walking distance of anything we needed. He and Mom would join us the following day, when we would all go together to the opening ceremony. Alex was not going to attend since the players were scheduled to go straight to their first host city, Hannover, where I would head the day after the opening.

Finally ready to leave the hotel, the girls and I headed for the elevator. We were discussing what to wear tomorrow when we were suddenly interrupted.

"Oo-la-la!"

All four of us froze and looked in the direction of the voice.

"Look who we've got here!" Four men in black-and-white tracksuits approached us. I recognised them instantly in a flash of anger – players from the German team. "The Pack!"

Angie started laughing. I wanted to slap her. Now the footballers were standing in front of us, next to the elevator, shamelessly sizing us up.

"Come on, we don't bite." The shortest one, Lens Petrov, was the one talking.

"We do," I said briskly.

"That sounds promising!" added the blonde on his left, and they all laughed like idiots, still blocking us from the elevator.

"So, you're staying here?" continued the short one. "How come? Your lover is in Hannover."

"My father is here."

"Wonderful! You girls fancy a dinner tonight?"

"I wouldn't be caught dead."

They laughed again.

"Why don't you just try? German food is good, and we're not so boring," said the blonde one, Ben Schwimmer.

"No, thank you. Would you let us use the elevator now?"

"Only if you ladies join us for a drink tonight," Petrov said, making me see red.

"Listen, you shrimp," I said into his face, "you'd better hold your tongue. You shouldn't dare to even look at us after all the rubbish you and your pals have said."

He was still smiling viciously. I wanted to slap him hard, but the third guy, Michael Krimm, must have understood that and moved him aside.

"Leave them alone, Lens."

The elevator arrived just in time.

"And you..." I turned to the fourth guy, Matthias Beller, ready to tell him what he deserved.

But I couldn't. My tongue simply got twisted.

He was staring at me, obviously confused, his mouth hanging open in shock, his face pale and child-like, eyes wide and black. I realised he hadn't even uttered a word. For how long had he been watching me like that?

The girls and I entered the elevator.

"You're not so loud as in the newspapers," I finally managed to say before the door closed.

"What the hell was that!" Angie broke the silence.

"A couple of bastards," I replied, still thinking of Beller's expression.

"This is unreal," said Lana. "Of all the hotels in the city, we had to stay in the same one as them."

"Unbelievable," I agreed. "If I see them one more time, I'll smash some glasses over their heads."

"Those two definitely deserve it. But Krimm and Beller were nice," said Angie.

"Yeah, because Beller was stuck staring at Jane like a puppy," Bea said.

"You noticed that, too?" I asked.

"From the moment they approached I don't think he even blinked."

Bastard! I thought. *God knows what game he's playing.* This behaviour didn't match the personality he showed in public. He was constantly bragging about his abilities, boasting that he was a world-class footballer who could win me over. I had been waiting for the moment when he would say something rude and intrusive like his friend Lens. To see him totally confused and speechless definitely wasn't something I expected.

I shook my head. *Hah, he's one of those guys who is brave when it comes to words, but in action will be the first to flee.*

*****

The opening ceremony was scheduled for five o'clock in the afternoon on Friday, the 11th of June. I was as excited as a kid. I made the girls get ready and head to the stadium way ahead of time so as to avoid the traffic and crowds as much as possible. My parents joined us half an hour before the ceremony started, after they landed and had lunch nearby.

At exactly five o'clock, the first note of my song with the other players' wives and girlfriends hit the grounds and I screamed in excitement. The video played on the big screens, where it looked even better than on a laptop. Crowds from different countries cheered as their girls appeared and the whole stadium shook when the Ukrainian flag covered the screen. The support was coming both from the Ukrainians and the English, as well as the American part of the audience. I knew Alex was proud while watching it in Hannover.

"So, you kind of opened the tournament," said Angie, making everyone laugh.

After the song, dancers wearing the colours of the participating countries spread over the pitch and waved the flags of their countries and the tournament. The vibe was good, and the crowd loved it. The party had started even before Bernd Becker, a famous domestic coach who won the last World Cup gold for Germany, stood up on the platform and uncovered the FIFA World Cup Trophy, which shone in its full strength and glory under the bright lights of the stadium and dying sun.

Fireworks burst spectacularly, making the atmosphere magical. Quickly and efficiently, the staff started removing the equipment and preparing the grass for the first game of the tournament between Uruguay and the host, Germany.

I noticed many important people in the world of sport who were also present at the stadium. Some approached Dad to say hi. A few of them I had met before. Those I hadn't, Dad introduced, and they all wished Alex luck during the next four weeks.

When everything was ready, a few minutes before the players went out on the pitch, I was approached by a member of security. He discretely handed me a note and withdrew before I had time to ask anything.

We hope to have your support tonight. M.B.

My hand shook and weird goose bumps broke out over my whole body. I read it at least ten times in three seconds. I opened my mouth to say something to the girls, but my voice was trapped in my throat. I knew the same second who M.B. was.

"What's wrong?" Angie asked. When I tried to reply, it was too late; Dad noticed my unnatural behaviour.

"What's that, Jane?"

I held out the note to him, still speechless, my hand slightly shaking.

He studied it quickly. It didn't take him much time to understand who it was from.

"Matthias Beller. What does he want?" I felt how angry he was, but this time it was directed at me. "Why does he think he can send you notes like this?"

"I don't know. I don't know anything," I replied clumsily.

"Maybe it's intended for all of us," said Angie, trying to save me.

"Then anyone could have accepted it. This was intended directly and solely at Jane." He gave me the look that always made my soul sink. "Have you had something with that brat?"

I was petrified. "No, Dad! Of course not!"

"For god's sake, Brad, don't make a scene," Mom intervened.

"You better not have," he continued in a slightly calmer tone of voice. "Alexander is a good man and doesn't deserve embarrassing incidents like this."

"But, Dad," I almost sobbed, "I don't know anything about this. We've never even exchanged a word. Ever!"

"Alright. Nothing happened. Make sure nothing else does. Or I will. I don't care what he says to the tabloids, this is too much."

I nodded in agreement and sat, still shaking.

I was experiencing a mix of feelings. I was upset that I'd made Dad angry. I was furious because that idiot had dared to write directly to me. I was sad because of how disrespectful all this was to Alex. I wanted to make Beller pay.

But at the same time, I couldn't help feeling tickles of excitement. *He knows I'm here with my parents. And he still dared to do this act! Brave!*

Or maybe this is all just a joke to him. Yes! That's probably it. He wants to provoke someone. Me, Alex, even my dad.

But, nobody has ever tried to provoke my father in this way, so audaciously! He must know he's risking a lot.

My mind was on fire, fuelled by the feeling of excitement in my belly. I knew I had to put an end to this. Matthias had caused problems with me and Dad, and he should know where his place was. I would make sure of that.

But, maybe, it suddenly occurred to me, *maybe I should take part in this dirty game he started, just to humiliate him and end it as a winner. Playing with fire isn't necessarily always bad.*

No! I cleared my mind of those thoughts. The next time I saw him, I would tell him off and make sure he realised his provocations were not interesting and he'd better stop.

The crowd cheered louder than before as the players made their first steps on the fresh grass, the Germans in black and white jerseys, the Uruguayans in dark blue. Some of them seemed worried but the majority looked excited. They had waited for this moment for four years, some of them their whole life, and it had finally come.

They formed a perfect line alongside some children from German orphanages. The captains of both teams each read a brief paragraph on anti-racism in sport, and everyone prepared for the national anthems.

Needless to say, when "Das Lied der Deutschen"[2] started with the live orchestra, I felt the ground vibrating, and I knew the whole country was watching that moment and singing along. They were such proud and supportive fans; they loved their players. When the going would get tough, they got tougher on them also, but throughout the years it had proven only to motivate the sportsmen to play better, work harder and give more. Even with the bad experience I'd had with their braggart

---

[2] "The Song of the Germans", German national anthem.

players, I was happy to be there to witness and feel all that German atmosphere first-hand.

It didn't take long to see that the hosts were the more powerful team. They ran as if they had engines. They passed the ball to each other with perfect precision. They were fast and fearsome, making the opponents lose their heads trying to get the ball, which soon resulted in a goal.

Lens Petrov, the short, loud show-off who was among the top five best strikers in the world at his twenty years of age, accepted the ball from Michael Krimm and from first contact sent it confidently into the upper right corner. The first goal of the tournament could not have been more beautiful, and he knew it. He celebrated by running all over the pitch with his teammates behind him.

Not even twenty minutes later, in a short action started by Lahrman, the goalkeeper, and mediated by Beller, Petrov got another nice ball that he used perfectly to increase the lead to 2–0. Even the coach, Rolf Gottfried, jumped to the grass to celebrate with him. As much as he was a loudmouth, he had the skills to back it up. He was a player of excellent quality and well aware of that.

"They are good," Dad commented during halftime.

"Yeah, every line is good," I agreed. "The strikers, the centre, the defence."

"I've read the statistics, too. These boys have different qualities than the English, Spanish or Italians. Individually, they are not so strong. I don't think they would fit this well in any non-German team."

"You're right, but all of them together form an unbeatable machine. I've read about the forecast for this year. They have the highest chance of winning," I said, despite not being very fond of how it sounded. "Nevertheless, I believe Alex and his team can trick them."

"No one expects them to."

We looked at each other and smiled.

"Which is their strongest point," I added.

The second half was equally interesting to watch. The Germans were stubbornly staying on their opponents' side. As much as the Uruguayans tried, they simply couldn't get the ball past Lahrman. Eventually, one imprecise shot from Uruguay placed the ball right at the feet of Friedrich Larsson, who couldn't help scoring despite being far in the defence line.

The whole of Berlin was on fire. We could see it on the big screen that showed the squares and pubs across the city where people were gathered to watch and support their team. They could not have made the German people happier that day.

After the game finished, we managed to pass quickly as a group through to the exit and into the cars that took us to the hotel. The ride took over two hours because of the expected traffic jams and happy, drunk people in the streets, but we didn't mind. That was the atmosphere we had come for.

"Ladies, let's all have dinner in the main restaurant in half an hour," Dad suggested. "I hope that's enough time for you to refresh and get ready. I'll go and welcome Peter and Sarah."

Bea's parents hadn't been able to attend the opening ceremony because of a last minute business meeting. Her father was as interested in football as mine, so they had more or less the same plan for the upcoming month. Lana's and Angie's parents were not that much into the sport, so they would follow the tournament from home.

I went to my room for a fast shower and changed quickly into a baggy, relaxed yellow dress and was back just in time. I greeted Mr and Mrs Lane and sat between Dad and Bea. The table was rounded, so we could all see and talk to each other. There was also a TV screen where a replay of the opening match was about to start.

We ordered food and champagne to celebrate the gathering. It was rare to have our families and friends together at one table, especially taking into consideration that Bea and I didn't live with – or even close to – our parents. It felt nice to be part of that atmosphere again, especially in a place like Germany was then – the epicentre of all important happenings.

I was halfway into my salad, talking to Bea's mother about the project in New York and why I hadn't had time to jump to Pittsburgh to see them, even for one evening, when loud noises came from the entrance and, one by one, the German players started rolling in.

I almost choked, clenching the fork in my hand. In a matter of seconds, I was covered in a cold sweat. I wasn't capable of even raising my head to see Dad's reaction. This was unbelievable! Yes, I wanted to see Beller soon to tell him what he deserved and put him in his place, but this was way too early!

Everyone at our table tried to ignore them and continue the conversation in a casual manner, but it was difficult to ignore the country's favourite twenty-three men. I tried not to look in their direction at all and made a point of listening and talking to my group – or I at least pretended to.

Suddenly, after less than ten minutes, Bea gasped. "Oh, god, this is not happening…"

I raised my head to see what she was looking at, and the next moment, felt my body go cold and numb. Matthias Beller and Rolf Gottfried were approaching our table, walking straight towards my dad.

"Mr Andersonn, it's my pleasure," started Matthias. "On behalf of the whole team, we came to thank you for watching us today and for coming to Germany. It's a great honour."

His voice was deep and confident, but I could see that under that stoic face, he was scared.

My dad was surprised, too. He clearly had expected the coach to talk, not the young player. Still, he decided to stand up and shake hands. I knew he was impressed.

"Thank you. We did enjoy today," Dad said.

"Did we live up to your expectations?" asked Gottfried.

"Definitely."

"Does that mean we have your support till the end?" asked Matthias, and everyone could see how his face went white and then red in a matter of seconds. So stupid of him to remind Dad of that letter from the stands.

Fortunately, Dad just smiled and replied, "Honestly, you would have it if it wasn't for the Ukrainians. They will get far this time."

Gottfried laughed. "Andersonn, that's a pretty biased and unrealistic opinion. Against all odds. I hope you're aware of that."

I then noticed Matthias staring at me like he had the previous day in front of the elevator. He was devouring me with his eyes, that boyish expression on his face again. I didn't know how, but I found him cute, even when I should've been angry with him. I was confused by what was going on in my head.

"You will see," Dad said. "Very few at this tournament are aware of the scoring machine Ukraine has."

"Better say defending machine," answered Gottfried. "Your daughter's boyfriend is beyond any class."

"Like she is," Matthias said, barely audible. But everyone heard it.

I froze with fear, confusion, anger and many more feelings I didn't understand, yet still kept my eyes on him.

The women giggled and even Dad laughed. "Boy, you've sure made up for that thank-you note back there!" He patted Matthias on the shoulder. "But I don't know how you will deal with Yanov."

"I will score on him," he replied. He spoke more confidently this time, still looking at me.

"After all this? I don't think you stand a chance."

"Luckily, I've got other players who can score," Gottfried said. "Others who control their whimsical hormones a bit better." He also patted Beller on the back.

"Well, according to what they've been saying about my daughter, they all struggle with that."

That sentence woke me up from wandering through Matthias's eyes and reminded me that I was supposed to be upset with him and his friends. At the same time, Mom intervened. "Why don't we leave that boy alone and you join us for dinner?"

"Thank you, Mrs Andersonn, but we have to be back to the rest of the boys," said Gottfried. "We only wanted to express our gratitude for having your support today. It means a lot coming from one of the most respected families in the world." He shook hands with my father again, pushing Beller to do the same. "Would you come to some of our next matches? We would provide the tickets and everything you need."

"If you can provide them for this whole lot," Dad said, gesturing to the full table where we sat, "then why not?"

"It's a deal, then." Gottfried then looked at me. "I'll talk to the boys regarding what they can and cannot say in public. It will be sorted."

"Thank you." I managed a smile.

My stomach started boiling up. This was something I was totally unprepared for, something I wouldn't have expected in my wildest dreams. After everything they had said and done, they now tried to get even closer; not just daring to approach my father, but doing it in a way they couldn't be rejected.

The girls and I gathered in my room after dinner.

"Beller's trying to get close to you and he's not even hiding it," said Angie. "But at the same time, he's doing it so nicely that you can't complain."

"Exactly. Everything is legit and friendly. Even your father can't say anything," agreed Lana.

"But, nobody ever…" I struggled to finish the sentence.

"Nobody has ever gone straight through Brad. You're right," Lana helped me. "That's what confuses me most. He's too brave for someone who just wants to fool around."

"Shouldn't you just…not care?" said Bea. "Regardless if he has any serious ambitions or not. You have a perfect relationship. Whatever Beller or any other man does or says shouldn't be of any interest. You simply say 'Sorry, I love my boyfriend, I'm not interested. Thank you and goodbye!' and that's where it ends."

"Yes, Bea, you're entirely right." I felt embarrassed, knowing she was completely right. "But I'm puzzled, and shocked, and angry, and confused!" I was playing with my fingers. "There's nothing I can do. They'll send us those tickets, and if Dad goes and I'm free, I *have* to go with him, because as much as I don't want to and as much as Alex will hate the idea, I can't say no to Dad, which means that I am literally going into Beller's path while he's orchestrating everything!"

Silence fell over the group. I almost cried in helplessness when the truth and reality of what I had just said hit me straight to my heart. After everything those bastards had said, after the numerous times they had made my boyfriend sad and angry, they now managed to cajole my father and get him and me to attend their games, which I hadn't had the least intention of ever doing, at all.

"She couldn't have put it better," Lana broke the silence.

"Now I can only pray that Dad isn't too interested in going to those games. Or if he is, that I have something unavoidable and un-postponable to do with Alex."

"Or you can be yourself," said Bea. "If you have to go with your dad, just stay with him all the time. He will protect you and make sure you don't end up in any uncomfortable situations. As long as you're with him, everything will be alright. He's not stupid. You heard what he said to Gottfried about his players and what Gottfried replied. Your dad knows what they think of you, and he won't allow anything bad to happen to you."

"She's right," Angie said. "You can even take it as a triumph. You go there, watch their game expressionless, be a cold bitch, and they can't say anything because their coach has told them to keep their mouths shut."

We all laughed and I felt easier at heart. They were right, after all. Dad has always been there to protect me.

*****

The following day, I headed to Hannover with Angie and Lana, while Bea decided to join us on the day of the match so that she could have more time with her parents. I surprised Alex at the hotel. I managed to sneak in with the help of the receptionist, who gave me the key to his room.

We decided that throughout the whole tournament, we would be in the same hotels, but officially stay in different rooms. We didn't want anyone to say Alex was neglecting his trainings for me. The other Ukrainian girlfriends and wives did the same. It simply looked better in public, although everyone knew who slept where and with whom.

When Alex returned from the training, he found me lying on his bed in my new turquoise lace underwear.

"Run for the shower, boy."

He threw his bag on the floor.

"I already had it at the stadium," he said, and next moment he was in bed.

Alex and I headed for lunch together before he went for his evening training, and I told him everything that had happened the day before. I had to because I knew he would find out sooner or later, and when the moment came, I would have to explain why my dad was going to German games and me with him.

Needless to say, he was furious.

"I will break his legs, I promise you! I will break his back and wreck that stupid face!"

"To be honest, I'd like you to. They are annoying. But for the time being, we should just let the situation develop at its own pace. And leave it to my dad to take care of everything." I covered his hand with mine.

"I want to do something, too! I feared this, but I thought they were all just weaklings who wouldn't go further than those stupid statements. Now I want to smash all their stupid faces. Including that coach's!"

"Alex, they won't do anything. They're just a bunch of spoilt, loud brats used to getting whatever they want. But they are aiming for too big a bite now, and they will choke. You'll see."

"Alright. But Jane, if I ever meet any of them, I can't promise there won't be any trouble."

"I'm not asking you to promise me that." I winked. "I'm gonna dish out some slaps myself if the situation calls for it."

"Deal!" We bumped fists like buddies and didn't discuss the topic anymore. We focused instead on what we were going to do the next day since it was his twenty-first birthday and our parents were supposed to meet.

CHAPTER 7

Alex and his teammates decided to celebrate his birthday the day after, when their first game was over, since they would, naturally, be more relaxed. Therefore, all Alex and I had to do on the day was make sure the family dinner went perfect. I didn't want to give either Dad and Mom or Mr and Mrs Yanov any reason to say later that the meeting "was good, but...". No "buts" were allowed that evening.

Alex found a cosy restaurant decorated old-style with modern touches that served international food. The players had only one training planned for the day, after which they were supposed to rest until midday tomorrow, when they would head to the stadium for a pre-match warm-up.

Alex left before me to make sure everything was in order. His parents would meet him shortly, and I waited for mine to come from the airport. We thought it best for the two sides to meet in the restaurant instead of the hotel. It would be more comfortable.

Dad and Mom never struggled to maintain impeccable appearances when travelling, so we left straightaway after they checked in. Dad stayed in his light grey suit and Mom wore a beige skirt and jacket set with golden dangling earrings. They looked beautiful together, as always.

The place was almost empty when we arrived, which made it easier to breathe inside, away from curious eyes. I had known Alex would choose well.

His parents stood up when we approached the table.

"Finally!" Tanya said, beaming. She hugged and kissed my mom and shook hands with Dad. Olexiy gave Dad a congenial handshake as well, then lifted Josephine's outstretched hand and kissed it.

She sighed. "Oh, true gentlemen are an endangered species nowadays."

Dad cleared his throat. "You are lucky to have married one."

Everyone laughed and then sat at the table. When Alex took his seat next to me, I held his hand under the table. We looked at each other and smiled. Everything was going to be perfect, just as we planned.

As the evening carried on and the courses rotated on the table, I felt myself relaxing. Our parents talked like old schoolmates. They shared stories, ideas and values; it all seemed natural and easy. My prayers were answered.

Later that night, when I escorted Dad and Mom to their room, Dad said, "They are nice people. They have brought him up well. I am happy for you." I felt another wave of relief. He hugged me and kissed me on the forehead, something that happened once in a blue moon. "Take care of this boy. He is good."

*****

June 14th, the day of Alex's first-ever World Cup game, began like something out of a movie. He was hugging me the whole night, waking up every two hours – sometimes scared, sometimes excited. I kept assuring him that everything would be alright. Even though his team had never had any real success in the championship, I was biasedly sure they would make it far this time. After all, Ukraine had never before had the best goalkeeper in the world – until now. This time I knew things would be different. The real struggle would begin in the later stage of the competition, not in the groups.

Apart from the Czech Republic, our other opponents were the U.S. and Colombia. We stood a chance against all of them. I don't even recall when I started referring to Ukraine as "us", but it just happened one day. "Us" now meant either Alex's team or the English. I'd cheer for the Americans, too, but I was never extremely passionate about their football team. They are much better in many other sports.

The atmosphere among the Ukrainian players was spirited during breakfast. I attended it with the girls. Everyone was excited and confident they would win, and the upcoming celebration of Alex's birthday that night only served to boost their enthusiasm.

"If we win, we have the right to be double drunk," spoke up Nikolay Pavlov. "If we lose, we can just get drunk."

Everyone laughed, but the coach cut them off by reiterating that they were not allowed to drink during the tournament – not even for "medicinal purposes", as one of the players had termed drinking to kill the sorrow in case of a loss.

The temperature that day was rather high, almost unpleasant for the boys to play in. I wore shorts and Alex's jersey instead of the tight dress that I had intended because that was the best way to handle the heat.

When the time came for the players to come out, it was like a dream. One by one, they confidently stepped on the fresh grass, one line in yellow, one in red. This was the first game for many of us there: the first World

Cup game for Alex, the first for his coach, Milan Andreyevich, the first for many of the players, and the first for me in supporting somebody so close. It sounded like a fairy tale and I was sure there would be some magic.

Surprising everyone around the world, I knew and sang every word of the Ukrainian national anthem. The camera caught me in the process and then switched to Alex, who beamed with joy. Video of that moment went viral within minutes. Alex was surprised, too, since I'd never told him I would learn the words for this occasion, nor had he ever asked me to. I knew it gave him extra motivation and couldn't help feeling that we'd just slapped all the bastards who thought our love was not genuine and that I would swap him for someone else during the tournament the first chance I got.

The first half of the game was calm. Both sides played as if they were in a warm-up session. The ball flew from one side to the other without a clear lead. I thought it was good, as long as Alex didn't receive any goals. He aimed to get the Golden Glove; anything less than that would be a failure for him.

The second half started in a similarly casual manner. One side would attack, the other would defend, then attack. The passes were smooth and the attempts probable but without result.

It started suddenly, in the sixty-somethingth minute. Alex passed the ball to Hrichko, who played a short, quick game there and back with Lomin and Krasinski, then the ball was with Rostov, who covered left middle without any Czechs intervening successfully. He sped up, unexpectedly passing through the Czech defence, and now there were only two players between him and the opponent's goalkeeper. He considered for a moment who to give it to, then chose Barnik, the youngest player on the team, who shot it confidently right at the keeper. We all gasped and threw our hands to our heads in despair over what looked like a lost chance.

But the ball did end up in the goal. The net was shaking. The referee whistled. It was a score for Ukraine.

I screamed along with the blue and yellow half of the stadium. The goal was as beautiful as it could be, perfect for the country's young star and to put the boys in the lead. The atmosphere heated up. Now our team was pushing hard on their opponents, who struggled to maintain their defence.

Another good action, prompted by Lomin and Volomin, continued by Hrichko, and transferred to the very front to Pavlov, Barnik and

Savchenko, resulted in another goal for my team. This time, Pavlov scored. I was happy for him. He had waited a long time to participate in this tournament and show his abilities, and there was no better way than this. Again, the stadium in Hannover shook under thousands of Ukrainians jumping and congratulating each other. We were on the good path.

There was no need for extra time since the game was clean, without interruptions or incidents. At the ninety-minute whistle, Alex removed his gloves and headed towards the centre, triumphant.

We returned to the hotel. The game between Colombia and the U.S. was at halftime by the time the girls and I met in the hotel restaurant for dinner with the guys. They came shortly afterwards in their team tracksuits and, of course, a celebratory mood, singing all the way from the entrance.

I kissed Alex when he came over to me.

"Great job, Big Boy. Zero again."

"I was motivated by you." He hugged me hard. "You were excellent up there. And singing also! It had never even occurred to me to ask something like that of you. I never would. But you, you are just amazing."

I melted at the sight of the gleam in his eyes and kissed him.

"Come on, lovebirds!" shouted Nikolay to us. "Stop it and join us. Tonight, we double party!"

After the dinner was over, the restaurant emptied out so only the team and their acquaintances remained to share Alex's cake, dance to some music and enjoy the success of the day. I had made sure the biggest cheesecake in town got delivered to the restaurant on time. It had three tiers with three different fruits: strawberry, cherry and blackberry, all Alex's favourites. He also blew out twenty-one candles and opened his presents: a tissue to clean his Golden Glove from Nikolay; from his other teammates, a custom version of the national team's and his club's jerseys with a zero as the number since that's how the sports journalists had been referring to him – Zero Goalkeeper, the guy who had received zero goals for the longest period in football history; some other funny accessories his friends had come up with; and tickets to Fiji from me, since we planned on taking a lengthy vacation after the tournament but hadn't decided yet where to go. Remembering our first date when we found out the island was a dream destination for us both, I thought it was a perfect present at a perfect time.

When we reached the room afterwards, we were both exhausted from the great things that had happened that day. Still, he hugged me from behind, his face in my hair. I loved when he did that. "Thank you for everything, Jane. You are a dream come true."

I turned and kissed him lightly. "You're exactly that to me, too. You give me everything. It's only right I give you everything in return."

"Something occurred to me today, Jane." He cupped my face. I always felt tiny and protected when he did that. "Before you, I used to imagine a perfect girl: how she would look, how tall she would be, how she would smile, behave, understand me, make me feel. When I saw you for the first time, you looked just like the girl I'd imagined, but something in your face assured me that inside, you're good too. The more time passes, the more I see that you have not only all the features of that perfect girl from my imagination but also so much more."

Shimmers ran through my heart and I hugged him harder, placing my head on his chest.

"You do things for me that I would like you to do," he continued, "and you do things that I would never even think of asking you to do. You make me extremely happy. On top of all that, my girl is officially the hottest woman in the world. Can this get any better?"

I smiled and kissed him again. "Just wait and see."

I jumped on him, hugging his hips with my legs. He swung me around and placed me on the bed. It didn't matter that we were tired. It never did. Every time we touched each other, we would suddenly obtain an immense energy that couldn't be tamed or controlled, only infused in passion, pouring out of us in gentle and wild moves that culminated in bliss. Our lovemaking was exactly that from the very beginning. After every time, we loved each other more.

*****

Ukraine's game against Colombia was in five days. The match, which we were all confident about, was in Hannover again, so they had plenty of time to rest, train and prepare. As much as I wanted to be by Alex's side all the time, I also wanted to attend other games, particularly the English team's. Their first one was scheduled for the 16th of June at three o'clock in Munich, which meant I would have to take a flight south early that morning.

Alex was understanding. He spent most of his day in trainings and meetings with his team. When he was free, he generally needed rest, which, outside of going to the gym, mostly consisted of lying around, relaxing, going for massages and abstaining from sex. He wanted the best results and I didn't want to tempt him or interfere. Doing my stuff made it all perfectly balanced.

When it came to the Germans, they indeed had stopped talking dirty about me in public. Since our encounter at dinner, there had been nothing in the newspapers nor on social platforms. It seemed that they really listened to and respected their coach.

That was another mysterious thing about them. Although individually they played mostly in different clubs in the Bundesliga, they performed best in the national team, led by Rolf Gottfried. At forty-two years old, he was rather young and was an ex-professional player with a glorious career, full of knowledge, wisdom and excellent tactics when it came to football. Bernd Becker said that having Gottfried coach the German national team was the best thing that could have happened to them.

Another thing I found interesting was the atmosphere he had created among the players: a sense of familial regard and trust. They all got on well with each other. Whoever didn't fit wasn't part of the team. There was mutual respect and admiration on all sides, but also an obvious feeling of awe from the players towards their coach. They looked up to him as if to a father, listened to him like kids, and as a result were the most successful team in the qualifiers. That was partly because they were scared of him but also because they felt they owed him success in return. He had made them stars by giving them a chance In return, they had to give him goals, wins and respect.

I was thankful to him for putting an end to all the distasteful bragging. I even wished I had gotten in touch with him earlier. However, I didn't like the fact that he offered tickets to my father. Something wasn't right there.

Dad called me in the afternoon. He was already in Munich." Hello, Jane! I hope everything's fine there."

"Yes, I'm just getting ready for the flight tomorrow. We'll reach Munich around eleven. I was thinking that we could join you for lunch and then go to the stadium together."

"Sounds great. Listen, there is something I have to talk to you about."

I immediately sensed what it had to do with.

"Gottfried called me this morning about the Germany–Jordan game tomorrow."

"Dad, it's in Berlin and we're gonna be in Munich. There is no way we can make it."

"Listen, I thought that too, but I did some calculations and talked to the pilot and the crew. They think we can be there without even being late."

I instantly grew anxious. I wanted to rebel, but I knew I couldn't.

"Was he really persuasive?" I asked.

"Kind of. I explained that it would be a rush for us, even taking the jet, but he said that many names from sports, politics and business would share the zone with us. After how we supported them in the first game, it would be great for people to see us again. Even Rottmeier, one of my partners for more than a decade, will attend with his friends. It would really be good for me to show up there. I'd refresh some friendships."

I knew the decision had already been made. All my cheerfulness from the last few days died out. "So, what have you decided? Who's going?"

"Josephine says it'd be too much for her, and I want to leave her with Matthew because he invited us for a dinner after the game. The Lanes are already in Dresden, since the Americans will be playing there in a couple of days. So it's only you and me."

"Can at least one girl come with me? In case you get involved in talks with men?"

"Sure."

I sighed but made sure he didn't hear.

"Alright," I said. "When are we coming back?"

"The day after tomorrow. You can take a flight back to Hannover and I'll go to Munich again."

I hated what was about to happen. I had no control over it. Bea once said that Jane Andersonn never let any man tell her what to do, which was true, apart from this one, who happened to be my father and who had all the power over me.

I persuaded myself that he knew better than me, that he knew what he was doing and what was good for the long term. So that was how I presented it to Alex.

He, naturally, raged over the room for almost half an hour. He was as helpless and as powerless as I was.

"They won't get anything, love, I'm telling you." I tried to calm him down. "We'll just go, watch the game and come back, that's it. Most likely we won't even spend more than ten minutes with them, in the worst case."

"I'm sure they'll book you in the same hotel as them, and that they'll invite you for a drink after the game."

76

He was right, but there was absolutely nothing I could do. I had to follow my dad and trust he would make everything alright in the end.

Angie agreed to come with me. When I asked the girls who wanted to join me, she was the first to speak up, while Bea and Lana were still frozen in surprise. "Those showy bastards. They'll see how it is to tackle The Pack," Angie said.

*****

Around nine-thirty the following morning, we were already on the way to the capital of Bavaria, and we arrived at the Allianz Arena for a three o'clock start. I was so stressed about the next game that I even felt nauseous and was stone-faced during "God Save the Queen", almost missing the lyrics.

We played against Argentina, and from the very first whistle I could see that the game would be interesting and tense. Players rushed each other, kicked, hit, shot. There were plenty of cards in the first twenty minutes, after which point they calmed down a bit so as not to lose players.

However, three minutes before the end of the first period, one guy in a navy blue jersey managed to put the ball in the net behind our goalkeeper Harold Dare. It wasn't a beautiful shot but rather the result of a clumsy defence, for which Dare was upset and angry at himself, kicking around water bottles at the side-line.

During the fifteen-minute break, all I could think about were the possible developments of the German game. I almost ignored the referee's whistle that announced the start of the second half.

"Fix that face, girl," Angie said. "You look like somebody forced you to come here, not like you're being forced to go somewhere else later. People will notice and think something's wrong."

I nodded and did my best to change my expression. I mustn't stress over something I couldn't change.

Luckily for the English team, Joshua Hadleigh managed to score halfway through to the end, cheering up the white side of the stadium and bringing a sincere smile to my face. Towards the end of the game, both teams were trying hard, but the tie held. At least we didn't lose.

"Let's go," Dad said soon afterwards. I swallowed hard and headed behind him.

On the plane to Berlin, I changed into a knee-length tight white high-waisted skirt and a matching top and shoes. With Angie's help, I fixed my hair and makeup to look elegant and presentable in case Dad introduced me to some of his business acquaintances.

He was right about the timing – we arrived at the stadium half an hour before the start of the game. Our seats had an excellent view, and the moment we arrived Dad recognised and started chatting with a few people. We were offered drinks, and fifteen minutes later received a note from Rolf Gottfried.

It's a pleasure to have you here tonight. I hope everything went well on your inbound flight. Ask the staff for whatever you need. We will meet in the restaurant in the hotel.

Alex was right. I repeated to myself that Dad knew what to do.

The game was great straight from the kick-off. The hosts flew on the waves of support that came from the full stadium. Almost all the stands were white with black, red and gold flags. Only a small portion was Jordanian. The atmosphere was wonderful: constant singing, shouting, support and cheering on of the players when they had a good move. These fans were invaluable.

The first goal came after twenty-something minutes. It was Michael Krimm who scored, with an assist from Ben Schwimmer. The goal was a beauty – the ball was long and precise, ending in the upper left corner, just in front of the keeper's fingers. The whole stadium roared, amazed, and started chanting his name. He just waved, hugged his teammates and went back to his position to get ready for the continuation of the game.

He was a calm type of guy, Michael Krimm. Clubs were constantly fighting over him, but he had stayed in the same one since he was a kid. He was deeply private, never appearing in public except for in sports news, and only because he was a world-class footballer – otherwise he wouldn't. His story was known to everyone, which was why journalists didn't want to mess with him or dig into his personal life – out of respect.

Namely, when he was ten years old, his parents died in a car crash in the mountains of Montenegro. He wasn't with them only because he had been attending a summer football camp. Otherwise, he wouldn't have survived either. That road was infamous for frequent accidents and Mr and Mrs Krimm were in the wrong place at the wrong time. Michael was left to his fraternal grandfather, who was a wealthy widower in the south of Germany. He had wanted a different career for his bright grandson, but when the boy showed an obvious talent in football, he saw how it helped him deal with the tragic loss and didn't try to change his ambitions. That support resulted in one of the most wanted players in the world now.

Back on the pitch, the game was heating up. The hosts pushed their opponents, finally scoring another goal minutes before the break. This time it was Beller. Unlike his friend, he ran all around the pitch to show off and celebrate. Others joined him.

"They look like idiots," Angie said. While everyone around us jumped and hugged, we remained seated, stone-faced.

"Complete idiots," I agreed, hoping that someone would put my I-couldn't-care-less face on the big screen so they wouldn't even want me to come next time.

On the other hand, Dad was enjoying himself. Plenty of people he knew were there, but he spoke in German to them, so I had another excuse not to get involved. I made sure I left an impression that I appreciated being there but wasn't really happy either.

During halftime, Angie and I went to the toilet to refresh a bit from the sun and heat. When we came back, cocktails were waiting for us. Answering my questioning look, Dad told me Gottfried sent them. They indeed wanted to impress.

The second half started energetically from the Jordanian side. They attacked wildly, piercing the famous defence that very few could break. The Germans were surprised, especially when it resulted in a goal for the players in red. I almost jumped with joy. It felt so good to see their smug faces give way to shock and disbelief.

Gottfried yelled and shouted, and on the big screen we could see the goalkeeper, Lahrman, doing the same. The goal was neither clumsy nor accidental. It was the result of a couple of excellent passes and the Jordanian striker's precision. They were the first in months to score against Germany, and even if they lost, they would be remembered for that.

However, it turned out that I had been delighted too early. That one goal just made the hosts angry and more aware of the importance of the game, the tournament and the fact that they were playing in front of literally millions of their fans. They had to correct what had been done.

Germany rushed to their opponent's goalkeeper straight from the centre. They had to repay the people who had come to watch them as well as those sitting in front of TV screens at home and in pubs.

There was one substitute in the middle, which must have given them extra energy. Fifteen minutes after receiving the goal, they scored another one, making it 3–1 for them.

Again, the whole Olympic stadium shook with joy, delight and song. Even I had to admit that the goal was good. Lens Petrov had sent it in from an angle that seemed improbable, yet he still managed.

The rest of the game was energetic and full of attacks from both sides, but the result stayed the same. At the final whistle, the local fans jumped and celebrated as if their boys had won the tournament. Angie and I finally stood up but only with the aim of leaving the venue as soon as possible. I didn't want too many reporters taking photos of me there.

That was another topic I was concerned about. I asked Dad about it in the car on the way to the hotel.

"So what about when all the local media start drawing assumptions as to why we're attending their games? It will come as a perfect conclusion to all those ideas the players have given them."

"Nah, they have already written so much trash. This is going to be nothing different," he said, disinterested.

"Are you sure about that? 'Cause the way they've gossiped and attacked me has been rather aggressive." I was irritated and couldn't believe he didn't see the scale of the interest we as a family held in this country, especially when connected to its most adored sportsmen.

"I guess that with all the experience I have, I can assure you that nothing bad will come out of this. It never has."

"Dad, it's already gotten out of hand!"

I saw how Angie cringed at the tone of my voice. When Dad looked at me, I immediately regretted my words.

"Yet I got it under my hand, did I not? I spoke to Gottfried and it was resolved. Am I correct?" He said the last word more loudly. I could only nod.

After returning to the hotel, we went straight to the restaurant. I wasn't even aware of how hungry I was until I started eating. I wanted to finish before the players came so that I didn't have to stay longer than needed.

As soon as we were done eating, they rolled into the room in loud spirits.

"I hate this, Angie," I said while Dad was in the toilet. "Now it even looks like we're waiting for them. So humiliating!"

"Just maintain your poker face and everything will be alright in the end."

They noticed us, of course, but sat in a different part of the restaurant, probably instructed by the coach. Once Dad returned, not even five minutes had passed when Gottfried approached us. They shook hands.

"Thank you again for coming and also for staying here," the coach said. "Would you do us one more honour and join us?"

I managed a curt smile, composed myself and followed him, shaking with anger and fear of the unknown.

He guided us to the table where Lens Petrov and Michael Krimm sat.

"I guess you know these boys," Gottfried said, but the two of them still stood up and introduced themselves to my father.

"Yes, we do," I couldn't help saying through my teeth. I didn't hold out my hand and neither did Angie. They all laughed and we sat, Angie on my right and Dad on my left.

"Would you like something to drink?" Gottfried asked.

"Yes, please," Lens answered longingly. Angie smiled.

"Only the guests, Petrov," Gottfried said.

"But, Coach, we deserve it!" he protested.

"Additional rounds tomorrow," he said strictly, like a father to a naughty kid. Lens reacted like a kid, rolling his eyes, which somehow made me smile, too.

"Do they get additional rounds whenever they contradict you?" Dad asked.

"Yes, they do," Gottfried replied shortly.

"Even when we don't contradict him," added Michael Krimm quietly and seriously. None of us could help laughing.

"Alright, let me recommend a wine for you," said Gottfried. He looked at Dad, who nodded.

Soon, we had glasses filled with a local white wine that smelt wonderfully tempting, I had to admit. The players had only fresh juice and protein shakes.

"It's the best German wine in the market," Gottfried explained. "I discovered it twenty years ago at an event down in Munich."

"It's a beautiful place," Angie said. "So complete. It has history, architecture, kind people, delicious food and beer, open-mindedness…I could easily live there!"

"You're more than welcome any time."

"Cheers to that!" said Lens.

"No, first we cheer to your win tonight!" Dad interrupted.

I liked the drink; it relaxed me. I started noticing that these guys weren't so bad. Lens and Michael could have a completely normal conversation with me, Angie and even Dad. I was impressed with their knowledge about America and England that spanned beyond football into politics, culture and weather. They also asked about my and Angie's careers and what our plans were for after the tournament. Lens was particularly interested in the music video I had made with the other footballers' girls.

"I had a very reliable source who said that you would wear our jersey and wave our colours. What happened to that?"

"Well, that source didn't count on my faithfulness to England and Ukraine."

"I respect that. But you have to admit that it would have looked so good. The hottest girl in the world representing the strongest country in the tournament."

"I already did that."

"Come on! I understand that you support your boyfriend, but you have to be objective. Ukraine stands no chance against us!"

"You stand no chance against Alex," Angie said. "After everything you've said about Jane, he's quite determined not to receive a goal from any of you."

"He can be as determined as he wants, but against Michael, he stands no chance," Gottfried said.

"I guess we will see," I said.

"But the video is excellent," Lens added. "Great job. I wish you were my girlfriend and that tournament was somewhere else. Waving a German flag into the faces of all our opponents must be an awesome feeling."

"It is, I assure you."

They managed to relax us. I don't know if it was the way they talked or just the wine, but I found them to be kind and fun. They didn't insult Alex nor did they talk about him in a condescending way. They admired me and my father and respected what we did. They were completely different from the guys they had presented themselves as earlier in the papers. I was telling myself not to be fooled, but after a while, I couldn't help laughing at their jokes and comments. I wanted to be uptight and to not get involved in their conversation, but they were confident and interesting and they dragged us in. I couldn't avoid them with the excuse that they were boring or stupid, because it simply wasn't true.

I liked the way they talked together, Michael and Lens. They worked well in tandem. Michael was calm and serious, while Lens was constantly funny, even without trying. We could see that his jokes were innocent and honest, though completely unintentional. After a while, I started laughing hard at whatever he said. I simply couldn't help it. I no longer thought that they were stupid, shallow footballers. Through our conversation about football, history and even fashion, I was impressed by how well-informed they were.

I was laughing at another one of Lens's jokes, this time about his coach, when Ben Schwimmer and Matthias Beller approached the table. When I caught Beller's eye, I couldn't look away. This time he was no longer confused like a puppy. He stared at me in front of my father, as confident as on the pitch.

"Brad, let me introduce you to Ben Schwimmer. He and Beller are both Bavaria-made. You met Beller last time," said Gottfried.

They shook hands.

There was no more space at the table.

"Would you like to go and have a chat with the other boys?" Rolf asked.

"Wouldn't that be kind of a betrayal to the English and Ukrainian teams?" Dad replied, sensing it would not be good to leave me alone with them.

"Definitely not. You'd just meet the winners of the tournament," said Matthias. He was way more confident than he had been the other night.

"I don't want to leave the ladies alone," Dad said.

Great job, Dad! I thought. The bastards had planned everything carefully, but they were still not smarter than my dad.

"We'll take care of them, Mr Andersonn. Don't worry," said Lens.

My father laughed out loud. "Petrov, you're the one here I trust least." Everyone started laughing.

"I'm gonna keep an eye on him, Mr Andersonn," said Ben.

"Didn't you two grow up together?" Dad asked, and the whole room shook with laughter.

"You can trust me, Mr Andersonn," Michael said suddenly, in a voice typical for him: calm, quiet, confident and serious.

Aware that the situation could only become uncomfortable if he refused, Dad looked at me, asking for approval. I couldn't give it because I was still dealing with the emotions Matthias's look had given me, so Angie stepped in.

"We'll be fine, Mr Andersonn. Go and enjoy."

Dad looked at me again and I nodded in confirmation.

Gottfried and my father walked away, and the two chairs left empty were filled by Ben and Matthias. Matthias sat right next to me. Instantly, I felt the sparks between us and tried my best to ignore them. I didn't like the guy. I had no idea where that awkward energy was coming from.

"Well, hello, Jane," he said. He moved closer to me.

I looked at him, wanting to slap him in that self-satisfied face while simultaneously controlling myself and being courteous because it seemed as if everyone at the table had forgotten about their conversation and was focused on us.

"Finally, we meet," he added.

He was no longer the confused boy I had met a few days ago. He was confident, winning, handsome as hell and looking me straight in the eye. Something cold and weird ran through my nerves, straight to my bones. Those black eyes captivated me again.

"Yes. You've been wanting that," I said, hiding behind my glass.

"For quite some time," he added, raising his lemonade to my wine. "Cheers to that!" He clinked his glass against mine.

"What's the purpose?" I asked. "I could've sent you a photo with my autograph without all this hassle."

Everyone laughed.

"You can still do that for me," Lens chimed in.

"I wanted to talk to you." Matthias still wasn't letting our eye contact drop.

"And you've worked hard for that. Even through my dad. Impressive!"

"I didn't want to come across as an insecure kid."

"No, you didn't. What you are doing is actually very brave. Audacious even."

"Anything to get to know you."

On my other side, Lens and the other guys dragged Angie into a conversation, leaving me alone with him.

"Why's that, Beller?"

"I just want to know first-hand what you think about Germany."

I smiled.

"*Ich liebe es!*" I quoted McDonald's.

"Nice to hear that."

"There you go. You got the answer to your question. Do I still have to come to your matches?"

"It would give me great pleasure." He took my hand and kissed it. I felt unforgivable tickles in my belly. "Knowing that you're up there, watching, would make me fly over the pitch."

I was confused by his eyes.

"Thank god there are other guys on your team who can fly without my support."

He smiled and weird shivers ran down my spine.

"Trust me, all of them like to see you," he said.

"Too bad for you," I managed to reply.

"Why? You didn't like it today? You didn't enjoy yourself?"

"I don't see any legit reason to come and watch German matches when I have two other teams to follow."

"That's why I am here – to give you the reason."

I couldn't hold it back anymore. I was upset, insulted and excited at the same time.

"Matthias Beller," I started, "are you aware that you are shamelessly, hard-core flirting with me when I'm totally uninterested and already taken?"

There was a brief pause, during which we looked at each other. Nobody else seemed to exist. I could literally feel the fire between us. A thought of those lips kissing me ran rapidly through my mind and I swallowed in fear of it.

He didn't get confused as I had wanted, which shook me a bit. I waited for his response.

"Firstly, yes," he said, "I am flirting with you, consciously and determinedly, on purpose. Secondly, I thought that by now you would have figured out..." He sipped his lemonade while I stared at him. "I don't care about your boyfriend."

In a matter of milliseconds, anger substituted all the excitement I had felt.

"And thirdly," he continued, "I am not quite sure about your total disinterest in me."

Only my sense of decorum prevented me from splashing the best German wine into his face.

"You arrogant swine!" I said, nearly shouting. I stood up and turned to Angie. "I want to sleep. Let's go!"

"No! Wait!" Matthias jumped up and caught me by the hand. "I didn't mean it like that."

"You did!" I looked at his hand holding mine tightly.

"I did, you're right," he admitted.

Everyone was watching and listening to us. I decided not to make a scene and took a deep breath, then sat back down. He smiled.

"Guys, how do you survive with this cocky brat?" I asked, still looking at him.

"We kick his ass when necessary," replied Ben.

"Could you do it now, please?" I sipped my wine and then felt Matthias's hand on my back. He had leisurely put his arm over me! Courageous bastard!

"If my father sees that arm, he'll rip it off!" I hissed.

"I'll risk it," he simply replied.

I turned my head to face the others, not wanting anyone to see me and think I was talking only with this one guy.

"Where are the other two girls, the Jessica Simpson and Lois Lane?" Lens asked. Puzzled, Angie and I looked at each other, but the next moment we understood and burst out laughing. We had never thought about it, but Bea did actually look like Jessica Simpson, and Lana resembled Lois Lane.

"Now I'm really curious to find out my nickname," Angie said.

"Miss Jolie." We all laughed again.

"And me?"

"You're just Jane," said Matthias. "You are one of a kind." I smirked at him. "I will elaborate on that but only once your father is not around. Otherwise, he'd rip my head off."

"Keep getting closer to me and he'll do it anyway."

"Not if you tell him not to."

I again felt as if only the two of us existed in the room, at that table. I prayed to god that Angie was entertaining the rest of the guys.

"Why would I do that? I don't like you at all."

"I can make you like me."

"Oh, really. How?"

"Depends if you want it fast or slow?"

The tone of his voice excited me, and that feeling spread from my chest down to my belly and up to my head, which was on fire now.

"Can you elaborate on that?" I asked.

"Well, fast would be we'd meet in my bedroom after dinner. I would make love to you in such a way that you would need one month to pull yourself together."

I almost choked on my wine.

"You cannot make love to me," I managed to say. "You don't know me, thus you can't love me. All you want is to get me on my back."

He smiled.

"All that you said is true. I don't know you; I don't love you yet. And yes, I do want to have sex with you. But I adore you. I have from the day I saw you. And I assure you, I can make love to you so well that you will be dying to know how wonderful it will be when we do get to love each other."

I almost couldn't inhale. I didn't know any longer if he was playing a game or speaking the truth. The whole time he was looking me straight in the eye, unblinking. Normally I would recognise a guy who only wanted quick sex with me, but this one seemed completely different.

"A-and slow?" I stuttered. Even my hands were shaking.

"Slow would mean going for coffee with me in the beginning. Give me a chance to do that, Jane. Only coffee. Like friends. If you don't like it, you will at least get to know me and have valid reasons not to. But I assure you that you'll enjoy it."

My breathing was shallow. For some unexplainable reason, I wanted to accept; but my brain was working hard, preventing me from it.

"What do you think?"

My mouth was dry. I was absolutely, totally confused. In my head, an angel and a devil were battling over the answer.

My dad and Gottfried approached the table, interrupting everything. Matthias moved back, so as not to be so obviously in my face. I went for another sip of wine and realised my hands were still shaking. I drank it and put the glass back fast before anyone noticed.

"We should leave now, ladies," Dad said. "It was a pleasure to meet you all."

"We are delighted," Ben said. "We hope to see you at one of our next matches."

"I can't guarantee that, but I can't decline it now, either." He looked at me, giving me a sign to move.

I stood up, probably a little bit too fast, and everything in my head spun and became a blurry mix of black and purple. Matthias stood up immediately and steadied me.

"I'm okay," I said quickly.

"It's a good wine, isn't it?" said Gottfried while my vision cleared. I could only think about how angry Dad would be with me for embarrassing him by being obviously drunk. I was surprised, too, because I hadn't even finished the third glass. I usually handled alcohol much better than this.

"That's a normal reaction for most people who try it for the first time," continued the coach.

Angie jumped to help me. "Yes, I feel it, too."

I was so concerned about what Dad would say that I didn't look at Matthias again. I held Dad by the arm, thanked them all briefly, and we left.

"So, what do you girls think about them?" Dad asked when we entered the elevator. I noticed by the tone of his voice that he wasn't upset with me, and I felt at ease.

"They're a funny lot," I said. "They were rather respectful, unlike the personalities they showed in the media. I think I can deal with them. I'm not worried anymore." I was actually worried about what Matthias had suggested, but I decided to think about it once I was alone in my room.

"I agree, but I don't like that man Gottfried," Angie said. "We know his reputation. He seems too kind and nice to us. Almost unnaturally."

"I agree," said Dad. "That's exactly what I've been thinking since he offered the tickets. I've got this feeling that he's up to something, but I still haven't figured out what."

"Probably some business idea or sponsorship," said Angie.

"Could be. I guess we'll find out by the end of the tournament. For now, leave him to me and you girls deal with the boys. If things become uncomfortable, I know how to solve them."

We walked out of the elevator and were almost in front of Dad's room.

"Jane, you stay gracious and loyal in all this. Like today. If we go to another one of their games, don't support them too much. It won't look nice, and it'd be disrespectful towards Alexander and Matthew."

"Don't worry, Dad. They still haven't won me over." I kissed him on the cheek. "Goodnight."

When we went around the corner, Angie took me by the hand.

"I want to know everything you two talked about."

"Sure. But tomorrow, on the plane. I can't deal with this mess in my head."

"You've got a headache?"

"Yes, Angie, and I've got no idea how. You know me. Three glasses of wine can't do anything to me. If we hadn't all drunk from the same bottle, I would bet they put some drugs into my glass."

"Alright, then. Go sleep now and tell me tomorrow."

I entered my room and removed my clothes on the way to the bathroom. All I could think of was my shower and bed. The day had been long, tiring and eventful. On top of that, my brain was spinning. *What the hell am I going to say to Matthias Beller?* I knew the answer should be no. But I was terribly curious to talk to him like a normal, ordinary person. Since the other guys had proved kind and funny, maybe he wasn't the bastard he presented himself as in the papers. His teammates had also made comments about me, but they were friendly during the dinner.

But he was different from them. While they made typical guy jokes, he was pretty honest that he wanted me – not as a friend but as a lover, a girlfriend even. Why was I thinking so hard about if I should see him again or not?

I hoped that the hot shower would make me exhausted so that I'd just stumble into bed and fall into a dreamless sleep. I had no answer to the question I posed to myself tonight. Instead, I started thinking about him. He had looked great on the pitch and without his jersey. When he'd sat next to me and put that arm over me, I could see his fine, solid muscles through his T-shirt. *It must feel great when those arms grab you and throw you on the bed. Or when that chest presses against your breasts while your bodies move, full of desire. He probably looks dazzling without any clothes. Like a Greek statue. Him taking me would be a sculpture of the highest form of art.*

I switched the shower off with my mind still on that thought. I felt sinful but decided to give myself a few minutes of those forbidden thoughts since I found it so difficult to push them away. To avoid feeling guilty, I told myself that that was the only way to get rid of them.

I thought I heard knocking on the door, but I assumed I was imagining things, drunk and tired as I was. I quickly applied some body milk and was about to put on my pyjamas when the knocking repeated. This time I was sure it was there. I covered myself with a purple nightgown and walked across the room, annoyed.

"For god's sake, Angie, I really can't talk now," I said, opening the door and starting to turn sideways to let her in.

Except that it wasn't her standing at my door.

It was Rolf Gottfried.

Instantly, I sobered up and was covered in a cold sweat. I only had on the light, short gown, and he was too close, looking at me with eyes that did not hold any of the respect or distance I had seen earlier during the day.

"What a nice welcome," he said.

I was absolutely shocked and confused. "H-how can I help you?" I stammered. His eyes ran quickly up and down my body. "Did you forget something?" I asked stupidly.

"Yes, I did," he said and simply entered the room as if it were his.

I stepped back in fear but only a little. I didn't want to show him I was afraid.

"Can we sort it out tomorrow morning? I am really tired now."

"No." He closed the door behind him, not moving his eyes off of me. "It has to be tonight."

I have to be brave, I have to be brave, I repeated to myself. No matter what he had come for, I must be brave.

"With all due respect, Mr Gottfried, you are not invited here. If there is something you want to discuss with my father, please, talk to him tomorrow. I am tired. I had a rather long day and I have the right to rest. Therefore, I'm gonna politely ask you to leave my room."

"Hah, now, when I'm in? No way! And I bet you won't call anyone to save you."

I shivered but wasn't afraid anymore. Stupid man. Like any other. I sniffed for the smell of alcohol, assuming he was drunk, but couldn't trace anything.

"What's wrong with you Germans? You all really think your arrogance works like a charm with me?"

"I know it does. You don't, but I do."

"Come on. Leave me alone."

"I know chicks like you. All this turns you on." He smiled viciously.

I brimmed with anger. "Will you leave now?"

He didn't move.

"You don't want me to leave. Look at you. You're not even shouting. And you could. Your father is just down the hall. If you raised your voice, he would be here in a matter of seconds and my career would perhaps be over. But you don't want that. You want me to stay."

I was shaking, but it wasn't fear. It was something else.

"Get out," I said weakly.

"I can bet you are turned on right now," he continued. "Tell me – when was the last time you had sex with Yanov? Before the start of the tournament?"

"It's none of your business!" I snapped.

He moved closer, but I didn't step back this time. The distance was dangerously small.

"I know it anyway. Playing as well as he is, he has to have been abstaining for quite some time. I know you're not a satisfied woman right now."

In a lightning movement I wasn't prepared for, he put one hand on my back, holding me to him, while his other hand went to my breast. He squeezed it and I moaned. His vicious smile appeared again. He repeated the move, and my eyes widened in shock at the wave of feeling that came over me. I was looking him straight in the eye, amazed at what he was discovering in me – something even I didn't know existed.

With one simple pull, he untied the bow on my waist and my nightgown opened. He touched my chin with one finger and then dragged it slowly down my neck, between my breasts and all the way to my navel. I was covered in shudders of excitement, barely able to move except to lean in to his touch. I only realised my mouth was open when he put his thumb on my tongue, and then trailed it down, resting over my nipple.

I couldn't believe what was happening. I wondered if it was a dream, but his moves brought me to reality and proved my wakefulness.

What is going on with me?

Both his hands were on my back now, stroking me. He was slowly pulling me towards the bed. He didn't kiss me. There was no need for that. The need we had was of a different nature.

He placed me on the bed. My body was slack underneath him. He bent over me and put his hand between my legs, then smiled at my disbelief that I was wet. He pushed me only slightly and I lay on my back. He put one finger inside me. I was wet and boiling.

"You're even better than I thought," he said, adding one more finger and unbuttoning his trousers. At the sound of his belt I shuddered with excitement. I wasn't afraid of anything anymore. His fingers were moving, teasing me, and all I could think about was how to extinguish the fire that he had lit.

When he removed his boxers, I moaned again at the view of how excited he was, how ready, and at the thought of what he could do with that, *what he will do to me.*

He sat on the bed. He didn't need to tell me anything. I sat on his lap, taking him in, and almost screamed in enjoyment. At first, it was mixed with pain because of the suddenness of the moment. But with every move, the pleasure was greater. I came fast and strong, almost ashamed at how quick it was. He saw how excited and eager I was.

I was still shaking in the remnants of the climax when he started kissing and biting my breasts. Then he took my hips and moved them up and down, taking me on another crazy ride. I held onto his shoulders, still strong and muscular, and wondered why he didn't play football any longer with all that strength. The more he helped me, the more I wanted. I was looking for another orgasm, and I noticed how he shook, experiencing the same pleasure. He didn't want to come too fast. He wanted to prove himself.

I didn't care. I wanted more, and I was taking it.

When I reached the last, highest step of those stairs, I couldn't help screaming. It was a scream mixed with a dirty laugh. He liked it and instantly came with me.

We both breathed heavily, lying on the bed next to each other. My heart rhythm was coming back to normal, but one thought swirled around in my mind on a loop. *What the heck just happened?*

He was the first to break the silence. "Frau Andersonn, I'm impressed."

"I bet you are," I replied calmly.

I started to understand what had been going on.

"So, this whole charade – talking to my father, inviting us to the matches, being too friendly – all that so you could get into my panties? And the rubbish that your boys were saying in the newspapers, that was just to distract the attention from you?"

He laughed. "You are a smart woman, Jane."

"And obviously very wanted among you guys."

"Almost like the trophy."

We both laughed.

"You are a very strange man, Gottfried. With this body and attitude you could have any woman without all this hassle – my father, the distance, arranging tickets, risking the public finding out."

"Yes, but I wanted Jane Andersonn. Like every bloody man in the world."

I laughed. I liked that this man, more than twenty years older than me, full of experience, complimented me so directly.

"And all the hassle and charade, as you called it, was worth it. You are a damn hot and active woman, Jane."

"And you are a very intruding and demanding man, Rolf."

"I definitely wasn't the more demanding one a few minutes ago. And I don't think you'll ever complain about my intrusion."

"Hah! Again with the German arrogance!"

"You like it, Jane. You know I'm right."

"Maybe yes, maybe no." I stood up and put my gown on again. "Would you please go now? I need to sleep and be fresh for tomorrow."

He started putting on his clothes. He was handsome. I never really paid attention to men my father's age. They were totally out of my scope of interest. But after this incident, I wasn't sure where I stood with my wishes, attitudes and values.

What shocked me more than the fact that I had just slept with the German coach was that I felt not a single twinge of guilt or regret. The next day I was to meet my boyfriend, who I had just cheated on, and I didn't feel bad about it. *When I wake up, everything will be normal, as if nothing happened.*

I remembered the day I found Luca alone in the apartment in Kiev and the surge of wild emotions I'd experienced, and thought, *Why didn't I do anything then? I should have. If it was so good with this old guy, with him it would've been absolute fireworks!*

CHAPTER 8

I woke up early in the morning feeling perfectly normal. I didn't even have a headache from the previous night's wine. I got dressed, applied makeup, fixed my hair, packed quickly and looked at the mirror. *You rock, girl.*

It was my routine. Somehow, I expected it to feel different this morning, but it didn't. I felt great.

In front of my dad, everything was normal. In front of other people, too. Nobody looked at me suspiciously like I'd expected. Whosoever eyes I met, they revealed only adoration and admiration. Nobody suspected anything. Nobody knew anything.

That gave me tickles of excitement. I had a big secret. I had received immense pleasure from one of the most wanted men on the planet, and nobody knew about it except for me and him. And there were no consequences. My boyfriend didn't know, and there was no way for him to find out. Ever. Why would he? And how? Only Gottfried and I knew what had happened. There was no way it would ever reach anyone we didn't want it to. He surely knew that it wouldn't work well for him if he told too many people, and he had no proof anyway. I would deny everything; nobody would believe him. Besides, why would he pick a fight with me? We had a good time together.

When I saw Alex in Hannover, I ran into his arms, kissed him, hugged him, had sex with him. Everything was as usual. He was happy that I was back. He had watched the game and seen how indifferent I was at the stadium in Berlin. He loved it. I told him that after the game, we had a drink with the players and that they were fun and kind, surprisingly different from the guys in the media. He didn't think they were entirely honest but trusted that I knew what to do and how to behave.

I cannot describe how well I compartmentalised around Alex. I had absolutely no sense of guilt. I just told myself to switch to the girl I normally was. The dirty Jane was left behind in yesterday. I had read in books that after a tryst, some women would feel filthy, or that they could smell the remnants of their lover on them. None of that related to me. I felt as if nothing bad had happened. Actually, I felt great. The sex I had with Gottfried was something new. Not that Alex was not good. He was perfect.

But Gottfried was different. And that change felt good for me, a girl who previously had slept with only one guy.

After Alex left for training, I gathered the girls in Bea's room to tell them the news.

"I had sex with Gottfried," I said straightaway.

Lana choked on her juice, Bea dropped her makeup pouch and Angie gasped.

"I knew it!" Angie said.

"You did?" I laughed, while Bea and Lana stared at me in shock, their mouths agape.

"The bastard was too friendly. I said yesterday he was up to something."

"Wait, wait, wait!" Bea raised her hands to slow us down. "You went after him or he came after you?"

"Well, he came to my room, didn't want to leave, kind of attacked me..."

"Then it's rape!"

"No, Bea, it was not. I didn't protest much."

She was in disbelief. And disappointed. I clearly saw that.

And it hurt.

"What happened to you, Jane..." she whispered.

"I don't know. That's why I'm talking to you girls. I don't know what happened, or how, or why. But I was in the shower, thinking about Beller – who is not so important now – and he just showed up in front of my door. I don't know. I was excited, he pushed me a bit and we had a mind-blowing session."

Dead silence.

Bea cut it. "And after that, you simply returned here and made love to your boyfriend."

"Well, yes."

Silence again.

"You cold bitch!" This time it was Angie who interrupted. She started laughing, making me laugh, too.

"It's not funny!" Bea snapped.

"At all," Lana agreed.

"Why are you two so uptight?" Angie defended me. "She's young and deserves some fun, and if she can get it with a hot, experienced guy, why not?"

"Angelina! She loves Alex! The whole world knows that! The whole world is *watching* that!"

"Nobody knows what happened apart from Jane and the coach."

"Well, we know best how every single piece of dirty laundry – dirty *underwear* – comes out sooner or later!"

"Not when you're the daughter of Brad Andersonn," I said.

They all went quiet again.

"She's right," Lana said finally. "However, Jane, bear in mind that right now you're playing alone. Your father doesn't know what happened —"

"And will never find out," I added.

"Of course. So now it's just you and Gottfried. He's dangerous. You have to be extremely careful."

"So you think he won't stop?" I asked.

"Would you like him to stop?" Bea replied.

I paused for a moment. "To be honest, I don't know. It was good, but I wouldn't venture something like that again willingly. It would be best if he stopped."

"I don't think he will," Angie said. "Neither him nor them."

"Why do you say 'them'?" I asked.

"I'm concerned about Beller." We all gave her questioning looks. "He sent you the message at the opening match, not Gottfried. All the guys talked about how they would hit on you during the tournament, but everything was rubbish, jokes. Only Beller took it further and openly invited you out."

"Wait, what? We're not updated with this." Bea said, puzzled. I recounted for them everything that had happened at the dinner before Gottfried came to my room.

"All that, plus the way he looks at you," Lana said.

"Is it that obvious?" I asked.

"Yeah," Lana and Bea said together. "Even a blind person could see how he gets those puppy eyes whenever he sees you," Lana added.

"So both of them are trying to get her?" Bea asked.

"I'm almost sure about that," said Angie. "It's just that I think none of the guys know what the coach is up to. Everyone seems to be helping Matthias. You know, encouraging him, letting him sit next to her, stuff like that."

That was a lot to consider. After Gottfried left my room, I had completely forgotten about Matthias. I thought he was just joking with me and assumed he was all talk. But what the girls said now made perfect sense. I started again thinking about those coal-black eyes, that arm behind me, how he would make me like him slow and fast...

However, I had to push all those thoughts into a box and deposit it somewhere at the far end of my mind. I was about to meet my boyfriend and no German thoughts were allowed.

*****

The next day, Alex had only one training, in the morning, because his second game was the following day. We had decided to spend the afternoon together and go for a small walk in the city, but I had other plans. When he returned from training, I was waiting for him in bed, naked.

"Jane, you're gonna pay for this," he said. "I didn't take a shower at the stadium."

"Pay for what? For you being too lazy to have a quick bath?" I moved to a sitting position and the sheets shifted, exposing my breasts. I loved his expression.

"I rushed to come back to you as early as possible." He threw his bag to the ground and started removing his clothes quickly. When I heard the water in the shower, I went to join him. My hair was already perfectly done, but I didn't care. Our shower sex was always memorable, including this time. He was already hard when I stepped into the shower, before he realised I was there. I helped him with the shampoo and scrubbed him over his back and chest. All that time, he never looked away from my face. I got wet just from seeing that desire in him. He didn't have to do anything.

He took the shower gel and started scrubbing me, starting with my shoulders and then moving rapidly to my breasts. He squeezed them hard and I moaned. In a sudden movement, he pulled me to his chest, one hand wetting my hair and holding my head so that I could not escape his kiss and the other going straight between my legs. I let him play with me until I felt hotter than the water coming from the shower, and then I moaned again.

"Take me now."

He obeyed, pushing me against the wall as I hugged my legs around him, my arms encircling his neck. He supported me easily as if I weighed no more than a feather. I loved that strength in him. He could hold me even with only one arm. He looked me in the eye, I smiled wickedly, he placed himself inside me. My eyes widened in immense pleasure.

I loved it – how he always treated me, caressed me, touched me, satisfied me. He was a perfect boyfriend. Of course I loved him.

I could barely stand on my feet when our shower episode was over, so I put my hair up in a towel, wrapped myself in a bathrobe and went to lie on the bed a bit. I had just put my head on the pillow when somebody knocked on the door. When I opened it, I couldn't see a person, but rather a large bouquet of pink and white flowers of all kinds. The smell they gave off was wonderful and instantly filled my nostrils and the room.

"Frau Andersonn, delivery for you," said the little voice of the poor courier from behind the bouquet.

"How did you know I was here?"

"The order came clear that the flowers be delivered to you, either in your or Herr Yanov's room."

"Oh, alright. *Vielen Dank,* then."

"There is a note also."

Thank god I was quick and decided to read it first. The courier was still holding the bouquet when I opened the note.

You haven't given me an answer yet. Kisses. M.B.

My heart stopped.

"Jane, what's that?" Alex came out of the bathroom.

My breathing stopped, but I still managed to react fast.

"Take this and throw it away," I whispered to the courier, shoving the paper into his jacket. Then I took the flowers and closed the door with relief. When I put them on the floor, I saw Alex's questioning look.

"Some big fan?" he asked.

"I have millions of them." I winked, and he managed to smile. I decided to be partially honest with him. It would save me lots of trouble in the future. "It's from the Germans. They are thanking us for coming."

He didn't like it but didn't make much fuss about it either.

"I bet your father got the same ones," he said and I laughed.

"I'll throw them out as soon as I get dressed." I kissed him deeply, and the argument was over before it began.

That Matthias was a crazy bastard! To be so brave as to send me those enormous flowers and so audacious and mean as to make sure the flowers reached me either when I was alone or with Alex – only a crazy or rude man could do that.

Or an extremely interested one.

I started dwelling on that and continued to throughout the rest of the day and night. I even had dreams about Matthias: about us going out and deciding after only one hour to just be together, about how I suddenly didn't care about Alex or what anyone would say.

I woke up in a cold sweat a couple of times that night. Every time I awoke, my dream would stop with the appearance of my father and his extreme anger at what I had done to the family reputation. But each time, I would look over and see Alex lying next to me and then breathe in with relief. *No one else. It 's just my guy and me. Forever.*

*****

The match between Ukraine and Colombia was scheduled for six o'clock in the evening, so after breakfast Alex belonged to his teammates and coach. The girls and I were lounging by the swimming pool until we were also supposed to go to the stadium.

"I have to meet my parents tomorrow in Stuttgart," Bea said. "They decided to go and watch Italy play Costa Rica and asked me to join. Any of you feel like coming along?"

"Me!" I was the first to jump in. "I need to relieve my mind of these thoughts and occupy it with something else. Right now football is the best option."

"I agree. You need to reorganise your priorities and come back to stability," Bea said.

"Alright. Lana and I can move down to Munich and meet you two there for the England–UAE game on Monday," Angie said.

"Deal."

"What are you gonna answer Beller?" Angie asked over her melon juice.

"To leave her alone, of course!" Bea replied instead of me. Silence ensued. She turned to me. "I hope?"

I hated when she looked at me like that because I knew she was completely in the right. But I couldn't help my honesty. I looked at Angie, asking for help because she obviously understood me on this matter better than my other two friends.

"Of course she's been thinking about that coffee," Angie said devilishly.

"Jane, don't tell me—" Bea started.

"I haven't accepted yet," I defended.

"Yet! *Yet!* What does that mean? Angelina, are you giving her these insane ideas?"

"He's so persuasive," I said. "I'm truly intrigued to find out if we can talk about anything normally. As friends."

"What friends?" She was getting more upset. "He wants to take you to bed, Jane! That's the friendliest you two will get."

"Bea, you know very well that before Alex, most guys were scared to even look at me because of my dad. Alex and Matthias are the only two men who have stood up to him. Matthias even more, because he went straight up to Dad and then to me. And you cannot say he has nothing to lose. As a young, rising player, he has everything to lose."

"This is really a funny, strange situation," Lana said.

"But I don't get it," Bea continued. "Why do you feel the need to give him any chance? You said it yourself – you have a perfect boyfriend. Although he's the first for you in everything, he is the best. You feel it. You've said it numerous times."

"Bea, I'm just curious to hear what he will say. I won't go to bed with him."

"Gottfried didn't say much and you went to bed with him in the blink of an eye."

"Beatrice, enough!" Angie said before I could reply. "As conservative as you are, you love Jane. You'll have to decide whether you're gonna stick with her or abandon her. This nagging is not helping. It's just destroying the mood and atmosphere."

"I cannot support something like this, Angelina! She's cheated on a perfect guy once, and she's preparing to do it again. And the tournament has just started. I dread to think about what's going to happen in the next three weeks."

Again there was silence.

I couldn't say anything to Bea because I knew she was only telling the truth. She knew me very well. We had grown up together, we lived together, we shared everything. She knew very well what was on my mind, and she didn't like it. Because it was wrong. Angie understood me, too, but for her, all of this was exciting, just as it was for me. It seemed neither of us could explain where my strange behaviour was coming from, but she stood by me nonetheless.

"Alright," Bea said. "Let's see what happens. But, Jane, please, don't ask me to lie to Alex. I can lie to your father but not to Alex. He is too nice for me to do that."

I agreed, and we changed the topic. It felt surprisingly pleasing to talk about clothes and what we would wear in the next few games instead of the guys who played them.

Around one hour before we planned to leave the swimming pool, a member of the hotel staff approached us.

"Miss Andersonn, you are being asked for," he said nervously.

We all looked at each other.

I was too puzzled to ask anything. I put on my beach dress quickly and followed the employee. I had absolutely no idea who my visitor could be. Anyone was an option: a persistent journalist, a fan, some local artist who wanted to collaborate with me, even Dad.

In the small salon behind reception, the employee said something in German to a man in jeans and a white T-shirt who was standing in front of one of the blue baroque chairs, facing away and observing a painting on the wall. The staff member then retreated quickly and discreetly.

When the man turned, I felt the familiar shivers in my chest and down my spine. He looked great in those simple clothes. I could see his strong shoulders and arms, and they made me think about the Greek statue scene I had had in my mind a few days ago.

He smiled, and I almost smiled back before I realised I was supposed to be upset.

"What are you doing here, Beller?" I hissed. "You're supposed to be in Dusseldorf!"

"Oh, you know my schedule?"

"You are insane coming here and asking for me so deliberately! Who let you? That's not allowed! I'll complain to the manager of the hotel—"

"I came for my answer." He smiled again.

"What answer? You are crazy! Leave before he comes!"

"I'm not afraid of your boyfriend, Jane." He was calm, as if he wasn't doing anything out of the ordinary.

"Beller, why are you doing this? Imagine what people who have seen you will think and say."

"What can they say? I came to see a friend."

"Oh, shut up!" I turned to walk away. I didn't want to be seen anywhere near him, not this far from the pitch. It was too dangerous.

In the next second, he grabbed me by the arms and held me close to his face. I got lost in the abyss of those eyes I had noticed even the first time we met.

"You've got no clue how much I want to shut your mouth right now and kiss you, because you look terribly, incredibly attractive without makeup in that purple swimsuit and shawl. But I don't want to rush you or scare you." I was confused like a little girl, just staring at his perfect face. "For now I'm just gonna ask you for one thing, and that's yes or no. Do you want to go out with me, Jane?"

My brain was dull but trying to work fast. I knew what I wanted to answer but also what the answer should be. At the same time, I was paralysed by the way he was looking at me, by his smell and his strong arms that I had imagined hugging me. He was so close. I became scared that Alex might pass by, and I knew that as much as I enjoyed being in his arms, I had to make Matthias leave.

He smiled again.

"Yes," I replied.

He let me go after a few too-short seconds. I could see on his face that he was satisfied. I knew I was excited, and the fact that it was prohibited only made it more exciting.

"I'll update you with the date and time," he said. "I gotta go now."

He looked at me for a moment and then moved closer and kissed me on the cheek with the clumsiness of a boy kissing his first school love. I managed a smile and he left.

*****

I showed up at the stadium in a simple blue and yellow dress. The girls brought flags and scarves. I was ready to support Alex and his team more heartily since this game was potentially a deciding match. If they won, they would for sure go to the next stage of the tournament. If they lost, well – I didn't see that as an option.

The game started calmly. The fans on both sides were amazingly supportive. They created a pleasant atmosphere and it felt good to be part of it. Tanya, Olexiy and Maria were also there to support Alex, seated in the row in front of us. Together we sang and cheered, waving the flags. Some fans approached us for photos, and as the game wasn't too exciting, I gave them as much of my time as possible.

That is, until we heard a whistle right in the middle of saying "cheese". We were all confused for a brief moment, and then I saw Tanya jumping with joy. I looked at the screen, saw that we scored and started jumping with the gathered lot.

We saw the whole action on the replay. Rostov had hit the ball that was passed to him by Savchenko. He had a clear view and couldn't miss. It was a smooth goal.

However, that didn't calm the boys down. They went on rushing the Colombians with their full power and eagerness, and in the last minute of stoppage time, they scored again. This time it was Vitaliy Koval.

During the break, we went to have a few beers with Alex's family. When we returned, the fans were already singing their hearts out.

"Never in the history of Ukraine have so many supporters attended World Cup matches," said Olexiy.

"And they still keep coming," Maria added. "I have no idea where and how they got the tickets, but they are arriving in buses, trains, planes."

"I've read an article that estimates that at the next game against the U.S., there will be more Ukrainians than Americans," said Bea.

"That's astounding!" said Tanya. "But Americans never really cared much about football, right?"

"Yeah, but these numbers are still historical," Olexiy said, "and our son is part of that history." He kissed Tanya on the head, beaming.

When the second half started, the opponents immediately wanted to fix the result and save themselves. They had already lost to the U.S., and if the current situation held, it meant that they were out of the tournament. However, it wasn't entirely easy to play against the Ukrainians. They were prepared for this kind of "attack in despair", as Coach Andreyevich called it. Not only were they impenetrable but they also surged forward with force and determination.

Milan Andreyevich was considered to be the beginning of this glorious chapter in Ukrainian football history. He picked up a team in shambles that had never achieved much, refurbished it and wrote pages and pages of winning articles. He first made the boys feel like they were brothers and cousins. He wanted them to get along and respect each other, and at the same time enjoy themselves. His success was proven by the fact that the boys were very good friends outside the pitch and training grounds. They spent holidays, birthdays and breaks together. Coach Andreyevich always said that was the key to his and their success. When they played together, they felt they played first for their family, then for their country, and then for everyone else. And the fans loved them for that, too.

Halfway into the second period, a third goal was scored for Ukraine, and not even five minutes later, a fourth. Both were achieved by the defending line. The game was over, and 4–0 was more than we could have asked for. The Colombians were shattered over the grass. They'd been expected to go further, to the knockout rounds, but they were caught by surprise.

As for us, it was certain that we were in the next round. Everyone had known and expected it, but now, when it was confirmed, somehow we all breathed out in relief. The next game was against the Americans. It wasn't important on the technical side, but it did matter to me because I cared about the country I was born in.

Back in the hotel, we couldn't help celebrating. The dinner was held in high spirits, with singing and toasts. The players were full of self-confidence, even while Coach Andreyevich said that the result was great but they were not even halfway through.

When he said that, I caught myself wondering what would happen to me along the way to the trophy if Ukraine was out. I would have the solution to the situation I had created for myself – all those men would be too far from me to cause any more problems. For now, I still continued to be in their vicinity.

Despite knowing very well that it was wrong, I felt damn excited about what was coming up.

CHAPTER 9

I put off my announcement that I would be leaving for two days until the next morning because I didn't want to destroy Alex's celebratory mood. I knew he wouldn't like it too much, although he did understand that during the tournament he was the one working while I was on a one-month vacation. I couldn't just sit in the hotel and by the pool waiting for him so that we could enjoy a few hours together between his trainings, matches and meetings with the team. I had to have a social life of my own, especially since the girls were with me and we were moving from city to city together.

After breakfast, the four of us left for the airport. Angie and Lana went to Munich, while Bea and I landed in Stuttgart in time to have coffee with her parents and then move to the stadium. Bea's mother, Sarah, was of Italian descent. That was one of the reasons they came to see the game; plus, her father, Peter, was eager to see the famous Italian team play.

We tried to make it a secret that we were there, so as to avoid any troublesome assumptions. However, it was useless. I had the impression that from the moment the reporters noticed us take our seats, they only switched between photographing the players and us. I constantly had to pay attention to how I reacted and what my facial expression was, especially because I didn't want to show too much pleasure in being there since even the Italian players had said things about me. Some of those vulgar statements included the girls also.

The first half of the game was boring compared to what we had seen the day before. The ball was passed from one side to the other by the players of both teams, and while there were some good moves and entertaining mistakes, no goals were scored – neither side even got close.

During the break, we took a chance to talk to some fans and snap a few photos while Bea's father went to get us some snacks. By the time he returned, the players were ready for the next part.

The second half was much better than the previous one. Shocking everyone, Costa Rica placed the ball behind the best Italian goalkeeper, Francesco Russo. It was unbelievable. I almost laughed, even though I was supposed to cheer for the team in blue. Italy had been one of the most common favourites for this competition since its start almost one hundred years ago, and this year they were considered one of the teams that would definitely take part in the semi-finals.

Now they were losing to Costa Rica.

As the game went on, the minutes seemed to be ticking faster than normal. I didn't want to imagine how the players must have felt. In a blink of an eye, it was already the eighty-seventh minute, and nothing much had changed. The Costa Rican defence was impenetrable, and the Italian offence now consisted of three players, with four in the midfield.

Then, out of the blue – literally – an Italian player took the ball and furiously rushed forward. On the big screen, we could see his distorted, red face. He was unstoppable. He was so fast that he escaped the enemy players and soon found himself alone in front of the goalkeeper. He had to react fast; and fast did he react. He hit the ball, and it flew to the upper left corner. The keeper jumped toward it and touched it only lightly – he couldn't stop it. It was 1–1.

The stadium, with an Italian majority, started shaking as if a train was running under it. The red-faced player fell to the earth and his teammates jumped over him. I thought he would suffocate being under them for such a long time, but when he stood up, he had regained a normal complexion. It was Marco Moretti, a twenty-seven-year-old player at the peak of his career. This was his first goal in the tournament.

The Italian coach shouted at his players to stand up and move before the last whistle. The extra time was only two minutes; there was still a chance for something to be done.

And, surprisingly, something was.

The opponents were still dizzy from the incident a few minutes ago. The fans hadn't even had time to rest their throats when the referee whistled again and the big screen showed 2–1 for Italy. This time, it was a midfielder who placed the ball behind the posts in almost the same move as Moretti. The fans in blue screamed, waving their flags and scarves, and the game came to a close very soon afterwards. Unexpectedly and somehow unfairly, the Italians had managed not to lose.

I had to admit that in the end, the game was not a complete waste of time. The atmosphere from the fans, combined with the plays of the second half, was worth stopping by Stuttgart.

By the time we reached the hotel, we were starving, so we went for a hearty dinner consisting of Italian dishes upon Bea's mother's insistence. "To my Italians," she said. I had pasta and Prosecco, which I hadn't tasted in ages. Halfway into the dinner, I'd already had one bottle myself while the pasta on my plate was barely touched. The drink was delicious and made me appropriately, pleasantly tipsy. Bea was on the same page.

"Do you girls often drink so much?" her mother asked.

"How much? This isn't much," Bea said and unintentionally hiccupped, making us all laugh aloud.

"It certainly is," said Sarah.

"Not according to the Andersonn's scale."

"Bea!" I snapped jokingly. "Your mother will think I'm an alcoholic."

"No, she won't," Peter intervened. "I often drink with Brad. His capacity is beyond belief."

"Cheers to that!" I said, and we all laughed again.

When the dinner was almost over and all four of us were laughing at everything anyone said and not at all feeling like going to bed, two men entered the restaurant, each holding a bouquet of roses. They looked around for a while until the one with black hair caught my eye. They both turned and approached us. I instantly recognised Stefano Silvi of the Italian team, but the black-haired guy took me a few more seconds. It was Marco Moretti, not with the red, distorted face I remembered from the stadium but with a normal one, smiling.

"What are you two doing here?" I said, surprised. Bea hit me in the rib to remind me of my manners.

"We came to say thank you for coming today. Nobody knew about it nor expected it," said Marco, looking at me.

"Well, you can thank these people. It wasn't really my intention," I replied, and Bea hit me again.

Stefano passed the flowers to Sarah. "Thank you for coming to our game and bringing your beautiful daughter and her friend."

I smirked at him. I had never been jealous of Bea, but a sentence like that was just ridiculous.

"You are welcome, boys," she said. "Join us for a drink."

"They're not allowed," I said.

"On this occasion, we might have one," said Marco. "If we keep it a secret."

"We'll have to negotiate on that."

My audacity was unassailably coming from the drinks I had been having, but I didn't mind it. I enjoyed being sharp with guys who thought too much of themselves.

I had to admit later, though, that they were rather well-mannered and kind, engaging in conversation equally with Mr and Mrs Lane, Bea, and me. I didn't feel as bothered as I thought I would. They were courteous, eloquent and knowledgeable. They even came well-dressed, in tailored trousers and shirts.

After half an hour, Bea's parents stood up to leave.

"We apologise, we have an early flight tomorrow to Munich," said Sarah. "But I believe the girls can stay a bit longer."

"Not too long, though," added Peter, "since we're going together."

"No worries, Mr Lane," said Marco, standing up to shake hands. "It was lovely to meet you. Hope to see you soon."

With Bea's parents gone, there were maybe ten people left in the restaurant, including the four of us. Marco turned to me and confidently said, "It is true. You really are a bloody brisk bitch."

Instead of being shocked and enraged, as would be my normal reaction, I paused for a moment and then started laughing out loud.

"And your face looks much better off the pitch than on," I replied, and Stefano started laughing. Marco hit him.

"Have a drink. Relax," I said, passing him my glass of Prosecco.

He took a sip and returned it to me. "Let's order another one. Better."

"I think we've had enough for tonight," Bea intervened.

"No, I haven't," I said. "Go ahead."

In ten minutes, another bottle of the sparkly, delicious wine was on our table. I didn't notice much difference from the previous one, but maybe I was just too carried away and tired.

Our conversation swayed from basic chit-chat to their beginnings in football, which were quite easy since they were born in a country where football was like a religion. Their parents supported them, they started earning money playing as teenagers and the rest came as a result of lots of hard work and commitment. They also talked about Sicily, where Stefano was from, and about Lake Como, near which Marco used to live with his parents. It would have been a completely friendly conversation if it hadn't been for Marco's occasional hand on my leg under the table. When he first did it, I twitched, electrified. Our eyes met, and since I liked the feeling, I didn't say anything.

"Italy is not possible to be entirely explored, ever," Stefano said. "The nature, the food, the sea. You have to keep coming again and again."

"Like being in a bed with Italian," added Marco, his eyes still on me.

"You are delusional," Bea replied.

"I'm telling you, there is no better guy than an Italian."

"I've tried. It's not true."

"You should try again." He turned and winked at her.

As the evening went on and we were not tired, we decided to play a game. Everyone asked a question, and whoever answered wrong had to take a sip. As if we hadn't had enough to drink already. I didn't rebel, though. I liked how things were developing.

We started with tricky questions in geography, but they were cunning and soon switched to World Cup trivia and football rules. Bea was a pioneer but I was no amateur. I knew everything they asked, from the first time thirty-two teams played (1998) to where the next match for the Italians would be (Leipzig). I could even recommend them what to see in Leipzig since I had visited a couple of years ago, attending an event with Dad.

"Very well versed, Jane," Marco said. "Impressive."

"Since you said a while ago that I was a brisk bitch, I'll take this as a huge compliment."

We laughed.

"And you dance well."

"Yes, I'm a hell of a dancer."

"Show me." He stood up.

"What?" I was taken by surprise. "I don't have to show you anything. Open YouTube and you'll see."

"I don't believe anything till I try it. Stefano, play something."

I hesitated.

"What? Are you scared? Come on, a good dancer can adjust to anything, right?" He held out a hand. I accepted it.

The moment he put his arm over my waist, I felt those same tickles of excitement as when Gottfried had touched me. I knew I should've stepped back immediately, but, then again, it was all just a game, wasn't it? His game, my game…it didn't matter anymore. I enjoyed it a lot, being the centre of attention of all those guys who thought so highly of themselves but then turned into puppies in front of a pretty girl. They were all fools who thought they controlled the situation, while the actual person in control was me.

"Tell me now sincerely," I whispered to his ear. "What's the real reason you and Silvi came here?"

He smiled. "You are not stupid."

"As I proved earlier."

"I wanted to have a word or two with you."

"So far you've had more than one or two words."

"I don't see you complaining."

I wanted to step away, but being held by him felt too good and comfortable.

"Not for now," I said.

"So, we can continue in this direction?"

I only smiled. An alarm in my head was screaming at me to stop, say goodnight and go to my room, but the devil in me didn't listen. Towards the last few tones of the song, I whispered in his ear, "Room 1050. I'll give you a guide for Leipzig."

He was surprised at first but very quickly regained that confident look on his face and winked in confirmation.

I didn't tell Bea what my plan was. We only wished the guys goodnight and headed toward our rooms. She was too tipsy and tired to ask me anything, so we separated, agreeing on a time to meet tomorrow and promising we wouldn't be late.

I was tipsy, too, but much more excited. I checked my phone. No text message from Alex. So he didn't miss me so much after all.

I wanted to take a quick shower, but I didn't have time. Not even five minutes after I entered the room, I heard knocking at the door. When I opened it, Marco was breathing fast. He'd clearly taken the stairs, and I laughed to myself. I stepped back from the door.

"Come on in," I said after he was still staring at me in disbelief. "What? Are you scared?"

He finally entered and closed the door behind him. "No, bella, I'm just admiring the view."

I knew he was already worked up, but I wanted to tempt him more, to play more. I walked to a shelf across the room and bent, pretending to look for something, conscious of how short my dress was.

"Oh, I'm sorry." I stood up. "It seems I haven't brought the guide with me."

"So why have I come all the way to the tenth floor, through the emergency exit?" He approached me. The blood in my brain was boiling, and my nerves were on edge.

"I guess you know the answer better than me," I said. His face was now millimetres from mine. I was already all excited, and something hot was pleasantly twisting in my belly. I didn't know if he could see it in my eyes, but the next moment he grabbed my head and held me so I couldn't move away from his kiss. It was wild and rough and full of desire.

He took me to the wall and lifted my dress. He tore my underwear, and I did the same to his shirt after the buttons annoyed me. He opened his trousers and dropped them to the floor. He was hard. I wanted him inside me as soon as possible. He wanted the same. He lifted me and entered me, strong and forceful. I let out a scream. He closed my mouth with his hand.

It felt so different than with Gottfried. It was pleasurable but in another way. His moves were different: faster, more demanding, selfish. He was like a kid in a candy store, wanting to touch everything, try everything, fast. Still, I loved it.

I was sensitive, my back tight against the wall, relying on him and chasing my orgasm, when I heard his moans get deeper. The next moment, he came.

He let me stand on my feet and gasped, his head on the wall next to mine. There was a brief silence, which I had to interrupt, having regained my breath.

"I see you were really excited about this," I said.

"Of course. What did you expect?"

"To come, to start with." I pushed him away and laughed.

"Are you making fun of me?"

"Not at all, boy. For your age, you performed excellently. How old did you say you were? Sixteen?"

That touched his ego. He freed himself of his clothes entirely and went after me. "This was just the beginning, hun. I had to relieve myself of the pressure. The best part is coming now."

He helped me out of my dress. I kept on my high heels and bra.

"Dear lord, you're perfect." He stepped back to get a full look at me. "If you were mine, I wouldn't get off of you for weeks."

"Can you condense that into one night?"

He caught me by the hair and pulled my head back, giving me another harsh kiss. I felt his other hand between my legs. He played, making me more and more excited. He opened my bra and bit my nipples, putting my nerves on edge. I started moaning. When he put only one finger inside me, I thought I would explode. He was hard again and big, like a few minutes ago. I wanted him inside me. Soon.

"Turn," he told me. I listened. He bent me just a little and then entered me with the same force as earlier, but this time the feeling was much more intense. I was about to scream, but he pulled my hair back. "No, you mustn't scream."

"Why?" I almost begged.

"It's much more intense if you don't make a sound. You'll see."

As he continued, different colours and clouds of pleasure and happiness drifted around in front of my eyes while I stifled my moans. I was on the way to the orgasm I craved so much, but I wasn't reaching it. "I want to go to bed," I demanded.

"No, you will come here," he said confidently.

"I can't—"

"I will make you."

He changed the angle, the rhythm, completely throwing me off track. I was caught, overwhelmed with feelings. The next moment I came once, strongly, but he didn't stop, so I came again. And again. He still didn't stop.

"Now, we will move to the bed," he said.

I lay down, still trembling from the force of the orgasms. He bent over me.

"Are you exhausted already?" he said and lifted one of my legs. "I'm not done with you yet." He entered me again.

First, I felt pain but then, another wave of enjoyment. He was going slowly now and that drove me crazy. When I was on the verge of reaching orgasm again, he stopped. My eyes narrowed in disbelief.

"Don't be disappointed."

He turned me on my side and entered me again. He moved slowly and then faster. When I felt I was coming, he stopped again.

"Now it's your turn to play," he said, moving to lie on his back. I was so full of demand that I stood up immediately and sat on him, but before I moved, he caught my hips. "You have to listen to me and do what I say." I nodded. "Promise?" I nodded again. He moved suddenly and entered me so strongly that I screamed again.

I listened to everything he told me to do. We changed positions numerous times. Whenever I thought there was no other possible angle, he showed me there was. I was up, down, bent to one side, then to the other, twisted, lifted, and finally, when my body was shaking because my nerves were completely on edge, he let me come. That lasted a long time. He was sweating because he didn't want to stop. While I was coming, he came too, and we both collapsed on the pillows and fell fast asleep.

Sometime in the night, I woke up. It was almost sunrise. My muscles were in pain and I laughed to myself about it. I realised I was all sticky and sweaty and went for a shower. I glanced at my phone when I returned to the bedroom. This time, there was a message from Alex.

I miss you.

I woke Marco up.

"You should go."

He didn't make any drama or even hesitate. He knew he was supposed to leave before anyone noticed he was missing from his hotel.

"When will I see you again?"

Stupid men.

"I don't know."

"Alright. I'll work on that."

"Don't act suspiciously tired in training today."

"Don't worry. After this, I have enough energy to last me till the end of the tournament."

He left without a kiss, without a hug. Like a real one-night-stand.

*****

Just before we boarded the plane, I received a text message.

Let's meet for breakfast tomorrow. You and the girls can come to our match afterwards. M.B.

Matthias. So sweet. He immediately diverted my thoughts from the eventful night I'd just had.

I replied I would see what I could do. Going to Düsseldorf meant finding a reason to give to Alex, which would be quite difficult if my father wasn't coming with me. But I knew I wanted to see him. This guy intrigued me more than any of them.

When I entered my hotel room, another bouquet was waiting for me, this one with a note: *To the most beautiful woman in the world. M.B.*

I felt pleasant tickles in my chest. This guy was trying hard.

We met my parents and Angie and Lana and all went for lunch in Hofbräuhaus, one of the best places in Munich if you're looking for excellent atmosphere, beer and food, and then headed to the Allianz Arena, where our Englishmen were facing the United Arab Emirates. We were certain that the match would end in our favour, so the basic reason for the gathering was to meet Matthew Vance since the previous time Dad and I had needed to rush to watch the Germans.

As we assumed, the game was pretty stress-free and smooth, and it ended 2–0 for us. The atmosphere at the stadium wasn't that heated up, so the crowd after the game wasn't as great. Thus, we were back in the hotel in decent time for a drink before the team returned. Dad asked that only we and the players be in the restaurant so we could all relax and talk loudly.

When the players and Coach Vance came, we all stood and were introduced to each other for the first time. I finally got to meet Joshua Hadleigh, the dream of thousands of girls throughout Britain, and my dream, before Alex.

He truly was charming, with his spiky hair and cockney accent. I didn't want to waste my chance to talk to him and the other guys, so I dragged the girls to the table where they were sitting, making space next to my and Bea's parents for the coach and his assistants.

It indeed felt great to have some English chit-chat and make jokes that everyone understood. It felt like a gathering at home in a pub. Angie stood up to get closer to one of the guys since they were engaged in a heated discussion about which city was better for living, London or Manchester, so I got to sit next to Joshua.

"I can't believe I've finally met you," he said.

"Why? You've been eager to?" I said without thinking. I realised that when it came to men recently, almost anything I said seemed to sound flirty.

"Yes, for years."

"Hah. I don't believe you."

"From the moment I first saw you."

"Okay, stop now. That's too poetic."

"November 12th, three years ago." He was staring at me, looking for a sign of recognition.

"Doesn't ring any bells." I sipped my wine.

"The fashion show by Sandra De Vee."

My jaw dropped. "You know my CV better than me. What were you doing there?"

"My sister took part in it, too."

I didn't remember any of the girls from the show since I was the most important one. I only recalled that the event was successful and was followed by some commending articles.

"So why didn't you talk to me?" I asked.

"I was stupid and shy."

"You don't appear to be either."

"I guess I was just mesmerised."

I took a moment to look him deep in the eyes. *Oh, god, how I love these games!* He looked at me as if he was still mesmerised and confused.

"I swear, there is something about you," he continued. "I saw it then and got absolutely petrified. I thought 'No way. This girl would not even consider going out with me.' So I didn't dare ask. And there is your father, as well."

"Well, I can't say anything except that you should've tried. You would've been completely safe." I winked over my glass.

"How do you mean?"

"How can I say it and not make you walk around full of yourself…" I hesitated.

"Say it anyhow!"

"You are the only British guy my father ever approved of for me."

Silence ensued, during which I smiled calmly. I could see a storm in his eyes.

"That can't be true," he said breathlessly.

"It is," I reassured him.

"No way…"

"Shall we ask him?" I immediately caught Dad's attention while poor Joshua was still in shock. "Hey, Dad, what have you always told me about Josh?"

He laughed. "That he would be a perfect match for you, up to all my standards. But, too late."

The other players laughed, too. I started feeling bad for Joshua, who didn't even smile.

"It's okay. Seems like we were not meant to be," I said.

"This is a lot to accept. To know that the most dangerous man on the planet actually wanted me for his daughter, while I did nothing." He put his head between his hands.

"Maybe you didn't want the daughter so much," I teased.

"Come on, Jane. What man wouldn't want you?" He was getting nervous, I could see it in how he had started playing with his fingers. "I cannot believe it. I think I'll regret this forever. It had been my dream to date you – have you coming to my matches, me going to your shows. I was just always too worried about what your father would say and do if I messed it up."

"I don't know what to say. I wasn't really ignorant when it came to you, either. But it's not the girl's part to take the first step, not in my situation."

"Oh, god, stop. I hate myself right now!"

"Hey, calm down. You have to be well-rested for the next game. You guys mustn't embarrass us."

"Yes, you're right. We won't. I'll do my best." He finished his water. "So, you and Yanov…You are a hundred per cent serious? I mean, that's it?"

I couldn't help laughing. "Yes, Alex is the love of my life. He is 'The One' for me."

I finished my drink and decided to go to my room. I apologised to everyone and said I needed my beauty sleep since I was tired from running here and there. The girls left with me.

Joshua was sweet. I wanted to say that I wished I had known about his interest in me earlier, but after being with Alex for nine months, I knew very well I wasn't missing out on anything. Still, I was interested to know how things would have unfolded with my teenage dream.

However, I had more pressing thoughts. Up in my room, I needed to figure out how to go to Düsseldorf without having a fight with Alex or making Dad suspicious.

"You'll have to tell Brad," said Angie straightaway. "You cannot go without telling him. If you do, you'll create a problem for yourself that you don't want in life. If he says yes, you go, if he says no, you cannot."

I felt as if a rough, cruel hand had squeezed my heart. I imagined Matthias's sad face if I told him I was unable to come.

"She's right. There's no other way," Bea said.

Think, Jane. Think! I was screaming to myself. But then there was a knock at my door – Dad and Mom were there. I invited them to enter, and Dad took out an envelope.

"It was delivered to me this morning. I just opened it now. Ten tickets for the German match tomorrow. Do you know anything about it?"

My brain was working furiously.

"Yes," I said. The girls paled and all looked at me. "They sent me flowers the other day thanking us for coming and asking us to come again. I assumed they would send something." Gosh, how well I lied! On the spot!

"So, have you girls any other plans, or shall we head to Düsseldorf?"

The four of us nodded in disbelief, and then, having realised how awkward that looked, I verbally confirmed that we were going. When Dad and Mom left, I fell on my bed, still feeling like it was all an episode of a TV show.

The girls left soon and I went for a shower. When I returned, Matthias had texted me.

Did you really think I'd leave it all up to you to sort it out? ☺

- *You are unbelievable. Thank you. We will be late for breakfast, though.*

I have a plan for that, too. We'll have a good time.

- *We better. I'm visiting and you are a local. You have to entertain me well.*

No problem. Just come.

A good thing was that the match was at four o'clock. In the last round, teams from the same group all played at the same time, to avoid games being set up – that is, to prevent teams from calculating what the best result for them would be in order to get a weaker or stronger opponent, or to eliminate some other team they considered dangerous. That meant we didn't have much time to waste and would need to head to Düsseldorf immediately after breakfast.

Needless to say, Alex didn't like any of it. Even over the phone, I felt the anger and powerlessness in his voice when I told him I had to again go with Dad to watch a German game.

"You know what, I can't believe your father can't see they are all assholes. I'm gonna talk to him to ask him to stop pulling you around."

"Love, please, calm down. You know that's not an option."

"Why not? Maybe he would understand it when I tell him from my point of view."

"I actually think that would only enrage him. It would look to him like you'd be teaching him how to behave and take care of his daughter. He thinks he knows best."

"Everyone makes mistakes."

"Not Brad Andersonn."

"Jane—"

"Alex, listen to me. I know very well – and so do you – that we cannot, must not make my father angry." He was silent on the other end. I knew exactly what was going through his mind. "Love, focus on your training and games. You know that I am all yours, and only yours. No one can change that. Ever. Even my Dad knows it. That's why he takes me with him. He knows me well. He knows all this – meeting people, making

117

friends, closing business deals and whatever else – it's all a big show. Empty all your anger on the grass, and when I return we'll make up for all the lost time. Okay? I love you."

"I love you, too," he said, and I already felt his furore retreating. "Come back fast."

I have to admit that, at that moment, I did genuinely feel bad for my actions; but it lasted only for a second. I remembered how excited I was to see Matthias, so I pushed Alex and our conversation to the far end of my brain and focused on what was about to happen. I had to act proper so that no one would notice anything strange was going on. Luck was on my side – everything was happening at such a pace that I didn't have time to be confused. It was all so fast that I hadn't even had time to tell the girls about Marco Moretti. Anyway, I'd funnelled my thoughts into a single-minded focus, so I wasn't worried about keeping my story straight. I wasn't even anxious. So far, I'd proven to be a pretty good liar.

In Düsseldorf, we again stayed at the same hotel as the players. A few minutes after I entered my room, I got a text message.

11:30 at the entrance to the bar. I ʼll be there.

I put on denim shorts, a plain white T-shirt and flat sandals and headed down exactly at half-past eleven. I was as excited as I would be before a date, although this was supposedly only coffee with a friend.

He was waiting, looking damn hot in jeans and a plain white T-shirt – we had unknowingly chosen almost the same outfit. Having eyed each other properly, we laughed at it.

"Hello," he said shyly.

"Hi," I replied, feeling blood rushing to my face.

"Let's move, so that we don't waste time."

He took me to another exit of the hotel, where a car and driver waited.

"We don't have much time since I have to be back in the hotel at one," he said as we slid into the backseat of the car, "but I've prepared everything for tonight."

"What if I won't want to go anywhere with you tonight?" I gave him a vicious look.

"Alright. You will decide after this hour and a half."

He didn't try to put his arm around me, nor did he try to sit closer to me. He was polite and courteous and stayed on his side of the seat. I remembered how intrusive he was that first time we had a conversation, when he'd put his arm on my chair and acted so confidently. Now we were both like teenagers.

"Where are we going?" I asked.

"You'll see. We'll have peace, for sure."

"Thank you." He answered my unspoken question: I was mostly concerned if anyone would see us. I liked that he knew what was on my mind and responded accordingly.

"How do you find football these days?" he asked. "It's your first World Cup, right?"

"Yeah, finally. I'm having the time of my life, to be honest." Gottfried and Moretti flashed in my head, but I dismissed them. "I was too young for the previous one. I didn't really care that much. Now, it's different. I am enjoying it, fully." I almost hiccupped.

"I can see that. You've been jumping from city to city."

"It's not so difficult with the jet. And the girls have lots of energy. But I'll definitely need a proper vacation after this."

"You feel more like going to the seaside or the mountains?"

"The beach. An empty one."

"Where?"

"I won't tell you."

"So it's booked already?"

We both knew if we continued in this direction, we'd inevitably mention Alex, so I didn't answer and he understood it.

"What do you prefer?" I asked.

"This year, after all this is over, I'd like some snowboarding."

"Where?"

"Canada."

"You'll have to go to the north."

"Yes, I've got some plans already."

"You're going alone?"

He stopped, looked at me and smiled. "Yes. I don't take my girls on those challenging trips."

"Because it's too dangerous?"

"Because I never take them seriously."

I smirked.

He understood what he'd just said. "I...you know what I meant. The majority of the girls are in it for the fancy part of the lifestyle. So far, none have proven brave and endurable enough."

"Endurable?"

I loved how red his face was becoming and how confused he was – totally unlike the bragger I met a few days ago.

"Yes. For the weather, adrenaline, all that. But let's change the topic."

I started laughing.

"Your first commercial that went viral was awesome. I had to tell you that in person," he said.

"The sports equipment?"

"Yes. I remember you looked too sexy for a thirteen-year-old. You even had boobs."

I laughed again. "As if you cared about girls at that age. Don't lie to me now. How old were you then, fifteen?"

"Seventeen. And I'm not lying. I remember that period very well. Everyone kept talking about you ever since: the media, the guys from my club. You've constantly been in my face. But you never came to any of our games when we played in England, neither with the national team nor with the club."

"I was busy. Whenever a game is not in London, it makes it difficult for me to attend. Nevertheless, I don't stay at home all the time. I go out. You could've passed by a bar and said hi."

"Yeah, sure, with your father always watching you over. I'm frightened of that guy. Tell me – does he have a huge telescope in Texas from which he monitors what you do and who mingles around you?"

I held my belly laughing at the thought of my Dad behind a telescope. "He certainly doesn't have any such device, but he is an expert in taking care of me."

"I know. I see. You are a true gem, Miss Andersonn."

I blushed again, feeling warmth in my chest. All these things he was saying were so cliché, but somehow I didn't perceive them like that. They made me smile.

The car stopped and we climbed out. I didn't know where we were, except that it was in the city, somewhere close to the Rhine. There was a park and people in it, but nobody paid attention to a couple getting out of a grey car. He had also thought about being inconspicuous. I liked that.

"Let's go this way." He pointed towards a tall tower. I saw his hand reaching towards mine, but he immediately realised what he was doing and retreated it, embarrassed.

"Thank you," I said. The appropriate reaction would have been to give him a criticising look, but I couldn't. His hand was what I wanted.

When we approached the entrance to the TV Tower, I noticed there were no people around. The staff welcomed us wordlessly and led us to the elevator.

"As far as I know, these venues are payable and swarming with people," I said, releasing the pressure from my ears as we ascended.

"I made sure that today, it's only for us."

I looked at him, and my eyes shone with girly excitement. The door of the elevator opened, and we stepped into a rounded room, equally empty as the entrance hall.

"Jane, welcome to the top of Düsseldorf."

I was amazed, staring down and trying to absorb the busy, football-festive city below me.

"You are crazy," I uttered, catching my breath.

The buildings all lined up next to the vast, wide river; in the noon sun, it all looked like a painting. "Why did you do this? In the highest season, of all the places in the city, it must've been damn difficult."

"I wanted us to have some quiet time, away from people. And this seemed like a perfect spot. In the heart of the city, but still far from the crowd." He stood behind me. I felt his closeness and turned.

"Thank you."

"It's the third time you've said that today." He smiled and put my hair behind my ear. Our eyes couldn't disconnect. "You don't need to thank me for anything today. I wanted us to enjoy ourselves and be as comfortable as possible, taking into consideration the circumstances."

"You are a good planner."

"I was well motivated."

I smiled back, feeling butterflies.

He showed me around and pointed out interesting spots in the city. We didn't have much time, so we sat for a drink. The staff brought an array of fruits, sandwiches and small cakes. I had only juice, in solidarity with him since he didn't drink alcohol during this month of football. Incredibly, I felt like I was having an absolutely normal first date.

"So, tell me, Jane – what was your first thought about me?" he asked over the table. I appreciated that he hadn't seated himself right next to me. I would have been completely confused by his closeness.

I hesitated a bit but then just chose to be honest. "That you're an asshole."

We both laughed out loud.

"When was that?" he asked.

"When you said the first dirty thing about me."

"You'd never heard about me before?"

"I did hear about you but never paid attention. You know, in England we have plenty of good football to watch. My eyes were all on Joshua Hadleigh."

"Hah, that midget with a speech problem! I don't know what you girls see in him."

"He doesn't have a speech problem! His accent is lovable." I was laughing again.

"To those who can understand it."

I held my belly as I tried to quash my laughter.

"I had to draw your attention somehow," he said.

I smirked. "With those stupid statements?"

"Now I know I should've done it differently. I only did what all the other assholes were doing. I should've been more..."

"Subtle?"

"I guess that's the word," he agreed. I neared the table to take a sip of my juice and he leaned on it, too, reducing the distance between us. "So, tell me now, Jane – why are you here?"

We stared at each other, and it felt endless. I loved it. I wanted to play a game with words, but I couldn't force my mouth to form any. Anything but the truth was too complicated. *Damn, I shouldn't say it. Or maybe I should. I cannot lie now. Or should I?*

"Because of the way you look at me." It was out before I could prevent it.

"How is that?" He wasn't arrogant, but curious. I liked the lines of his face, the depth of his eyes.

"Like this." My voice was close to a whisper.

"Would you elaborate on that, please?" He took my hand that was on the table and started playing with my fingers. Excitement rushed through my whole body like electricity. I looked at our intertwined hands but didn't withdraw mine. I returned to his eyes again.

"Other guys...who've also said dirty things...they have eyes of...predators. Around them, I feel how they want me. With you...I don't feel that. It's different."

Damn it, Jane! Could you be more honest? You stupid girl! You're just running into his net, letting him play with you instead of vice versa!

He let my hand go, releasing me from the tremors I had.

"Well, that's nice to hear. That I don't look at you like a creep or a sexual maniac."

I immediately relaxed again and managed a smile.

"I'll be honest with you, Jane. Initially, most of my thoughts regarding you were similar to those guys' – only, I thought about it more in a long-term sense, like if I wanted to be with a girl seriously, I should be with the hottest one. But that day in front of the elevator...that changed everything."

I remembered clearly the incident he was talking about, the day before the tournament started.

"Lens was so excited and reacted in a second, while I just..."

"Froze," I finished for him.

"Yes. Seeing you in front of me in the same hotel, the same hallway. It just seemed unreal. You were too good to be real. I couldn't stop staring."

"It was noticed."

"Indeed?" I nodded. "I thought only the guys noticed it. They know how I normally behave around women. I'm embarrassed now."

"No need. My girls keep secrets."

"That's good to know, since my friends keep bringing up the fact that I look and sound like a complete idiot when you're around."

"You mean like an arrogant swine?" I referred to our first conversation.

"Yes. That wasn't an excellent start with the woman I am into."

"Still, it didn't completely ruin my impression of you."

"And that is?"

The feelings of excitement and pleasure that accompany attraction were boiling in my chest. I wanted to share that with him but knew it would sound too affectionate, and I didn't want him to know how intrigued with him I already was.

"I might tell you later."

"Does that mean we'll meet after the game?"

I blushed and looked down. *Damn, I behaved like a girl!*

"Depends what you're planning," I said.

"If you're thinking about that 'making you like me fast' way we discussed last time, I'll have to disappoint you and say no, that's not what I've prepared." He leaned back in his chair. He was again so confident, and it worked like an inescapable magnet on me. "Unless you insist. I wouldn't mind wrapping up the night with that."

"No, I don't," I whispered again.

"Don't worry about it, then."

"So what have you planned?"

"Let's keep it a surprise."

I felt a surge of excitement and fear. He was scanning my face and could see that.

"Jane, remember this – I'll never do anything to damage your reputation in any way." He again bent over the table and put his hand over mine. I immediately looked around, glancing unconsciously for the waiter. "Even if he sees something, he's been well paid to keep his mouth shut," he answered my thought. "I really mean it, Jane. I completely understand the situation you are in. Just because I am not afraid of your boyfriend, that doesn't mean I'll pretend he doesn't exist. Those flowers I sent the other day were reckless, but now I understand how you have to behave, and I will not force you into anything you don't want. I am going to make us enjoy the time we have together, and in the end, you will decide." My mouth was open as I tried to process my mix of feelings. "Yes, you heard me well – we're gonna play a game, but the main rules are yours."

I breathed out in relief.

"So, about tonight…" I started.

"Trust me. For the beginning."

I was caught again by his deep, coal-black eyes. I couldn't escape them.

"Can the girls come?" I uttered.

"No. Just you and me."

I could have bet the energy between us was bursting out like sparkles.

"Only the two of us? Not your friends?" My voice shook.

"Not my friends, not your friends. Only us. We don't need them. They would attract too much attention."

"And we won't?"

"I've made sure of that."

I breathed in heavily and finally said, "Alright."

He smiled and lifted my hand off the table, starting to play with it again.

"So, tonight after the game, I'll pick you up from your room. Be ready at eleven. Most likely we won't make the dinner, because very early tomorrow we are leaving for Hannover, so Rolf decided not to organise anything. He'll speak to your father, though, as a formality. But that's it. I don't think your dad will insist on leaving tonight, since you have basically just arrived. Which leaves you with me for the whole night." He winked and I smiled, a tempest of excitement in my stomach.

But then I remembered something.

"Matthias, does he know? Your coach?"

"I haven't told him anything myself, but he suspects because of my idiotic behaviour when it comes to you."

"And he's fine with that?"

"Yes. He's even supportive. He hates Yanov. We want Lahrman to get the Golden Glove, but with your Blondie it's gonna be very difficult."

"It's gonna be impossible. He will get it."

"Not if they play against us and I put seven shots behind him." I gave him a stern look. "Alright, sensitive topic. I'll change it."

"I've got the impression that your coach cares about the image of the team quite a lot. Yet now you're telling me he doesn't mind one of his players mingling around an occupied woman?"

"Not when that woman is Jane Andersonn."

Normally, I would say "Makes sense" and move on, but that fluttery Jane who was all girly and enamoured with this hot guy only blushed. At the same time, my brain was working hard trying to understand the actions of the cunning coach. If he was so supportive of Matthias's interest in me, why had he gone for me himself? If he was like a father to them, he should've stayed away. *I have to talk to the girls about this and be extremely cautious when it comes to the old guy.*

"Unfortunately, we have to go now," he said, interrupting my thoughts. "Gottfried doesn't mind you, but if I'm late for the game, he will mind everything."

"Let's not risk that."

Back in the hotel, we took the same door we used to go out. When we were about to part, we both stopped and stared at each other.

He touched my cheek and goose bumps ran down my spine and limbs. "Till tonight, Jane?"

I nodded.

"At eleven o'clock."

I smiled in confirmation. He started moving towards me. My legs melted. I closed my eyes. His hand cupped my face and I almost moaned, parting my lips. But then I felt his lips, lightly, at the corner of my mouth. Although I wanted a real kiss, I loved this one, too. It was pure and innocent, and I liked him more for it.

"See you," he said, stepping back and smiling like a teenage boy.

"I'll be ready."

"Oh, yeah, I've almost forgotten – dress…inconspicuously. Is that okay?" I looked at him questioningly. "You look too hot in dresses, and we don't want to be so easily noticeable. So something more…calm would be great. You got me? Not so much in people's faces."

"Alright. I'll manage something calm."

He winked and left. I waited for a minute and then practically floated to my room.

Before I saw the girls, I rummaged through my suitcase. I found white jeans and a black silky shirt. Basic and modest. When I met them, there was no time to tell them everything since we had to go straight to the stadium. We agreed to gather after the game, as there wouldn't be any official dinner.

For the match, I decided to wear a black dress with a big, wide red belt. It looked casual and elegant at the same time and felt light in the summer heat.

"You're only missing gold, you bitch," Angie said first thing when she saw me. She was right, I was wearing the colours of the German flag.

"I'm not." I showed her my golden earrings and matching bracelet.

"So the sex was good?"

"There was no sex."

"What?"

"We went out."

"Like, seriously?" Her face changed. She didn't seem to believe it. "I thought the breakfast story was just a cover-up."

I didn't understand what she was aiming at.

"Angelina, enough for now," Bea interrupted. "You'll hear all the details after the game."

My parents had been shopping in the city, so we met them at the stadium. For this occasion, I wasn't the cold bitch like at the previous game. On the contrary, I was all smiles – and people loved it. I noticed thousands of flashes around us. It felt great. I enjoyed taking photos with the fans and supporters from both sides who we met on the way to and on the stands.

When the players went out on the pitch, Lana told me to sit still and refrain from jumping like a cheerleader. I did my best to: I only clapped a few times, like Dad.

"Gottfried informed me that there would be no gathering tonight," he said, "so what do you say we leave together for Dortmund?"

"You're going with us?" I asked. I thought they would skip this last game and go straight to Dresden, where England would play the last group game against Morocco.

"Of course. I'm not missing my son-in-law playing the Americans."

"So, when do we leave?" I knew I risked a lot by giving him the power over that decision, but I had to be careful in covering up my actions.

"Tomorrow morning sounds good? After breakfast?"

"Ideal!" I breathed out in relief.

Once the anthems were finished and the players spread over the pitch in their positions, the whistle sounded and the game began. Our seats were excellent, just behind the benches. We could see everything properly. The players were dispersed everywhere. Both sides were full of confidence. The hosts knew they were going through and were in the first place in the group. The Tunisians didn't stand a chance, but it didn't affect their competitive spirit: they had lost the two previous games, which meant they now played like they had nothing to lose. On a couple of occasions, they gave a really hard time to Dieter Lahrman.

The first half ended with no scores, but it still was neither boring nor calm. Calm – I smiled every time I thought about that word and how Matthias had used it.

"Girl, you'll have to be more careful," Lana told me while we were getting refreshments. She was on her phone.

"Because?"

She passed it to me wordlessly. There were already photos of us up, and news – assumptions, more than anything – accompanying them.

DIFFERENT FACE OF JANE
SHE'S ON OUR SIDE NOW
WHO WAS IT? BELLER? PETROV? SCHWIMMER?

"Lana, this is typical bullshit." I gave the phone back to her. "Why are you wasting my time and destroying my mood?"

"I'm just warning you that you'll have to explain yourself to your boyfriend."

"How the hell do you want me to behave?" I said arrogantly. "Am I not allowed to be happy?"

"Nobody said that. But as a girl who has a boyfriend, that poker face suited you better," said Angie. "Now you look like you're here for one of those guys down there."

I wanted to snap back, but I took a deep breath instead. I knew they were honest and only wanted what was best for me.

"Much better," Angie said, nudging me.

Back on the stands, I got in the role of a haughty girl who had been forced into coming. I paid attention to how I reacted and knew that I was already fixing the damage done.

My excellence as an actress was proven by my calm expression during the three consecutive goals the Germans scored within fifteen minutes. It started with Friedrich Larsson in the sixty-seventh minute, then continued with Sascha Roth in the seventy-seventh, followed by Matthias in the eighty-second. Of course, the last goal was the most difficult to ignore, but I managed, even though the whole stadium shook like an earthquake under all the exhilarated fans. It took everything within me not to show how happy I was for Matthias's team.

The moment the game was over, Dad stood up, which meant we were leaving. We reached our cars and then the hotel very shortly. Dad and Mom decided to have room service since they were tired, which made it perfect for me and the girls. We opted for room service, too, and gathered in my room so we could finally talk.

However, they did not share my excitement as I thought they would.

"Jane, this is not good," Angie said, surprising me with her disapproval.

"The guy is cute. What's not good about it?"

"Jane, having sex is one thing. I'm okay with what happened with Moretti and Gottfried. Great. You had fun. They had fun. Awesome. But going for a date and having emotions is something else. It's dangerous."

"Oh, come on."

"Don't you 'oh, come on' me! I support you in your 'mischiefs' with those guys, but not for *really* cheating on your boyfriend."

"She's already cheated on him, Angelina," said Bea.

"Yes, but emotionally cheating is way worse. Alex is the first guy Jane had sex with. I understand if she wanted to try something different before settling down. But this thing with Beller is gonna get out of control. And you will suffer, girl."

"I told you, he said we would play according to my rules. This is all a game." I tried to explain myself.

"Yes, a game where you look like a tipsy turkey even when you're not playing it."

We couldn't help laughing. That eased the atmosphere a bit.

"I think it's cute what Matthias is doing," said Bea, "but still it doesn't change my initial attitude about all this. I think that you and Alex are perfect together. You work great together. Absolutely everything about you two matches: how you look at each other, how you talk, how committed you have been from the beginning. You two are clearly made for each other. So regardless of these other guys' behaviour and efforts, and whatever chemistry you feel with them, I think that sooner or later it will all fade. It's not, and can never be, as strong as what you have with Alex."

I again felt guilt. I loved Alex. That was indisputable. But I couldn't resist playing these games. And when it came to Matthias, I felt as if I had no option to avoid him. The desire was unearthly, and I had to quench it. Otherwise, I would suffer both mentally and physically.

"What about Gottfried?" I asked, changing the topic because I started feeling a headache coming on.

"He's rather strange," said Lana.

"Nah, I don't think so," said Angie. "It's simple. He wanted to get a good fuck, so he tried, and he got it. Everyone knows what a tough bastard he is, how strict and authoritative. I wouldn't even be surprised if, in his head, he thinks what he did is perfectly fine. He's older, more experienced and he kind of 'checked the ground' for his 'son'."

"Yeah, I agree," said Bea. "Plus, he knows it will all just stay a secret between you two. No one else has to know, no matter what happens between Beller and you."

"Or he simply assumes nothing will happen with Beller, so he doesn't care," said Lana.

"How do you mean?" asked Angie.

"He may think that Jane will never leave Alex for Beller. As Bea said – everyone who sees Jane and Alex can see that they are perfect for each other. Not Beller, nor Petrov, nor anyone else can change that. So now he's playing the role of a good, supportive fatherly figure, and all the while he knows the outcome."

"Could be," said Bea.

"Or maybe the old man actually hopes for you and Beller to work out in the end, so that he can be closer to you," Angie said, laughing. "Then he would be able to blackmail you and fuck you regularly."

I threw a pillow at her and we all laughed. "You bitch. This is not a telenovela!"

"Well, hun, I'm not sure about that anymore. Actually, I'm looking forward to the next episode."

"Angelina!" Bea threw another pillow at her.

"Let's hope this will all finish the best way for everyone," said Lana after we finished the pillow fight. "I'd just be careful with Rolf. See how he behaves and respond accordingly. Don't tell Matthias anything against him, because we never know how deep their connection is or what they do and don't talk about. Be cautious." I nodded and noted that in my brain. "And now, if you don't mind, I'd like to have some dinner."

Eleven o'clock seemed never to come. I was ready way ahead of time. Before leaving, the girls assured me I looked "calm" in my plain white jeans, black shirt, sandals and quilted bag. I wished Alex goodnight, having convinced him that what he'd read in the media was rubbish as usual. I compartmentalised him and switched into the fluttery, excited girl I was that morning.

When Matthias knocked on my door, I thought my legs would betray me. Nevertheless, I managed to walk across the room.

"Let's go," he said immediately, grabbing my hand. "I heard someone coming."

I followed him wordlessly. We went through the emergency exit and onto the stairs. There, we stopped for a moment. He eyed me from head to toe.

"Whoa, Jane, I said inconspicuous."

"You said calm."

"Never mind. Obviously, you can't go unnoticed."

He looked great, too, in simple dark jeans and a light blue shirt.

"You're not entirely calm either," escaped my mouth. I think his cologne confused me.

He smiled and showed me the way.

We took a different exit this time, and again a car and driver waited.

"So?" I asked when we sat inside.

"So, what?"

"What are we doing?"

"We're going out."

A mix of shock, disappointment, disbelief and something else I couldn't name flashed in front of my eyes.

"Out like…where people are?"

"Yes."

"What the hell, Beller!" I yelled.

"Wait—"

"No, you wait! Let me out of the car! I'm not going anywhere with you."

He took my hand. I shook it off.

"Don't touch me! Tell the driver to turn back!"

"Woman!" He caught my shoulders. "Calm down and listen."

Our eyes met.

"What did I ask you today?" he continued. "To trust me, right? And you agreed. So, trust me now."

"You're taking me out in public. How can I be fine with that?"

"Jane, I already care too much for you to do anything you might not like." His voice aimed to soothe. "Trust me."

I wished there was some whiskey so that I could have a shot or two to relax. Instead, I just breathed in and out and counted to ten. "Alright. But if something happens – something I don't like even a bit – I'll disappear, and I'll make sure something unpleasant happens to you."

"Deal." He spoke with such confidence that I released myself of the fear. He tried to make small talk but my replies were short, just for the sake of giving him a hard time for exposing me – us – to such a risk.

After a short drive, we stopped. He helped me out. There were nightclub noises coming from somewhere between the buildings.

"Tell me, Jane, when was the last time you partied?"

"I can't really say. Weeks ago."

"But it was something for work probably. I meant like party – going out purely with the aim of having fun."

"It's been ages." I tried to remember but I couldn't. It was definitely some time with Alex, probably in the late winter, before this year when things had become extremely busy for both of us.

"So, we'll do it now. Come." He held out his hand and looked at me in the same way he'd looked at me since the beginning. I couldn't refuse and I knew it. He had asked me to trust him, and at that moment, I knew I did. I took his hand and followed him.

We went towards the source of the sound. I liked it. The music was driving and catchy.

"Matthias, this place is going to be full of people. How do you explain that? They will all see us."

"Jane, I know this area. This is quite a dodgy place. It's very dark inside; you can't see much. Even if somebody recognises you, they won't believe that the actual Jane Andersonn came here."

"Is that your only guarantee we won't end up in trouble?"

"I've been here many times. The people inside are relaxed. They won't bother us."

"Very enticing," I said sarcastically.

"I'll have to google that word," he said, making me laugh.

This was indeed bloody crazy, but I knew that if anything went wrong, I could just escape to a taxi and return to the hotel in less than fifteen minutes. I was safe, I told myself.

Inside, it was as he said – dark, dodgy, basic and chill. The entrance security let us in without blinking an eye. There was no coat check, just a long bar and a DJ corner. The rest was a dance floor. There were already people on it, but it wasn't too crowded. There was enough space to enjoy ourselves and have air to breathe. Nobody paid attention to us.

"If you want to have a drink, I don't mind," he said.

"I'm fine. I'll stay away from it, too. I don't want to be suspicious tomorrow when Dad sees me."

He laughed. "I feel like I took an underage girl out."

"According to some standards, you did. I'm not twenty-one yet."

"But you're a hell of a woman."

Goose bumps covered me entirely.

At that moment, one of my favourite songs started playing. I hadn't heard it for ages. Nobody even played it anymore in the clubs. I screamed in surprise and jumped to the podium. Matthias joined me. I returned to my early teenage years when the girls and I would go out and lose our voices screaming out the lyrics. I was in a great mood, somehow relaxed without a drop of alcohol. After my song, others followed, all in German. I didn't know them, but he did, so he sang along while I tried to imitate him, making us both laugh.

He was right. Nobody cared about us. Even when I would look around, it was too dark to see any faces clearly. There were no flashes or aggressive lights. I felt relaxed and like I could completely enjoy myself. I was happy that I had trusted him on this. It was so crazy! I couldn't recall the last time, if ever, I was out in a club without any bodyguards, any kind of protection. And now, I, Jane Andersonn, was in a dirty underground German nightclub with Matthias Beller! Who would ever think about that?

"You should do crazy things more often," he said, interrupting my thoughts.

I saw he was looking at me again with that adoration from before.

"I cannot. I've never been able to."

"I'm not gonna ask you why, because it's obvious. But what I will tell you is that there are plenty of places like this around the world. There is always a way to do something crazy, to unwind a bit and still keep everything secret."

"I prefer not to risk it. It's not only about me. It's about Dad also."

"I'm not sure I entirely understand."

"I'm not sure you will ever be able to." He twitched a bit. "I don't mean to be rude, but there are certain things you people who haven't spent every minute of your life under a spotlight can never understand."

"Would you elaborate on that?"

I sighed and took his arm, steering him over to the bar. I asked for a sparkling water and then turned to Matthias, leaning close to be heard over the music. "I'll try to be short, but it's a complicated topic. The fact is, you don't often see stories like ours – the Andersonns, I mean. And I'm not being show-offish. I'm just stating the facts: a handsome, self-made English billionaire marries a gorgeous American millionaire; they have a daughter who is a perfect blend of the two of them; they have a perfect, peaceful and successful life; no adultery, no intrigue, no divorce; the daughter is not a troublemaker or a drug addict. Everything about this family is perfect. People like them and hate them at the same time. They want the same for themselves, they love them, but they are also jealous. They are constantly waiting for something bad to happen. You understand me at least a bit now? We are under scrutiny 24/7. Especially me. Dad already takes care of loads of bad stories that would otherwise arise about us, although all of them are lies. Imagine if he had to handle something that was more than just a rumour – he'd never forgive me. He doesn't want anything to smear his reputation. That is why I don't risk things like this."

"You are risking it now, with me."

"If I had known you had this on your mind, I'd never have left the hotel tonight."

He laughed. "I'm smart for not telling you the surprise."

"Am I risking everything by trusting you?"

He stopped and looked in my eyes again.

"I'm too into you to let anything bad happen to you. I told you that already." His face was serious.

"I guess you'll have to show me, too," I replied.

He smiled. "As long as you give me the chance."

The bartender passed us the water we had ordered, interrupting the sparks between us.

"Sounds like you have a tough life, Miss Andersonn," he continued. "Not entirely red carpets and shows as it seems from the papers."

"I cannot complain, taking into consideration everything that I have. I've always worked hard, from school until my most recent project, but I've never had to. There's a huge difference between me and someone whose dream depends on the success of their hard work. I've always had a stress-free life on that side. On the other hand, I can assure you that being always held up to such high standards is not entirely easy." I sighed.

"Yeah, don't disappoint dad, don't disappoint mom, what will people say, think well before you do anything, don't do this, don't do that – I already have a headache from thinking about it," he said, making me smile again.

"I'm glad you got at least a slight idea of how it is. But how do you do this? People also know you, especially here in Germany. How do you go out and do these crazy things, yet escape any trouble?"

"I do what people would never expect me to. Like this. Who would ever think we would show up here? Yet here we are. Nobody will believe it. And even if someone notices, we'll just run away before a big hassle starts. In the end, that's it: no photos, no statements, if anyone asks anything, we simply deny it. Do you think that anyone sane would ever believe that Gottfried's player spent a night out clubbing during the World Cup?"

I laughed hard at that. He had a good point.

We kept ordering sparkling water, which was the only thing that made the bartender smirk suspiciously since everyone else around us was rather drunk, but he didn't say anything. Our mood was getting better with every minute. The DJ somehow knew what we both liked. He played a mix of everything: new, old, 80s, 2000s, pop, rock, punk, rap.

However, I certainly didn't expect to hear my New York project song to play immediately after "Geronimo's Cadillac". I screamed and jumped, almost dropping my bottle of *Sprudelwasser*[3] (that by now I knew how to order in German).

---

[3] Sparkling water

I had practised for this song a million times, so my moves were smooth and natural. I was entirely absorbed in the rhythm. Matthias being there as my partner just made it more intense. I felt so audacious that I broke the barriers in my head and pressed my body to his. He was surprised at first but immediately accepted the game. We waved, jumped, rolled on the floor, stood up, all the time perfectly synchronised as if we had practised it before. When the tune came to a close, I almost couldn't believe what had just happened.

"This is unbelievable!" I said. He hugged me from behind and put his head on my shoulder. I breathed heavily, resting on his chest. I suddenly felt as if I wasn't Jane anymore. Or, better said, as if I was exactly the same Jane, but in another life where I was normal, ordinary, like millions of others – just a girl out with her boyfriend. Damn, it felt good!

"Are you thinking what I'm thinking?" he asked.

"This is beautiful."

"Yeah, it feels good to just be normal sometimes." He kissed me on the cheek. "Come on, let's go."

"Where?"

He was already pulling me through the crowd towards the exit.

"Some girls were looking at us suspiciously. Better to get lost."

I was a little sad and disappointed that the night was over. Although hours had passed, it felt like minutes.

"Are you tired?" he asked.

"No."

"Perfect." As we climbed in the car, he spoke in German to the driver, and then we were off to the next location.

We stayed in the next place for only one hour. It was more a bar than a club, so we had another few sparkling waters and enjoyed the music. No one paid us any attention again, and we left just before closing time. My feet hurt from dancing to every song they played, but I didn't care. I had fun, and adrenaline was rushing through my body, keeping me awake and excited.

"Still not tired?" he asked on the way out and smiled when I replied in the negative.

The next stop was close to the TV Tower where we'd had snacks earlier that day. It was a park filled with bushes of blooming purple flowers. There was no one except for us. He brought a blanket from the car and put it next to the small pond. We sat, this time tight to each other. I was in front of him, and he hugged me so I could relax back, bent on him.

"Tell me this is really happening," he said.

I snuggled in his lap.

"I like you, Jane. I can't help it," he whispered.

I turned to face him. It felt great, different, like nothing before. This was all so crazy and...I didn't know how to express myself. He was looking at me in the same way he had the first time we met. My stomach was swarming with emotions and excitement. We were millimetres away from each other. He still wore his cologne that made me dizzy with infatuation. He cupped my cheek. God, his hand felt so good!

The moment the connection between our eyes was lost, another connection commenced. His lips, which had been on my mind the last couple of days, finally met mine. My whole body shook, every nerve vibrating. I thought he'd be a good kisser, but this was something beyond my imagination. Our tongues danced together in perfect synchronicity like our bodies had a few hours previous in the club. His taste was captivating. The more I had of it, the more I wanted. We split only to catch some air and then connected again.

"For goodness sake, Jane..." he whispered, pulling away. I moaned because he stopped, and he hugged me, completely enclosing me in his chest.

I was happy, though I knew everything was wrong. I had told myself earlier that day that I would enjoy the game, and right now I was enjoying the moment. I didn't want to think about why it was wrong.

We sat there for a while and then decided to move back to the hotel. In the car, we didn't talk much; we only held hands while my head rested on his shoulder. I loved being close to him. It filled me with excitement and pleasure.

The entrance to the hotel was clear, so we stepped onto the emergency stairs. When we reached my floor, I turned. I didn't know what to say or how to part ways – whether to promise a next meeting or not, whether to say how much I'd enjoyed it or not – taking into consideration that god knew when and if it would happen again. I wanted it. I was certain of that.

In the dark, he caught my eyes and pushed me gently against the wall, holding my hips. I wrapped my arms around him and he held me in a long kiss that contained all the emotions the two of us had created in this single day.

"It feels so unreasonably hard to let you go now," he said, smiling. "I don't know when I'll see you again. As soon as I figure something out, I'll let you know in the next few days."

I was drenched in his scent. We stood still, silent, staring at each other. I, too, felt the pain he talked about, the pain of physical separation.

"I wish we could stay here. I'd just hug you. I wish you didn't have to go."

Something crazy whizzed through my mind.

"I don't," I said. "At least till breakfast time." He was still confused. "Let's go to your room."

He was puzzled but didn't want to waste time. He took me by the hand and we headed down a few floors. We were lucky that no one met us in the hall. When we finally closed the door behind us, I started giggling like a kid who had done something naughty – which I actually had. He smiled, too.

"I didn't want to ask too much there," he said, bending over me to give me another kiss, "but will you tell me now what you have in mind?"

"I want to sleep next to you these last few hours before everyone starts waking up," I said honestly. "Then I'll run to my room and pretend I slept there the whole night."

I could see the happiness on his face. "Whatever you want." He lifted me and spun me around. I shared his excitement. I didn't know where all this joy was spurring from. This guy, who I had thought an asshole, made me fluttery and happy in a way I had not been happy before.

I only removed my shoes, as I didn't want to waste time dressing up in the morning, and, somehow, I didn't want him to see me half-naked already.

I found it weird, taking into consideration what I had done two times already, but on the other hand, it seemed natural. With Gottfried and Moretti, it was all about sex. With Matthias, it was like dating. I couldn't have sex with him on a first date, and he didn't mind that. He was more than happy to just sleep next to me. He didn't even expect anything more than that.

He also didn't remove his clothes. I liked that silent respect towards me. The moment I laid my head on his chest, I only felt peace, tiredness and the fading scent of his cologne. I fell asleep as easily as a toddler.

CHAPTER 10

The alarm woke me up just after seven. I felt like I would have given half of my earnings to anyone who would let me sleep a couple more hours, but I knew very well I had no option. Matthias and I were still hugging each other, tightly and softly. He woke up, too, and smiled when he saw me.

"I am awake, right?" he asked.

I smiled back.

"If somebody had told me yesterday I would wake up next to Jane Andersonn today, I'd tell them they were out of their mind."

"Well, we kind of are out of our minds."

I squeezed out of his arms and looked for my sandals.

"I wish you didn't have to go now," he said. "I'd make you a perfect breakfast."

"Sounds tempting. Maybe next time." I was tying my sandals.

He stood up from the bed and sat next to me. Our shoulders touching gave me those pleasant tickles all over my body.

"When will the next time be?" he asked.

I looked him in the eyes and paused. They were shining with boyish excitement and just a little trace of worry in the expectation of my answer.

"When and if we manage," I said, not moving my face away from his.

He smiled and drew a hand to my cheek. "I will do everything in my power so that we manage."

Before our lips touched, I thought only about how happy I was at that moment. There was still some of the excitement of the previous night, and I knew I wanted it repeated. Soon. And if it took a bit of a struggle, I didn't mind.

I took my belongings and he escorted me to the door. We stared into each other's eyes endlessly before we finally gathered the courage to kiss and part.

I returned to my room all joyous but didn't have much time to dwell on everything that had happened. I took a cold shower to pull myself together. I was not to look like I had spent the night out in front of my parents. My eyes burned from tiredness, so I even ordered ice cubes to tap around them so they didn't appear so swollen.

I was the last one to show up for breakfast, but the look the girls gave me was encouraging so I concluded I looked good. My parents didn't suspect anything. I wasn't late, and if they asked why I had arrived after everyone else, I could always say this tempo of life was exhausting – running from city to city, attending even two matches a day sometimes. I had prepared several valid points in my head, just in case I needed them.

When we arrived in Dortmund, I was all excited about seeing Alex; Matthias was at the far end of my brain. It had to be like that if I didn't want to disclose anything. Besides, I missed Alex a lot. I knew he was upset because I'd been gone for three days instead of two, and the reason for that were the Germans, who he didn't like at all. To make it up to him, I wanted to prepare something for him as a reparation. By the time we got to the hotel, the Ukrainian team were already gone for training and wouldn't be back for two hours, which gave me enough time to go to the nearby supermarket and get the ingredients for the healthy muffins Alex loved. I asked to be admitted to the hotel kitchen where I could prepare them. In the end, a cook assisted me to make sure I finished on time and even gave me a lovely traditional plate to keep as a souvenir.

In Alex's room, I set the muffins on a little desk next to the door and decided to lie on the bed for a few minutes. As it turned out, I was so tired that I fell fast asleep.

"Hey, Love." Alex nudged me gently.

I opened my eyes sleepily and saw him. I stretched out my arms, dragging him into a hug and onto the bed, next to me. "Let's sleep more," I mumbled.

"No problem. Except for my afternoon training."

"Argh, skip it and blame it on me." I snuggled up on his chest like a cat.

"If you continue like this, that's exactly what I'm gonna do." He kissed me on the hair. "See, those flights every day are exhausting you. You'll get sick. You should calm down a bit."

"It's okay, Alex, I can manage. It's only for a month." I kissed him on the cheek. "Which happens to be the most exciting month in sport in the last four years."

"When you say it like that, you make me understand you." He kissed me again. "I'm truly lucky that we're on the same page when it comes to football. So many women don't get it."

"'Cause they don't know what they're missing."

The devil in me laughed at this, while the angel almost made me choke.

He went for a bath and returned quickly, taking the plate of muffins to bed. I closed my eyes and felt the weight of him next to me. "Delicious," I heard him say. A few minutes later, he finished all of them and snuggled under me, and we both slept.

Perfect routine, perfect calmness, perfect happiness. Everything was alright. Everything was as usual.

Around four o'clock, his alarm woke us up. He left shortly afterwards and I moved to my room. I didn't even check my phone. I felt too groggy for any brain functions. I knew I was supposed to meet the girls at some point, probably for dinner, so I started getting ready.

The phone rang, taking me so by surprise that I jumped.

"Miss Andersonn, there is somebody here who wants to see you," said the receptionist.

"Who?"

There was a short silence, then ruffling, and then a male voice spoke in a whisper. "It's me. Can I come up?"

"Who are you?" I didn't recognise the voice, though it sounded familiar.

"Lens. It's urgent."

"Are you serious?" I wasn't groggy anymore. "I'll come down."

"No, there are too many people here. Just allow them to tell me your room number. I tried everything, they won't give it."

"Tell them they are about to get the biggest tip any hotel has ever gotten."

"So?"

"What's going on, Lens?"

"There are too many people here. Same in the bar and the restaurant. And for this topic, it's best if nobody hears us."

"My boyfriend is coming soon from his training."

"I know he's just gone. I saw their bus leaving."

Now I was silent. What was I supposed to do? He said it was important. I had no idea what it could be related to. I was thinking fast. He had come all the way to Dortmund, when he was supposed to be in Hannover with the rest of the team, to tell me something personally. It had to be important – either to me or to Matthias.

I thanked the receptionist for doing her job and allowed him to come upstairs. I had wanted to order a huge cup of coffee, but Lens changed my plans, so I decided to wait for that small ritual until he left. I was beginning to feel anxious, so I was thankful that he came shortly. When I heard the knock on the door, I ran to open it a bit too eagerly.

140

He stood at the door, smiling. His relaxed appearance calmed me down but at the same time puzzled me.

"So?" I asked when he closed the door behind him.

"Give me a minute. I've just arrived."

I offered him a chair next to the desk. "If you want drinks, take them from the minibar." I sat in the other chair. "I'm listening."

He took a thorough look at me.

"I don't know where to start," he said.

"I guess you don't have much time, so it'd be better if you began soon. Is everything alright with you guys?"

He smiled secretively. "Everything's fine health-wise, if that's what you're referring to." There was something in his expression that gave me goose bumps. "Some other things are wrong."

"Go ahead."

"I know you slept with Gottfried."

It was as if lightning struck me. For a moment, I got dizzy with shock, but I composed myself fast.

"That old bastard!" I started laughing.

Lens was taken aback in surprise.

"What does he want now? Why are you telling me this?" I continued.

"I came to warn you. You seem to be pretty relaxed about it all."

"Is he sending me a warning, or what?"

"No. When he told me, I didn't believe him. But then I realised you have no idea how dangerous he is."

I smirked at him. "I don't really get it."

"You think he's just a horny old man who wanted to get a good fuck. Actually, he's up to something more."

"Like?"

"I don't know yet. I couldn't figure out from what he told me, but I can assure you he's pretty damn vicious. And you, playing with Matthias in front of his nose—"

"I'm not playing with him."

His face showed confusion.

"Why did you do it, then?"

"I like Matthias. Rolf simply happened. I didn't have a pretty high opinion of you lot at the time."

"I'll try to understand that. However, I still can't emphasise enough how careful you gotta be with Gottfried. He wants you, same as any other guy. He tried to get you, he managed. Now I wouldn't be surprised if he's devising some method to get you permanently."

"Lens, that's ridiculous!"

"Could be, could be not. The fact is, you would have been safer if you'd refused him."

The tone of voice when he said that sentence gave me chills – but only for a second.

"I still think he's just a horny old guy who wanted to get a good fuck." I relaxed again. "Nothing to worry about."

"Jane, I've known him personally for years. The fact that he told me means he's up to something."

"Does he know about Matthias and me?"

"Of course he does."

"Yesterday Matthias told me he wasn't sure."

"He didn't lie to you. They haven't talked about you yet, and whenever you come up as a topic, Rolf is discreet. But he knows everything. He told me that when we talked this morning."

Something in this whole story was still odd.

"Have you told Matthias?" I asked.

"No."

"Why not?" I looked at him sternly. "Shouldn't you protect your best friend from a girl like me?"

He didn't reply. Then I saw the glow in his eyes, which soon transferred to his lips as they turned up into a smile.

"Apart from that," I went on, "you could've told me all this over the phone, or in a message." I stood up from my chair and bent over him. His eyes wandered to my breasts, which he now had a good look at, and back to my face, which was a few centimetres from his. "Why are you here, Lens?"

"To get the bribe for keeping my mouth shut."

I knew very well what I wanted at that second, and he knew it, too. Despite how wrong and forbidden it was, there was no question about it. I knew exactly what was going through his mind because the same thought was in mine: *Why not?*

In the next instant, when his hand was on the back of my head, dragging me into a kiss, I didn't act surprised or pretend to refuse. Instead, I decided not to waste time. He tasted too good for that.

Also, I was thinking about how impressed I was with myself. So many girls around the world would give everything just to spend a few minutes with this guy who I had become acquainted with. And here he was, coming to me alone while he was supposed to be hundreds of kilometres away preparing for a match. I didn't think about Alex. I didn't even think about Matthias. All I thought about was that I couldn't miss this opportunity, could I? Lens Petrov was high on the list of the hottest men in the world – and damn hot he was – and he had materialised in my room. I didn't need more persuasion than that.

We moved to the bed, every step removing a piece of clothing. He took off my bra and dove into my breasts. I let myself disappear into receiving. It was pure enjoyment. He seemed eager to give a lot without demanding much. He was aggressive, and I liked it. It was exactly how I imagined sex with a guy like him would be.

I helped him out of his boxers before he lifted me and threw on the still-made bed. He went down my neck, over my belly and removed the last piece of clothing I had on. By that point, I didn't want anything else – no more playing or games, only him.

"I could just enter you now and give you what we both want, or—"

"Give me!" I interrupted him.

He smiled confidently.

"I never really thought I would hear that from the hottest woman on the planet."

"Don't disappoint her."

"I sure won't."

He sat on the bed, between my legs, then lifted my hips and pulled me towards his crotch, entering me.

I nearly shouted in a wave of excitement and almost painful pleasure. When he started moving, I struggled not to moan, but at the same time, the suppression made me feel him more intensely.

I didn't regret at all that I was having sex with Matthias's friend less than fifteen hours after I'd felt like a silly girl with him on a date. In my heated-up mind, there was no space for him or any other man. It was all about my pleasure and how to attain more of it.

When Lens started rubbing me, my sight got blurred. I thought I wouldn't make it to the end of the ride, but he soon proved me wrong. I came shaking and in spasms, once, and then a second time. And then he came, growling and strong, squeezing my thighs.

He toppled next to me while we both breathed heavily. When I completely understood what had just happened, a thought crossed my mind: *one more*. I started laughing aloud.

He looked at me questioningly. "Are you mocking me?"

"Absolutely not, Lens. This was mind-blowing."

Soon, I made him dress and leave. None of his friends nor anyone in Hannover knew why he was absent and it was better it stayed like that.

"Lens, I am very serious about this – what happened in this room is top secret. No one, not even Gottfried, can know. I don't care about how you guys like to show off to each other. If you endanger my reputation or my relationship with Alex, I am not forgiving."

"Got it, Miss Andersonn. But what about Matthias?"

"Shouldn't I be asking you that?" I smirked.

He got confused. "Well…nothing. I wasn't planning on telling him anything. He's so into you."

"Why did you come here, then?"

"I didn't want to miss my chance with you. And Matthias has never been serious with girls."

"So you think he'll get fed up with me soon?" I didn't like how it sounded, or the thought of it, but I had to ask.

He was silent for a while. "I don't know. Maybe it's different this time, with you. On my side, I know I won't tell him anything. It would just ruin our friendship and whatever you two might have," he said, looking at the floor. On his face, I could see the fight going on inside him. He wanted to regret what we had just done, but he couldn't. I almost laughed at it.

"We have a deal, then?" I wanted to conclude the evening.

"You can trust me, Jane," he reassured me.

As soon as he left my room, I realised I had better shower up and prepare to meet the girls and tell them everything before Alex returned from his training. Needless to say, they were in disbelief. Their reactions fluctuated from anger, to sadness, to fear, to shock.

"Who have I been living with these last couple of years!" Bea said. "It seems that I never knew you."

"I never knew this side of myself, either," I said.

"Sexual monster," said Lana.

"I don't know how you don't understand," I protested. "All these guys are attractive. We've watched them on the TV, in the games. We wanted them, dreamt about them. And now, all of them are at an arm's length. How can I refuse?"

"By thinking about your faithful and committed boyfriend, Jane!" Bea criticised.

"Then I would be missing out, wouldn't I?"

"You're now basically telling us that at no point with those four men did you think about Alex, not even for a second?" Lana asked.

"No. How would I? If I had thought about him, I wouldn't have been able to do it. Nor would I be able to sleep at night. Every time it happened, I would kind of…switch him off."

A brief silence ensued.

"Switch him off?" Lana asked.

"Yeah. I simply put him out of my brain, enjoyed myself, and when I was about to come back to normal – to him – I put the event out of my brain."

Another silence.

"You are a bloody psycho!" Angie said, laughing. "I wish I was able to do that and sleep free of nightmares."

"I can give you some acting classes," I said, and we all laughed – even Bea and Lana, who were disapproving out of sincere, motherly concern.

"You gotta be very careful, Jane. What Lens said about Gottfried really worries me," Lana said. "Even if you play everything well and manage to keep it all a secret, he might boil up a storm for you, just out of vice."

"Also, he's not afraid of your father like the younger guys," Angie added. "He's accomplished, wealthy, good-looking. Even if your dad got him retired, he would have plenty of means to enjoy the rest of his life."

"The question, also, is if your dad would support you if he found out that what you've done is actually true and not some lie a few Germans came up with," Bea said.

My head was heating up with all the thoughts and suggestions. I knew they were right and I had better think about it all with my head cool. I decided to give it some time tomorrow before the match. Tonight, I was supposed to spend a regular, relaxed, normal evening with my official boyfriend.

Everything was perfectly alright with Alex when he returned from the stadium. He was satisfied and optimistic, confident that he would not receive any goals tomorrow. While he was talking and removing his tracksuit, I observed him, listening carefully and thinking how perfect in every way he was. His look, his attitude, his English, even his accent, his behaviour on the pitch and off the pitch, his care for his family, for me. Attractive, big, strong, with those ocean-blue eyes and blonde hair, he looked like an illustration from some art book. I loved him with all my heart.

Why then, did I enjoy meeting other guys, giving them my body and receiving theirs? Why did I like so much the guy who was Alex's complete opposite? Matthias was taller than Alex, slimmer, with black hair and coal eyes, audacious, a bragger and an impolite bastard when he'd first made it known he had an interest in me. He even played as a striker, while Alex

145

was a goalkeeper. They were two absolute extremes. What was going on with me? Did I actually know what I wanted?

*****

The day began in great spirits. My and Alex's parents, the girls and I all attended the breakfast with the team. They were highly optimistic, partly because they knew they were going through to the next stage and partly due to the fact that their trainings over the last few days had been particularly tough and exhaustive. They felt like Spartans – invincible. The only concerns they had were whether they would be the first or second in group E and who their opponents from group F would be; Belgium and Italy were fighting over first place. Nobody said it out loud, but everyone knew that the guys wanted Belgium and dreaded the Italians, with their strength and long football history.

Coach Andreyevich told them to focus on the upcoming match and on the next opponent when the time came. I, too, listened to his advice. I found it difficult to even think about the possibility of Ukraine being eliminated from the tournament. It was inconceivable in my mind, and I wanted it to stay like that. I was rather confident that my boyfriend wasn't going to take any goals, even – or perhaps especially – from the Italians. One of their players had already "scored" with me and karma always balanced.

The boys left and we headed to the stadium shortly after them. The atmosphere there was thundering. Everything shook with the singing and support coming from both sides. The American ambassador to Germany was seated next to us with his family. He teased me about who I supported, and in response, I only pointed to my yellow dress and blue shoes.

I sang both anthems, and soon afterwards the game kicked off. The fans sang even louder and more energetically than they had before the game, and it wasn't ceasing. Bea's parents, born Americans, were particularly loud, in company with my mom, who was also born and raised in the U.S. Dad looked reserved. He only observed the game, chit-chatting with people around. By now he was already English-American, but he always loved and supported English football more.

Nevertheless, when the first goal was scored, he couldn't keep his face composed. The action was beautiful to watch. It all started with Alex, who put the ball back to the game by blocking a goal and kicking it halfway across the field. A couple of passes followed, from the back lines forward, and the strikers exchanged the ball between each other three times, creating a clear opportunity for Savchenko to shoot. He did, and he was

146

precise. There was nothing the goalkeeper could have done. He jumped to the right corner but was unable to reach it on time. Ukraine led by 1–0.

The boys ran around the pitch in celebration and returned to the game more confident. Twenty minutes later, when the team went for their break and we had drinks in the stands, the majority of us were more relaxed than we'd been before the game.

The second half was equally as exciting. The Americans showed much more fire and aggression than in their previous games, but against Ukraine's readiness and skill, it wasn't enough. Seven minutes before the end of the game, the action accumulated to another beautiful goal. When everyone thought the ball was about to go out of the pitch, Pavlov showed up out of the blue, rushing faster than ever. In front of him, he had two American players who didn't expect him and failed to react on time. By the time they stormed after him, he was already ahead and unreachable. The only opponent in front of him was the goalkeeper. To everyone who was watching, it seemed impossible that he'd score, but not to him – as he later would tell us – he knew he was going to.

The game ended, the final result 2–0 for my boyfriend's team. I was jumping with joy but did my best not to overreact out of respect to the country where I had been born and lived most of my life.

We headed to the hotel with the aim of reserving the whole restaurant for us and the team so that we could watch the Italy–South Korea and Belgium–Costa Rica games to see who would be our opponent in the knockout stage. According to the boys' calculations, we were supposed to cheer for Italy to win and hope for Belgium to lose so that we would play the Belgians instead of the Italians. I still believed that whatever happened, our opponent would be afraid of Ukraine. Alex was the only goalkeeper in the tournament who hadn't yet received a goal.

When the guys entered the restaurant, I couldn't help running into Alex's arms before his parents and sister could.

"I'm proud of you. Your whole country is proud of you," I whispered into his ear as I hugged him strongly.

"Thank you, Love. You're the best supporter ever."

I kissed him and then let him go to his family.

By the time everyone settled down, the games in Leipzig and Stuttgart had already begun. At the end of the first period, the Italians had scored once, while the Belgians were at a draw, so the guys' mood was up. However, the next forty-five minutes were very exciting for both stadiums and all four teams played with their hearts. In the end, when Belgium won

2–0 and Italy 2–1, dead silence ensued. Ukraine's next opponent was the multiple-time world champion.

"And that's when the ship sinks," said Nikolay Pavlov pessimistically.

Vlad Starovsky threw a fork at him. "Shut up!"

"Thank you," said Coach Andreyevich. He took a deep breath. Everyone was looking at him. "Boys, we can do this," he said confidently. "We have trained the past two years for this. I have prepared you for this tournament, and so far, my methods have proved successful. If you don't believe me, read the newspapers. I don't care if the Italians have won dozens of trophies before. This year it is ours."

Damn it, Jane! What are we gonna do now?

\- *What do you mean, Matthias?*

Your Blondie. He got the Italians. In three days he's out.

\- *The Ukrainians will stay. They are good.*

Honey, I think you're too optimistic. Unreal even. They stand no chance.

\- *I'll just remind you that Alex hasn't been scored on yet.*

Which doesn't mean anything. Please, let's see what we'll do. I can't imagine you leaving Germany while the tournament is still on.

\- *Me neither. I'll plan something with Dad in case the Ukrainians lose. But that won't happen.*

Alright. As for our next meeting – can you come to Hannover on Saturday?

\- *I'll do my best.*

On the way to Dresden, I had plenty of time to think about how I would go to Hannover the next day. I didn't tell Alex anything. His mood was swinging from good to sad to confident. We'd spent a few morning hours together by the pool before I headed to the airport with Bea's parents, Dad, Mom and the girls. England was playing against Morocco in Dresden and we, of course, had tickets.

"Dad, how do you like the German matches?" I spoke up on the plane.

"They're rather exciting. Lots of goals."

"Would you go tomorrow to watch them against Portugal?"

He looked at me discerningly. "I would. Why are you asking? You've heard from them again?"

"Yes. Beller has spoken to me."

The girls were looking at me in shock and disbelief that I'd said a semi-truth, but I remained confident.

Dad laughed out loud. "I was waiting for that boy to step up again. He likes you a lot."

I swallowed hard before I smiled. "He does."

"Unfortunate kid. Like the rest of them."

"What do you mean, Brad?" Mom asked.

"All of them drool when these girls are around. Even Gottfried."

I almost choked, and I was sure the girls did, too. I turned pale in shock and was thankful for the makeup I had on.

Mom laughed. "Come on, Brad. You must have perceived it wrong. That behaviour is normal when men are in the company of pretty girls."

"It is, but it should be among girls of their age. I wanted to punch Gottfried that first time when I saw how he looked at Jane. As if he had seen a piece of meat. But I held myself. Thank god my daughter is a lady."

This time I couldn't control myself and did choke but managed to turn it into a cough.

How could I be so naïve to think Dad wouldn't notice anything? Thank heaven he hadn't figured out what had actually happened between his only daughter and that vicious man. I felt feverish.

"But, yes, tell Beller we can come tomorrow," Dad finished.

I was silent the rest of the flight, though the girls did their best to keep me chatty so that my parents wouldn't suspect anything. When we finally landed, we separated into three cars. I was with Lana and Angie while my parents took another and Bea went for lunch with her parents.

"Interested to hear some more crap about yourself, Jane?" Lana asked. "Just to relax your mind for now."

"Throw it. I'm listening."

"*In his recent statement, Cody Swinston said: 'The reason Alexander Yanov plays so well is because he is refraining from sex with his girlfriend.' The American goalkeeper added: 'Which shows how damn professional he is, since I don't know how I would stop myself from jumping on Jane whenever I saw her.'*"

It helped. We laughed.

"This one is more polite: *Robin Braam hopes the Netherlands will get to play against Ukraine in the quarter-finals because he'd get to be in the same city as Jane. 'I'd invite her out for dinner.'*"

"Too cute," Angie said. "Give us more of the dirty stuff."

"'*I'd show her what an orgasm is,' says Paolo Reis when asked who he'd take to bed if he could pick any woman. 'She'd move to Porto after that,' he adds.*"

"This is sweet also. It's from today: *We asked Mati Beller if he knew the reason for Jane's recent attendance of German matches. He replied that she had got to know them a bit better and probably saw they were not as bad as they had appeared earlier. When questioned about how much he liked her as a person, Beller said: 'She's smart, kind, funny and beautiful. Anyone could like her.'*"

After the girly "awws", we were already in front of the hotel. Inside, we went straight to the restaurant where the players were finishing their pre-match meal. Coach Vance greeted us and some of the players also approached. We all felt hungry and decided to stay for lunch, after which we would change quickly and head to the stadium.

The moment we sat, I noticed how Joshua Hadleigh was staring at me. He was all red. I couldn't quite discern what he was trying to express to me, but I certainly understood his head movement towards the door when they all stood up. Curious as I was, I couldn't ignore it, and when they left the restaurant I announced I was going briefly to the toilet.

He was waiting for me at the door.

"You look wonderful," he said in his cockney accent. "Will I get to see you tonight after the match?"

"I'm afraid not. I'm watching the Germans tomorrow. We're leaving tonight."

"They are more important than your country's team?" He was visibly saddened.

"They are not more important. We're just going for the sake of fun. They're playing Portugal. I'm sure it's gonna be a good show."

"I'm sure you can have more fun at any of our matches." He was persistent. "And after the matches."

"Oh, really?" He'd stepped into the field I was already experienced in. "What would you do with me so late?"

I could see his face turning red again.

"We'd play cards," he said.

"I don't know any."

"I could teach you."

"Like a private session?" I smiled.

His mouth went open. "Kind of."

"Be careful, Josh. You're playing a dangerous game," I answered and turned away, hiding my smile as I returned to my friends and family.

On the way to the stadium, Dad announced he and Mom would not be going with us to Hannover.

"I've attended two games already," he said, "and the chances are I will be able to watch them again. Josephine is tired and we'd also like to stay with Matthew."

"I entirely understand," I said.

"If you want to avoid it, tell them I'm not letting you go. But if you want to go, of course, take the jet."

I wanted to jump and hug him but knew that'd cause more trouble than good, so I held myself back.

"Thank you, Dad."

"But be careful. Be a lady, like you always are."

Something within me twinged, but I had to quiet it down and forget it. I reminded myself that Dad didn't know about my adventures and never would, and I forced my mind to focus on the good outcome of this conversation: I would be in Hannover with only the girls – no parents to worry about and hide from.

I texted Matthias as soon as I was alone. He was on cloud nine. He booked us rooms and organised everything. We would meet before the game and also after it. He wanted to wait up for me to land from Dresden, but I convinced him to sleep because he had an important match. Plus, I didn't know when I would arrive since the England game wasn't ending until eleven at night. I also reminded him how his coach was supportive of us, and there was no need to upset him by changing his focus from work to a woman during the most important month of football in the world.

I found it hard to pay full attention to the game, knowing how exciting the following day would be. I didn't even inform Alex I would be coming back to him a day later than planned. I decided to postpone it and again compartmentalised him at the far end of my mind. All the circumstances were playing out too favourably for me to let my conscience mingle with my happiness about the events that would follow.

The game itself wasn't as interesting as Joshua had claimed it would be. The three goals for England were scored in the first half, leaving the Moroccans hopeless and sad. They managed to turn one action into a nice score towards the middle of the second period. When we heard the last whistle, we checked the result of the other group H game: Argentina had won against the UAE 1–0, which positioned them at the head of the group while England followed up second. That meant the next opponents for England would be the Norwegians, who were the best in group G.

"That will be an interesting game to see," Dad said, and we agreed on all attending it in three days in Düsseldorf.

I wished goodnight to my parents and Bea's as well and then urged the girls to hurry up and leave for the airport, using the night flight curfew as an excuse. We managed to take off just before midnight and arrive in the hotel in Hannover before three. We all left wordlessly for our rooms, overwhelmed by our exhaustion.

I prepared myself for bed and was about to crash when a big paper note slid under the door.

Open up. Special delivery. P.R.

*****

The first game of the round of sixteen was scheduled to start at five. I woke up at noon, feeling nauseous. *I should not have drunk that,* I thought, but I couldn't say it was entirely a mistake. At first, I couldn't remember everything that had taken place. He was gone, but the bottle of red wine he had brought wasn't. It still stood on the table we'd finished it at. Where it all started.

My phone rang, making me jump.

"Thank heavens, Jane! Are you alive? Where are you?"

Fuck! I was supposed to meet Matthias!

"Where are you?" I asked, still putting the picture together and trying to remember what my next step was supposed to be.

"In the lobby. Waiting for you. It's been one hour already. I thought something happened."

It did happen. "Nothing happened. I overslept. I don't know how I didn't hear the alarm this morning." *I didn't even set it.* Plus, Jane Andersonn never overslept. That was why agents and directors liked working with me. I had always been responsible with time. But thank goodness Matthias didn't know that.

"Oh, you poor, tired woman." He sighed. Even groggy and hungover, I could sense in his voice that he was upset but didn't want to take it out on me. "Alright. Let's forget about going anywhere for now."

I took a look around my room, knowing there was only one right thing to say. "No, don't cancel anything. I'll get ready and come down fast."

I knew I wouldn't look presentable at all – not even half-decent – but I had to meet him, after all the effort I'd put into flying here and he'd put into organising a quiet place for us to meet. But I couldn't have invited him to my room. That was out of the question. The smell of adultery stemmed from every crevice of the bedsheets.

I got up too fast, causing my eyesight to turn purple, but I didn't have time to care about that. I called housekeeping to ask for a complete and thorough clean up and then rummaged through my suitcase to find a suitable dress. No time for makeup, not even mascara. I only showered, sprayed some perfume on and ran to the elevator.

"I don't remember the last time this happened. I wasn't aware I was exhausted," I said. I wanted to avoid apologising. I thought that would sound suspicious.

"It's alright." He touched my hand on the table. "At least you're here. That's more than I hoped for."

"And without my parents to satellite me. Imagine!"

"Everything has worked well for us."

We sat in a cosy, quiet café nearby. Nobody else was inside. Everyone had opted to sit in the garden because the weather was nice – or maybe because Matthias had asked the owner to keep them there, I didn't know.

We shared the breakfast and talked over a delicious coffee. Every sip was clearing my mind, helping me compose myself and regain the presence of mind not to slip in some improper tell-tale remark.

He wasn't upset anymore that I was late. He was more concerned than anything, but we managed to divert to more cheerful topics such as our school days and childhood memories.

We grew up similarly, for the most part. His family were well-off, too, but never drew attention like mine. That was always the incomparable part. Also, he had both parents' support for his football and snowboarding, which he'd been interested in since he was a kid. He always had what he wanted – worked for it, of course – but without the pressure of failure. It was like for me: you work hard to get something, and if you succeed, excellent; if you don't, well, not a big deal. You still have a house to live in, a car, paid bills and the ability to go somewhere for vacation to freshen up your mind and prepare for the next try.

"But in order to get into *Die Mannschaft*, I had to fight as if my daily meal depended on each training," he said. "Even Heinemann, the coach before Gottfried, picked players extremely cautiously. The guys from our club who were in the team when I was fifteen told us stories about how they shed blood and sweat to give him the results he wanted."

"From what I understand, Gottfried is even worse?" I said.

"Yes, he is, but at least I know I am giving my best. I earned it. The boys, too. Otherwise, none of us would be here."

I understood. I did work hard. It had taken me years to become fluent in Italian and Spanish, it had taken me weeks of sweat and muscle pain to dance professionally for the New York project, and, simply, it took harsh exercise every day to keep my body in shape and thus in business. On the other hand, I was lucky to have been born with the appearance I had, and in a family who always attracted attention. It was inevitable for me to be onstage, whether or not I tried or wanted it. I was grateful to my parents and the girls, who over the years had made me aware of that and appreciate what I had. I had all the conditions to always be happy, and I valued that and was grateful.

But what am I doing right now? I am happy with my wonderful boyfriend, who is as committed, loving and caring as he could be. And a hard-worker, too. Why am I here, with this man, cheating on him? Am I not right now disrespecting everything my parents and friends have taught me?

I knew those thoughts would just ruin my date, so with the utmost effort, I pushed them aside and focused on the handsome man who sat opposite me.

We changed the topic. He told me how his friends had teased him over the past few days. The guys who knew about us, that is: Lens, Ben and Michael, his closest friends. The others suspected something was going on, but nobody said it out loud. It was like a big family secret. I grew a bit uneasy at the thought of so many people knowing about my double life, but he reassured me everything was under control since he'd never let anyone or anything hurt or smear my reputation.

"So you're telling me that the girls and I are completely safe to come to your room party tonight after the game? Nobody will find out or tell the journalists?" I asked.

"Exactly. Nothing to worry about. I stand for my guys. They would never do anything to damage any of us."

Well, your best friend fucked your girl. If that's not damage, I don't know what is, hungover Jane thought but kept it to herself.

"Alright. We'll meet you here, then."

"Yes, most likely we'll be in Lens's room, 'cause he's the one who can stay awake the longest and still be ready and good the following day."

"Deal."

"Now, tell me, what about next week? In case your Ukrainian goes home?"

"I could stay with Dad. He took this month off from work and won't return home before he sees the final game. We have most of the tickets already. So I'll stay with my parents."

"It can't be better for us then, can it? The blonde nuisance gone, you here alone, awesome!"

I kicked him under the table, to which he replied by catching my hands on the table and bending over as if to kiss me. I was instantly petrified, both thinking how crazy he was to do that in public and captured by his coal-black eyes.

"You've got no idea how much I like you," he whispered.

"I like you, too, Matthias," I whispered back and closed my eyes. His lips fell on mine and felt like a soft touch of something I needed but wasn't aware how much. His tongue knew perfectly well where and how to roam me, exciting me to the point of making each of my hairs stand up.

If his kisses were like this, I could only imagine how his lovemaking was. I was looking forward to it but somehow, wasn't yet ready. I knew it was completely contradictory to my previous actions, but I also understood myself to some extent. With other guys, it was only about sex. With Matthias, it was much more. We needed to take our time.

When we separated back in the hotel, I neatly folded up the lovely two hours we'd had and placed them in a box with all my feelings for Matthias, locked it, took a deep breath, forgot about it and called Alex.

I had sent him a message before I found the note under my door last night, but the answer I'd read before meeting Matthias got me worried. It was too short and curt.

He didn't pick up straight away, which stirred up my belly, but after the seventh ring I finally heard his voice.

"I'm sorry I haven't called you earlier. I was asleep, then had to meet the girls, and now I'm finally alone."

"So?"

I shivered. He was upset.

"I wanted to explain everything properly. Dad has messed it all up. They invited him, initially he accepted, but then during the day he changed his mind, and in order not to offend anyone he asked me to go instead of him and Mom."

He didn't speak for a few seconds.

"Is that really what happened?" Alex asked.

I swallowed hard.

"Yes."

Silence again.

I didn't know if I should say anything, or defend myself, or explain more. I wasn't sure if that would put me in more trouble or make him angrier than he was.

"Alright," he finally said. "We'll talk when you return."

I had never imagined he, my Alex, was capable of presenting coldness like that. I tried to think rationally about everything. He didn't know about Matthias and me, or about any of the guys. He was just jealous and upset that I was attending the game. That was it. I'd have to deal with that and explain everything to him in person. I'd make him understand. He just didn't like being informed about such things via a text message. He didn't like the Germans. That was the cause of all this.

When I sorted that out in my head, I put it aside and started going through what had happened during the night.

Dear lord!

*****

Special delivery by a P.R. When I opened the door, I had no idea who the P.R. could be, so when he entered the room, it took me at least ten to fifteen seconds to fathom that it was him.

"What…" I tried to utter.

"… am I doing here?" he finished.

I nodded.

"And…"

"How come?"

I nodded again.

"It's simple. I heard Jane Andersonn was in town, so I didn't want to miss it." He walked to the table and put a bottle of wine on it. "Come, have a glass. It's the best wine in Portugal."

I closed the door. He'd already found glasses in the cupboard and was opening the wine. We didn't say anything until I accepted the glass he offered and took a big, long gulp. I immediately felt more confident.

I sat on the chair opposite him. "What are you doing here?"

"Drinking wine with you."

"Before your game tomorrow?"

"Yes. This is like water for me, babe. It won't affect me." He was relaxed. "So, how are you? What are you doing here?"

"I heard Paolo Reis will be in town. I didn't want to miss it." He laughed hard at that. "Especially after the trash he said about me just a few days ago."

"Oh, you wanted to make it certain?"

I finished my glass. "I've never even liked you."

Paolo seemed impressed with my drinking speed and poured me another glass.

"Shame. You'd look good on me."

He was arrogant, just like he presented himself in the media. Girls around the world fell for that bravado.

"Unlucky you. I'd never be with you. You're too much of a braggart."

"Who said we're talking about relationships? I meant you'd look good on top of me."

That familiar excitement stirred in my belly. I sipped my wine. "Keep dreaming."

Paolo laughed again. "You're pretty bitchy, Jane."

"What can I say about you, who came to my room at three in the morning with a bottle of wine?"

"Determined."

Now I laughed. "That's a smart answer."

"Let's see if you're a smart girl, too." He finished his glass and poured more. "Why do you think I'm here?"

The wine got to me. I was bold enough to do anything. "To try and realise some of the things you've publicly said."

"You're half smart."

I smirked at him.

"I won't just try. I'll do them."

I took another huge gulp and laughed.

"I assure you," he said. "In the next thirty seconds I'm gonna get you out of those miserable panties you're wearing and stick my dick into you so deep you'll wish you'd never tried any other."

My eyes widened and my mouth went agape. I visualised all he said and felt instantly warm between legs.

I stood up and finished my glass. "I bet you're just talking. Thank you for the delicious wine. I'm going to sleep now." I started towards the bed.

Within seconds, he'd stood up, grabbed me by the hand, and turned and slapped me with an animalistic kiss. I tried irresolutely to push him away but actually wanted him to continue. I was absorbed in his aggressive cologne and pressed between his hard muscles. Indeed, his body was exactly how it looked in all those girly magazines I'd read: solid, strong and demanding. I couldn't refrain from enjoying it.

I heard his jeans being unzipped and pulled down, and I reached down and helped him out of them without breaking the kiss. He moved my underwear aside and put one finger in.

"Damn, you've been ready since the moment I entered the room."

He turned me again, bending me over the table, and entered me.

It was again different. It was ruthless, with animal force, in this position. I let out a scream, forgetting about the time and place I was in. After only a few more moves, I came and he followed. I breathed heavily and went slack, but he pulled me up.

"We're not done yet," he said and pushed me to the bed.

In less than ten minutes he was hard again. My body wanted more, too. That was all I could think of. Not Matthias. Not Alex. They were both somewhere in the distance – vague, mist. They didn't matter.

My intruder made me sit in his lap, helping me move up and down while biting my breasts. I experienced multiple smaller orgasms while again climbing to the strongest one. On the way, before I had reached the top, he came first. I wasn't disappointed. I could see he was determined to make me remember him.

When Paolo got hard again, I was sitting on a shelf, embracing him with my legs – another feeling unknown to me. He first entered me soft, and as we moved, he got stronger. My eyes widened in surprise. He smiled. "There are so many new things I could teach you," he said.

"Teach me as much as you can tonight." I bit his earlobe.

My breasts were tight on his chest while we moved energetically towards the next orgasm, stronger than the one before. I was about to scream my heart out, but he pulled me by the hair, preventing me. I was grateful.

We then moved back to bed, eager to go for more. I didn't know where I had found that energy. I'd been extremely tired, even before he came over. I was definitely carried by the strength of the wine. And some madness.

He placed me on my belly and started touching me. I kept my legs tightly closed, but he separated them.

"You have an incomparably wonderful body, Jane, and I haven't said that to many women."

I already knew that but still was proud, especially to hear it from a womaniser like him.

The next moment, I felt his tongue on my back, sliding up to my shoulders and then down, down, ending in a brutal bite. Instead of hurting, it made me more excited. He understood, lifted me slightly and entered me again. This time I came moaning into a pillow.

*****

What I couldn't recall the next day was if we'd had one more mind-blowing session before we fell asleep or if that image of me sitting on him in the armchair was a dream. I knew everything else was real because when the phone had woken me up, the room was filled with the smell of alcohol and sex. During that short phone conversation with Matthias, I'd even noticed traces of semen on the bed and floor. It had all happened.

Now it was time to get ready for the game and leave for the stadium. The girls were ready, waiting for me in the lobby. We all wore loose summer dresses because it was scorching hot outside. I had opted for red that day. It went well with a beige hat and big, dark sunglasses, and, as it would turn out later, it looked great in photos, also.

On the way to the stadium, I was too overwhelmed with the information I wanted to share so I asked the driver to take us to a place where we could have a quick, quiet coffee.

The girls were not as shocked as they had been before. They listened without interrupting.

"Lend me some." Angie was the first to speak.

"You'll have to sleep in my room, then, so when they come, we'll just share them."

We all laughed, except for Bea. I looked at her with subdued fear.

"You are sick, Jane," she said, controlling the furore within herself. "You need help."

"Come on, Beatrice, you're overreacting!" Angie defended me. "It's not entirely right what she's been doing, but it's far from a psychological problem."

"Then you don't love Alexander at all," Bea continued.

"I do love him. He is the love of my life. He's the most dear, caring man in the world."

"So?"

"I can't resist having fun. Isn't it exciting to do all these things while nobody knows, even suspects?"

"Well, Alex has started to suspect."

"No, he hasn't. He's just jealous."

"Jane, Bea is right. You need to stop this," Lana said. "You've slept with three different men within five days, plus you've got more involved with Beller. I'm saying this as your manager. It's a quick tempo and the number is quite high now. News may spread easily. All somebody has to do is accidentally let something slip publicly, then some smart journalist will dig a bit deeper, and there you go."

"And how did Paolo Reis know we were here, anyway?" Bea asked.

Another slot of silence ensued as I realised I had no idea.

"You didn't ask him?" Angie asked.

"I did," I stammered, "but he didn't give a clear answer."

"Somebody from the Germans told him, then," Lana said. "Only they knew we were coming."

"Why would Matthias or any of his friends talk to their Portuguese opponent the day before the game? Especially about such a sensitive topic?" Bea asked.

I was about to say I didn't know and defend Matthias, when Lana said, "It was Gottfried." We all looked at her, shocked. "I can almost bet it was him."

We dwelled on that for a couple of seconds.

"You're right," said Angie. "It all matches. He obviously likes to babble, since he sent Lens to you. And it seems like Lens truly had good intentions – when he warned you about him, at least. Gottfried knows everything and is up to something bad."

Bloody old man! Why is he sticking his nose in other people's business?

"I'll talk to him," I said. "I'll tell him to stop whatever he's up to."

"You think he'll listen?" Bea said. "You're only going to provoke him."

"I can't just let him do whatever he wants. Especially things like this. Now he probably knows that Paolo and I had sex last night."

"Cunning bastard!" Angie said. "This makes me wonder if he also guided Moretti, or if that one came on his own."

"Could be," Lana said. "I definitely wouldn't be surprised if he knows about him, too."

"Damn it!" I swore loudly, making a few heads turn. Things seemed to be getting out of my control.

Then again, these were all assumptions. Maybe Gottfried wasn't so dangerous. Maybe he didn't want to do me harm or expose me to anyone. Perhaps he just enjoyed playing these vicious games.

"I'll definitely have to speak to him," I concluded. "Before that, I can't know anything. Not even if what we've just discussed is true. There's no use stressing and fearing. Let's move on from this for now. Anyway, none of them have any proof of what happened between us. Whoever decides to speak up to Alex will lose, since Alex trusts me unconditionally. I know he loves me above all and I can convince him of anything. Right now, he's just jealous. I'll sort it all out."

At the start of the game, the German team comprised the German Four: the media's name for the inseparable friends Matthias, Lens, Ben and Michael. Gottfried didn't like when commentators mentioned "the strongest formation" in relation to his team, because he had worked hard with his players so that all twenty-two men who wore the German jersey were at their best at all times. If one was injured, they wouldn't suffer for his absence because there was always another equally capable. Those tactics made the team strong and fierce, and their opponents feared them.

It was beautiful to listen to thousands of voices singing "Das Lied der Deutschen"[4]. Everyone was proud, waving their black, red and gold flags and scarves. I had goose bumps throughout that whole minute.

The game was aggressive from the first whistle. Everyone wanted the ball, the opportunity to pass, to run and reach the opponent's posts. The Portuguese were definitely under more pressure with two-thirds of the stadium bearing down on them, constantly singing German songs. The remaining third was loud, too, but could not outvoice the hosts.

---

[4] "The Song of the Germans", German national anthem

The players also fought with each other, full-on shouting matches stemming from minor incidents. The atmosphere was electrified. That was why when the first goal was scored, I felt as if the stadium was imploding. It happened so fast: I saw the net shaking, there was a complete void for a second, and then the exhilarated masses started shouting in awe. Lens Petrov had scored without even looking at the goal. When he received the ball, two Portuguese players were running up on him. He knew he had no time, so he turned, kicking the ball instinctively, and it landed exactly where he wanted it to.

Lens was lying under a pile of his teammates while the ground shook as we all watched the replay on the big screen. It was miraculous.

The game heated up even more. The Portuguese players in red used every chance to attack and didn't risk any more reckless moves. It became very difficult for the Germans to even take possession of the ball, which was mirrored in the statistics towards the end of the half: seventy-three per cent in favour of the Portuguese. The Germans didn't like that and fought with their heart and soul to do something about it, but, as combative as they were, nothing was working.

That was, until Friedrich Larsson managed to slide tackle a Portuguese defender without fouling and push the ball to Finn Barthel. They couldn't waste this opportunity. Suddenly, each player in white was positioned exactly where necessary, and after a few fast passes, the ball was with Kiefer Hermann, a midfielder, who kicked it at the empty corner of the net.

The audience roared in amazement. It was a beautiful play to witness, and it replayed multiple times on the screen, the stadium shouting in approval each time. I couldn't refrain from taking part in it.

When the referee whistled for the end of the first half, I felt as if I had been working out. I was completely unaware I'd been jumping up and down and supporting the guys in white. It was like my body was moving on its own; the game was that good. No wonder people say football can so easily get under your skin. I felt grateful to Dad for having taken me to matches whenever he could during his visits to London. He taught me to enjoy the game itself. It was only later, as I was growing as a woman, that I became interested in the players. I was lucky the girls were on the same page as me. A model with a footballer boyfriend – such a cliché, but inevitably always a fairy tale.

I went down from the stands to have a mug of cold beer to refresh and clear my throat. Fans rushed to us the moment we sat down. While sipping the gold drink, I took photos with excited boys, girls, men and women of all ages and nationalities. Most of the Germans could speak excellent

English so we had some short chats. They expressed how proud and happy they were that "The Pack" had come to their game and supported them.

"Hey, Jane," shouted one funny, round middle-aged man in lederhosen. "Can you do something to Yanov so that he finally gets scored on? Poor Lahrman deserves a reward before his retirement."

"And what are we gonna get in return?"

"You can switch to our side. Those boys are all lined up for you four."

The whole crowd in the bar roared with laughter.

We returned to the stands, where the temperature felt some twenty degrees higher. It was still scorching hot, and the atmosphere from the supporters made it hotter still. The singing and chanting began even before the players went out onto the grass.

There were no substitutes in the German line-up and only one in the Portuguese. The whistle blew and the second half started. The action unfolded at the speed of light. The ball was flying from one side to another, from one player's foot to another's; it was almost difficult to follow where it was. For the first fifteen minutes, the game was purely focused in and around the centre of the pitch.

Then, finally, Paolo Reis lost it in anger. He got the ball and started running towards Dieter Lahrman. He rammed through the German defence, leaving the players in shock. By the time they started after him, it was too late. In the next second, it was only Paolo and the goalkeeper. The latter stood no chance. Paolo Reis was considered one of the most precise strikers in Europe. This wasn't as marvellous a goal as the previous two, but it counted. It was now 2–1 for Germany.

Germany should have been nervous, but Gottfried was suspiciously calm and composed. He gestured something to a few of his players, and within five minutes the game had turned into a real battle. The white jerseys were dispersed all over the pitch. They seemed to be everywhere. Lahrman observed from his side of the field as his teammates fought the game they were already winning. The next goal was inevitable; they were attacking with such force that the opponents couldn't keep up.

In the seventy-seventh minute, Schwimmer passed to Beller, who shot the ball straight to the centre of the Portuguese goal. The keeper was too far to the right and couldn't make it back. As the audience roared "Beller!", the scoreboard changed to 3–1. Matthias jumped to Michael, who was closest, for a bear hug, and the others joined in. He then ran over to his coach, who gave him such a sincere and paternal hug that I couldn't help seeing that despite how cunning he was, the old man truly cared about his players.

A couple of minutes later, the Germans proceeded to secure their victory by placing one more shot behind the Portuguese goalkeeper. I felt bad for the guy because as much as they were trying, they couldn't handle *Die Mannschaft*. The last goal was accomplished by Finn Barthel, the defender who had assisted the second one. The fans cheered as if it was a golden goal and I was again amazed. It was an absolutely electrifying feeling to be a part of the German-supporting mass. We hugged each other, jumping and shouting as if the team had won a medal. It was a fantastic and memorable afternoon.

I was dead tired upon my return to the hotel, so I decided to take a nap before meeting Matthias and the others. I noticed slight bags under my eyes and realised I'd have to sleep more in the upcoming days if I didn't want to look washed out.

A text message waited for me when I woke up.

Shall I pick you up or do you girls wanna come alone?

- *I'd appreciate if you came for us, Mati. Thank you.*

As the girls and I were getting ready, I could feel myself getting nervous, but it was more like the positive, jittery feeling before something good than real anxiousness.

"Jane, are you sure it's safe for us to appear there?" I heard for probably fifth time that day.

"Beatrice, will you shut up for once and act like a twenty-one-year-old girl instead of a middle-aged woman in menopause?" Angie told her.

"Alright. I'm just saying. I'm gonna have an awesome time, but I'm not the one with a boyfriend and a strict dad."

I refrained from replying to that because I didn't know what to say. She was right, and her worry was justified. I just didn't want to think about it. All I cared about was the upcoming evening. I was going to be with Matthias and his friends. I would get a chance to experience what hanging out with them was like.

Matthias knocked exactly on time. He was so punctual that I was almost sure he'd arrived earlier and waited in front of the room until the exact minute he was due.

He was as handsome as a teenage dream in jeans and a black team T-shirt, his hair still wet from the shower and those coal-black eyes meeting mine. I couldn't speak up, mesmerised as I was, so he initiated.

"Ready to move, ladies?" He smiled, not drawing his eyes away from mine.

I knew it was crazy, but I couldn't help it: I propped up on my toes and kissed him right there on the doorstep. "Congratulations," I whispered.

He loved it. I could feel it. He hugged me and kissed me on the forehead. "Thank you."

When I turned, the girls were staring at us, all three with different expressions: Bea disapproving, of course, Lana worried and Angie perplexed.

As we walked, I asked him about the game from his perspective. He was excited to tell me everything, so he didn't stop talking until we reached Lens's room. Listening to him soothed me significantly.

"One more question, Mati," I asked in front of the door, behind which I could already hear loud laughs and conversation. "How are we gonna behave inside?"

"As friends, but I'll be next to you all the time. Sounds good?"

I nodded, relaxed.

A wave of many emotions ran through me seconds after we went inside. I expected to see Lens, of course, and the other players. But not Gottfried. And I certainly didn't expect to hear someone say, in English, "The lovebirds are here!"

"*Halt die Fresse!*"[5] snapped Ben Schwimmer, throwing a pillow at a guy in the corner.

When Matthias pulled me in by the hand, I realised I was petrified. All of them were looking at us in silence.

"Welcome to the den, girls," finally said Finn Barthel, the scorer of the last goal today.

"Thank you. It's the perfect place for The Pack," said Angie, and nobody could help laughing.

Matthias quickly introduced us to everyone in the room, thankfully skipping the handshakes. I wasn't sure I could have stomached touching Gottfried after everything. There were some other girls, wives and girlfriends of the players milling about. Debora was there, too, Friedrich Larsson's wife, who'd been on standby to represent Germany in the video with the footballers' girlfriends – the role that I had been pushed to accept. I didn't know how she felt about that. I knew that I certainly wouldn't be happy, but she appeared carefree.

---

[5] Shut up!

164

The boys freed up a sofa for Matthias and me, and Lana sat next to us with one of the guys. Bea and Angie stood off to the side, already engaged in conversation with some others.

It was easy to make small talk with them, even with Lens. He behaved normally, as if nothing had happened between us. Even Gottfried was relaxed. I did catch him two or three times scrutinising me with his cunning eyes, but by then I had already regained my courage and didn't fear him as much as I had at the beginning of the night.

"So, Coach, what brings you here?" asked Angie, her bravery supported by the drinks she'd had.

"How do you mean?" he answered, grinning.

"You're quite…infamous for being very strict. How come you allowed your boys to have alcohol and a whole lot of girls in their room?"

He smiled. "Everyone needs some time off to unwind."

"That's not how we know you," said one of the players.

"Schneider, mind your manners in front of the guests." Gottfried turned back to Angie. "As for your question, Lady Jolie. I am not too old to be able to take on parties like this. Actually, I'm not much older than you." He leered at her like a predator at his prey.

Angie's eyes sparkled in surprise, while some guys whooped and whistled.

"I'm sure you're at the best age right now," she replied flirtatiously over her glass of wine.

Everyone laughed again, including me. I loved her for being so brave, wild and silly. Sometimes I wished I had her freedom to do whatever she wanted with men, whenever and with whomever she wanted, without thinking of the consequences. Angie didn't have to worry about what would happen if people found out, if she got caught. All that was impossible for the daughter of Brad Andersonn.

What am I talking about? Am I not doing exactly that?

I swallowed hard and redirected my thoughts back to the conversation with Ben and Michael, who had moved next to us when Lana and Finn Barthel got up. Ben had a very pure, almost English-sounding accent. As it turned out, he studied English and Art History in high school and loved it, but had postponed university while his football career was soaring. He was just a year older than me, so he had plenty of time.

Michael was mysterious as always. He didn't speak much or joke around. It became clear to me very quickly that he didn't like me being there. Not because of me personally, but because he knew about Matthias and me. When Matthias and Ben left for a moment, I tried to pick up a conversation with Michael.

"What do you plan to do after the tournament?" I asked. "I've read you're wanted in England."

"I'm not going to leave Germany. I'm going to stay in Munich with Lens, Ben and Matthias." He was straightforward. "What about you?"

That question struck me like a thunderstorm. I turned my face away briefly as many scenarios rushed through my mind.

"That's a good question," I almost whispered.

The question I had been avoiding posing to myself – or even considering – was what I would do on the last day of the tournament. A few days ago, before my date with Matthias, I was sure it was going to be only Alex and me in the end. We were the only thing that mattered after this summer storm of excitement was through.

However, now, after getting to know this wonderful German guy better, after discovering he was not a cretin like he'd seemed at first, my mind started creating visions of the bright and successful future we could have together. An English lady and a German knight, as some magazines referred to us. It was such a believable fairy tale. The Conqueror from the East, as they called Alex, sounded beautifully romantic, too, but at that moment, I just couldn't decide which story I liked more. One thing was certain: I loved Alex. Whether I loved Beller…well…it was too early for that, but I couldn't ignore the attraction we felt towards each other.

"If the final game was tomorrow, what would your answer be?" Michael continued.

I looked at his face, trying to figure out why he was pushing me. I knew it wouldn't be smart to lie, so I almost stuttered, "I would go with my boyfriend."

"Why did you come here? Did you lie to him?"

In a normal situation, I would have been shocked and appalled at such a question coming from a virtual stranger. But I couldn't snap at him. I started sweating.

"I didn't lie. I told him the truth – that I was supposed to come with my Dad, but he was unable to, so the girls and I had to come by ourselves."

He was looking at me straight in the eye.

"You are a good manipulator, Jane," he finally said. "Better use it to stay out of trouble."

I didn't have time to reply anything since Matthias returned just then with a cocktail for me. I hadn't wanted to drink, but the glass was colourfully loaded with different fruits and simply tempted me.

"Debora makes them," Matthias said. "She's our bartender wherever we go."

"I spent all of high school working behind a bar," she said while still mixing drinks. "Until they noticed I would look good in boutique windows."

Debora was known from shopping malls throughout Germany and some makeup commercials. She had a simple, classical face with balanced features which worked excellently on camera. She could emphasise whatever was required.

"Lucky you," said Bea. "I've seen some of your stuff. They're amazing."

"You are the lucky one. Born blonde like that, with that shape and build. I bet they picked you for modelling as soon as you learnt how to walk," Debora replied without a trace of jealousy.

She was right. In Pittsburgh, where she was born, Bea was famous for her fairy-like beauty, even as a child. In supermarkets, people had stopped her parents to ask about her and if she could be featured on their advertisements. Whenever they travelled, flight attendants had loved her and taken her to play with them. On their holiday travels, other families had found her wonderfully cute and polite and invited her over, so she always made friends. It was clear to Mr and Mrs Lane that Bea was meant to be a model, and she didn't even try hard.

I felt slightly bad for her because she was definitely overshadowed by me, just like Lana and Angie. Lana had almost given up her career to work on mine. Angie was still rather successful, as was Bea, but they did receive attention and offers to some extent because they were my friends. They always dealt excellently with it, for which I loved them unconditionally.

Gottfried decided to leave us with an excuse that he had some paperwork to look into, so I felt significantly more relaxed. The moment he closed the door behind him, Lens spoke up.

"Since the boss is gone, I suggest we play a game and find out more about each other. Especially now The Pack is here."

"What do you have in mind, Lens?" asked one of the players.

"Truth or Dare," replied Ben instead. Lens nodded.

"Are you sure you two aren't twins separated at birth?" I asked.

"He wishes he was my blood, but no," said Ben.

"Alright. So, whoever's afraid can leave now," said Lens.

Friedrich Larsson, Debora, three other guys and their girlfriends stood up.

"Knowing you, Petrov, it's better that we skip it. The amount of distasteful viciousness you're capable of coming up with is endless," said one of them.

"Anyone else?" asked Lens when they left.

"No. I choose truth," said Angie. "Shoot."

"What are your measurements, Jolie?" He couldn't have been more straightforward.

"Ninety, sixty-seven, eighty-seven," she replied without blinking.

"Can I check that?"

Everyone started laughing.

"That's why they left," Matthias whispered to me. "He'd do that to one of their wives, too."

"No way!"

"Yup. And never take a dare from Lens. That's heartfelt advice. Never."

"Got it."

After Lens "measured" Angie with his hands, it was her turn to ask. She turned to Michael.

"Truth," he said.

"What's your secret – how do you handle these three brats all the time?" We all laughed again. "After a couple of hours, I can see how similar they are. You're much more mature. How do you handle them? How come you're even friends?"

"We grew up together, so I can't really ditch them," Michael said, managing a smile. After everyone's laughter ceased, he continued, "To be honest, we just somehow happened. When I joined the club, they were there, laughing all the time. Back then, their jokes were much smarter. I found them interesting. So we stuck together. It's not a matter of choice anymore whether we'll be friends or not. We're simply there for each other."

"Like us," Lana said. "Even if we piss each other off, there's no question about destroying the friendship. We just are."

It was Michael's turn to ask now, and he turned to Bea.

"How is Jane to live with?"

It seemed like everything Michael said had a hidden depth. Even in this stupid game, I felt like he was criticising me for what I had been doing. I was sure he was really asking how it was to live with someone who cheated on her boyfriend in the disgusting way in which I was doing it. He wanted to know how she could share and support all my lies.

I knew Bea understood it in the same way. She smiled courteously, avoided looking at me and said, "Tough at times, but I'd never have a different flatmate."

Dear, lovely Bea. I sent her a kiss across the room.

A few more questions were exchanged before it was my turn. I knew it would come and that it would not be easy. It was Lens who asked me:

"When did you first have sex, Miss Andersonn?"

I felt red hot inside, but on the outside I went pale. Taking into consideration what had happened between us, this was an inappropriate question. From anyone else, it would be fine. But him!

However, I forced myself to calm down. Everyone was watching me in silence, waiting for a response. I realised it was a stupid reason to take offence and create an uncomfortable atmosphere. It was just a regular question asked in these sorts of games.

I took a breath. "The end of December."

All the guys' mouths fell agape and the room went silent as a cemetery. Angie broke it with her laugh.

"Seriously?" Matthias took me by the shoulders and looked into my face.

I nodded.

"You're joking," said Lens in disbelief. "You didn't have a guy before Blondie?"

"No, and I can't see why everyone's so shocked about it. Did you ever see or hear of me dating anyone before him?"

"No, but we thought you had kicked it off way earlier," Ben said. "A hot chick like you, who was attractive even at fifteen, would start exploring early."

"Not me."

"How come?" asked one of the players. "You have lived on your own for the last five years. You've had all the freedom."

"I did, but I always knew what I was and was not allowed to do and how I was not to behave. Even with my Dad on another continent, he knew everything going on around me. Even if something slipped past him, there are plenty of people who could inform him via the morning news."

They finally understood and we moved on. I purposefully chose the oldest of the guys, the goalkeeper Dieter Lahrman. I wanted to hear the opinion of the most experienced of them. "How do you take the behaviour of your coach? Is he sometimes really deserving of a fist in the face or do you always admire and respect him?"

Lens protested that the question was too nice and not dirty at all, but I wanted to hear the answer.

"He is a pain in the ass most of the time," Dieter said reluctantly, taking a look around the room as if to make sure the coach really wasn't present. "All that shouting, ordering us around, punishing us for no good reason. But we see results. Every time he yells, we know it's good for us. And off the grass, he's like a father to all of us."

"Maybe because he doesn't have kids of his own," said Lana.

"Probably. He says he never wants them. Always having a team of grown-up kids is enough for him." We laughed. "Happy with the answer?"

"Basically, whenever he's strict and arrogant, you guys accept it?" I had to confirm.

"Yes." Dieter lay back in the chair. "Why are you asking?" He was scanning me with his narrow green eyes.

"Is that your Truth or Dare question to me?"

"Yes."

"Come on, guys! This game is losing its point!" Lens interrupted.

"*Halt die Klappe!*"[6] Lahrman said.

I felt everyone's eyes on me, as if all of them knew. Instantly, I was covered in cold sweat, but I composed myself at the speed of light. *What are you thinking, Jane? Don't be stupid! Of course nobody knows!*

"He seems very strict with you guys, giving you orders like you're his soldiers and he's some kind of big, badass boss," I said. "The Ukrainian coach is much warmer with his players, and Matthew Vance, too, and they both have great teams. So I thought that asshole-ness wasn't necessary."

"But neither the Ukrainians nor the English will win the Cup," said Lens.

"We'll see," I said curtly. I was becoming belligerent.

"With all due respect, you guys are out on Monday," said one of the players – Sascha Roth. "We got the easier side of the table, as unfair as it may be to you, so we're kind of in the final already. On your side, you guys have Italy, England and Norway. There's no chance you can get through that."

"You won't be saying that when they kick three goals behind your back and leave you stunned!" My voice was louder than I meant it to be.

---

[6] Shut up!

Everyone was surprised at this attitude coming from me. I knew I wasn't supposed to be so defensive of Alex, not in front of them, but I couldn't let them make fun of his team. I had known those boys for a while now and seen first-hand how hard they trained and how committed they were. I couldn't stand to hear them being disregarded as losers.

"This topic is not perfect for the company we have tonight, so let's change it," Matthias said, putting a hand on my shoulder.

I looked at him, grateful. "Thank you," I said warmly.

The game ended shortly afterwards. Nobody was in the mood for it anymore. Everyone was too tired and sleepy, especially the players. They were lucky to be staying in Hannover while they waited for their opponents to be decided tomorrow – either Ecuador or Sweden. The girls and I had to head back to Munich, where the Ukrainians were preparing for their first game in the round of sixteen.

All the couples had already left, and soon Angie announced she was about to fall asleep and insisted that we leave, too (to which Ben and Finn simultaneously invited her to take a nap in their room that was "just next door"). We wished goodnight to everyone, and Matthias escorted us to the hall. I let the girls go a few steps in front of me and turned to Matthias. He made sure nobody was looking and cupped my face.

"The evening was wonderful. Thank you for coming."

The glow of joy in his eyes made me feel warm. This man truly cared.

"You're welcome. Thanks for inviting us."

He smiled and placed a quick kiss on my lips.

"Jane, shall I…"

"Yes. Come to my room."

I could almost feel his pulse accelerating through his palms still on my cheeks.

"Alright. See you in a while. I'll just get rid of them." He gestured to the room.

The girls and I left together and separated on our floor. I entered my room and before I managed to place my card in the holder to activate the power, someone grabbed my hand, pushed me all the way inside and closed the door. Before I could scream, I was against the wall and a tongue was inside my mouth.

I was turned on instantly. Even in the dark, I recognised that cologne and those hands that ran up and down from my hips to my breasts.

"You again. You really can't stop yourself," I said, returning the wild kiss. I ran my fingers through his hair and pushed my body against his. "You're insane. How did you get here so fast?"

"I wanted to taste you this whole fucking evening," he said.

I froze.

That voice wasn't Lens's.

I pushed him away and frantically shoved the key card into the power holder.

Friedrich Larsson was standing in front of me. Debora's husband.

"What the hell are you doing?" I screamed.

"Shh, Jane!" He tried to put a hand over my mouth.

"What is this? Are you insane? With your wife nearby!"

To be honest, I didn't care about his wife at all. I just mentioned her because in the wake of such a shock, I felt I had to defend myself somehow.

"Alright, calm down. Don't shout. I apologise. I shouldn't have…but I couldn't hold myself back, Jane. It's just…you. So close. I couldn't fall asleep."

"It's better that you leave right now. Matthias will be here any minute."

"Alright." Friedrich gave me sad puppy eyes, but I couldn't sympathise. I wanted him out of my room as soon as possible. Lens or Friedrich, my head was clearing fast, and I had no time for any games or adventures.

Suddenly, his face became serious. "Wait – why did you say 'you again'?"

I felt the blood leaving my face.

"Wh-what do you mean?"

"Who did you think I was?"

I thought the bones in my legs had vanished and that I would stumble down to the floor, speechless, in front of him.

"Matthias, of course," I said automatically and instantly regained my self-confidence.

"But you've just left him."

"For a moment, till he says bye to his friends. Then he will come here. What are you aiming at, Friedrich?"

He was looking me straight in the eyes, searching for any traces of deception, but by then I was so good at lying that there was nothing for him to find.

"You'd better leave now and never mention this to anyone." I opened the door.

"Sure," he said on his way out, then paused. "You'll keep this away from Debora? No matter what happens?"

"You don't worry about that, as long as you don't say anything."

I closed the door and sat on the floor in relief.

Dear lord! I was so close to exposing myself! Me, exposing myself! Not someone else – me! So stupid of you, Jane! Thank goodness he is just another stupid man. He'll never remember that I actually touched his hair and should've known even then that it wasn't Matthias kissing me. All he'll worry about now is Debora finding out.

I went to the bathroom to take a shower, and when I put on some modest black lingerie, Matthias was already at the door.

"I missed you," he said, closing the door and taking my face in his hands again. The kiss he gave me this time was longer and deeper, abounding in care and adoration. It gave me pleasant butterflies in my belly. We moved to the bed and hugged under the blanket.

"Nobody believed you girls would show up," he said. "They thought I was fantasising."

"I'm glad we showed them. The girls enjoyed the evening, too."

"You all are more than welcome to join anytime."

"Thank you, also, for the help and support when they started talking about Alex."

"Of course, hun. I understand it's a tricky topic for you. Better not to mention it until you've figured it all out." He kissed me on the forehead.

"That's a very mature attitude from a guy in your situation."

"There's no other way. Otherwise I'd go nuts and kill him." He laughed and I kicked him. "I'm serious. If I thought about how every night you're not here, you're in bed with him, I would go mental. It makes it easier to focus on the fact that despite all those nights with him, you still choose to spend time with me. It gives me hope."

I rose to give him a kiss and make him stop talking about Alex. It made me feel uneasy, and I didn't want to destroy the limited time we had together.

"Tell me about your work after the tournament. Do you already have something planned?" he asked.

"I don't know much about the new offers. Lana is getting all the information on that and we've agreed to talk about it later. We'll have to read through some scenarios and decide what to accept. It's probably gonna be another movie, and there will be some fashion projects, like the one in New York."

"All in London?"

"They don't have to be. That's the best part."

"I love that about our games, too. We go from city to city but always come back home."

"What about you? Have you got offers abroad?"

"Yes, but I still don't know if I will accept."

He was looking at me with that adoration that always made me feel so valued when I was next to him.

"Where are the offers from?"

"London."

"No way!" My heart started pounding faster. A crazy thought occurred to me: if I stayed with Alex after the tournament and Matthias moved to London, we could still keep seeing each other. But I immediately disregarded it as impossible since that was what it would be – entirely impossible. There was no chance we would be able to meet without someone noticing. London wasn't a dodgy German nightclub.

Then something else occurred to me, and I knew the answer before I said anything.

"Mati, don't tell me—"

"Yes, Jane. Whether I'll accept depends on you. I didn't want to tell you, but since you asked…"

This man really cared. *Maybe even more than Alex. So far, Alex hasn't mentioned moving anywhere to be closer to me. Yet this man, who has fallen in love with me from afar, is ready to do so much after only a few meetings. He is so sure of me!*

But Alex had also got some offers, I reminded myself. He'd decided to wait until the end of the tournament, when *we* would decide what to do. Yes, I remembered: last time we talked about it, he told me he got an offer from Italy. He said we should wait until the end of the World Cup and then decide. So, it wasn't that Alex didn't care. He just expressed his love in a different way. My perfect boyfriend. How dare I look for flaws in his behaviour!

I pushed Alex out of my mind again so as not to spoil the night with Matthias. I cuddled on him. "That's very lovely of you. I don't have anything to say except that you are an extraordinary man."

"For an extraordinary woman." He kissed me on the forehead. "Thank you for this happiness, Jane." He hugged me hard and we fell asleep.

CHAPTER 11

When I woke up, the room was full of light and the wonderful smell of roses. My eyes couldn't miss the colossal bouquet that rested on the table by the window. Next to it, Matthias was standing in his boxers and a T-shirt with the *Deutscher Fussball-Bund* emblem, putting breakfast together. My eyes might as well have been heart-shaped at that moment. He looked at me and smiled, and I was spellbound.

"I went out earlier to pick the flowers myself," he explained. "The breakfast I ordered in my room and then brought here."

I crawled out of bed and walked over to stand next to him.

"Shall I assume you'll have tea or do you perhaps want coffee?"

Instead of answering, I hung my arms around his neck and kissed him.

It felt great to do such basic, simple rituals with him, to be normal and relaxed, to share casual events and stories. Sitting there in front of him, in my underwear, without makeup, my hair messy, I felt stronger than ever that we could indeed work as a couple.

Unfortunately, as soon as we finished the food, I had to get ready to leave for the airport. The girls had already texted me that they were packed and waiting for me. Matthias and I parted as star-crossed lovers, unsure when we would meet again.

We arrived in the hotel in Munich some three hours later. I checked in, dropped off my suitcase and immediately went to Alex's room. He would be returning from training any minute. I relaxed in the armchair next to the window and was scrolling through the news and social media when he entered.

From the moment I'd arrived in his room and breathed in his signature scent, I realised how much I missed him. Initially, I wanted to jump and hug him, but the expression he had on his face made me freeze in my seat.

He threw his bag down. "Finally," he said.

I stood up and walked to him.

"Alex—"

"How was it? Did you have an amazing time?"

I tried to touch him, but he stepped back.

"Did you enjoy yourself with your new *friends*?" His voice rose with every sentence.

"I wouldn't have gone if I hadn't been forced to, Alex," I said as calmly as I could. I knew I had to be cool-headed if I wanted to get a good result. If I became emotional, I would just expose myself.

"Oh, yes, you were forced to go. By your father."

"Alexander, I am not sure you entirely understand my situation, but I can't blame you. We grew up in different circumstances."

"Clearly, we did. I can say no to my father and stick to what I believe is right!"

"I cannot." I swallowed hard. "And you knew that before we started dating, didn't you?"

He didn't have a reply to that, so he changed the topic.

"You didn't seem very upset to be there. I saw everything."

"Alex, they are not so bad as you think. I can say they're even kind and courteous. And I enjoyed the game."

"What makes you think they aren't assholes after everything they've said about you?"

"We met them a few times for lunch and in the hotel. They were always polite and respectful towards me, the girls and even you." I swallowed again at this last lie.

"I'm not an idiot, Jane!"

I was stunned and frozen again. He had never yelled at me like that. Never before had I seen his face so distorted in anger.

"They've said some pretty disgusting things, and I'm sure they still think them! The reason you keep going has nothing to do with your father. It's because you *like* it! You like them and the attention they are giving you! It makes me sick."

I felt relief. He knew nothing about Matthias. He was just upset, for obvious reasons. It was only jealousy.

"Alex—"

"And the worst part is that you're enjoying it! Have you got any idea how disrespectful that is towards me?" He was shouting so loudly I could almost hear the windows shaking.

"Is this only about you?"

Now he was stunned. He looked at me in surprise. *Great job, Jane. Offence is the best defence.*

"You are at your trainings every single day," I continued, "and when you're not, you're playing a game. We see each other not even two hours a day, and even then you're tired and need to rest. I understand all that and support you. Have I forced you into anything since the tournament started?"

He was quiet so I went on.

"When you wanted to sleep, we slept. When you wanted sex, we had it. Have I ever complained about the amount of attention I've been receiving these last two weeks?"

He didn't say anything, but I saw the change on his face. His anger was dissipating.

"Apart from that, you know what my relationship with my father is like. Josephine is easy to deal with, but what my dad asks of me, he gets. No excuses. No exceptions. I love him and respect him. The first time I went to the German match, I didn't like it. I am sure you could see that. But they apologised, stopped saying bullshit and turned out not to be complete idiots, so I don't see what's wrong with having fun when I can't avoid the situation I'm in. And I'm sorry that my trips don't coincide with your obligations entirely, but I deserve to enjoy my free time when you're not there to fill it."

Mic drop! Excellent, Jane!

His furore evaporated.

"Jane, I..." He was even embarrassed. "I wasn't aware. It's never occurred to me that I neglected you at any point." He had those sad eyes that I always saw when we parted at airports. It took me an enormous effort not to be moved by them now. I kept looking at him strictly. "Which was so stupid of me. Now that you say it, it's obvious."

He felt bad.

"That's because I haven't complained about anything," I said. "I don't mind standing by you. But there is absolutely no need to freak out when I'm gone for a day or two." He tried to take me by the hand, and although I wanted it badly, I moved it away. "As for the fact that I was with them, there should be no space for jealousy, Alex. Yes, I could have any of those men, but I choose you. Every day when I wake up, when I go out, when I work or rest, I choose you. I thought you knew that."

This time, I didn't step away when he stretched his arms out and drew me into a hug. I was instantly captivated by his closeness, by the smell of his deodorant and clean T-shirt. His heart was pounding loud under my ear, and I squeezed him.

"I'm sorry." He kissed me on the top of my head.

"It's fine. Just don't shout at me again like that. You frightened me."

"I promise I won't."

"We can always talk about anything, just without escalation." I raised my head to face him.

"Alright. Let's go to bed now. I want to hold you."

I propped up on my toes and kissed him.

Needless to say, I exaggerated my reaction, but it was all a part of the performance. I had to win his trust back, and playing the victim was a good idea. I had never felt neglected by him. I understood his busy schedule and what was required of him during the World Cup. If I didn't understand, we wouldn't have lasted long distance for eight months. I had my life, my parents, the girls. I had things to do while he was training – things that excluded having sex with other men. But in order to keep myself clean, I had to turn the tables. I had to overreact. I had no choice. And it was for his own good, too. If he found out what I had been doing, he would be tremendously hurt. This way, I just made him feel bad for being angry with me.

I made Alex feel so guilty that it didn't occur to him that even if he hadn't paid enough attention to me, there was nothing else he could have done differently. His job was football, and he had to be at peak performance at all times.

Anyway, I was happy, as were the other Ukrainian players, that Alex was back to normal and happy and optimistic again. Nikolay later told me during dinner that my boyfriend had been irritable the whole time I was gone, not his usual self during trainings and impossible to have fun with.

Now we were all ready for the match against Italy.

The day was dry and bright and the Allianz Arena was packed with fans: Ukrainians and Italians, of course, but also heaps of Germans. The number of Germans was surprising, but after speaking to a few we got to know they "couldn't miss the show".

"Next time I see you, we'll be celebrating the quarter-finals," I told Alex, kissing him in front of the hotel before he got on the team bus.

As it later turned out, Olexiy Yanov and I were the only ones thinking like that. Everyone else, including Tanya Yanova and my parents, had disquieted expressions on their faces the moment the bus pulled away.

"What's all this?" I asked, gesturing to the gloomy group while we were all having a beer before the game. "Thank god the boys didn't see you. The game would already have been lost."

"Jane, sweetheart, I'm trying to be positive, but I can't help being realistic," Tanya said, catching my hand. She was dead cold in the heat.

I shook my head. "The reality is that Alex hasn't received a single goal in the tournament, while the Italians have. Our boys are all young and full of enthusiasm and energy, while those guys are only full of themselves based on what others before them have accomplished. I bet they're not even ready for this game."

"It's so wonderful to see how much you trust Oleksandr." Tanya hugged me. "I'll take some of that confidence from you."

Before going to the stands, we also allowed some time for the reporters and gave some statements. Lana thought it professional to keep them in the loop, assuring me it was better than letting them draw their own faulty assumptions.

"Jane, you were observed being a very passionate supporter of the German team," said one reporter. "Why is that?"

"Your players are indeed a very funny group. I enjoyed attending the games, and they are good hosts."

"How does that sit with Alex and your friends from the English team?"

"Nothing has changed there. I still support them the most, with all my heart."

"Do you enjoy Ukrainian or German matches more?"

"German games are always memorable. However, you will see now where the real show is."

"Are you confident that the Ukrainian team will reach the quarter-finals?"

"I'm a hundred per cent sure about that." I winked and the little conference was over.

Up on the stands, the supporters were already singing fan songs, making the whole arena shake. On the big screen were commentators discussing the teams' statistics and supporters.

"As it's turned out, hundreds of buses are heading from all parts of Ukraine into Germany. Fans who weren't sure their team would reach this far are now frantically buying tickets at any cost and crowding in Munich, as well as in Nuremberg and Berlin, where Milan Andreyevich's team will play if they pass to the quarter- and semi-finals and the finals. Something like this has never been recorded in Ukrainian history. Despite good forecasts by experts throughout the year before the tournament, the average Ukrainian didn't think the team could do much. However, now they are more confident than ever that they will wave their flags at the Olympic Stadium in Berlin and even take the trophy."

It made my heart leap to hear this, knowing that my boyfriend was responsible for this writing of his country's history.

The girls and I wore Ukrainian jerseys; they dressed in yellow ones while I, of course, wore Alex's black and red one with matching black shorts. The four of us were a show for the cameras with blue and yellow flags on our cheeks, posing with other fans for selfies.

When the players came out onto the grass, every soul in the stands clapped, jumped and shouted in support. I was overcome by the positive nervousness that signalled something good was about to happen. This was going to be a hell of a match.

We were the first ones to sing the national anthem. I hugged Alex's parents while we belted the lyrics out along with thousands of Ukrainians at the stadium and throughout Munich. With every passing second, I felt more confident that the night would finish in our favour, and I wanted to transfer some of that vibe to the players on the grass.

I saw Marco Moretti out on the field. He had sent me flowers earlier that day. He'd timed them well; they were delivered once Alex left for the stadium. I was thankful to him for that. The note he added was boastful but made me laugh.

You're more than welcome to switch sides today when we kick them out. Always in my good memory. Marco M.

Now, on the pitch, he was equally confident, his chin held high up, glancing at the Ukrainians as if they were just a nuisance on his way to the final. I laughed at that. All of them were so naïve.

After the starting whistle, I was on my feet nonstop. I couldn't rest. I had to sing along with the crowd. As it turned out, major people from the Ukrainian showbusiness world had showed up, too, and they approached us to share their enthusiasm. Tanya and Olexiy helped me by explaining who they were and translating when necessary. I was brimming with pride to be there as Alex's girlfriend and accept all the congratulations and good wishes.

As for the field, I wasn't sure how the grass hadn't gone up in flames. It was hot and dry in Munich on that 28th of June, and the players were running over the field at the speed of light and with unbelievable strength. They were falling and getting up before the referee even had time to call a foul or stop the game. Both teams wanted to score as soon as possible to secure their way to the next stage.

However, it wasn't happening. The Ukrainians had expert possession of the ball but couldn't break the Italian defence line. The Italians did manage to approach our goal but couldn't get enough space to shoot. Even when they did, Alex was always in the right place, making it impossible for the opponents to score. I liked to see that he was calm and composed, just as he normally was for his games. He looked confident and ready, and he relied on his teammates, who were doing an excellent job by not leaving him stranded.

In the thirty-third minute, the hearts of every Ukrainian skipped a few beats. Finally, one of the tricks the Italians had devised worked, and in the blink of an eye, the ball flew over the middle line right onto the foot of one of the Italian strikers. None of the four defensemen in yellow were in their places, so the player in blue rushed maniacally towards Alex as another one joined him by his side.

It was two of them against Alex.

I felt a pain in my chest as if somebody was gripping my lungs and stopping them from expanding. The other Ukrainians were running after the two sprinting players but weren't fast enough. Alex was right between the posts. Was this going to be his first goal in months? Would this be the end of so many dreams?

The two Italians spread to both of Alex's sides so that he stood no chance. I tensed when I realised the other blue jersey was Moretti's. His face was red and distorted in his intensity. He wanted the ball. He got it.

Alex crouched, focusing.

Moretti now had a clear path. He didn't hesitate; he knew what to do. He shot with all his force. The ball skimmed through the air to the right corner, towards the empty space.

It seemed over. We could see the ball rocketing toward the net.

Alex jumped. We didn't think he'd make it – no one on earth did.

When he boxed the ball out from the pitch, for a couple of seconds there was a grave silence over the whole stadium. The net wasn't shaking. Then someone from the Ukrainian crowd screamed, and the whole fandom roared. My hearing cut out for a moment until Tanya pierced through, crying out, "That's my son!"

By the time Alex stood up, I was screaming, too. His teammates surrounded him and knocked him to the ground as if he had scored a goal. The stands were jumping and singing; I thought they might collapse.

The big screen was replaying the whole action over and over again, each time causing the yellow crowd to cheer as if nobody could believe what had just happened. The chance the Italians had just had was a perfect one, impossible to be wasted. But as I'd said before the game, they didn't count on Alex and his unearthly skills. He was way better than even the best goalkeeper before him. He had redefined the goalkeeper's job and skills and was the perfect infusion of talent, hard work, commitment and passion.

"Good choice, Jane," my father said. "He is truly the best in the world." He turned to Olexiy and Tanya. "Great job with this kid. He does the impossible."

Dad didn't know that the sentence he'd just said would, within a few minutes, become a headline on every social network. As if somebody had overheard him. *The Goalkeeper Who Does the Impossible* – it was catchy and sounded great.

I was proud. My guy was the best, and he'd proven himself to every person who didn't believe in him before this game started. After those shocking few seconds, I regained the feeling that everything would turn out good for us.

The game continued in the same manner as before the Italians' sudden attack. Neither side could reach the other goalkeeper, despite their best efforts. On the stands, nobody was sitting. We were all on our feet, every second expecting something crucial to happen. It took only seven minutes.

Due to the clumsiness of one Italian striker, Pavlov took the ball and started running through the middle of the pitch. He passed two midfielders and found himself facing only three blue defenders, flanked by five more Ukrainian players. He passed the ball to his teammates and ran forward. The boys managed to go around the three Italian defensemen and shot the ball back to Nikolay.

The pass went too high. The crowd sighed in disappointment, but before they'd even drawn their next breath, Igor Krasinski showed up out of the blue from our defending line and rebounded the ball on his head.

In an angle that was perfectly measured but achieved with a gallon of luck, it bounced off his head straight into the net. He started shouting, the whistle followed and all the players in yellow ran towards him.

Up on the stands, we were all still in disbelief. It seemed impossible. We waited, expecting the referees to cancel the goal because of an offside or some other breach, but no – the goal was legit and rolling on the big screen.

Ukraine led 1–0 against Italy.

I was jumping so high that I almost fell into the row in front of me. When the game continued, we were still hugging each other. A group of fans sitting next to us started up a chant, and Alex's sister, Maria, and I joined in. My parents and Alex's mom finally got the proof that the Ukrainian team was good enough to stand up against the powerful Italians.

The first half ended with both sides relaxing a bit. The Italians were tired, and the Ukrainians didn't want to rush and make a catastrophic mistake. We went behind the stands to grab another beer while the crowd went on singing. Despite being behind, the Italian fans still sang in support as well. The atmosphere was wonderful. It seemed that with every game as we approached the final, the mood at stadiums was soaring higher and higher. I could only imagine what it was going to be like later, for the final games.

The second half kicked off, and within the first few minutes, it was obvious that the losing team had reverted to aggression. They slid and hit, earning four yellow cards and even sending one of our players out. Nikolay Pavlov was also badly hit in the ankle, but he refused to be substituted. On the other side, Alex was working hard. He had to take care of plenty of shots aimed at him. Most of them hit the posts themselves, but he couldn't risk it. He was flying in all directions and had to react almost every three to four minutes.

Coach Andreyevich wanted one more substitution. I saw him talking to one of the guys who played in the middle, and soon he was subbed in. Andreyevich managed to communicate something to a few other players before the game continued, and somehow, we saw a slight difference in the Ukrainian style. They were swifter and avoided the hits and slides the Italians were trying on them, suddenly becoming the team attacking. The Italian goalkeeper was now the one who couldn't rest for a minute.

It was natural for us to score again.

Andriy Barnik – "The Kid", as they called him, since he was the youngest on the team – stood in front of the goal, perfectly placed where he wasn't offside but also where the Italians didn't expect the ball to fly to. One pass, two, three, and the ball fell on his left foot. *Damn it!* I thought. He was right-footed. But he knew he didn't have time to change, so he took a chance.

This time, the crowd shouted immediately. It was a beautiful, remarkable goal. Unassailable. The big screen replayed Barnik's confused face the moment he shot. He didn't believe it had gone in. Before he could fathom it, he was under a pile of his teammates. The audience went berserk.

"Pinch me," said Maria. "Pinch me, Jane! Is this really happening?"

I knew millions of Ukrainians back at home in front of their tellies were doing the same. The repeating video on the big screen convinced us it was all taking place. Having seen the angle in which the ball had bounced off Barnik's foot, we knew luck was on our side. Only a few millimetres further to the left or right would not have sent the ball under the crossbar.

It happened in the sixty-third minute; there were still approximately twenty-seven minutes to go. Anything could yet happen.

Contrary to what we expected, those last minutes didn't take ages – they actually seemed short. The Italians were completely disoriented, dispersed over the pitch without any idea what to do next. As I had assumed before the game, they were not ready. They were overconfident about their abilities and believed the game against the Ukrainians – all that stood between them and the quarter-finals – would be a joke.

Well, they were in the wrong. And it was too late. Milan Andreyevich's team now understood they were the more powerful one and were capable of scoring against the multiple-time world champions, so they kept storming onto the net with the aim of getting more.

That resulted in an amazing show at the Allianz Arena. In the days that followed, the highlights from this match would get millions of views on every network and maintain relevance longer than any other game until then. The whole game was action-packed, full of excellent attacks and defences. It unfolded almost like a movie; it was a pleasure to watch.

Of course, being there and seeing it all live felt much more intense. Few could doubt any longer which team was going further, but there were still spectators who were unsure if such a good game was really taking place in the round of sixteen and expected a turnover.

On the final whistle, the blue players fell to the ground while those in yellow ran towards their coach.

What the heck just happened? ran through my mind, even though I was the one who'd believed in them from the beginning. I couldn't imagine how the other fans must have felt. My heart wanted to pound out of my chest as I jumped and shouted like a cheerleader. Tanya started crying and was hidden in Olexiy's shoulder while Maria screamed like me, hugging a guy standing next to us.

On the big screen were the faces of the Italians, some of them in tears, some still slack in disbelief. Their coach sat on the bench, stunned, finally realising their mistake. They hadn't taken this match as seriously as they should have.

On the other side, Milan Andreyevich and his boys were dancing, hugging and jumping around. They'd proven to themselves they could do it. They felt invincible.

I couldn't stand in one spot any longer, so I decided to find a way to reach Alex. I headed down the stands. I didn't know if what I was doing was allowed or illegal, whether it would get me prohibited from future games, but I knew I had to do it. This moment was perfect.

And I managed. In the next second, I was on the grass, running towards Alex before too many people noticed me. I caught his eye because he was looking for us in the stands. He separated from the group; I couldn't stop running. Damn it! He was the sexiest human being on earth, all tired and soaked in sweat, with those wide, strong shoulders and those eyes that shone with the purest, swirling joy.

When I ran into him, he hugged me hard and spun me around.

"Love, you were the best! I knew it all along."

"Even when that ball was about to get in?" He smiled.

"Even then."

He kissed me on the forehead.

"Don't be shy in front of the world," I teased him, raising my chin for a kiss.

"It's not the world. It's our parents."

I laughed hard as he removed the hair from my face. I propped up on my toes and he briefly, sweetly placed his lips on mine.

There you go, world! All the articles that assumed I supported other teams more fell into the water with that one simple kiss. I wanted everyone to see that Alex and I were still a strong unit, despite all the stories.

Later, I found out that move had been a very smart one, but in that moment, all I cared about was being in his arms and feeling him. I didn't think about Matthias even for a second, not even to wonder how he might feel about the little show I was making. I couldn't quite differentiate if I was selfish, or wanted to cover my wrongdoings, or simply loved Alex unconditionally and wanted to show that. I was happy. He was happy. Ukraine was going to the next stage. No one I loved was going home. That was all that mattered at that moment.

That night, Coach Andreyevich finally allowed the team to unwind a bit, but not before they promised him the highest level of commitment the following day in training. We stayed up late singing, dancing, playing games, telling jokes and reading articles about how we'd shocked the world that day. We watched videos and highlights endlessly. Alex became, as my father had said, The Goalkeeper Who Does the Impossible.

*****

I didn't want to leave Alex again the following day, especially after all the events that had taken place and how fresh our first-ever fight was. I wanted to stay in bed with him, have breakfast with him, wait until he returned from the training and then relax by the pool with him.

But I had no choice. England was playing Norway in Düsseldorf. My dad was too excited about this game for me to miss it. "My older roots against my fresher roots", as he'd described it. He was always proud to explain to everyone who'd ask that he was English through and through, but that his last name was Norwegian, thanks to a great-grandfather who came to Britain, fell in love with it and stayed. That was the reason he felt a connection with them and had learnt the language, too, and that was why he was looking forward to the match.

I quickly packed after Alex left with his team, and my parents and I headed with the girls and Bea's parents to the airport again. This time, I promised Alex I would return the next day at the latest, and I planned to stick to my word.

Matthias texted me in the morning to say how good the game had been, not mentioning what I had done at its end. I knew he wouldn't like it, but I chose not to mention it either. Instead, I told him I missed him after the wonderful time I'd had, especially the morning we'd spent together. I wasn't playing a game. I meant it. Judging by his texts, that swayed his mood to cheerful, and he suggested we talk that night to arrange our next meeting.

I was anxious that day at the stadium in Düsseldorf because Ukraine's next opponent was to be one of the two countries I'd come to watch. It was shocking how things on the other side of the table had worked so in favour of the Germans, who didn't have a strong opponent, while the Ukrainians couldn't have gotten a worse path. Aside from facing Italy, the multi-time world champion, in the next stages Ukraine could get England, Norway, Sweden or – worst of all – Germany. I believed in Alex's team, but it wasn't entirely fair. I mentioned that to Coach Andreyevich on one occasion, but he expressed that he didn't worry much about it since the boys were ready to take on anyone. Yes, they would eventually grow a bit tired, but it was nothing they weren't capable of dealing with. The players themselves weren't always so optimistic, but the match with Italy had boosted their self-confidence.

For me, of course, it would be much easier to watch Alex kick Norway out of the tournament than England. The idea of seeing Matthew Vance, Joshua and the other funny boys we'd met go home without a medal was heart-breaking. But to have to watch them clash against Alex and his friends would be even more disturbing.

"Don't think about it, Jane," my mom said. "It will be what it's meant to be."

"Mom, you're American. It's easy for you to say," I joked.

"Yes, but for the last twenty-two years, I've been hearing all about the Andersonn family tree." She looked at Dad, who smiled.

"And you will for the next twenty-two," he said.

They'd been together their whole life. Sometimes I wondered how. They met very young – he was twenty-five and she twenty-three – and decided to marry and have a kid two years later, running their businesses along the way without intervening with each other's jobs. I guess that was what made them so strong in their careers and in marriage over all these years.

It had never occurred to me to wonder until I cheated on Alex whether one of my parents had ever done that to the other. I assumed I'd never find out. If one of them had, then the other one clearly didn't know anything about it. Otherwise, I knew them both well enough to know that they wouldn't tolerate even the suspicion of infidelity.

What I admired most was that both of them were exceptionally good-looking. They always had been. Josephine was a school and town beauty who many ranchers wanted to marry, but she'd ignored them all, wanting to pursue a career. Dad was charming from the moment he learnt to walk and talk. That's how he got through life, going from a poor working-class family in London to the top of the business world. He was smart and educated, of course, but unassailably handsome. He could have any woman of any age at any time. Had he always been faithful to Josephine?

Something in the way they looked at each other told me yes; but, on the other hand, would anyone suspect anything by observing Alex and me? We were also a perfect couple, and nobody knew what I had been doing. Maybe my parents were also good actors. Or maybe it was me who was sick, as Bea had said. Maybe I had a unique, wicked ability to lie without showing any tell-tale signs of it.

I started feeling a headache coming on, but it was, fortunately, time for the game to begin, so my thoughts deviated to more pleasant topics.

My parents and I went to greet some of Dad's friends and partners from Norway. I had met all of them when I still lived in Dallas. They spoke excellent English, but Dad exchanged a few sentences with them in Norwegian. It still impressed me to hear him talking in another language, especially knowing he learnt at a later age, in his late twenties.

We re-joined our group and some other people from England's business world. All the chit-chat helped us shorten the time until the first whistle.

The day had been heavy from the morning onwards, not too hot but oppressingly humid. It would definitely influence the players' performances. At the start, everything seemed great, but as the time dragged on painfully, the game turned torturous. It wasn't the kind of football the Ukrainian and Italian teams had presented the day before. It was a game in which the utmost effort was put in, with few results. The passes were good but unexceptional, the kicks were powerful but imprecise, the tactics were intentional but unproductive, the players were full of energy but didn't score.

It started raining but didn't get cold, so instead of being refreshing the rain made the air even heavier. The players had to do something to avoid going into extra time. The first half was finished, with the statistics equally distributed: possession, shots, fouls, cards. Nobody at the stadium could say which team was better and deserved to go further.

The rain stopped some ten minutes into the second half but it was still terribly humid. We couldn't wait for the game to be over so we could go to the hotel for a shower and then either discuss or celebrate the game with the English team, depending on the result.

Joshua Hadleigh performed excellently. He was giving his soul to the pitch and motivating other players to do the same. When he finally scored, I was happy for him first, thrilled that his efforts had paid off, and then for England, who had waited for this goal for so long.

It was a nice, smooth goal, the result of a couple of good passes combined with luck. Josh initiated the action and finished it. It was entirely his doing and the others thanked him by hugging him and piling over him in the minutes that followed.

Nevertheless, our happiness didn't last for long. The English had just started showing their power when the Norwegians went wild and, after a couple of forceful but proper attacks, equalised the score.

No one saw that coming, not even the Norwegian coach. They'd done everything by the book and it worked. I was glad to see them happy, although I didn't know how much longer the game would last now. The stuffiness in the air had become unbearable.

Unfortunately, we had to go into extra time: thirty more minutes of draining play, both for the players and the fans. As the sun went down, it became a bit fresher and easier to breathe, so the fans cheered up again just as the game started.

Both coaches introduced a substitute each, one of which was Keaton Flanagan, a forward who entered the game fresh-faced and enthusiastic. When Flanagan scored alone three minutes after the first whistle, I could bet every Englishman at the stadium thought Coach Vance should've put him in earlier and saved us all the suffering and anticipation. Now, with twenty-seven minutes to go, there were plenty of opportunities for another equaliser from Norway, which would lead to penalties. That was too stressful to even think about.

However, Norway couldn't catch up. The final whistle sounded a few seconds after the one hundred and twenty-second minute, and the match was finally over. Norway lost; England was going to face Ukraine in the quarter-finals in four days.

We had a while to wait for the players to return to the hotel, so I used that time to make a phone call to Matthias. I got pleasant tingles on hearing his voice.

"What a day for you, girl."

"Yes. I don't know if I died more yesterday or tonight."

"Those guys are not good to watch. I've told you. With us, you're at least certain."

"You show-off." I laughed. "What are we gonna do?"

"There are two options – I can come to see you the day before our match with Sweden, or you can come to Hannover again on the match day. Or both."

"Both sounds ideal. I just don't know how to make the first happen."

"Well, that's mostly up to you. I've already devised a plan with Lens, Ben and Michael. Rolf wouldn't find out anything. You have to take care of Blondie and your family."

"I don't think that'll be entirely easy. Even if I manage, that'd be for only a short period of time. One hour, two max."

"That's worth the hassle for me."

I felt warmth around my heart. "Seriously?"

"Of course. I would take a ten-hour flight if it was necessary."

Just then, Lana knocked on my door, which meant that the English team had arrived at the restaurant. I hung up, promising we would organise something for sure. I wanted to see those eyes again.

The atmosphere at the dinner was cheerful and raucous, with the distinctive noises of excitement, pride and happiness at a big event or celebration. Dad and Mom were engaged in conversation with Matthew Vance and some of the players when Joshua sat next to me.

"You look stunning," he said. He had been devouring me and my tight orange dress from the moment I entered the restaurant with Lana.

"Still thinking about what I told you last time?"

"I can't get it out of my head. You could be my girlfriend now if I had been braver."

I liked flirting with Joshua. He looked so confused with those puppy eyes. In the end, I only laughed, disregarding it all as a joke and avoiding giving him too much hope, which would border on inappropriate. He was different from the other guys who wanted me. He thought I was sweet and saw me as a swan princess, something clean to be nurtured, so I had to play that role. I didn't know why I wanted to play games with him. Yes, he was attractive and at a time would have been my dream boyfriend, but now I had no such feelings – only the wish, the compulsion, to play games.

He took us to the table where Bea and Angie already sat, engaged in conversation with some of the guys. I saw something then that made my heart leap.

Bea was red-cheeked and smiling, her eyes downcast, talking to Harold Dare, the English national goalkeeper. I had seen her like that only twice, both times with guys that had really made her world. Neither relationship worked out, but she had been deeply in love with them nonetheless. Now, she had that same expression. Finally! After months of rejecting guys around her, here she was, blushing.

She saw me looking at her and smiled. Her eyes shone. I winked at her, mouthing, "You go girl." Harold didn't even raise his head when we approached. His arm was on her chair as if he wanted to pull her closer, which was impossible considering they were already at the nearest decent distance from each other; an inch more would have been unsuitable for the public.

I was over-the-top happy for her. I had never really paid attention to him and neither had she. Otherwise she would've told us. I was dying to hear when they'd discovered their attraction.

"He's been talking about her for quite some time," Josh said, answering my thoughts.

We sat at the table and I moved closer to him so that the others couldn't hear us. "Tell me about that."

"Well, while all of us are drooling over you, he would always say something like, 'Yes, Jane is very hot, but her blonde friend is just heavenly gorgeous.' If we talk about women, he'd always be like, 'My wife will be blonde, a natural one, with long legs, elegant posture, bewitching eyes. Something like Jane's friend Beatrice.'"

"And you tell me about that now! We could've introduced them earlier!" I elbowed him in the ribs.

"Come on, I wouldn't do that to him. Plus, has she ever expressed any interest in him?" He poured some white wine and passed it over to me.

"No," I said. "You're right. This is better. Let's see how it develops." I raised my glass to him and his alcohol-free beer. "Cheers!"

Josh managed to keep me involved in conversation with only him for the rest of the dinner. I glanced occasionally to Dad to see if he thought what was happening was inappropriate, but he was too busy celebrating with other people. I decided to keep my distance as much as I could, but that seemed to attract Joshua even more.

I couldn't help thinking again about how things would have turned out for me if he'd had the courage to approach me before Alex. I had certainly wished for it, and Dad had approved of him. All Joshua had needed to do was take me out. We both lived in London. I was literally in front of his nose. We would have been English and international stars in sport, fashion, modelling, anything we did. We went perfectly together: he was taller than me, outrageously handsome, charming, and, as I'd gotten to know, kind and devoted. If he had only...

But I had all that with Alex already. The only difference was that Alex was based in another country, and in order to meet, we had to take a three-hour flight. That wasn't such a big deal; sometimes commuting through London would take that much time. Plus, he was still bigger and more handsome than Joshua – more than any other man I'd met.

I forced those thoughts out of my head and eventually managed to escape and make casual conversation with other people present. Soon after, the end of the evening approached, and the Andersonns decided to go to bed. We would all be going to Nuremberg the following day, us immediately after breakfast and the players later in the day.

I hadn't even removed my shoes when the room phone rang, making me jump.

"Hey, Jane. I feel a bit stuffy in this room. Would you go for a walk with me?" I recognised the cockney accent.

I knew I should've declined and made a scene about how rude and intrusive he was, but after all I could manage were several seconds of silence, we both knew I would accept.

Still wearing the orange dress, I went down to the lobby. I had approximately half an hour before meeting Bea and the girls for the full report on what had happened between her and Harold. We took a back exit to a side street where only few people roamed. He had changed from the team tracksuit they'd all worn for the dinner. I couldn't help noticing how he looked like he belonged on a teenage magazine cover in his light jeans and green T-shirt.

"You're going out?" I asked.

"Just round the corner. I thought you'd wear something more casual, too."

"You didn't give me time to change."

"I don't mind. I love that dress. That length suits you perfectly."

I smiled. "Now you're a fashion expert as well?"

"Trying to be. My sister constantly coaches me."

"Where is she now?"

"In London. She says she'll be here for the next game. She didn't bother coming earlier 'cause she thought we had no chance of getting anywhere."

"She's not much into football?"

"No, but it's alright. You're all the support I need."

"Is that why you scored today?" I met his eyes. They were absorbing me with unquenched desire.

"Absolutely. Seeing you there, I couldn't let us lose. I wouldn't forgive myself for another mistake with you."

This time, I stopped. The breeze blew vigorously along the street, making me shiver. He used that as an opportunity to get closer to me. I got goose bumps.

"You're cold," he said, pulling me in a hug, his arms all over my back. The angel in me screamed to step away, push him back and politely refuse. But the devil couldn't resist.

I raised my head and met his eyes, a few millimetres away from mine. I breathed in his aftershave.

"Not anymore," I said.

For a moment, he played with one of the locks of hair hanging from my half-bun, rolling it around his finger and scrutinising my face. I wondered what he could see in my eyes, if he was seeing the same picture I was at that moment: the life we could have had if he had been brave. Or was he thinking about something else?

"You're the most stunning woman there has ever been, Jane," he whispered. "I thought that when I first saw you, and I still think that now."

I didn't say anything. It was too late for his dreams. He didn't have the courage when it was necessary. Now, all we could have was a taste of the life we would've shared, a taste of what would've been ours.

I closed my eyes, parting my lips only slightly a second before he kissed me. I didn't do anything at first; I didn't resist, didn't add to it. I just accepted him, as if through that kiss he could show me what he was able to give me, how he could make me feel. I surfed on that wave of desire and longing. I eventually responded, taking him in with shyness and modesty, just like he wanted.

But the feeling wasn't good enough. It was not what I expected after so many years of fantasising about him. I was more excited in the second before he kissed me than I was during the kiss. It was plain and somehow empty. Lovely, but hollow. He desired me, I could feel that, but my reaction to him completely disappointed me.

When I stepped back, I understood I hadn't missed out on anything. He just wasn't it. Now I was thankful that he had never tried anything with me. I would've wasted my time, maybe even years, living in an illusion that he was "The One" based on my childish fantasies about him.

No, he definitely wasn't it.

Alex was The One.

"Jane, we have to meet again," he said, still hugging me.

"No, Joshua. I'm someone else's woman."

"I will make you mine."

"No. This was enough. Goodnight."

CHAPTER 12

It turned out Bea and Harold got along really well. As I had assumed, she had never been any more interested in him than the rest of us – he'd been discussed but seldom beyond the acknowledgement that he was a hot guy we didn't mind watching play. But Harold had carried a flame for Bea from the beginning. Seeing her a couple of times now at the tournament, and so close, made him too intrigued not to try and talk to her.

She certainly liked him now. We could see that from the glow on her face while she was recounting the night from her angle. She'd sensed him before he approached her while she was sitting with Angie.

"I suddenly caught this awesome scent and thought, 'Wow, this man has taste.' The next moment, I felt his hand on my shoulder, and when I turned, he was there above me, asking if he could join us at the table. I bet my face was white and dumb, because at that point in time he was the most good-looking man in the universe."

She'd thought it was just a fickle first impression and was sceptical at first, but as the minutes went on, she found herself more and more enticed by him.

"Yeah, I saw, you couldn't stop giggling," said Angie.

"He is so unbelievably interesting, so sweet," Bea continued. "We have so many things in common. Even our favourite horror movie is the same!"

"Seriously? Somebody else knows about *The Devil's Pass*?" Lana popped in.

"Yes! That's what I'm telling you! And it was he who said it first, so he can't be lying to trick me. Apart from that, we read the same books, love the same TV shows, everything. When the night was over, I felt sad 'cause we could have talked for another twenty hours." She sighed, blushing. "And he's so attractive."

She didn't know what Josh had told me, so when I shared that piece of information, Lana and Angie screamed while Bea went completely red.

"Now I seriously can't wait to see him again," she said.

"When's that gonna be?"

"In Nuremberg, of course. Jane, I'm afraid for the next match I won't be able to stay neutral."

"You traitor," I said without malice and threw a pillow at her.

*****

Everything was great back in Nuremberg. Alex returned from his training at lunchtime, and I was already waiting for him at the hotel. For the rest of the day, he was mine. We went for massages and relaxed next to the pool, just the two of us. He was happy, calm and confident when talking about the next game. Later, we stayed in and watched movies, which eventually turned into making love for hours. He reminded me how much I adored everything about him. I loved him.

Despite what I had done.

I still didn't feel bad for any of it. Instead, I appreciated Alex's every touch and kiss because it was truly warm and genuine, unlike anything I'd had with the other guys. Although I was only twenty, I knew he was the man for me. I felt it in everything we shared, in what he did for me and I for him, in the jokes only we understood, in the silent approval or disapproval that we communicated through a single look. We were made for each other. That was obvious to me nearly from the beginning; after only a few months of knowing him, I was certain he was mine.

Was it why I assumed he belonged to me, no matter what I did?

*****

When I woke up around ten in the evening, Alex was still sleeping, so I stretched and went to the open window to get some fresh air. My phone was loaded with texts. *Well, better than flowers and notes under my door,* I thought.

From Marco Moretti: *It was nice meeting you, Hot Woman. Shame I'm going home.*

From Paolo Reis: *I can't believe I miss you. Tell me when you're back in London and I'll jump on a plane for another night like that.*

And a long message from Matthias.

The first two I didn't even bother to reply to. I only deleted them. Those two were not interesting anymore.

But Matthias...

I wanted to come today, but you weren't replying, so I assumed you had to...deal with Blondie. Anyway, it all turned out good today, I reorganised everything for tomorrow. The guys know what to say and what not to say. If you want, I can be there early in the morning, when Blondie goes for his training, and will return here for my afternoon training, or most of it. What do you think?

- *Are you seriously gonna skip a training to come here?*

Yes.

- *What about your coach? I wouldn't piss him off if I were you.*

Don't worry about that. I've organised everything with the guys. I'll tell you. It's gonna be fine. Don't think about it too much. Just tell me yes or no – can you make it tomorrow morning?

I wasn't supposed to. It was way too risky with my parents and Alex's family all over the place. Somebody would notice Matthias for sure unless we stayed indoors the whole time. Alex had two trainings, one in the morning and one in the afternoon, and I didn't know when exactly he would return from either.

But I wanted to see Matthias. The fact that it was all so risky had me excited rather than scared. I was also curious to see if he was indeed as crazy about me as he seemed – if he would follow through with his insane plans, or if those were just words. After all, if I was considering leaving the perfect guy, I had to be sure about the guy I was leaving him for.

But was I really planning to leave Alex, ever? I looked at him lying peacefully in the bed where we had made love only a few hours ago. The thought of walking out on him made me nauseous and uneasy. I understood in that moment that I could no longer imagine my life without Alexander Yanov. He was my man.

Still, I inexplicably liked Matthias. The chemistry between us was unavoidable, and the idea of meeting him rushed adrenalin through my blood. I liked the feeling. What was one more meeting? I stopped myself from overthinking and replied.

- *Yes.*

He immediately typed back the whole step-by-step plan of how and where we would meet, what door we would use, which room, for how long, and what we should do "in case of emergency". He made me laugh and I was already mentally prepared for tomorrow's exciting morning.

I presented excellent self-control in hiding my exhilaration when Alex woke up shortly after to have a bite and quick shower. We put a movie on to play, but he fell asleep after less than ten minutes; exhaustion from the previous few days had caught up to him. He slept on my breasts while I scratched his hair, wide awake, thinking about how much I loved him and wondering why I was doing this to him.

*****

I managed to sleep well, surprisingly. After breakfast, I pulled the girls aside and told them the plan. None of them liked it, which was a clear sign that I was overdoing it and risking too much. Even Angie didn't understand.

"Woman, his parents are here! His sister is here! If she sees you with Beller or doing anything suspicious, you are over!" she said.

"I think Alex trusts me enough not to believe his sister's stories. Apart from that, I think all three Yanovs love me too much to suspect me," I defended myself.

"You're playing with fire. Don't overestimate your importance. They're a family which you're not yet a part of."

"I don't have time for this," I snapped. "Can I rely on you? If anyone asks for me, will you tell them I'm in the sauna?"

They rolled their eyes and agreed. What else could they do?

I went to the stairs of the emergency exit Matthias had told me to look for. In less than five minutes, he was there. I was trembling with excitement.

"You really came," I whispered.

He cupped my face and gave me a long kiss.

"You didn't believe me?"

"I was a bit reluctant to. This is insane."

"Yes." He kissed me again.

He already had a room key, so we headed upstairs. It was the only available room on the penultimate floor. Going up the stairs, I was breathing as if I wasn't fit at all. The first room next to the emergency door was ours, which was excellent for avoiding hotel cameras.

Inside, there was already a breakfast set up and an enormous bouquet of all kinds of pink flowers, the scent of which wafted throughout the whole room.

"You are wonderful." I turned and kissed him when he closed the door behind us. "You think about every single detail."

I loved being drowned in his eyes. They were dark and deep, and provided both excitement and comfort.

"Of course I do." He smiled. "I'm not stupid. I understand your situation and simply want to win you over, fair and square."

I couldn't smile back, so I kissed him again instead.

I joined him for breakfast but only had tea because I was already full. We talked about everything that had happened while we weren't together and how he'd managed to escape his morning training by claiming to Gottfried that he had to sort out a family problem.

"Are you sure he doesn't suspect something?" I asked worriedly.

"Nothing. I lied very well, and Ben, Lens and Michael are my accomplices."

"I am serious, Mati. I think he can be very dangerous if you make him angry."

"You're right, but trust me. He doesn't have any clue where I am now. He has great respect for Michael, and when he tells him something, he takes it as a solid truth."

"What would happen if he found out?"

"Better not to think about that. He won't. Don't worry about me, Honey. I covered myself well." He sent me a kiss over the table and I felt a rush of butterflies to my belly. I stood up and walked over to kiss him.

"I just wouldn't want you to end up in trouble." I hugged him.

"I have told you already – you are worth getting in trouble for."

I couldn't help diving into those eyes and kissing him again.

"Are you sure Michael will support you and lie to Gottfried?" I asked when I sat back in my chair.

"If you're asking because he's on such good terms with Rolf…"

"No, I'm asking because I have the impression he doesn't like me. Or let's say, he doesn't like what I'm doing."

Matthias was quiet for a second before he replied, "He doesn't." I moved uneasily. "But, it doesn't mean he won't do me a favour." I looked at him questioningly. "He is my friend above all. And, you know, friends support you, even when you do something reckless."

"I know, but the way he talks to me makes me…embarrassed."

"Don't worry about him. He just can't hide his honesty, but for me, he will lie to Rolf. Same with your girls. I am sure all three of them know very well what you and I are doing is not entirely moral, but they will lie to your parents, to Blondie, to whomever necessary. Right?" I nodded.

"Alright, I'll get those negative thoughts out of my mind," I said. I wanted Alex and my infidelity out of our conversation as soon as possible.

Time was ticking slowly and we enjoyed every single minute together. He sat on the bed and I cuddled on him, inhaling all of his scents, wanting to keep them with me as long as possible. He gave me five tickets for the game between Germany and Sweden tomorrow and said that I should come with anyone willing to join me, even my parents if they wanted. I had to think thoroughly about that. It was now my turn to do something silly for him. I really wanted to be at the stadium in Hannover the following day. I knew I had to make it happen, one way or another, whether it enraged Alex or not.

I knew that, being a good actress who had already lied so much to both my father and my boyfriend – the two men who knew me best and still didn't suspect anything – I was capable of creating another convincing story. And I determined to. I wanted to go and watch this man play.

While we chatted, we finally tackled the topic of women in his life. I'd seen him in the papers with many, always different. He changed girlfriends so fast that the girls and I couldn't catch up or remember any names. Now I wanted to hear his history from him.

"Tell me!" I elbowed him in the ribs.

"Maybe you don't want to know that part."

"Maybe I know most of it already, so there's no need to hide anything." I gave him a stern look.

"Well, there were…some girls."

"Don't play the mysterious card with me. How many?"

"I would tell you if I knew."

"I'm not asking about the women you've slept with. I mean serious relationships."

"I rarely took any of my girls seriously. Come on, why would I? I just turned twenty-four." I pierced him with my eyes. "Which doesn't mean I haven't matured," he added quickly. "I'm not gonna lie to you, Jane — I've been seen with many girls. I'm not even sure how many of those can be defined as proper relationships. Simply, that wasn't my aim at the time. Football was the only thing I cared about with all my heart. Until…well…until I met you. Since that day in Berlin, I can't help thinking about how life with you next to me would look. And it's not only because you're the most attractive woman in the world. There is something else to it. I noticed that how I felt about you was different than how other guys thought of you. Their stories mostly consisted of what they'd do to you, while I, actually, most of the time, imagined how it would be waking up next to you, kissing you hello and goodbye, cooking with you, cuddling on the sofa with you in front of the TV, going home knowing you'll be there."

I covered his mouth with my hand. As he was talking, I could clearly imagine those scenes, and they filled me with happiness and excitement. It all seemed possible and beautiful. It would be a completely fulfilled, carefree and joyful life. It could all be ours easily.

"You are capturingly romantic," I whispered.

He kissed my hand and caressed my cheek.

"Because you are capturingly beautiful," he said, gently drawing me closer until our lips connected.

I snuggled up on his chest, not wanting to let go.

"You know what fascinates me about you, Jane?" he continued. "That you are so pure."

I swallowed hard and suppressed the discomfort his last word caused.

"I've been thinking about that since our room party last time."

"After you heard that I was a virgin until a few months ago?" I laughed.

"That, too. But whenever I think about you and what makes me crazy about you, I understand why half of the world is crazy about you, too. You are smart, funny, hard-working, committed to your job and, well, your boyfriend. You are beautiful inside and out, and somehow, your whole body has the perfect shape. Some nights, when I would dream about you, you'd turn out not to be human at all, but a fairy or mermaid, because in my mind you are still not real. But then again, I know you are because I see you, I feel you now, and as unbelievable as it is to me that you are here, I know you are true."

I had to raise my head to look at him, fathoming everything he'd said.

"Matthias, have you read some romance book since we last met?" I tried to make a joke, but his face was serious.

"I'm deeply in love with you, Jane."

I was paralysed for a moment, letting the words resound in my head in case I hadn't hear him well. In the next one, I forgot everything bad I knew about myself, everything wrong I had done, all the feelings of uneasiness I'd had. It didn't matter now. It was all worth it for the adoration and love I could see in his eyes.

If we'd had time then, we would have made love. I wasn't sure at that moment if I loved him equally as he loved me; it was still too early for me to be certain about such a strong feeling. But I knew I adored him. Maybe it was because of the circumstances, because he was forbidden and I was somehow prohibited from him. Maybe it was because of all the hiding and secrets, the lies and manoeuvres, that our feelings for each other came on so fast and were so inexplicably, irrevocably strong. It might have been infatuation, but we both knew it was deeper than that. We weren't just blindly falling for each other. We were honest from the beginning because we had nothing to lose and everything to gain. Yes, I had Alex to lose, but if this man was better for me, at the end of the day, I was a winner.

After Matthias left, I ran to the sauna. I needed to be alone with my thoughts. He had sent an eruption of emotions through my body and mind, and I had to sort them out before seeing Alex again.

What the hell am I going to do? I almost screamed at myself. I was alone and needed to unwind myself a little so I put my head between my knees.

I didn't cry; that was out of the question. But I felt I might vomit, like knives were mangling my insides. It was not an unfamiliar feeling, brought on by suppressed tears and anger in emotional and overwhelming situations. I remembered it from when I was child, from my first memories of Dad teaching me not to cry ("That's for weaklings," he would say) and how to swallow the pain and tears and push them down. I would feel instead as if I'd overeaten and was about to explode. The nausea was almost unbearable.

I spent almost an hour in there, trying to find a solution. I loved Alex; I liked Matthias. I wasn't ready to lose either of them now, that was for sure. I would go on with this, enjoy both, and then when the time came, I would know what to do. I always knew.

Come on, Jane! What is this behaviour? I chastised myself. *You are not like this! This is weak and embarrassing. You wanted Matthias, you got him. You don't regret anything, so why are you troubling yourself like this? Pull yourself together, woman! Go out there and be the best, how everyone knows you.*

If I wanted to enjoy everything life was giving me, I had to stop overthinking and act as I had at the beginning of all this. I told myself I was not to think about breaking up with Alex or giving up on Matthias. Why worry, when I didn't know what would happen in the following few days? There was still a week and a half till the end of the tournament. I had to make the best of it.

*****

"Alex, since you and the guys will be busy the whole day tomorrow, is it alright with you if I go to Hannover? I'll be back after the game."

He agreed, but his face said a different answer. I swallowed hard and tried to disregard his expression.

"You can't have peace. You always have to move," he tried to joke, but his voice was gravely serious.

I sat on his lap and hung around his neck.

"I just want to see everything I can at this tournament. It's so exciting, watching all those games. The German ones, too. You have to admit that."

"I still think you're wrong and that they only pretend to be nice in the presence of four pretty girls."

"You know that I'm not stupid, right?"

"I know." He ran his hand through my hair. "I trust you."

I kissed him.

"If you had time to come with me," I said, "you would see for yourself what I'm talking about."

It was another one of my shameful lies, but I knew I had to tell it to protect myself. Inside, of course, I was thanking all the higher forces that gave him long and tiring trainings whenever I had to go and see Matthias – or someone else.

*****

We reached Hannover in time for breakfast with the German Four. They had finished all their obligations with the team and decided to wait for us. Matthias and Lens welcomed us at the entrance and guided us to the restaurant. I saw in Matthias's eyes and expression how happy he was that I'd managed to come.

It was difficult for me to control my emotions when I saw him. Although we all knew that I was having an affair with him, the hotel was still a public place, and our suspiciously close behaviour could attract too much unwanted attention.

My happiness and excitement dwindled significantly when I saw one more person sitting with Michael and Ben at the table: Robin Braam, a player for the Netherlands.

"What is he doing here?" I asked Matthias, seeing red.

"I knew she wouldn't like it," he said to Lens. "He is a friend of ours. He played with us in the same club in Germany and then got transferred to Spain. Some of our guys from the national team play with him there."

"That doesn't explain him being here." I could hardly control my anger and rudeness.

"They lost a few days ago to Argentina, so he is on vacation now. He decided to come and watch our game tonight."

"Matthias, that still doesn't explain what he's doing right here right now. Or, you know what? I'm gonna ask him myself."

I headed to the table, my heels clicking loudly on the tiled floor.

"Did he know I was coming?" I asked Ben.

Ben went white and didn't dare speak. He looked helplessly behind my back, probably at Matthias.

"Did he?" I didn't stop staring at him.

"He knew," said Michael calmly.

Now I turned and looked Robin straight in the face. "Do you think it's really appropriate for you to be here?"

He smiled and his tiny grey eyes shone confidently. "I thought I would drop by and explain myself," he said calmly. "Would you ladies sit for a while?"

Bea approached me and squeezed my hand, which meant that I was making too much of a scene and it was better to sit down, compose myself and behave. Wordlessly, we filled the vacant chairs at the table.

"So, where's the tulip?" asked Angie.

Surprisingly, Michael Krimm was the first to laugh, then the others. It took me a couple seconds to remember what she was referring to: *Robin*

Braam Says He'll Give Jane a Tulip First Thing When They Meet. The article dated a few months back.

"I saw you girls attended some of the German matches, and when the guys confirmed you would come for this one, too, I felt I shouldn't miss a chance to meet you," he said. "As for the tulip, it has to be Dutch. I was trying to find one, but they don't have them here in the city."

"Oh, so kind of you," I said sarcastically.

I was thankful that Matthias sat next to me. I tried as best I could to talk to him and Michael, who was the closest, and to completely ignore the Dutchman.

"Does he bother you?" Matthias whispered after a few minutes.

"He does, but I'll manage."

"If you want, we'll hurry this up and go to the room."

"It's alright. Does he know?"

"About us? No."

"Then better to stay. If I leave now, it'll be suspicious."

I managed to lighten my spirits over the next hour. Ben and Lens were really trying, and the girls were relaxed, too. Still, I avoided even looking at the newcomer. Any time I did, he would glance at me and smile; a couple of times he even winked. At first, I wasn't sure if it had happened, but the next wink was unmistakable. I wanted to throw a plate at him, but I composed myself again. There was no need for unnecessary drama.

Soon, the guys had to leave to get ready for the game. Matthias and I had agreed earlier that I would pass by his room to wish him luck before they left, but the girls and I had little else to do in the meantime so we stayed a bit longer in the restaurant with Robin. Now, with Matthias not around, I could freely take a good look at this guy. I couldn't not notice that he was handsome as hell. His grey eyes mysteriously, wantingly shone under his blonde, almost bleached eyebrows, the same hue as his hair. He liked the gym, that much I could see under his white, almost transparent shirt. His square face was turned to me, deciphering what was behind the look I was giving him.

"I see you ladies get along pretty well with my friends," he said, moving his eyes over each of us and ending on me.

"Yeah, they're good guys," said Lana.

"And quite hilarious," added Angie.

"I'd say you're maybe on too good of terms with them, considering that you already support other teams."

"You're the least entitled to speak about what's too much, Tulip," I said, to which he started laughing.

"I see you won't forgive me any time soon for my childish excitement."

"I'd rather call it stupidity."

Bea sighed. I knew I'd been too rude again.

"I could fix it, if you gave me a chance," he said calmly.

I instantly imagined him "fixing" the damage he'd made. Still, his brazenness took me aback. I didn't expect to hear such a bold statement in front of the girls. He was staring at me, and I didn't want to turn away for a long time.

It was maybe too long before I said, "I'm going to my room to rest before the game."

He stood up with us, trying to make us stay. I could see then that he was almost the same height as me, maybe an inch taller.

"Really? You're gonna sleep now?" he asked.

"Yes," I answered and we left.

As I was getting out of the elevator on Matthias's floor, Bea caught me by the hand.

"Jane." I looked at her. "Don't."

I knew what she meant, and she knew exactly what was on my mind. Still, I couldn't offer her any reassurance. I left for Matthias's room in silence.

I didn't have much time with Matthias – less than half an hour – but it was enough to catch up a bit and go over what we would do the next time we met. I had to go back to Nuremberg that evening for the Ukraine–England game the following day. I kissed him goodbye, for now.

In front of my room, I slowed down and looked at my watch. There was enough time. I had just scanned the card to open the door when I heard the expected "Ahem".

I smiled to myself before turning to face him.

"You wanna go for a drink?" Robin asked.

"It's better here. Less crowded."

He entered and closed the door behind him. When I sat in the armchair, he was still standing, undressing me with his eyes.

"What will you offer me?" he asked. I gave him a questioning look. "To drink," he added.

"What would you like?"

I was proud of my red dress that exposed my breasts perfectly enough to tempt but still hid enough to encourage the fantasy. His tiny eyes were running from them to my face and back.

"Anything you have." He approached and was now looking down at me.

I stood up, entirely closing the distance between our bodies.

"For example?" I asked.

I was on fire; his touch was all I needed to ignite. His finger started on my lips and then moved down my neck, over my breast and ribs. It circled my hip and ended low on my back.

"All of this," he said.

Instead of saying anything, I pressed my belly against his, wetting my lips and parting them slightly.

He didn't need another signal. The next moment, his teeth were biting my lips in a way that sent shivers up and down my body. I imagined how they would feel everywhere, and the next second he moved to my neck. I loved it, even though I felt he was slightly too harsh and I might have marks later. I didn't care at that moment; I couldn't. He was too good.

When he moved further down to uncover my breasts, I had to warn him not to damage the dress. That made him laugh, and he found the zipper under my arm with ease. I saw in his eyes how excited he was, how bedazzled. He didn't wait long to remove my bra, too. I was happy for it, because when he started on my nipples, all I could feel was bliss.

I didn't expect an orgasm that would leave my legs shaking, barely stable, but he was so skilled. He felt I couldn't keep standing in my heels, shivering with excitement and pleasure, so he started pushing me towards the bed. I sat and finally looked up at his shirtless body. His skin was white and smooth, his muscles strong and defined, compiled in a perfect picture. He bent over me and I moved up to rest my head on the pillow. He kissed me, deep and gentle, not violent this time.

"I've wanted this for so long. You have no idea what I want to do to you."

That instantly recovered me from my previous orgasm and prepared me for a new one. He knew we didn't have time to spare. His lips were everywhere on my neck. I closed my eyes and let my skin feel and enjoy him. He moved down between my breasts, skipping past them with tongue but still cupping them with his hands – hands that, in the next moment, caught my hips. His tongue was now on my navel and still moving downwards. *No, he won't do that! Unbelievable!* But he was going further down. My head was spinning. *He is! No way! I thought...I thought guys only go down on girls they love. I didn't expect it now, this is just quick sex!*

At first, my legs were tense in anticipation, and I was reluctant to spread them, but he helped me. When he touched me with his mouth, I felt as if he'd added oil to the fire that was starting down there. I immediately grasped him with my legs, an involuntary spasm, and the fire spread, all-consuming. When he bit me on the inside of my thigh, I moaned with a pleasure I couldn't tame. When I lost count of the bites, I was already on an endless wave of the wildest, most sinful satisfaction, enjoying something great and wondrous but forbidden and secret. I loved it.

He stopped, which confused me. Then he took his shirt and put it over my mouth.

"Trust me," he said.

I understood, and clasped the shirt with my teeth, closing my eyes again.

He went back down and licked and bit me again, and then slowly put one finger inside me. I was swarmed with tingles. All my nerves were on edge, electrified. He started moving his finger and that sent me on a new wave of climaxes. I was thankful for the fabric in my mouth because I couldn't help my moans.

When he put the second finger in, my mind had no room for any thoughts other than the pleasure this man knew to give.

I came again and again, in the end thinking my body wasn't able to take more. I was almost relieved when he stopped, but the very next moment I understood that he hadn't yet got what he'd come for. I couldn't rise from the bed, but I heard his jeans falling to the carpet. I was still lying on my back when he placed himself between my legs and entered me, easily, filling me with another cloud of pleasure. I managed to open my eyes to meet his. They said it all; I could see everything that was going through his mind. Neither he nor I believed we were actually together, doing this.

*****

The match was not entirely easy for the Germans, but they still managed to bring it to the end with zero goals in their net and two in the opponents'. The Swedes played an excellent game and put on a good show, of which the fans and spectators enjoyed every minute.

The only truly difficult moments were those when I would catch Robin, only a few seats away, looking at me – or when he would catch me looking at him. He would always smile, and I would smile back, while carnal scenes flashed in front of my eyes. *What the heck was that?* resonated through my head.

After the game, we went to the hotel to congratulate the guys before we were to leave for the airport and return to Nuremberg. I was happy that we didn't have to wait for them too long. I was growing tired and didn't want to spend too much time with Matthias while Robin was around. He could do something stupid and expose us, although I had made it clear to him when we'd parted that he must not, at any cost, reveal to anyone what had happened between us.

The girls and I first went to Ben's room, where the majority of the players were gathered. We congratulated them and Matthias escorted us out soon after. While the girls stood guard, Matthias and I hid quickly behind a corner to share a goodbye kiss that still, somehow, awoke the familiar butterflies in me.

Not even two minutes later, on the same floor, I heard someone calling me: another familiar voice. All four of us stalled and turned around in slow motion. Weren't there already enough surprises for one day?

"I'd like to talk to you, please," said Gottfried, appearing from behind the corner.

"We're actually in a hurry because of the late-night flight curfew," Bea said. I looked at her thankfully but told them to go ahead and I would follow.

We already knew this man was dangerous. I had to play this carefully. I went behind him into his room, certain that no matter what, there would be no physical contact of any kind between us. He didn't speak but stared at me, sizing me up from head to toe until I became uncomfortable.

"I don't mean to be rude," I began, "but why do you want to talk to me now?"

He scanned me one more time and grinned.

"I want to suggest something to you."

I smirked at him. I didn't want any dealings with him.

"After the tournament, when all this is over, come with me."

I felt as if somebody had slapped me, hard. The blood drained out of my head.

"Wh-what do you mean?" I asked.

"I'm serious. Fuck Beller, fuck Yanov, fuck everyone and come with me."

"Come with you where?" I was flabbergasted.

"You're still not getting me? Jane, I want you to be mine. Officially."

How could we all be so stupid? I felt dizzy and needed to sit, but I didn't want to look weak or vulnerable, so I plucked up all the energy I had to stand up against him.

"Rolf, no. You're mistaken with your feelings."

"No, Jane. I am forty-two, a mature man, and I know very well what and who I want."

"No, you're confused. You just want me for sex. You'd get bored in time. I need love. You need it, too. We can't give that to each other." I wanted to be as polite and reasonable as possible. I needed to avoid enraging him, simply because he knew too much.

"Jane, I've thought about this a lot. All this time, while watching you, what you're doing—"

"I care about Matthias. I care about both of them," I interrupted him.

"I meant all of them. Not just those two."

That left me breathless. My pupils widened in shock.

"Yes, I know everything. Even about the Dutchman today."

I felt nauseated.

"H-how?"

"I have my connections. What did you think? How else could Moretti and Reis know when and where to look for you? Or why would Braam insist on coming today? I've been conducting a little experiment and it proved my theory. That's why I've come to you with this suggestion. I know you, Jane. I know you better than any of those boys, better than you know yourself."

I struggled to stay stable on my feet.

"Tell me, why aren't you happy with Yanov? Why did you go to Beller? Why isn't either of them enough? I'll tell you – because they don't know what you need. They're too young."

"I am too young for you, too," I uttered.

"We were pretty compatible two weeks ago."

"That was only sex. I can't be with you! Ever!" I started losing control. "What would my parents say? What would the world say?"

"Your father would approve of me because he'd know I'm serious and someone he can confide in. I would charm your mother. As for the world – they would say we're the best damn looking couple ever."

I was silent for a second, consumed by the gleam in his eye. It made me shiver with fear.

"It doesn't work like that, Rolf. You think you know me, but you don't." I couldn't stand anymore. I sank into the chair. "Even I don't know myself."

He crouched next to me and caught me by the shoulders. "Trust me when I say that I know you and what you need. It all started with me, right? Do you think I would ever have approached you if I wasn't certain you wanted me?"

I was growing more and more confused.

"I thought you came to me that night out of sheer arrogance."

"That partly, yes." He slid his hand down to my waist.

It didn't make me excited as it had the first time. Instead, it sent a nauseous feeling up to my throat. I shuddered at the thought of everything he was suggesting. I didn't want that, however smart, mature, accomplished and handsome he was.

"We would take on the whole world, Jane."

Suddenly, I remembered what Lens had warned me about. He was right, even though it had seemed absolutely impossible then – and now, too. However great a liar I was, I couldn't fake anything now. I knew that even trying to act would get me in more trouble than I was already in.

"Rolf, listen." I tried to sound as kind as possible. "What you're saying would work well in some other life where there's no Alexander. But in this one, I'm afraid it won't. I'm not saying that I don't like you. You are an attractive man. But I love Alex and can't go against that." I saw he was getting upset. "What we had was just sex, excellent sex. You know those things better than me."

He let go of me. "I told you already that at my age and with my experience, I know quite a lot about life."

"So you also know you can't force anyone to love."

"Fuck your love!" I jumped at his suddenly loud tone of voice. "You're not on the right path, Jane. I wanted to help you, to put you under control."

"I know I'm wrong, Rolf, but I have yet to discover what it is within me that's making me do all this. I can't go with you. It would be just another mistake."

"Do you regret your other mistakes, Jane?"

His question came over me like a quick, cold shower.

"Tell me. Do you?"

"No," I uttered faintly.

"That's what I'm trying to tell you, damn woman! You don't regret it, and you never will. You know why? Because you are only looking for the love your father hasn't given you."

My heart skipped a beat, and my chest somehow squeezed my lungs. The next moment, my temper was rising.

"What does my father have to do with all this?"

"Oh, my darling Jane, he has everything to do with it." He laughed viciously.

"Don't involve him into this!"

"I told you I knew chicks like you, girls who grew up with strict fathers. They always like older men."

"You are the only man I've had sex with who is significantly older than me!"

"That doesn't change the fact that you need love and attention from an older guy."

"You are talking nonsense!"

"Do you remember all those moments when you wanted a hug from your father but didn't get it?"

I felt like I had swallowed a wire ball.

"Remember those evenings you'd come home from school with an excellent grade, expecting him to be happy and proud, and he'd just say 'Good job'? Remember when you weren't so successful, and he'd put you down for not devoting yourself enough?"

The wire ball moved down my throat.

"Do you remember when you'd come up with an idea or suggestion, but he'd just disregard it, finding a million flaws and reasons why it wouldn't work, and all the while you felt as if those flaws were yours?"

"Stop it!" I managed to scream breathlessly. I was already covered in a cold sweat.

"Maybe you even remember when you were just a kid, even a toddler, upset about something and crying, and he wouldn't even touch you, let alone hug you. Instead, he pointed a finger at you, shaming you, saying you mustn't cry because that's for the weak and you were embarrassing him."

"Rolf, stop!"

"And you would swallow all the pain, tears, anger, frustration and disappointment that he again didn't hug you—"

I slapped him with all the force I had. It just happened. I didn't even know where all that strength came from.

It was too much – everything he'd said. I couldn't control myself. He'd brought back too many memories, way too much pain. I had no clue how he knew such a huge part of my childhood, basically all my life as an Andersonn, as Brad's only child. I was beginning to believe he knew me after all. I just didn't know how. Where had he got all those details?

He touched his cheek. I could already see the two thin, shallow scratches my nails had made. He would be furious when he noticed them later.

"The last time a woman slapped me was thirty years ago, and it was my mother."

"I'm not gonna apologise. You went too far." I tried to justify myself, but I knew the damage had been done.

"Do you understand now why the two of us would work?"

"I don't like you, Rolf. I love Alex."

"You just don't get it! He will never be enough!"

"He will. And I will talk to Dad, sort it all out. Then—"

He interrupted me with his malicious laugh.

"Jane, you're smart enough to know that won't work. Your father won't change. That's how and who he is, and you will keep searching for love in other men in order to compensate for what you missed out on when you were a child. It has nothing to do with Yanov. You will always need a *daddy*."

I lost it again and moved to hit him, harder this time, but he was prepared. He caught my arms.

"Calm down, Jane. I don't like hysterical women and you've already enraged me a lot. Fine, you don't like me. Have it your way. But you will regret it."

I saw in his grey eyes that he was serious.

"You haven't mentioned at all if you love Matthias. I'm curious to see how he'd react to that."

"He knows how much I care about him." I was defiant.

"I don't think that 'caring' will be enough for him. He's totally, whole-heartedly into you. To hear you babbling solely about the man he hates most, without even a mention of him, would deeply wound him. It'd be a show for me to watch."

"Why would you do that to him? I thought you cared for your players."

"*Because* I care. I don't want him stuck on a woman who can't decide."

"Why are *you* stuck on her, then?"

I wasn't thinking when I said it. It simply slipped off my tongue. He stopped for a second and then smiled in his vicious way.

"See, that's why I like you. You're a bitch, Jane, not afraid to tell me anything. Everyone else is intimidated by me. It gets boring at times."

I took another deep breath, knowing that this was not going to end easily and peacefully.

"Rolf, what I did with you was amazing. I enjoyed it and – as I said – I don't regret it. You were great. However, for me, it ends there. I can't go on with you, and the reason is simple – I already love two other men. In two different ways, yes, but I love them. I can't be with you."

I saw on his face that his rage had reached its peak.

"The two men you love." He laughed again, but it was hollow, belligerent. "Do you even hear yourself? I thought you were smarter than this, but you're childishly stupid! Alright. Have it your way, but you will regret it. You'll see!"

"Don't threaten me!" The Andersonn in me didn't like being talked to like that. My courage plucked up instinctively. "I am young but not so dumb as you think. I have more experience than you would imagine!"

He caught my shoulders. "Don't shout at me. I'm warning you. You will lose everything," he said, leaning in close to my face, his voice dropping cruelly.

Carried by that surge of fear and anger, I managed to smile in his face. "You've got a lot to lose, too. Never underestimate the power of a beautiful woman."

I saw a flicker of worried surprise in his eyes, but it was quickly replaced by anger. He let me go.

"You've got no idea who you're dealing with," he hissed.

"Neither do you. Better think twice before you do anything. I am an Andersonn, and I'm not alone. Even alone I've been doing quite fine, don't you think? You're the only one who somehow happens to know my whereabouts. But no matter what you say or do, I will always get away with it. Why? Well, because, look at me – I'm Jane Andersonn."

I could see his face getting red. I had infuriated him with my rejection, attitude and words. I decided I didn't have time for any more talk. I left while he watched me, silent.

I was in a rush to meet the girls and took a moment in front of the elevator to pull myself together and hide all the stress that was visible on me. When Michael Krimm exited the elevator, I almost commented out loud that everyone seemed to be stalking me today. This was too much. I was tired.

"Hi, Jane," he said politely.

"Hello. Why aren't you with the others?" I asked.

"I'm just clearing my thoughts from all the excitement."

I managed a smile. "Well, people have worse reasons for clearing their minds."

He smiled, too.

"Well, I guess I'll see you around?" I said.

"Yes." He stepped aside so that I could enter the elevator.

Before the door closed, he turned.

"Jane." He was looking at me in a way I hadn't seen from him before – sympathetic, somehow. "You could be a perfect girlfriend, if only you hadn't…"

He couldn't finish, but he didn't need to. Instantly, I was again covered in a cold sweat. He turned his eyes away before the elevator door closed, to my relief. I couldn't have endured his critical look for much longer.

He knew. He knew it all, too. Not only about Gottfried. He knew about everyone.

CHAPTER 13

Needless to say, none of the girls liked what I had done with Robin, though they didn't bother me about it since we had a much bigger problem now. I didn't have time to stress about it. I left all my anxiousness on the aircraft when we arrived in Nuremberg. I didn't have the luxury of taking anything with me – not when I was going to Alex. I wouldn't ruin his night and the following day that he needed to be mentally and physically ready for. I told myself I could do it; I could do it all, like always. I compartmentalised everything into a matchbox and kicked it out of my brain. I was now to be my boyfriend's perfect girl.

"I know you know everything you should and shouldn't do," said Lana on our way to the stadium, "but, please, in order not to complicate things more, don't even think about getting too close to Joshua today."

I understood. After how emotional Joshua had been the last time we met, I knew it was best for us never to meet again at too close a distance. I wasn't interested in him at all anymore, but I couldn't say the same for him.

Bea had painted an English flag on my cheek, and I wore jeans and Alex's jersey. It looked sweet. Nobody could say I was betraying either side. My and Alex's parents were there, too, as well as Mr and Mrs Lane. We had great seats in the stands closest to the pitch in a neutral area. There were both Ukrainian and English supporters around us, so if I got carried away, I wouldn't be alone.

I was growing nervous with every minute as the kick-off approached. Never before had I been in a conflicting situation when it came to football. I had always been proudly English, though half-American, and was well aware of my identity. This time last year, I still had hopes of one day dating Joshua Hadleigh. I had never thought I would be seriously in love with a guy from another country – a country that would now be confronting mine at the World Cup! I didn't even know who I wanted to win.

I knew I would be on TV throughout the world, so I sang along with both anthems in order not to upset either side. I'd been sure to have a drink before the game, so by the time the players went out on the grass, I felt a bit more relaxed.

The girls were more worried than me: Angie and Lana because they were English through and through, but especially Bea, because Harold had a fifty per cent chance of losing tonight. However, I'd decided to have fun, whatever the outcome, at least until the final whistle. I was lucky that Dad was in a good mood with so many of his English friends around. He treated us all with frequent rounds of beer, which only made me more excited and easy-going.

The moment the game started, I felt as if I was sat in a racing car. I sang fan songs with my parents and then with the Yanovs, while the game on the pitch lit up. Both coaches were constantly on their feet yelling advice to their players, who were doing so excellent that neither Alex nor Harold had much work to do. Joshua was losing his head trying to break the Ukrainian middle and defending lines, as were Pavlov and Barnik. There were dozens of wonderful, beautiful moments and passes that could've become goals if not for the magnificent defence of both teams.

The atmosphere on the stands was great. The girls and I were on the big screen every now and then – and how couldn't we be, when we indeed looked like "four beauty queens" out there (as the headlines later read)?

When the referee announced the end of the first half, the players were already tired and ready for the break. The 0–0 result didn't suit any of them if the game was to continue at the same pace. With everyone giving their maximum, they would use up all their stamina before going into extra time. That meant something had to be done in the forty-five minutes following the break, and it had to be done at the right moment so the other team wouldn't have the time nor the energy to recover and react.

While I was waiting for another beer, a few groups of fans from both sides approached us asking for photos. We chatted with them and cheerfully encouraged them that everything would be alright in the end, even though that was impossible. When I turned to check on my parents, I saw them looking at me and smiling, glowing with love.

It was rare. Though I always knew how much each of them loved me, it was something that was understood, not said. I received more affection from Mom, but it was Dad's love that I had always longed for. I knew he adored me more than anything, but I only wished he showed it more, instead of…well, instead of what Gottfried had said. Moments like this somehow compensated, at least for a while, for everything I wished I received from him – yet they never fully did.

I knew I was risking being hurt again, but I had to try. I stepped up to them and hesitated, only for a millisecond. Dad spread out his arm and drew me into a hug.

My mind nearly shut down in disbelief. At that moment, it was the best feeling ever.

"I am proud of you, Jane."

I had certainly heard that before, but it was years and years ago. I definitely didn't expect it now, after everything I had done. Of course, he didn't know about my wrongdoings, but I did. Hearing these words now, from him, I didn't know how I was allowed to react. Why now? I felt I had no right to his affection.

"What's wrong?" he asked.

"Everything's great," I managed.

"You look puzzled."

"No, it's just that you don't say that often."

All three of us laughed.

"Well, it doesn't mean that I haven't been proud of you every minute since you were born. You've always been a perfect child."

That was almost too much for me to handle. I wanted desperately to cry but I pushed it down, feeling that terrible nausea instead. I hid my face in his shoulder and hugged him hard. He didn't say anything. He knew that I didn't need any words, only his hug.

Mom interrupted us after a while. "Come on, you two. You'll steal the show. Two Andersonns being overly-emotional in public. I already see it in the newspapers tomorrow."

"Three," Dad joked and drew her between us.

The game continued a few minutes later with my spirits higher than before. Everything Gottfried had said yesterday was nonsense. Whatever I had done was over now, behind me. All those men were in the past. Gottfried was wrong. I wouldn't need some older man to feel loved. I had my father's love. I had Alex. I had Matthias, if I wanted him; there was still time to decide what to do. The most important concern for me was sorted now: I knew where I stood and that the malicious coach was wrong about me.

The first fifteen minutes of the second half went on with many close calls but still no scores. Alex had now made a couple of dangerous interventions, but he was cool-headed so everything ended well for his team. Harold was similarly adept on the other side. However, we all knew something had to happen. A penalty shootout would not be an acceptable end to this night. Both Alex and Harold were excellent goalkeepers, but penalties were more about luck than skill. I didn't want to see either team get lucky in a shootout. It would devalue the title they would win later.

216

Somehow, as the match went on, the Ukrainian part of the stadium became louder than the English. I saw the fans in white trying hard but couldn't hear them for the yellow mass. Tanya and Olexiy were polite not to join them with their full heart but I saw how patriotic they were.

As if carried by the renewed wave of support, Lomin and Volomin – the defence duo from hell, as the sports journalists called them – pierced the middle of the terrain and charged forward, urging the other players to do so and leaving nobody behind to protect Alex. It was all or nothing. They passed the ball between each other so fast that the English players couldn't intervene. Now, it was Hrichko who had it on the right side, with four players in front to kick it to. It was Rostov who received it, hitting it hard towards the English keeper.

Harold boxed the ball but not out of the pitch; it fell right onto Barnik's foot. Three Englishmen rushed him and he rapidly sent it over to Savchenko on the other unguarded side. He reacted well, seeing that Harold was looking in his direction, ready to defend, and kicked it to Nikolay Pavlov, who was just on the verge of being offside. It took him a precise jump to catch the ball on his head, where it changed direction, straight into the unprotected corner of the goal.

I couldn't refrain from screaming my heart out. The players were piling up over Nikolay, and I was jumping between my parents, the Yanovs, the girls and the Ukrainians around me. It was a beautiful goal, achieved by excellent tactics and months of hard work. Milan Andreyevich obviously knew that if they were going to win against any of the powerhouse teams, they had to plan well – and he just proved to be an excellent planner.

It took almost five minutes for everyone on the grass to pull themselves together: the Ukrainians to calm down and go back to the game, and the English to gather up their shattered confidence and stay active, now aiming not for a winning goal but an equaliser.

When the game resumed, the action was more intense, even wild and aggressive. In the urge to do something, the English made a couple of (un)intentional clashes that the Ukrainians felt they had to react to. Three players got yellow cards, Nikolay being one of them. The clock was ticking, and the show was beautiful to watch for anyone, but especially for me, because whichever team won, I was winning, too.

We reached the ninetieth minute and the stoppage time announced was five minutes. Alex now had an even harder job than before, with a few balls missing the posts by a hair's breadth. It was the longest five minutes of the day, with every second stretching to its maximum. At times, I could almost see the ball going behind Alex's back, but then I would blink and see it was just a hallucination from tiredness, excitement and beer.

When the final whistle announced that Ukraine was in the semi-final, I was squashed under a pile of hugs coming from everyone around. I'd believed that it could happen, but millions around the world hadn't. How could anyone predict that Ukraine, a nation which had never been particularly good at football, would kick out two favourites for the trophy in a row? The English had followed the same fate as the Italians. It wasn't the wonderful 2–0 result of before, but even 1–0 showed who was better this year.

In another situation, I would've found a way to reach Alex on the grass again, but since my country was the opponent, I decided to stay and act as polite as possible. My good image had to be maintained.

The streets of Nuremberg were crowded with Ukrainian fans who couldn't help showing their excitement and joy for the historical success of their country. Nobody could blame them; even the police were kind to them while moving them aside for the cars to pass. It took us quite some time to reach the hotel, and it took the guys even longer. They felt obliged to answer as many questions as possible and stayed late at the press conference, which was overfilled with journalists from all over the world. They were the third semi-finalists.

It didn't strike me until Bea's father mentioned it that Ukraine's next opponent would be Germany. I had somehow hoped that having Alex and Matthias on the same pitch could be avoided. Now, it was inevitable. What a game of destiny: my keeper against my striker. What a game it would be for all three of us!

I knew then that I wanted Alex to win, despite the fact that it would crash every German's dream of taking the FIFA World Cup Trophy on their own home turf. I knew they were excellent and probably deserving, but I deeply believed this needed to be Ukraine's year.

When the guys finally arrived at the restaurant in the hotel, they were already singing and chanting on the way in. Everyone forgot about the food; all we wanted was to sing and celebrate. When I saw Alex, I almost dropped my mug of beer and rushed into to his arms.

"You are the best damn goalkeeper in the history of sport!" I kissed him. "You're gonna win this thing."

He dropped his bag and lifted me. "I saw you up there. You were like a fan leader. You are the best, Jane."

I hid our faces with my hair and we shared another deep kiss that sent tremors all over my body. I couldn't wait to be alone with him that night.

The evening's festivities were prolonged till the early morning, despite how tired we all were. We simply couldn't stop celebrating. For us English, it wasn't a particularly painful defeat because we had already seen England play in the World Cup semi-finals, but the Ukrainian exhilaration was beyond description. They didn't have a sip of alcohol, but they were drunk with joy. It was the joy of having something extremely special for the very first time.

Up in the room, I pushed Alex into the shower and then we barely reached the bed in our excitement for each other. I missed him: feeling him, his touch, everything about him. We went wild that night, every breath a moan, scream or gasp. It wasn't making love; it was the wildest possible sex. I was glad and happy to see once again that with him, I could have absolutely everything.

*****

On the plane to Munich, where the first semi-final game was to be held, I thought about the previous night and wondered why, despite everything with Alex, I still had wandered off to other men – five of them, to be more precise. Six, if I counted Matthias, who I hadn't had sex with. Or eight, if I counted Hadleigh and Larsson, who I'd kissed. *Oh, gosh, I almost lost count of them. It would sound like a joke to somebody.*

But it wasn't a joke. In less than three weeks, I'd cheated on my perfect boyfriend with eight men. Bea was right: there was something wrong with me, especially because I still didn't regret anything. Looking out the window at the German landscape so far below me, I waited for some feeling of remorse to begin, but it wasn't coming. Why would it, anyway? I was twenty. It's not like those men had forced me into anything. I'd known very well what I wanted every time, even though most of them came as a surprise. I had wanted them. I had wanted to feel how it was to be possessed by someone who was different, forbidden.

Part of me wanted to see how far my lies could go. My parents always taught me I shouldn't lie because people would always find out in the end. I'd never lied to them, nor to my friends. Now I wondered if it was really true after all. After weeks of mischief, nobody even suspected me. Was it because I was a good actress and an even better liar? Maybe what I had done was too atrocious to be believed. *Hah! Imagine Jane Andersonn sleeping with six different men in three weeks.* Nobody in their right or wrong mind would believe such a thing.

"Why are you smiling?" Angie asked me.

"I was just thinking about something."

"Why do I think I know what you were thinking about?"

"'Cause we're the same."

We laughed.

"What are you gonna do, Jane?" asked Bea. "The Cup is almost over."

"I know. It's over for me, too. All that. I feel like I've had enough."

Lana and Angie couldn't help bursting into laughter, though Bea stayed serious.

"Of course you've had enough. It was high time," said Lana, justifying herself.

"After yesterday, after Dad hugged me like that, I'm done with everything. I guess I don't want to take these risks any longer. I especially can't risk disappointing him."

"You didn't know he'd always loved you and been proud of you?" asked Bea.

"I knew, but he never shows it to the extent I would like. It's as if what Gottfried said was true. But I don't know. I don't fantasise about an older man as a partner. It's not like that. I just want Dad to be proud of me. Alex is enough. Alex is perfect."

"Well, I am glad to hear that, finally. What are you going to do with Matthias?"

I inhaled deeply. "I think you know the answer. It hurts me to say it out loud."

*****

The Ukrainian and German teams didn't stay in the same hotel, for which I was extremely grateful. Matthias was persistent in asking to meet, but, despite how much I wanted to, I couldn't give him the time he was asking for. Alex's trainings coincided with Matthias's both days before the game, so they were free at the same time. I had risked enough, as I had said, and I didn't want to exhaust my luck.

I was also avoiding him because I dreaded what I would feel when I saw him. At this moment, I was determined I would leave him and stay with Alex. That's how it was. That's how it had to be. That was the only right thing. But the emotions that meeting Matthias would evoke again…was I able to deal with them? Could I solve the situation properly with him standing in front of me?

It was the Fourth of July, so we had a little celebration for American Independence Day during dinner, after which both Alex and I went to bed ready to sleep. I was dreaming deeply, his arms around me, when my phone woke me up.

Come at least to the window.

I managed to squeeze out of Alex's hug with the excuse of needing to go to the toilet. When I was sure he was again fast asleep, I approached the window and opened the curtain. We were on the third floor, so I could see Matthias clearly in the parking lot. His face shone with excitement when he saw me. He smiled and blew me a kiss. My phone buzzed with another message.

If you could only come down.

It was as if some monster's fist was clenching my heart. I felt physical pain as I watched him down there with that puppy-eyed look on his face. He adored me like he had from the first day. One of the reasons I liked him so much was how he made me feel just by looking at me with those eyes full of admiration and care. I was devastated to know that the next time we met, it would be goodbye. I wanted to run down the emergency stairs again and jump into his hug. I didn't know why I wanted that so much, when I loved the man who had been hugging me only minutes ago. Was it possible...no. It couldn't be.

It couldn't be possible for a woman to love two men equally.

Then, what is this?

The two of them, they were so different. I liked them both for everything they were. Yes, I didn't entirely know either of them – one never gets to know everything about their partner. But I was sure about Alex. Maybe Matthias was also able to give me everything Alex did. Would I ever know? How?

The need to cry was rising in me to the point of suffocation. *You mustn't cry, you mustn't cry,* I repeated to myself. I managed to blow him a kiss before retreating from the window.

-   *I need to be back in bed.*

Alright. I miss you. Hope to see you tomorrow. At least for five minutes.

-   *Let's see.*

Promise me.

-   *I can't.*

Have I ever put you in danger of being discovered? You can trust me. I will make it work tomorrow. Five minutes, Jane?

-   *Alright.*

I knew it was wrong to say it, but I had no other option, did I? Tomorrow was the day when I would tell him I was staying with Alex.

I was thankful to God for letting me sleep peacefully and without nightmares. As soon as I opened my eyes, I immediately remembered all the pain that had twisted in my chest the night before. The pain felt so physical that I instinctively looked at my breasts to check if I had a bruise.

"I was admiring them, too," Alex said, smiling. He was sitting at the table, preparing toast for breakfast.

"I just had some weird dreams," I white-lied.

I straightened up in bed, surprised by how different and easy it was to deal with things in the light of day. Nothing seemed so bad as it had a few hours ago while I watched Matthias in the parking lot.

Alex came and sat next to me. He handed me a glass of water and a plate. On the toast, he'd made a heart out of berries and jam on peanut butter. "For the best girlfriend," he said, kissing me on the hair.

It wasn't the first time he'd done something sweet like that, but now I felt it stronger than before. I put my overflowing emotions aside and hugged him hard.

"I love you, Alex. You are the best man I've ever met and will ever meet."

He kissed me on the shoulder.

I would never be able to live life without those little things he gave me.

Tonight when you go to bed, let me know. I got a room on your floor, in the same hall. It was a bloody difficult job for a five minute meeting, but I don't care. I'll be there from ten o'clock. When he falls asleep, text me and sneak to the room. I'll keep the door open.

I texted back, agreeing to everything without showing too much affection. I was sure that by now he understood something was odd but didn't want to ask over a text message – better for me.

I spent the whole day bracing myself for that moment, for those five minutes. When Alex left for training, I went to the gym with the girls, who immediately knew something was wrong but didn't want to ask many questions. I didn't blame them. I whiled away the hours at the pool, then the sauna, then the spa. I wanted the day to pass quickly, and at the same time, I didn't. Tomorrow was the final game, either for Ukraine or Germany, for Alex or Matthias. I was confident the Ukrainians would move forward, but the idea of Alex and three of the men I had cheated on him with on the same pitch aggravated me.

After dinner, Alex and I lingered at the rooftop pool, watching the sunset.

"Jane, tell me honestly." He was hugging me from behind. "Do you now believe we can win against them?"

"I do," I replied without hesitation, kissing his arm under my chin. "I believe it and I know it. Just do as your father told you – don't lose your head out there."

"As long as I have your support, I won't."

"Of course you do. I'm gonna show the world whose biggest fan I actually am. Your mom helped me order that blue and yellow dress and matching shoes. They're ready in the room."

He kissed me on the head.

"I am somehow calm. I cannot describe it. I should be more excited, frightened even. It's my first World Cup semi-final. It's Ukraine's first semi-final, and I'm not stressed."

I turned around to kiss him.

"That's because you know who's the best and who's gonna take that trophy home in seven days."

When we went to bed, it was difficult to stay awake while listening to his peaceful breathing, which always managed to calm me down. However, there was a job to be done. Around half past eleven, I put on my nightgown, texted Matthias and left.

I was determined in what was about to happen. I wouldn't let him touch me. I would be cold, as cold as possible. I would tell him I didn't care enough for him to leave the man I loved. I would be brief, strict, say what I had to in less than five minutes and go back to my room without letting him say anything.

The door was slightly open. I squeezed in with the elegance of a ballerina and closed it behind me. It was dark inside; there were no lights except for a small, diffused lamp in the corner. At first, I didn't see him, but then my eyes found the tall, dark, athletic figure standing next to the window.

I had a flashback of everything that we had shared over the past few weeks: how he'd treated me, how he'd cared for me and ensured that nothing bad happened to me, how respectful he'd been towards Alex in front of me, even though he hated him. I let all the memories fall over me: how attractively arrogant he was when he first interacted with me, how lovely our first date was when he looked at me longingly over the table, how awesome and unforgettable our night out in Düsseldorf was, how our every meeting was full with emotions and teenage excitement, how he adored me, how I enjoyed him.

He was beautiful.

I stood, frozen in my steps. He turned and faced me with his deep, wonderful coal-black eyes.

He smiled. "May the lightning strike me now if you're not the most beautiful woman in the universe."

It was the combination of everything – how he looked, what he said, how he smiled, all that he was – that made me instantly dump my plan and run heedlessly into his arms.

He hugged me, strong, wordless, sensing something was wrong. I didn't dare let go of him, certain that I would fall apart. When he took me by the shoulders and made me look at his face, my eyes were big and swollen with withheld tears and pain.

"Jane…"

Neither of us knew what to say. He knew what was on my mind. I saw how his eyes saddened before he touched my cheek and drew me closer. Oh, how I loved his taste, his smell, his touch. He glided over me with such pleasant ease it made my hair stand on edge.

We moved slowly towards the bed. He sat and I snuggled up in his lap, our lips not parting even for a second. He slid his hands under my gown and drew them over my back. I removed his T-shirt and pressed my body against his, absorbing his warmth with my every nerve. His fingers never lingered on one place; they were exploring my skin. When he kissed the corner of my neck and shoulder, my whole body shook, even when he did it again a few inches over, and again.

We lay down, intertwined in a hug, my head on his chest. I wanted to be his but couldn't make myself do it, and he didn't want to push me.

"There is nothing stronger now than my wish to have you," he said, "but we're not gonna do it like this."

I raised my head to look at him wonderingly.

"You are my petite little Jane. I'm not gonna take you in five minutes as a goodbye."

I hugged him harder.

"There are many reasons for that. One of them is I need more than five minutes for the first time with you."

I managed a weak smile.

We stayed like that significantly longer than five minutes, and it was he who reminded me I had to go if I wanted everything to end well. The pain was agonising when we separated our bodies to stand up from the bed. I was hugging him again at the door, reluctant to leave.

"Another one of the reasons," he said, devouring me with those eyes, "is this is not goodbye."

"Matthias—"

"I'm determined. If I wasn't sure about you, I wouldn't persist. I'm not giving up on you, Jane Andersonn."

I should have said "You'd better" or "I've given up on you already" or anything similar, but I couldn't. I'd already had enough pain for one evening. If I'd said something so hurtful, it would have backfired and destroyed me entirely. Instead of anything right and sane, I touched his cheek again, and with all the strength I had, turned and went back to my room.

*****

Alex noticed I was absent during the night, but I told him Dad had called me to make a plan for the remaining week in Germany. That was something I had already discussed with my parents, so I felt it was just another one of my minute lies, nothing big. He was okay with it; he had other things to think about.

Namely, the time was ticking terribly fast towards nine o'clock, when the game was scheduled to start at the Allianz Arena. The city was on fire. Every TV and radio station was broadcasting live from the streets swarming with a bevy of people in yellow and blue and locals in white waving black, red, and gold scarves and flags. It was Tuesday, but that didn't prevent any football lovers from starting drinking beer in the early morning.

The Ukrainians were euphoric. There were thousands of them in the streets hanging around together, regardless if they knew each other or not. The celebratory mood was high from the beginning. After their team had kicked out Italy and England, they were confident they could serve the same dinner to another favourite.

The Germans were in the same mood. The fact that the Ukrainians had pulled some miracles at the tournament didn't sway them in their firm belief that they would reach the finals and lift the trophy. If they won this game, their next opponent would be either Brazil or Belgium, and the statistics were on their side when it came to those two countries.

I again took control over my mood, mind and body, and nothing on my outside betrayed how stressed and sad I was inside. When I put on the blue and yellow dress and stepped into my matching blue court shoes, I shone with pride, even while my soul was twisting in pain for the other man I also wanted to win. I repeated to myself a dozen times that I had to act my best that day; otherwise, everything would go to ruin.

I was successful. Alex didn't notice anything while getting ready. When he picked up his bag, I hugged him.

"Good luck, Big Boy. Next time we meet, you'll be in the World Cup finals."

He smiled and kissed me.

I joined the girls and the others in the hotel lobby, and we headed to the stadium. The day was beautiful, sunny and fresh. The sunset was straight from a movie, and the evening brought more magic with it.

Surrounded by people, I settled into my role quite well and my good spirits weren't acting any longer. I was the perfect girlfriend of Alexander Yanov, and that's exactly how I behaved.

We had seats behind the team benches and could see pretty much everything. The stands were already shaking under the thousands and thousands of supporters who were trying to out-sing each other. The sight of it all was stunning, and it was intensified by the fact that my boyfriend was about to play.

I refused to drink; I thought it would make me vomit. Alex's father was the one ordering for everyone this time. They got on very well with each other: my parents, his parents, even Bea's. It was another sign to me that I had made the right decision. It made my heart melt to see all of them talking cheerfully, this time supporting the same team.

Exactly on time, the players came out onto the grass. They lined up, with the captains standing next to the referees. The Ukrainians were wearing blue to contrast from the hosts in white. Alex was still in his black and red jersey, the same one I'd worn at the previous game against England. I was glad to see that he looked calm, although I knew how anxious each and every one of them was inside.

Matthias had that boastful expression on his face that was both annoying and endearing. I knew a million things were going through his mind, as well. This was a doubly important game for him. If Germany were the victors, he would win over two opponents: his professional and personal rival.

When the whistle blew, my blood pressure soared.

Both teams had their most famous names on the pitch, and the spectators were hoping for a world-class clash with lots of good moments, if not goals. Everyone knew that Alex was still the best goalkeeper, and most probably would keep the title no matter what happened at this game. He hadn't received a single goal since the beginning of the tournament; that had already set some records, and every sports journalist and expert claimed he deserved the Golden Glove.

The ten-minute warm-up went smoothly, but then the real, heart-pounding game started. I was in great form, jumping and screaming, whole-heartedly supporting the blue team and occasionally yelling at the referee when he called fouls on us and not the Germans. The host team was way more aggressive than their opponent. They wanted to score and were rushing at the Ukrainian players with a force bordering on excessive.

Five minutes later, there was a clash between Savchenko and Sascha Roth very close to Lahrman. The German defender had reacted too wildly in preventing our forward from shooting, so we got a free kick.

It was a good spot. I stood up to see better. Pavlov said something to three players, who all took their positions as Hrichko prepared to shoot. They were too dispersed; I couldn't see everything. I heard the whistle and saw Hrichko accelerating, then the ball flew over most of their heads and bounced from Pavlov, to Barnik, to Volomin, ricocheting off his right foot straight into the net.

Lahrman tried his best but couldn't make it in time. The ball was lying behind the posts. I jumped in ecstasy and disbelief along with the forty-thousand fans in blue and yellow. I was pulled into hugs from the Yanovs and then my parents. I managed to squeeze out in time to see the replay of the goal.

The Germans were frozen in place, shocked. The Ukrainians were making a pyramid of each other on the grass. Alex was there, too. I felt bad for Matthias and the other guys who had become my friends, but I knew how much this meant to the people of Ukraine.

The replay showed how brilliantly positioned the Ukrainian players were, and it was all Pavlov's idea. What a marvellous plan! Even the local commentators admired the whole action and gave it a respectful report as the game continued.

The Germans were pushing harder now. The attacks were more fierce, more forceful. They reached Alex a couple of times, and he reacted well. There were even three close calls when he was one-on-one with an enemy player, but he dealt with each successfully. Matthias was one of the three. My heart skipped a beat when I saw him getting close. *If this was a movie*, I thought, *he would score*. But he didn't.

After the thirtieth minute, the Ukrainians seemed to have drawn energy from some secret source and started attacking ferociously again. They did make a few fouls, with two players earning yellow cards, almost seriously injuring one German, but the game continued.

Five minutes before the end of the first half, the fans seemed to be as exhausted as the players. We all needed a break. Alex kicked the ball from his area back into the game. Starovsky was waiting for it and settled it before heading forward. It was another move in a series of attacks that managed to pierce the German defence line. I saw Matthias and Lens running to help, but it was too late.

We had three players lined up onside in front of Lahrman. Although the next second, each of those blue players had a white one attached to them, that didn't prevent them from rapidly passing the ball between each other. The last one to touch it was Barnik. He ran, turned and, three metres from the goal – before he fell – managed to hit the ball and direct it behind the line. It was a legit goal for Ukraine at the forty-second minute.

After another wild and emotional celebration, I caught myself staring at the result box. The Ukrainians were definitely and obviously better than the mighty Germans. Was this real? Was this really happening?

The blue boys on the pitch were full of confidence as they brought the first half to an end. The most difficult part was still yet to come, but it was easier to deal with when in the lead by two goals. When the referee announced halftime, the Ukrainian fans jumped and screamed as if their team had won the game already. I couldn't help joining them, anticipating a good end to this night. *Eventually, it's going to be like in the movies*, I thought and smiled to myself.

I tried not to look at Matthias because I knew it would hurt me and affect my mood, so instead, I watched Alex and his teammates walking towards the tunnel. He was about to pass right by us and I wanted to catch his eye.

Staring at him, mesmerised by how good he looked, I didn't notice Gottfried approaching him until too late. Gottfried said something to Alex, who stopped in his tracks. Gottfried smiled – not a good sign.

The next second, Alex started at him violently, poised to throw a punch. One of his teammates held him back, and then Gottfried started shouting his heart out.

Everyone in the vicinity could hear. The blood left my body.

"Did you really think she was faithful, you moron? I can tell you she is not! She fucked like a rabbit! I couldn't get her off of me! And it was all in front of your eyes, you idiot!"

Time stopped, then lengthened. I went numb. When I sat back in my seat, I didn't feel my legs. I could only feel the pounding of my heart, every beat like an earthquake in my head.

Somebody was holding my hand while I struggled for air: it was Angie. She was telling me something, but I didn't understand her. It was as if she was talking in a foreign language. Instinctively, I looked around, searching for Dad.

"That bastard! He's gonna pay for this!" he shouted as he left the stands, taking his phone out of his pocket.

I then looked down to the pitch. Alex was being dragged to the tunnel by five players. On the other side, Ben and Michael were holding Matthias back from getting in Gottfried's face.

Everything was ruined. I was discovered. The day after I'd decided I would go back on the right path, I was destroyed.

It was Bea's voice that broke through the darkness.

"Jane, come on! Are you really gonna be affected like this by some horny old man's words?"

That jolted me awake like an electrical shock. I raised my head to face her blue eyes that were now shimmering with power.

"Get up, girl! It's just another wishful bastard!" Some of her power transferred to me.

Of course. Nobody will believe him if I deny everything, if I behave as if nothing really happened. Dad is already sorting it all out. Alex was upset because I was so rudely insulted, not because he believed him. What Gottfried just said was absolute nonsense, not the truth at all! And that's how I have to behave!

I saw in Bea's look that that was what she wanted of me. Oh, lord, how much I loved her in that moment, how grateful I was for everything she had done for me.

Mom brought me some water and soon I was my old self, or at least looked it. I knew millions of cameras in the world were now directed at me, and I had to look good. I had to be confident and composed. I felt even better when I heard the Yanovs commenting on how disgusting the German coach's behaviour was.

"To say something like that about a kid! To go so low! Such an accomplished and professional man with an admirable career! Abominable!"

"He saw there was no other way," said Maria. "Alex is playing at his best. He wasn't going to take any goals. I just hope he will calm down and continue at the same pace."

I worried about that, too. I knew how well players separated their private lives from their jobs, but, then again, I remembered some big football stars who had made emotional mistakes in the heat of the moment. I prayed that the same would not happen to my boyfriend. He didn't deserve it.

Fifteen terribly long minutes eventually came to an end. Dad returned just when the players started coming back out.

"Some things are sorted already," he said. "Some will be tomorrow. But one thing is certain – that idiot will regret every sentence he said down there."

"Thank you, Dad." I squeezed his hand.

However, I couldn't calm down. Alex took worryingly long to come out of the tunnel, and when he finally did, he was arguing with Coach Andreyevich. We all saw it but couldn't hear anything. In the end, Milan said something strictly and Alex gave up and walked over to stand between his goalposts.

"This is not good," said Olexiy as the second half started.

"I know. I just hope you're wrong," answered Tanya.

Surprising everyone, Gottfried didn't get any penalty for the disruption he had caused, probably because others got involved before something seriously bad happened. Still, I wished everything were worse for him and promised myself I would make him regret what he'd done, though I didn't know how. My only chance now was that the Ukrainians win.

The atmosphere on the pitch was like a gang war. It was tense, and everyone could feel it. The Germans were attacking and we were defending, then we were attacking and reaching their goalkeeper to no result, then we were running back and they were attacking – the action circled relentlessly. It was exhausting even to watch.

One action started by the German defence lead to all the players gathering on Alex's side. The players in white seemed to be everywhere, and they were fast. Our guys were after them and the ball, preventing them from positioning for a shot.

However, Lens was too skilled. He was short, skinny and fast, and managed to escape a Ukrainian defender. The ball fell on his left foot – the one he didn't normally use – but the goal was close enough. He went for the shot. The ball flew. Alex saw it coming in time but it was as if he couldn't move, couldn't react.

Thousands gasped. The net was shaking. Alexander Yanov was scored on for the first time in seven months.

My head went numb. I fell in my seat, hearing Olexiy and Maria swearing in Ukrainian. This wasn't good.

There was no time for shock and anger. The Germans didn't want to celebrate too long. They picked up the ball and headed towards the centre point. Their fans were in a trance like hungry beasts. They'd had a wonderful taste, and they wanted more. And their players were determined to give it to them.

Coach Andreyevich made one substitute and left in Alex, who I could see was disturbed. He was trying to focus, but his face was contorted with worry. I prayed for him. I knew his confidence was now destabilised, but the Germans still needed to score two more times to win, and even with this one goal against him, Alex was still the best.

The drama dragged on for another fifteen minutes. The Ukrainians were trying their best to score again and defend well, and they were doing great. However, it was difficult to maintain such balanced tactics with an enemy who had nothing to lose. It seemed as if Germany didn't care about their defence at all, only how to reach Alex's side again.

It came in the sixty-sixth minute. Alex defended one hit, two, three, four, each time boxing the ball away but not managing to catch it. The fifth time, Leon Schneider had the empty net two metres in front of him. He couldn't miss – he didn't miss.

The equaliser came as a shock to the entire football world that night. After a wonderfully played first half, the sports media were in favour of Ukraine and thought nothing could beat them. Now, opinion had fallen back to the popular belief that the German machine was too powerful for the young stars from this Eastern European country.

The only man who held himself composed was Coach Andreyevich, who calmly gave some guidelines to the players on the pitch. Gottfried was jumping around with his players, hugging and congratulating them. *On what?* I thought. *On his own malicious work! Bloody bastard!*

When the "party" was over, the ball again moved from the centre. There were still more than twenty minutes to go. A lot could be done, and nothing was entirely lost. It seemed for a while that the Ukrainians had regained some of that power and forcefulness they'd shown the first half. They almost scored two times but were unlucky when the ball hit the posts and bounced off the wrong direction. The fans in blue and yellow felt as if the third goal was coming – it was just a matter of minutes.

Some ten minutes before the end, the Germans were again pushing hard on the opponent. It was an intense battle between almost seven players. The ball escaped and rocketed off before being caught by Matthias, who ran towards Alex with his full strength. It was obvious he couldn't score – I knew how much he wanted to – so he acted smart instead of emotional and passed the ball over to Lens.

Alex was too focused on Matthias. Whatever was going through his head in that moment stalled him – he reacted unusually late. When he finally turned to face Lens, he was already in full swing. Alex jumped after the ball, but he didn't make it. Germany had scored their third goal, and it was entirely Alex's fault. No one could argue with that. It was lost. Everything was lost. I didn't even think, let alone care, about what Gottfried had said about me and how that would affect my image and career. I was consumed, devastated that the tournament was over for Ukraine, for Alex.

There was no hope in the last ten minutes. It could only become worse by the Germans scoring again. They seemed not to care anymore, though. They were exhausted from the game, which had taken more energy than they had planned to give. They were the winners, and they knew the morale of the Ukrainian players no longer existed.

Germany's supporters were singing, outvoicing the other half of the stadium, whose mood had now swayed from furious to despondent. Women and men cried, beholding the last minutes in absolute shock and disbelief. Twenty-five minutes ago, their team was about to win, and then everything changed. The dream of millions was destroyed.

Upon the final whistle, our players quickly retreated to the changing room while the locals stayed to celebrate. I was glad only for Matthias, but it was a hollow joy. I couldn't stay for too long – none of us wanted to. Despite a wonderful beginning, it was a terrible night that desperately needed to be over.

When we reached the hotel, the receptionist informed us the players had already arrived. They kept the press conference to a minimum and had a police escort all the way from the stadium, while it took us almost three hours to drive through the cheering crowds of exhilarated Germans, now World Cup finalists. Coach Andreyevich met us outside of the restaurant.

"Some of the guys are in there. The others are still in their rooms. You are most welcome to gather here. It will help them feel better." He turned to me. "Jane, go talk to him. You're the only one who can now."

I nodded in agreement and ran up the stairs. All I could think about was how hard I would hug him and try to make it less painful – for both of us.

He was in the shower. I almost couldn't see him through the steam. I threw off my shoes and stepped inside, still dressed. When I saw his ice-cold eyes, I slowed my pace and my breath. I realised I might have been wrong in my overconfidence. Maybe he did believe what Gottfried had said. Still, I knew I mustn't make a mistake, so I didn't move. I stared at him, immobile, water running all over me.

And then I saw the change. His eyes filled with a familiar warmth, and I knew I was safe again. I raised my hand to touch his jaw. He hugged my waist. I propped up on my toes to kiss him lightly.

"You are still the best."

He squeezed me into a wet hug.

"No, I'm not. I destroyed it all."

His voice was shaky. He was crying.

I felt terrible but knew I mustn't show it. I had to be the strong one at that moment, even knowing very well that everything was entirely my fault.

"Even the best mess up sometimes. Remember Beckham in 1998 and Zidane in 2006?"

He managed a smile. "You are wonderful. I don't know if I would make it through this disaster if it wasn't for you."

I squeezed him harder. Of course he would say that. He'd forgotten that without me, there wouldn't have been any altercation on the pitch in the first place. But I didn't want to bring that up.

"I shouldn't have let him provoke me like that. But I couldn't control myself. He and the others pretended to be nice to you, inviting you to their games, being your friends…and then to say such things! Such disrespect towards you! It infuriated me in a second. It totally uprooted me from my normal self. I couldn't focus anymore."

He cried again, hiding his face in my hair.

I kissed his chest. "It's alright, Love. You are still the best. You're still young. Who would have expected that a professional man like Gottfried would do something like that? He took us all by surprise. But that's it, now. He used his dirty card. There's nothing else he can do in the future."

"You are right about everything, Jane. But how am I gonna face my teammates, my friends, my coach, my family, the people of Ukraine back home?"

I raised my head and made him look at me. "With a bronze medal and the reassurance that in four years, you'll fix this."

I saw in his swollen eyes that he was starting to believe what I was saying. I knew it would take days, even weeks, to recover from this loss, especially if the media went hard on him. But there had been worse failures in the history of football, and making a mistake in one game and still ending the tournament as the best goalkeeper in the world wasn't so bad as it could have been.

I encouraged him to finish his shower, get dressed and move downstairs to be with the rest of his team. Coach Andreyevich gave a nice motivational speech for the third-place playoff in four days and we all retreated to our bedrooms soon after. I knew the night would be long and difficult. Despite the influx of optimism and positivity that we'd built up in the last hours of the day, the fact of the matter still was that Ukraine had been so close to entering the World Cup finals until one man – my boyfriend – destroyed it all.

Because he loved me.

The following day, straight after breakfast, we all moved to Frankfurt, where the match for third place was to be held. We had yet to see who we would face, Brazil or Belgium, but whoever it was, the guys were now confident that they would win. The rage of loss had been transformed overnight into an incredible surge of positivity.

I decided to go with Alex on the same plane. The articles in the newspapers were too much for a calm, kind guy like him to handle. As it turned out, everyone believed Gottfried. I was taken aback to find that out. I hadn't thought anyone in their right mind would believe such nonsense. It was obvious Gottfried had only wanted to infuriate Alex because Germany was losing. But the media had clearly been waiting for a juicy story like this to pounce on.

Dad was upset, too. His lawyers were dealing with everything, but it would take some time – at least two or three days. On that first, most difficult day, I wanted to be by Alex's side.

At Frankfurt Airport, we were welcomed by a swarm of reporters and photographers. We didn't comment; we just walked away, holding hands and protected by security.

"I hate this."

"It will pass, Alex, you'll see. Right now, they're only trying to distract the world from the fact that Germany is the weaker team who would've lost to yours. Their coach had to resort to something very ugly to prevent that from happening, and they're trying to get a reaction out of us to cover it up. It's as simple as that. After a few days, it will be a different story – you'll see."

I was right, of course. The very next day, the English media changed the direction in which the wind was blowing and turned against the others, accusing the German papers of yellow journalism and slander for ignoring the indecency of what their coach had done. I was proud of my people. After a few hours, the Americans and Ukrainians joined them, too, and by the end of the day, photos of me attending Alex's training and the two of us having dinner in the city were all over the Internet.

Everything was coming back to normal, to how it should be. Not everything was lost, as I had thought at the end of that terrible match. I still had my Dad's trust and my boyfriend's love. Alex was going to win the award for the best goalkeeper and, as we were all confident, the bronze medal in the match against Belgium on Saturday.

We were also planning to attend the final game on Sunday. Brazil had just beaten Belgium in the semi-finals, so the guys wanted to watch the match and cheer for Luca Ferreira. I was relieved that Alex would stay with me until the end of the tournament. I didn't want us to be separate much, knowing that it was all my fault.

*****

Although everything was going great for me again, there was one thing that kept me awake at night.

Matthias.

He hadn't spoken to me since the incident with Gottfried. I knew I should've been relieved that he had given up on me – and made the choice for me – but I didn't want it to end like this. I wanted things resolved peacefully and with common sense, but not with him thinking that I was a whore. He believed his coach. I knew it.

It felt strange to spend the days without his text messages. I knew I had better get used to it because that was how it was going to be in the normal, faithful life I was to have with my boyfriend.

The day before the third-place match, Alex was at his last training and I was sitting with the girls in a café overlooking the vast pool. A waitress approached me and said quietly in my ear, "Miss Andersonn, Mr Beller is here and insists on seeing you."

I went white and almost sunk into my chair. I braced myself rapidly because I didn't know what Matthias was capable of doing now.

When I saw him at reception, I couldn't help thinking again how handsome he was. He turned to face me, and I could tell he was furious.

"Hello." I decided to say something friendly to avoid creating an awkward situation in front of the hotel staff. "Why don't you join us by the pool?"

"That will not do," he hissed through clenched teeth. He showed me a room key. "Let's go."

Speechless, I followed him without rebelling in order not to attract more unwanted attention. In the elevator, there were two other people who of course recognised us but judged from Matthias's face that it was not a moment for any friendly chit-chat. I was telling myself that we were doing nothing wrong. We were just two friends talking about something ugly that had happened: nothing more, nothing less.

However, when we entered the room, I let myself unleash. "Who the hell do you think you are? Taking me to a room like this! In front—"

"Shut up!" he cut me off and I stopped dead. "Is it true?"

His face was distorted, almost unrecognisable. His dark eyes, usually so soft, were black with fury.

"Is what true?" I almost whispered. *No, Jane! No, no, no! You mustn't fall now. Stand up! Stand up and fight!*

"That you fucked my coach! Is it true?"

I took a deep breath, reminded myself again how well I could act, and did it again.

"It seems like you've already formed your opinion. I don't know what you're doing here."

"Tell me, Jane! Did you sleep with him or not?!" He was getting louder with every word, while I kept my tone deliberately calm.

"You expect me to abandon everything I have built and be with you after the tournament and yet you think so little of me. Your coach already now stands between us more than your mother ever would." I admired how harsh I was on him. "Leave me alone. I'd better go to the man who trusts me. Thank you for making this easier for me."

What he did next surprised me. He took me by the shoulders and shook me violently with his full force. "TELL ME! DID YOU HAVE SEX WITH GOTTFRIED?!"

In spite of my shock, I looked him straight in those coal-black eyes and saw that, under the grave confusion and righteous anger, they still adored me. That encouraged me more, so I simply, almost effortlessly said, "No, I did not."

He eased his clench on my arms. I knew I would get bruises later. No man had ever treated me like that.

"Now let me go, you monster."

"I don't understand," he said, holding his head in confusion. "I don't get it at all. He's never lied to me. About anything. I thought it was all a made-up story to enrage Yanov and make him lose his head so that we could win. But when I heard it, it was...it was as if he was talking to me. I was so angry. It made me sick. Just the thought of you two together...I asked him right there on the pitch. He confirmed it."

"Matthias, he didn't want to admit on the spot that he'd lied."

"I asked him again later in the changing room, when everyone was calm and we were alone, and he again said you two had been together, before...before you and I started seeing each other. He even told me to keep trying with you, 'cause your...skill is worth it."

I looked at him and was satisfied to see he wasn't so sure anymore about the story he had come here with.

236

"I can only say that I have no idea how he can know anything about my skills in bed. I understand why you trust him, but from my point of view, he's just another guy who wants to get between my legs. Nothing better than those idiots Braam and Reis."

I knew I was playing a dangerous game turning a player against his coach. That bloody old man would do anything for football and his players, as he had shown a few days ago. I knew Matthias trusted him with his full mind. But what about his heart?

He was confused.

"I understand everything you say, but, damn it! He is like a father to me! He'd never lie to me about something so serious."

"Why are you here, then?"

He looked at me with mixed feelings of anger and adoration. "Because I fucking love you, Jane. I love you! I love everything about you! I love your smile, your looks, I love your mind, your jokes, your smell. I love how you cuddle on me when we sleep, your skin on mine, the sound of your voice, your soft hair. I love your eyes, even when they are not looking at me! I love you, you damn woman!"

Shock, pain, tears, joy – everything stirred up in my heart. I no longer had control of my body: my legs that stepped towards him, my hands that reached to his face. When I touched him, he calmed down in an instant, like a tamed tiger under a hand he trusted. He was all I could see and think of at that moment.

"I love you, too, Mati," slipped off my tongue before I could think of what good or harm it could cause.

It seemed that was all he needed to hear. He hugged me softly, the total opposite of how violently he'd handled me a few minutes ago. His touch felt good. I closed my eyes and rested my cheek against his chest. He was patting me on the head, running his fingers through my hair.

"Come to the game on Sunday, will you?" he asked.

"We will all be there."

"I hope by then you will make up your mind. This waiting and hoping is eating me like acid."

I gathered my courage and looked up at him.

"You also have some decisions to make."

*****

Saturday, July 10th was considerably different than the gloomy, tragic Tuesday before it, thanks to the efforts of the Ukrainian people. They travelled in crowds from Munich and even Berlin – where some of them had prematurely gone, expecting their team to play in the final – and when they reached Frankfurt, their mood was again lively and upbeat. The streets were covered in blue and yellow colours and people already wearing plastic bronze medals around their necks. We all admired their cheerfulness and how fast they had recovered from the loss earlier in the week.

When the match kicked off, our fans were obviously louder and more supportive than the opponent's. The girls and I were like cheerleaders up on the stands, jumping and chanting with Tanya and Maria. I wanted to show everyone that nobody, especially not an old prick like Gottfried, could ruin what I had with my boyfriend.

Encouraged by the fact that *"Yanov actually can receive goals"*, as some papers put it, the Belgian players strode hard and fast on the Ukrainian defence, giving it their best. However, they could do nothing against Alex, who was back to his old self: impenetrable. He was there to stop every ball and assist every time the last line of his teammates was pierced. He was again the best.

Nobody saw the first goal coming, so there was a slight silence of surprise when the ball shook the net behind the Belgian goalkeeper. It was achieved through a few long passes and sent into the goal by Savchenko in a beautiful arc. The ball flew over two Belgian players and the goalkeeper, ending up right where it needed to be.

It was excellent motivation, and when the Ukrainians came back to the pitch for the second half, it was obvious who was stronger. Try as they might, the Western Europeans simply couldn't handle them. The ball possession statistics were in favour of our team 72–28, and it was just a matter of time when the next goal would be scored.

It happened in the fifty-seventh minute and then again in the sixty-ninth. By then, I had already almost lost my voice shouting and cheering. The bronze medal was ours: the first ever for Ukraine at the World Cup. My boyfriend had written history.

The ceremony was beautiful. Germany did a great job as always when it came to organising events. I'd had a wonderful month and managed to make it to all the games I wanted, thanks to their excellent management of everything in and out of the stadiums, in the streets and hotels, even in the air. I doubted we would see a better organised tournament soon.

Alex, his teammates and their coach were shining proud while being awarded the medals. It was official by then that Alex would get the Golden Glove. No matter what happened in the final game, he was still the goalkeeper with the fewest received goals in the tournament. Best Young Player would be awarded to Andriy Barnik, which came as a slight surprise because we thought the Germans would pick up everything except the Glove. The top scorer would likely be Lens, and the best player probably someone from *Die Mannschaft*, or perhaps Luca Ferreira. All the awards would be given out the following evening, together with the gold and silver medals. That was why we had already planned to go to Berlin after winning third place.

That night, we could finally all celebrate properly, which meant drinks. It was an immense relief for the guys. They had been professional and respected their coach's conditions for a whole month. Now, they could unwind. My dad and Olexiy Yanov made sure the hotel was supplied with enough of everything. It was a hell of a party. We danced, drank, sang karaoke, danced again – even on the tables – smashed glasses, invited staff to join us and went for "one more", even when we were dead tired and about to collapse.

Alex was happy about Ukraine's first medal in an important international competition, but he wasn't exhilarated. I could see in his look how every now and then his thoughts dwelt on what they could have achieved if he had kept his head cool. It was his fault that Ukraine wasn't about to play the final game. At the same time, it was all Gottfried's fault. And, in the end, it was all my fault.

Already used to that action, I forced the unwanted thoughts out of my mind and did my best to help him do the same. In a way, they were still winners, and that's how most of the world saw them. They would fix it all in four years in Brazil.

Sometime around six in the morning, the sun through the windows chased us to bed. We decided to go for a nap, promising to continue the celebration on the way to and in Berlin, and then back in Ukraine, where everything was being organised for the arrival of the best football team in the country's history.

*****

Everything was ready for the big finale in Berlin. After we arrived at our hotel, I went to see a hairdresser with the girls. We wanted to look perfect for this last game, as we were sure we would be under constant media watch, especially since we'd be with the Ukrainian players. Harold Dare was coming, too. The English team had left the country the day after we beat them, but as soon as he renewed his contract in London, Harold flew back to meet Bea. They weren't yet officially together, but there was sure to be buzz when everyone saw them together on the stands.

Alex and I decided to go to the stadium separately. I was to go with my parents and he with the guys from the team, so we would meet there.

This time, I decided to wear white with black court shoes: simple but perfect and very subtly the colours of the German jersey. Since Alex had lost, I truly wanted to see Matthias win. I knew I would have to pretend I supported Brazil and refrain from jumping every time the Germans stood a chance to score, but after so much lying and acting, I thought that would not be a problem for me.

Music was blasting at the stadium, cheering everyone up and getting the crowd excited before the players came out. We were there on time; however, Alex and the guys were late, which was quite unusual. The first to show up was Coach Andreyevich and a few players.

"Where are the others?" I asked.

"Following," he answered reassuringly.

The German and Brazilian players started coming out and we saluted them with screams of joy and ecstasy. They all looked wonderfully warrior-like, particularly the Germans. I barely spared a glance for the guys in blue. When the anthems were over, Nikolay arrived with the rest of the guys but without Alex. I looked at him questioningly.

"He texted me he had to finish some stuff and he'd come alone," he replied.

"That's odd. What does he have to finish now?"

Nikolay just shrugged his shoulders. "Probably something about the award."

I turned to Alex's parents. "Has he mentioned anything to you?"

They shook their heads.

"I looked for him," said Andriy. "I went to his room and knocked, but nobody answered."

I tried to remember if he had mentioned having something important to do, but I couldn't think of anything.

"Don't worry, Jane. He probably has a valid reason to be late," said Olexiy. "He'll be here shortly, I'm sure."

The game began with a thundering roar from the audience. The guys started so well that soon I forgot about my worry and focused on the turf. The players on both teams were running at an impressive speed from one side to the other. Luca Ferreira was doing great. He was an amazing motivator and leader to his team.

For a brief moment, I remembered Alex's apartment a few months ago, when I'd seen him almost naked.

Maybe it all started then, and I was just unaware.

Suddenly, I was shaken out of my very private thoughts by a situation on the pitch. There was a crowd of white players on the Brazilian side.

240

Their first try for the goal missed, but the ball ricocheted off the post, and with a well-placed second hit, the ball was in! Germany was in the lead, thanks to Ben Schwimmer. The goal was marvellous: unplanned but precise. It was midway through the first half of the game – a perfect time to score.

Without realising my actions, I jumped and screamed in exhilaration. The girls joined me so that I didn't look too awkward surrounded by so many Ukrainians, who had lost directly to these guys less than a week ago.

"Ahem!" Nikolay said jokingly.

"I'm sorry. They're just friends." I raised my hands innocently and he laughed. "And you have to admit that the goal was awesome."

The aggressive game continued, and it was almost difficult to watch how brutally the players fought each other. Even the referee gave up calling every single foul since there were so many. The Brazilians were stubborn, and with a hard push in the last ten seconds, managed to equalise the score. The crowd was in awe. It was a perfect way to end the first half. Nothing was certain now. Both teams were playing well enough to be deserving of the golden trophy that waited for them in front of the tunnel.

I remembered Alex. He still hadn't showed up, and in an instant I was filled with worry. Something had happened. He hadn't texted either me or his parents. I tried calling him for all fifteen minutes of the break, but he didn't pick up.

"Don't stress yourself so much, Jane," Tanya told me. "I'm sure he has a good reason for being absent. What's the worst thing that could happen? He probably got stuck in traffic or something like that."

"He should've texted us. Any of us."

"Maybe he forgot his phone or it's out of battery. It happens."

"Not to Alex."

"Honey, calm down or you'll make me worried, too."

The second half kicked off, and I again put my fear aside. Of course nothing bad had happened to Alex. I was just overreacting. The game was heating up to the standards of a real World Cup final. The night was fresh and the air perfect, and the footballers played with all their body, mind and heart. It was truly a pleasure to watch them. Pass by pass, the action was growing more exciting. Nobody knew who would be the winner: one minute the Brazilians were about to score, the very next the opposite was happening. Seconds moved on for minutes, and minutes seemed to drag on for hours.

It was only the fifty-first minute when Lens scored his eighth goal at the tournament. It was brilliant to watch the replay of the action, which started with Lahrman and fell into place in the middle line before being forwarded to the best striker they had.

The Brazilians weren't giving up, so, afraid of being scored on, our team couldn't rest even for a second. Germany had to fight not only to maintain the result but also – since it was in their nature – to try and score more. It was torture. I struggled to control my reactions at times.

Fortunately, Michael Krimm put an end to everything – Brazil's dreams and Germany's fears. At the eighty-first minute, he alone squeezed through the enemy defence and, in a move no one expected, launched the ball over the keeper and placed it in the corner between the goalposts. It was 3–1 and over, ten minutes before the official end.

The celebration started in the stands, and the girls and I couldn't help joining in. I knew people around me disapproved, but I would explain it away later. Everyone had seen me attending German matches over the last couple of weeks. Being happy for them now was nothing unusual. If I'd had any self-awareness, I would have been ashamed of how ridiculous and disrespectful in my audacity I was. But at that moment, my only thoughts were of rejoicing.

The referee decided there was no need for more than two minutes of stoppage time, and when those long two minutes ticked off, the whole of Germany was on its feet. My hearing cut out completely for a moment from all the noise and roaring. It was beautiful.

The Brazilians lay on the grass while the Germans ran all over the pitch, hugging each other and their coach. Red, black and yellow flags were everywhere and the stadium looked as if only Germans existed. The other half was quiet and calm in their seats. After having celebrated with each other, the German players ran to the closest stands to join the euphoric fans. Security wanted to separate them, but they refused. Michael was with his grandfather, Ben with his parents, Lens among some girls, and Matthias…

Matthias hugged his parents, cheered with some fans, took a large flag from them and then started running towards the centre – towards us. My legs went numb, my stomach stirred, and my heart filled with love and adoration for this man.

He stood under us and stared straight at me with that same look I had fallen for.

To hell with everything! I thought and ran down towards him. I didn't care about anything or anyone at that moment. Whatever people might say, I would reply that we were just friends, only friends. They could believe it or fuck themselves with their opinion.

A security guard wanted to prevent me from jumping over, but I sternly told him to let me go. Matthias was staring at me with a wide smile on his face. I ran into his arms without thinking. I understood only partially the gravity of what I was doing when he took me by the waist and then hugged me hard. Before I could say he was crazy – as if I weren't, too – he put the flag over our heads and kissed me with all the strength of his emotions. It was full of excitement, joy, his sweat, my perfume, our love. It was one of the most intense feelings I had ever experienced. I knew I would never regret it, no matter what happened afterwards.

"It's over, Jane! It's all over!" he said. "The trophy is ours! You are mine!" He kissed me again, but my mood died out immediately.

"Congratulations, Mati, but—"

"It's over! Everything's over! Now it's just you and me. I am so grateful that you came! I thought...I feared he would do something to you, but when I saw you on the stands, I knew everything was alright. That gave me such an injection of confidence for the game."

My heart didn't function any more.

"Mati, I don't understand. What are you talking about? Who would do what to me?"

"Yanov, of course. Now that he knows."

The feeling I experienced next was something absolutely and completely foreign, a level of agony I had never thought the human body could feel. The strength of my emotion wracked my body like a physical pain. Some invisible fist was squeezing my chest, preventing me from breathing, while another one was doing the same to my stomach, sending bile up into my throat. My legs let me down, and I was now relying fully on Matthias to stand. My skin went as white as my dress.

"He knows?" I whispered. "About us?"

"Yes."

"Alex knows about you and me?"

"Yes, about us. And the others."

Now I experienced a series of cramps surging through different parts of my body.

"I thought you knew. That's why I was scared he might be violent with you. But when I saw you here, I thought everything was right. I knew we would win, because you came."

"H-how does he know?"

"Lens told him. He told me, too. Rolf was furious that you refused him, so he put pressure on Lens and convinced him it was the right thing to do. But it doesn't matter. I have forgiven you for everything. I wasn't sure before the game, but when I saw you here, I knew I had. All that is behind us. I know that you were always honest and true when we were together, and that's all that matters."

It took me time to understand what he was actually saying: he knew I had slept with his coach, his best friend and three other guys, and he still forgave me. He must be insane. Absolutely insane.

And Alex...*Dear lord! Where is he? That's why he hasn't come to the game. That's what he had to deal with!*

"I have to go," I said.

"What?"

"I have to go see him."

"Jane, you didn't know any of this?"

"No. Alex...he's nowhere to be found. If he has done something to himself because of me, because of what I've done, I won't be able to live with myself." I was swallowing tears and trying to squeeze out of his arms.

"But, Jane, it's all over with him. He doesn't want to see you anymore. There is no need for you to go and risk your life!"

"He'd never hurt me. I know him. I have to see him. I cannot leave him like this."

He let me go.

"Are you gonna come back?" He was looking at me sadly.

My mouth almost said, "Of course." Almost. Alex wouldn't want to see me ever again after this, that was certain. But would I be able to have anything with Matthias after all this? He knew everything, too. Maybe he was forgiving now, but later he would hate me for it. How would I step out publicly anywhere with him?

I loved Matthias. I loved Alex. I couldn't promise anything now.

"Are you leaving me for him? Again? Even when he doesn't want you?" he asked.

"I'm sorry, Mati. I don't know."

I turned to go, still under the flag.

"I love you, Jane. You are the only woman I will ever love with such intensity. There will be no other in my life after you."

"Don't say that, Mati."

"I know that. I've known that for some time already. I'll be happy either with you or with no one else."

"I love you, too."

244

I gathered all the strength I had, removed the flag from my head and started running, fighting back tears, nausea, pain, shock and everything else my body was capable of feeling. I wanted to be invisible more than ever in my life. I had gotten used to the presence of interested people with cameras and those who loved my work, but at that moment, after I was unforgivably, distastefully and inappropriately intimate with Matthias at the place millions of people were watching, I desperately wanted all of them to stop staring, flashing, screaming, asking. I couldn't look up. I was terrified.

Still, I ran. I asked the closest security guard to assist me to the nearest exit, where they got me a car to take me to the hotel.

It was terribly difficult to move over the streets since every breathing soul was out and celebrating the gold medal. I died a million times before entering our hotel and breathlessly bending over the reception desk to demand a key to Alex's room. They didn't argue much, probably because they saw what condition I was in, and after they passed me the card, I ran all the way up the stairs, tripping once.

When I swiped the card, the light on the door showed green, but it wouldn't open when I pushed. I tried again and realised something was blocking it. I tried harder.

"Alex, let me in!" I shouted, to no avail.

I used all my force and managed to open the door just enough so that I could squeeze in. What waited for me inside looked nothing like a luxury hotel room.

Everything was broken.

Pieces of wood and glass were on the floor. The bedsheets and pillows were torn, the curtains ruined, the bathroom door displaced out of its frame. All that, done by the man who was sitting on the destroyed bed, his back turned to me.

What have I done?

This was it. I knew I was discovered. There was no point lying to him anymore. I had done terrible things, and there was no way to fix it – not this time. With all her ferocity, dauntlessness and beauty, Jane Andersonn was exposed and downright defeated.

"Alex…"

"I can't guarantee I won't hurt you if you get one step closer," he said threateningly.

I didn't care. I walked halfway across the room when he suddenly turned and threw a bedside lamp at me. "WHY?!" he shouted.

It hit me on the arm, scratching me. I didn't care. I was lost in another wave of shock after having seen his distorted face.

What have I done?

"I gave you everything in my power! I loved you, cared for you, treated you with respect! And you persuaded me you felt the same! Why? All this time! If you weren't happy, why did you let us reach this point? Why were we flying from one end of Europe to the other to spend time together? Why did you introduce me to your parents? Why did you let me introduce you to my family? Why did you come here as my girlfriend and support me so publicly when you weren't happy with me?! When behind the scenes, you were fucking anything that moved!"

What have I done?

The nausea bubbling up in my throat was increasing and I felt on the edge of losing consciousness. I was doing my best to fight it, but it was overwhelming.

"I never lied to you about loving you, Alex. Everything with you and your family…that was all honest," I managed to say.

He stood up and approached me furiously. I knew I was about to get hurt, but I didn't care. He squeezed my arms so strongly I thought he touched my bones.

"So what do all those men mean?!" he shouted in my face. "You wanted to get experience? Help them laugh behind my back? I thought I had the best woman in the world by my side! While that woman spent her time fucking around – not with one, not two, but *eight* other men!"

There weren't eight, but it was not time to correct him. Nausea was still rising in my stomach and I almost couldn't speak at all for fear I would vomit.

"Why?!" he demanded.

"I don't know!" I screamed it out. "They just happened. I was never looking for any of them. They came to me themselves. All of them. I don't know why I didn't stop myself. I can't explain it! I guess I just wanted to have some fun, and before I could prevent anything, things were already out of control. But what I know for certain is that I love you. I never faked it. Whenever I told you how special you were to me, I never lied. I always meant it with my full heart."

He let go of me, his face contorted with disgust. His beautiful ocean-blue eyes that had always loved me were now filled with hatred. I prayed this was just a nightmare.

It wasn't. It was the result of what I had willingly done. Why? I still didn't know. Even now, while facing the logical consequences, I didn't know. I regretted it, yes, but was it because I was losing Alex or because I truly understood I had done something terrible? He was a perfect boyfriend. We'd had everything together. Why had I done it all? Was it all just pure boredom? Was it simply because I could do it, because I'd faced so little misfortune that I'd thought that nothing bad could come from my actions? Jane Andersonn always had everything and got away with everything. Jane Andersonn was a winner. Had I thought I was completely invincible? Had I thought myself immune to any kind of redress? What a selfish, conceited, careless idiot I was!

He went to the wardrobe and kicked it hard. I moved to approach him, but he threw a chair at the wall.

"You are the worst thing that has ever happened to me!"

My senses went numb. His words resonated in my head and the meaning of what he said reached my mind fully. The pain was skyrocketing. I couldn't stand on my feet anymore; I was losing my sense of gravity.

And then it happened.

My breathing became shallow and turned to gasping. I'd been trying to suppress my breath to keep the bile at bay, but I had no choice but to release control or else I would've suffocated. One by one, large tears started rolling out of my eyes, over my face and down my neck.

After more than sixteen years, I was crying.

It astounded me. I wasn't familiar with the feeling. I didn't know how to do it. My throat was making animal noises, fighting for air.

Alex turned and looked at me, his face changing, anger giving way to surprise.

"Jane, are you…"

I could still hear the echo of what he'd said, and my heart cramped so hard that I had to crouch; but, unstable as I was, I fell, cutting my knees on the broken glass and splintered wood. It hurt punishingly but not more than the pain in my chest. The tears were now a flowing river. I was ashamed, somehow worried Dad could see me. I hid my face in my hands, still fighting for air.

Alex observed me for a while, taken aback by what he was seeing, but eventually he winced and approached me. He crouched next to me. "For christ's sake, Jane, get out of there!"

I tried to stand up, but when I put a hand on the floor, I felt more pieces of glass in it. I looked at my already bleeding hand and brought it to my face that was dirty with makeup. I didn't want him to see me like this.

He tried to remove my hands from my face but I resisted, so he helped me stand up and put me on the bed. I couldn't stop crying. I was falling apart.

He came with tissues, forced my hands apart and started cleaning my face. I took the tissues from him, embarrassed, trying not to meet his eye. I was covered in blood, dirt, makeup and hair. I'd never looked worse, and I still couldn't stop crying.

"Alex, I'll go. Just don't say that again, not while I'm here. I'll calm down and I'll disappear, just don't say it again."

I was in the foetal position on the bed, my legs smearing it with blood. He sat next to me, watching me, neither of us believing that I was actually crying.

"Jane—"

"I can also stay if you want. Do whatever you want to me tonight. Anything. And tomorrow you can tell everyone what happened. I'll be able to live with that somehow, somewhere. But I can't live with what you've just said. You are the best part of my life. You are the best thing that has ever happened to me. And if I am the opposite to you, let me at least believe that what we had was real."

I was caught in another wave of tears and spasms at the thought of tomorrow. I hid my face in the torn mattress, feeling the slices of pain in my knees and hands.

What's going to happen tomorrow? How will I survive? What will I tell Dad, Mom, the world? How will I behave? How will I ever save face after the show I made at the stadium? How can I move on without Alex? Why have I done this to myself? I had everything. Why was I so unappreciative of my career, of my family, of my wonderful boyfriend? I could've stopped earlier. I had a chance. Why did I sink deeper and deeper into the sick corners of my mind? How could I ever think I would get away with this?

He didn't speak. He only stared at the carpet endlessly. When I felt his warm hand on my shoulder, I thought he was going to squeeze it again and braced for the pain.

"Come on, Jane. Come here."

He pulled me up and passed me a wet towel. I cleaned my face while my crying ceased slowly.

"Look at me."

I forced myself to.

"What you said last…I don't need more lies. Obviously, with you, I can't distinguish what's true and what's not."

"I didn't lie. You will see in the days that follow. I have no reason to lie about anything anymore. My career is gone. The life I knew is gone. When Dad finds out, even my name will be gone. You will see it tomorrow. Jane Andersonn is finished. Forever."

I dreaded what was to follow and almost started crying again.

"What..." He took a deep breath. "What if nobody finds out?"

My breath stopped halfway in my throat as if lightning had struck me.

"What do you mean?" I asked.

"Like that. If people don't find out. If your father doesn't find out."

I stared at him, the corner of my mouth twisting up humourlessly. "I am still not getting you. Everyone saw what I did at the stadium tonight. Everyone in the world knows about Gottfried. After they find out about our breakup tomorrow, the others will surface. It's inevitable."

"I got an offer from France. I've accepted it already. It was supposed to be a surprise because we would be closer to each other."

I started sobbing again. I still didn't understand what he was aiming at.

"Come with me to Paris, Jane, if you really love me as much as you say."

The shock was so strong that I stopped crying instantly. This was something I definitely didn't expect, even in my wildest and most audacious hopes. *He isn't leaving me! He doesn't want to end things!*

"H-how do you mean?" I asked.

"I mean that you move to Paris to live with me."

Paris? I'd never liked that city! I had always made my visits there brief and couldn't wait to come back. London was my city, my home. I had a life there. My best friends were there. My job was there. I had my corners there. Paris had never been worth the thought of spending more time than necessary. I found it too grey, too gloomy at any time of year, even more than London. How could I live there?

How could I not? I had already ruined his life enough. He had every right to demand anything from me. I swallowed hard, feeling as if a rock had moved down my throat.

"Alright, let's go to Paris," I said.

He looked at me as if he didn't believe I had agreed.

"Alright. Go get your passport."

"We're going now?"

"Are you having second thoughts?"

"No! I'm just gonna change."

"There's no time for that."

"Alright," I said obediently and stood up to go to my room.

"Jane, we're leaving immediately. No phone calls to parents, no messages to anyone. Nothing."

"I understand."

I ran to my room before I could give my brain time to fathom what was happening. I didn't have much to grab, anyway: only my passport, my British ID and one credit card. My phone and everything else was in my purse at the stadium.

I returned to Alex's room, and he looked surprised to see me, as if he expected me to have run away.

"Alex?"

"Yes?"

"I don't understand."

He walked towards me. I expected he would shake me violently again or hit me. The Alex I knew would never hurt me, but I had hurt this one so terribly that I didn't know what he was capable of doing.

"Breaking up with you would mean admitting to everything. I would have to face it all with my parents, my friends, my acquaintances, my teammates, my future colleagues. It would follow me every step of the way for my whole life. Millions know us. Millions would know what has happened. Every time they look at me, they would think about how the most beautiful woman in the world cheated on me. That's something I am not capable of living with. I don't know if anyone would be."

Tears started rolling down my cheeks again, burning in the scratches.

"Petrov, he told me Gottfried had put pressure on him – if he didn't tell Beller and me, Gottfried threatened to sack him from the national team. While leaving, he said that he would try to reason with Gottfried so that it doesn't go public. And apparently, Beller loves you, so he will also talk to Gottfried to protect you as much as he can. But even if it goes public, if we stay together, no one will believe them. They will gossip and talk for some time, but it will stop when people see that we're not separating. People will forget. They'll move on."

I understood what he was talking about. It was the best decision he could've made for us, especially for me. Whatever the papers said over the next couple weeks, if nobody believed them, my relationship with my father was maintained, my career was saved, my name was clean – and the same went for Alex.

Nevertheless, I was covered in cold sweat and fear. Was his public image the only reason he was staying with me, despite everything? How good was it for me really to stay with a man who hated me? What kind of life was this going to be?

I felt I had no right to complain or ask anything. After everything I had done, I was getting out almost undamaged, all thanks to this man. Was there still some hope he—

"You're probably wondering now if those are the only reasons I've suggested this," he said, reading my thoughts, like always. "No, they are not."

He put his hand on my cheek. It felt wonderful, his touch so warm on my damaged face.

I needed to hear it so badly: I needed to hear he still loved me. He did. I saw it in his eyes. But he didn't say it. He couldn't make himself.

We left the room, my dress dirty, my face swollen and my eyes red. We had nothing in our hands except for our documents – no bags, no suitcases. "Nothing from our previous life," he'd said.

"I've organised everything so that we reach Paris as inconspicuously as possible, but we'll still have to make an effort," he said. "Go to the toilet, pull yourself together and be again the Jane Andersonn people know."

I nodded, went to the bathroom, washed my face and looked at myself in the mirror. *Come on, Jane. Another role. This time, for him.*

We didn't speak in the car nor at the airport. We walked next to each other looking straight ahead and serious – no holding hands, no touching. My face was cold, expressionless and confident on the outside, although I was a carcass inside.

People noticed us, but they didn't approach, partly because of the security nearby, but I was sure also partly because of our faces. We boarded a small plane and I sat by a window, Alex next to me, still not touching.

It hurt. It bloody hurt. I wished he'd hit me with all his strength. It would have felt better than this distance. I had never really been aware of how much I needed touch to feel loved and cared for. He did love me. He did care for me. We wouldn't be doing what we were doing if he didn't. But he refused to touch me, as if I was contagious, diseased.

I was telling myself it was normal. I had no right to expect anything more. I had done enough. I was lucky to be in the situation I was. Still, it hurt. Everything pained me. My heart, my body, my wounds, my memories of everything. I regretted my actions.

But Matthias. *How can I ever regret Matthias? That insane man who fell for me like a teenager and did incredible things to make me happy. Where is he now?*

How does he feel? Is he gonna feel better one day, or is it really going to be as he told me at the stadium? I was going to miss him, terribly.

The plane accelerated and took off. We could see Berlin, all lit up and celebratory. I wished I had been part of it. I wasn't because I had ruined it all – for myself and by myself.

Alex was looking straight ahead, not at me, a million thoughts in his mind, too. I didn't dare look at him. I was doing my best to seem composed but felt I might shatter apart at any second.

Like never in my life before, I was afraid of the uncertainty. It was a new feeling, to have no faith that things would work out. What was going to happen to me? What was tomorrow going to bring? I had the man of my life by my side, but under what circumstances? I knew I had to be strong like Dad had always taught me, but I couldn't stop thinking about the last month, the last few weeks, the day that was ending, the new one that was just beginning. Those thoughts fraught me with terror. All this time, I was pulling my luck. I'd surrounded myself with lies and disguise, going further and further with every step, every day. I had been doing great. But I had completely ruled out the other players. I'd thought I was the only one involved, when, actually, everyone I had got involved with was a protagonist in their own right. In my brazenness, I had failed to see that. I was selfish and cared only about myself and my own wellbeing. I got what I had been tempting destiny for. I had no right to complain now. The only thing left for me was to face this unavoidable uncertainty, this agony of vagueness, of unclarity, of not knowing what would happen the next day, the next hour, not even the next minute. I didn't even know if I was alone or not.

Below me, the German landscape flew by at an alarming rate. Inches away, Alex's arm next to mine was unmoving. For the first time, life felt cruelly real.

ABOUT THE AUTHOR

Jovana Iv was born in 1992, and lives and works in Southwest Asia. She studied English Language, Literature and Culture, and so far has published two short stories. She also has a travel blog, but recently she is focusing more on writing novels. *There Are Other Ways to Score* is her debut novel and the first out of four books about Jane Andersonn.

You can find more about the author and her books on her website, www.jovanaiv.com, and the Instagram and Facebook profiles for *There Are Other Ways to Score*.

www.ingramcontent.com/pod-product-compliance
Lightning Source LLC
Chambersburg PA
CBHW070004120726
47909CB00003B/794